MURDER ON OAK STREET

If you're in the mood for romance, try these novels written under my pen name: Andrea Matthews

Thunder on the Moor Series

Thunder on the Moor
Ride with the Moonlight
Shake Loose the Border

The Cross of Ciarán Series
The Cross of Ciarán
The Book of Carraig
The Cave of Rúin Ársa

www.imfostermysteries.com

Facebook Page: IMFosterMysteries
Twitter: @IMFosterMystery
Instagram: @imfosterauthor

MURDER
ON
OAK STREET

A South Shore Mystery

I.M. Foster

Inez M. Foster

Murder on Oak Stret

This is a work of fiction. All characters and events in this publication, other than those clearly in the public domain, are products of the author's imagination or are used fictitiously and are not to be construed as real. Any resemblance to real persons, living or dead, is purely coincidental.

Cover designed by Jenny Quinlan, Historical Fiction Book Covers

ISBN 978-1-7333375-7-1 (Pbk)

Inez M. Foster
New York

Website: www.imfostermysteries.com
Facebook Page: www.facebook.com/IMFosterMysteries
Twitter: www.twitter.com/IMFosterMystery
Instagram: www.instagram.com/imfosterauthor

To my dad, who passed on to me his love
of history and storytelling

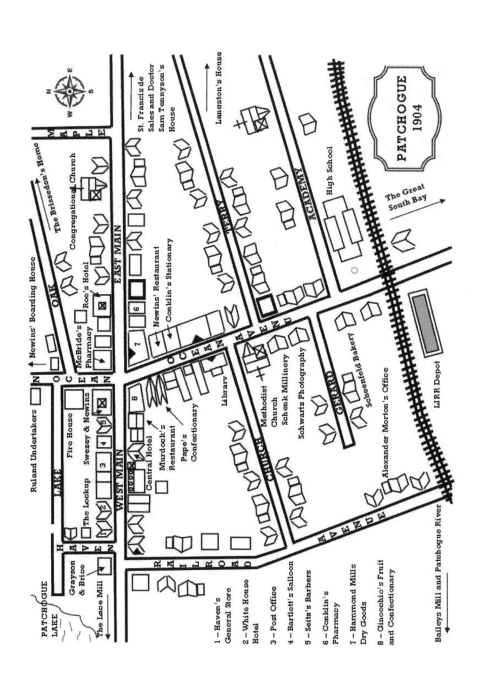

PATCHOGUE
1904

The Great
South Bay

PATCHOGUE
LAKE

Ruland Undertakers

Grayson
& Brice

The Lace Mill

Newins' Boarding House

The Brissedon's Home

Newins' Boarding House

HAVEN

LAKE

Fire House

The Lockup

Swezey & Newins

OAK

McBride's
Pharmacy

Roe's Hotel

Congregational Church

EAST MAIN

St. Francis de
Sales and Doctor
Sam Tennyson's
House

Langston's House

WEST MAIN

Central Hotel

Murdock's
Restaurant

Pape's
Confectionary

Library

OCEAN

TERRY

Newins' Restaurant

Conklin's Stationary

CHURCH

Methodist
Church

Schenk Millinery

Schwartz Photography

AVENUE

GERARD

Schoenfield Bakery

Alexander Morton's Office

ACADEMY

High School

LIRR Depot

Baileys Mill and Patchogue River

1 – Haven's
General Store

2 – White House
Hotel

3 – Post Office

4 – Bartlett's Salloon

5 – Seitz's Barbers

6 – Conklin's
Pharmacy

7 – Hammond Mills
Dry Goods

8 – Ginocchio's Fruit
and Confectionary

PROLOGUE

Friday, April 3, 1902 – 4:00 p.m.

Cornelius Desmond crept up the staircase of the crumbling tenement. Each step creaked and moaned with the pressure of his heavy boots until, at times, he felt sure he would plunge through to the floor below. Pausing momentarily, he wiped his sleeve across his brow, then grasped the dilapidated banister once again. Though he was careful not to exert too much pressure, it wobbled and shook all the same as he moved his sweaty palm along its splintered surface. Then, just as he reached the top step, a piece of railing broke off in his hand, and it was all he could do to keep from tumbling over the side to the dingy floor two stories below.

Utterly shaken by the experience, Cornelius sat down on the darkened landing, instinctively fumbling for the white linen handkerchief his grandmother had given him when he left Ireland. His hand was so clammy that he nearly dropped the crumpled cloth before he was able to wipe away the perspiration that had accumulated on his forehead.

He sat blinking for a moment, taking deep breaths to calm his frazzled nerves. As his eyes gradually adjusted to the dim lighting, he began to gaze around at his

1

surroundings, hoping to see the haggard man whose nephew had come to him, begging that he go to the rooms of his dying uncle. Too ill to speak for himself, the man had sent his only relative with the message, and as usual, Cornelius had responded immediately.

Perhaps his wife was right, and he was getting too old for this. Having just turned fifty, he noticed his joints ached a bit more than they had a few years before, and strands of silver had begun to mix amidst his coarse auburn hair. Still, he felt compelled to help those less fortunate than himself. He had done well with his lumber business, far better than many of his fellow Irishmen, and what better way to put his fortune to use?

With a frown, he took stock of his condition. A small tear rent the sleeve of his frock coat, and his rich leather riding boots were terribly scuffed. Forbes would not be pleased, but there was no help for it. He gazed around the darkened landing once more, chuckling to himself. None of his business associates would ever expect to find him in such squalid surroundings, but here he was, sitting precariously on the crude landing of this dilapidated building, his creased black pants covered in dingy gray dust. Still, he had given his word, and he was, above all else, a man of his word. With the greatest of caution, he pulled himself up, taking time to brush the powdered debris from his pants as he continued to look around the dimly lit hallway.

At the end of the corridor, a single gaslight flickered dismally, revealing the most deplorable conditions he had ever seen. To his left, the once elegant railing hung hazardously over the narrow staircase, evidence that at some time in the past at least one poor soul had plunged through to meet his death, or at best had sustained a multitude of broken bones. Almost everywhere huge chunks of plaster covered the floor, exposing gaps of wood and brick in the wall from which it had fallen; a convenient escape route for the various forms of vermin that made the building their home, no doubt. Even the once elaborate rug had become a veritable bed of lice, for here and there inebriated bodies sprawled across its worn pattern of maroon and gray.

Cornelius cringed at the sight, for even in poverty he had never tolerated such utter filth. His mother had taught him better than that. A promise was a promise, however, and the detestable conditions in which he found himself only made him more determined to assist the mysterious man who had so recently implored his aid.

"Excuse me," he said as he nudged one of the men who lay half-comatose on the rotting carpet. "Me name is Cornelius Desmond. Was it yerself who called for me help?"

The man opened his eyes momentarily but then spewed up some awful green bile across his chest, causing even Cornelius's usually strong stomach to turn slightly. He hoped desperately that it was not the man he sought but bent down by his side just the same.

"Can I be of some help?" he asked, but the drunken man just moaned and rolled over, much to Cornelius's relief.

Finally, in an effort to evoke some sign of recognition, he called out the name of the man who had beseeched his help, but he received no response save the sullen drip of water that ran along the ceiling and onto the floor. He was about to turn and leave, convinced that he had come on a fool's errand, when a short way down the hall a door opened, letting the musty glint of a streetlamp filter through the grimy window. A dirty-faced young woman peered out from amongst the shadows and smiled sweetly. Though she couldn't have been more than sixteen, Cornelius could see she was worn far beyond her years, and he gently placed a few coins in her shaking hands before speaking.

"I wonder if ye could be helping me?"

"Right this way, sir. Whatever you want," she said sensually.

"Oh no, darlin'! Ye misunderstand me meaning. 'Tis a large gentleman I'm looking for, about six feet or so, I believe . . ."

"I don't know nothin' of that sort," she said. "Ye'll have to go elsewhere for that!" Then she slammed the door in his face, making sure to secure the money in her bodice before she did.

"Wait! Please, 'tis nought like that! He's ill, ye see, and needs me help. I must find him at once lest it be too late."

After a moment's hesitation, the door opened and a thin ivory arm pointed out the crack and down the hallway. "I reckon ye're looking for old Joe."

"Thank ye, darlin'," Cornelius said as he placed a few more coins in her hand and continued down the musty corridor.

At the end, a broken door swayed on rusty hinges. Cornelius pushed it open slightly, peering around the edge, and there, on a flea-ridden mattress flung in the corner, was a discarded lump of humanity. His gray hair was terribly knotted and had begun to fall out, and his skin sagged around the decrepit bones that remained. Though his eyes were closed, they were sunken deep within his face and gave the impression that they had not been opened for years.

Taking care not to stumble over the debris that covered the unvarnished floor, Cornelius moved to the old man's side, gently touching the putrid skin surrounding his neck, for he feared he had indeed arrived too late to offer anything more than a proper burial. Still, if that was the case, he was determined to see that the poor soul was laid to rest with dignity. Unfortunately, he had no sooner bent down than there was a loud, shattering crash. A searing pain shot through his head as heavy glass fell around his feet, and he dropped to the ground, half-conscious.

A brown-haired man, a bit older than himself, quickly lifted Cornelius's bleeding head in his arms and began pouring whiskey down his throat and over his clothes. Though Cornelius tried desperately to protest, he was too dazed to move and could only shake his head from side to side, groggily attempting to push the man's arm aside, but to no avail. He could do no more than blink in disbelief at the man, whose wild eyes gazed down at him.

Hastily, the stranger dragged Cornelius back out into the hallway. "Now everything ye have will be mine," the villain whispered with a grin. Then without another word, he tossed Cornelius over the broken railing, sending him sprawling to the hard wood floor two stories below.

Cornelius lay in a pool of blood, pain shooting through every part of his body. The mysterious man stood glaring down from two stories above. Did he know that face? He couldn't think. The pain was too intense, and it was all he could do to retain consciousness. He heard a woman scream. Was she gasping for air? Where were the other tenants?

Footsteps thumped from above. The clink of metal caused him to open his eyes. A bloody knife lay inches from his fingers. The mysterious man knelt beside him, still chuckling. Almost casually, without any feeling whatsoever, he reached into Cornelius's waistcoat pocket and retrieved the gold watch Brigid had given him.

"I'll give me best to yer wife." With a vicious cackle, he stood up and, tucking the watch in his pocket, walked out into the evening mist.

Recognition dawned just as the darkness engulfed him, but there was little he could do about it. "God forgive me sins," he uttered with his last breath.

Saturday, April 4 – 8:00 a.m.

Daniel O'Halleran stared down at the crumpled body, blood spreading out in a deep crimson pool beneath the man's head. He reached over to close the victim's turquoise eyes. Something wasn't right here, aside from the fact that a body was lying battered and broken on the rough wooden floor. He couldn't put his finger on it, but then that wasn't his job, now was it?

"Well?" Sergeant Timothy O'Halleran asked, a frown creasing his aging brow. "What killed him, then?"

Trying to suppress a smile, Daniel stood up, brushing the dust from his pants. His uncle knew very well what had killed the man, but clearly wanted to make Daniel feel important in his new position as a coroner's physician for the city of New York. "You're well aware what killed him, Uncle Timothy."

His uncle gave a quick glance around before slapping him on the back of the head. "Ye're a professional now, lad. Act like one, eh? Yer da didn't spend all that money for a medical degree for ye to be acting the fool."

This time Daniel did laugh, but he removed the smile from his face quickly as his uncle's frown deepened. He was right. Richard and Sarah Adams had raised him as their own in every respect after his mother had died. For all intents and purposes, they were his parents, even though he'd insisted on retaining his mother's surname. He did want to make them proud of him.

Wiping a hand across his face to remove any remnant of tomfoolery, as his adoptive mother called it, he took a deep breath. "He's cracked his skull and bled out." Daniel bent down again, sniffing the man's clothing. "Probably drunk, but I can't be certain."

"Sure, I can smell it from up here," Timothy said. "Whiskey, I'd say. I'm thinking ye need to be getting out a bit more if ye've any doubt."

"It's not what he's been drinking I question, but the amount that made it into his stomach. Most of the smell is coming from his clothing, not his mouth. What self-respecting drunk would let that much liquor go to waste?"

Timothy nodded. "Ye may be right, me boy. I know the man, and he's not one to be found tipping more than a glass or two, especially in a place such as this."

Daniel rubbed a thumb beneath his bottom lip, hesitant to say what was on his mind, but the thought was apt to come out anyway. He nodded up the stairs. "Maybe he was here for other reasons. I've no doubt that girl was pregnant. If he wanted her to have it aborted . . ."

This time Timothy shook his head. "I'll not be believing that. More likely he was here to talk her out o' such a drastic act, and someone caught him at it. The father, perhaps." He scrubbed the day-old stubble on his chin. "What about the wretched sod in the corner room?"

"I suspect that was natural causes, but I'll be able to tell you more—"

"I know, when ye get a better look." His uncle rested a hand on his shoulder. "Ye'd best be quick about it, though. The chief will be wanting this one wrapped up before the widow gets any ideas. She's way out on Long Island, so 'tis not likely he'll be spending a great deal o' time or resources on it."

"But if the man's been murdered . . ." Daniel stood, indignant to think the chief might put other considerations before the truth.

Timothy pointed a finger at him. "Now ye listen here, boyo. 'Tis the way things are. If the widow wants to hire someone to investigate, she's free to do so. The city's not likely to be spending good money on a drunkard found dead in a tenement, especially with a pregnant lass stabbed to death two floors above. Saints preserve us, lad, the knife's lying at his fingertips."

"There's no proof it's his knife, or that it was even used in her murder. Perhaps I could try and use that new fingerprint system I've heard mentioned to see if—"

"It doesn't matter," his uncle said, cutting him off. "'Tis lying beside him, and that's how the bigwigs will see it, whether ye like it or not."

"Then why ask me at all?"

"This is a good job, and ye won it fair and square, but ye can lose it just as easily. Give the boss yer opinion and leave it at that. And for the love o' God, don't be going making any waves, or ye might find yerself unemployed with a reputation as a troublemaker. Fingerprints, indeed!"

Daniel sighed, his shoulders slumping as if a weight had been laid across them. "It may not matter one way or the other."

"And why's that?" Timothy narrowed his eyes. "Out with it."

"Prudence wants me to resign and go into practice with her father." He shrugged, trying to shift the heaviness from his shoulders, and rubbed the scar on his forehead. "It certainly pays more, and she's used to the finer things in life. Besides, I'd actually be helping living people, and if the department's not going to follow up on anything anyway . . ."

"Humph!" His uncle grumbled in Gaelic, words Daniel didn't understand, and pulled a cigarette out of his pocket. "That's all a bunch o' malarkey, and ye know it. Ever since ye've been a wee lad ye've spoken o' naught but joining the police force. Yer da saw how important that was to ye. Sure, he wanted ye to have a grand education and all, and yet he found a way for ye to have both, didn't he? Now here comes this society lass, asking ye to give it all up. Yer da put yer dreams above his own. He always has. I can't be saying the same for this lass."

"Let's not get into that again." The longer they dwelled on the topic, the more his forehead ached. "You don't like Pru. I understand that, but she does love me, and I her. Shouldn't that count for something?"

"Then she should be wanting what's best for ye."

"And what about me wanting what's best for her? I have to think of her needs as well."

His uncle gave a half shrug. "'Tis why I never wed meself."

Daniel chuckled, the ache along his scar easing a little. "You never wed because you eat and drink your job, and you couldn't find a woman who would put up with it . . . or you."

"True enough, though when I see yerself all grown like ye are, I do regret it from time to time—not having a lad o' me own." He sniffed before continuing and gripped Daniel's arm. "That aside, I just want ye to be happy, lad. Ye know that."

"I do, Uncle, though if you don't let me get going, I'll be sacked regardless." He picked up his medical bag, the one his uncle had spent a fortune on for his graduation. "I'll see you for dinner Wednesday night, seven o'clock sharp. You know how Hattie gets if you're late."

"Now there's a woman that might have turned me head once upon a time."

"She'd have knocked that thick Irish head of yours off its block." Daniel walked outside with his uncle and looked up at the dilapidated building. "I know Dr. Scholer will do his best, but if we rule it a murder, will the department at least see if any of the other tenants saw anything?"

Timothy scratched the back of his head. "Ah, Danny! I'll do me best, but the truth o' it is there's likely not a soul in there that heard a thing. Aside from the drink, I'm thinking there might be a good deal o' opium use going on."

Daniel nodded. "But you will try?"

"O' course I will."

Daniel squeezed his uncle's shoulder and headed back toward his buggy, his uncle's voice calling after him.

"Ye'll be letting me know what ye find?"

Daniel waved his hand, a smile crossing his face once more.

After taking an hour for lunch, Daniel returned to the morgue. He opened the windows that sat high in the wall of the autopsy room as far as he could, both for the light they offered and the fresh air. The more he thought about it, the more he was convinced the man had been murdered. Turning back to the table that sat in the middle of the room, he looked over the pale figure that rested on it, oblivious to the fate that was about to befall him.

"Well, sir, whether they like it or not, I'm going to do my best to get to the truth, so what secrets do you have to tell me?"

The cause of death seemed clear enough. The right side of the man's skull had been cracked open, likely on impact. Splinters had pierced his cheek, and from the looks of it, he'd bled out within a minute or so. Of course, the obvious didn't always tell the full story. The question here was whether the fatal blow had occurred before he went over the railing or after.

Daniel explored the man's scalp and noted a small sticky patch of hair on the back of his head. Blood, no doubt. Sure enough. On looking closer, he could see a small laceration buried beneath the auburn strands. Taking a comb from his instrument table, he ran it through the stiffened locks. Bits of what appeared to be glass fell onto the table, and he picked one up, walking over to the window with it to get a better look.

A yellowish olive in color, it was most likely from a whiskey bottle. So he had been hit over the head first, though the small wound he'd sustained wouldn't have been enough to kill him. The hard landing on the floor had done that. The blow would have dazed him, though, enough for someone to pour a bottle of whiskey down his throat, perhaps. Daniel doubted the one used to hit him over the head had been full. Still, he needed more than just a gut feeling.

After dropping the pieces of glass in a small bowl, he removed the man's jacket. The lapels were still damp, and the stain could be seen clearly in the rays of sunlight that shone through the windows. The shirt was damp and stained as well. A bottle of whiskey crashing into his skull could have done that.

Removing the man's stiffened shirt, he checked the skin around his neck and shoulders. Just as he'd expected. There was bruising, as if someone had held him down. This was no accident. He'd bet his fancy medical bag there were drag marks along that second-story landing as well. If he could only go back to the tenement and take a look . . . but that wasn't his job, even if he thought it should be. The detectives would handle that.

On a hunch, he scraped beneath the man's fingernails and placed the resulting material under his microscope lens. Skin. That clinched it. He pulled over his notepad and wrote down his findings. Daniel sighed. The coroner would conduct an inquest, of course, but he doubted much would come of it.

It was already noon by the time he moved to the raven-haired girl. She couldn't have been more than sixteen years old, but she had definitely been sexually active. The child she'd been carrying had died with her. The poor thing had never even had a chance at life. Daniel couldn't help but wonder if the father had known about the child, or if it would have mattered if he had. *It hadn't in my case.* Shaking off a burst of anger, he looked back at the table.

Thinking about his mama always brought a lump to his throat. God, this could have been her lying there, and by extension, himself. But no, his mama hadn't been a soiled dove, just extremely naive. He shook his head, banishing the thought of the heartbreak his mother had gone through, and concentrated on the girl before him.

Focus, man. You have a job to do. As he suspected, she'd been about five or six months pregnant. She was still barely showing, but then she was petite to begin with and probably undernourished. The womb had been pierced, likely killing the infant even before its mother breathed her last. The stabbing blow that had ended her life was through the heart. He picked up the knife, examining it as well as the wound. There was no question about it being the murder weapon. And yet it didn't sit right with Daniel. None of it did.

There was a third party involved here, another responsible for both their deaths. He stretched, straightening his back to get a kink out of it, and glanced at his watch. Already three, and he still had the old man to look at.

The tramp's eyes and skin were yellow, with red spider-like veins visible on his upper chest. The liver itself was a large yellow mass and nearly hard as a rock. Natural causes, though he supposed some would say the man had killed himself with excessive drink. While the younger man and girl had died somewhere between two and six the previous afternoon, the old man had been dead for an additional twenty-four hours at least. Rigor mortis had completely disappeared, and decomposition had set in.

Daniel completed his notes, then went to clean up. Pru never wanted to know what he'd been doing. In fact, she'd stated in no uncertain terms that if she found out he'd been touching a corpse, she'd not let him near her until he'd bathed thoroughly. The church bells down the road rang out the time.

Shit! He was going to be late for dinner again, and it was with Pru's parents. She would not be happy.

By the time he finished cleaning up, dropped off his report with the coroner, and caught the El connection to Brooklyn, there was no chance they'd be waiting on him for dinner. His cursed under his breath again. And what difference had any of it made? Dr. Scholer had been attentive enough and promised to see the evidence introduced at the inquest, but once it had been declared a murder, the investigation would be turned back to law enforcement. Both he and Scholer knew there was little chance the murderer would be located. His uncle would try, to be sure, but with his long hours and the lack of interest on the part of the department, it was unlikely he'd uncover the truth. Perhaps Pru was right, and this wasn't the job for him.

He walked up the steps of the handsome brownstone just blocks from his own and knocked on the door, which was promptly answered by the butler, Carleton.

"She's waiting in the parlor, sir."

"What mood is she in?" Daniel asked, his scar tingling again. He really didn't want another argument.

"Let's just say she's not pleased, sir."

Taking a deep breath, he walked into the fashionable parlor to find Prudence Davis with her arms crossed over her chest and her lips pressed firmly together. After an awkward moment of silence, she finally spoke. "We were meant to dine with Mother and Father tonight."

"Well, I'm here now. I know I'm a bit late, but . . ."

"It's after nine. Mother and Father finally ate and headed up to bed." She let out a sigh of . . . what? Annoyance, frustration, disappointment. Daniel couldn't be sure, but she came over and touched his cheek with her hand. "We really can't go on like this, Daniel. We have obligations, commitments. Tonight was just my parents, but what if it was someone important?"

"I don't know anyone important." He rubbed his scar again, and she nudged him down on the sofa before sitting beside him, her slender fingers massaging his forehead.

"It's bothering you again, isn't it? Not because of me, I hope?"

Unable to manage more than a feeble smile, he reached up, pulling her hand down to his lips and kissing the palm. "No, it's just all so useless. They found a body down at the Bowery . . ."

"Oh, Daniel, you didn't have to go alone, did you?"

"Of course not, but that's not the point. I'm sure the man was murdered, that it was covered up to look like an accident. There'll be an inquest, of course, but it's all just going through the motions. Dr. Scholer will do his best, but with no more than a cursory investigation by the department, it will likely end up being declared murder by persons unknown."

"Well, you've done your job. The rest is up to men like your uncle Timothy."

"But I'm sure I could discover more if—"

Pru placed a finger over his lips. "Really, Daniel, don't you work enough hours as it is? This wouldn't happen if you were working for my father."

"Your father gets called out at all hours."

"On occasion, and it is a bother, but it's not on a daily basis, and the pay is far better."

15

"I don't want to argue over it, Pru. Not tonight."

"Fine, then." She stood up, glaring at him. "You didn't have to *touch* this corpse, did you?"

"No, the cause of death was obvious." Good Lord, he'd just out-and-out lied to the woman he was going to marry, but it was her own fault. She was being irrational about his work. What she didn't know . . . Before he could finish the thought, she spoke again, her tone much softer.

"I think Cook's kept some food warm for you. Sit at the dining table, and I'll have it brought out." She took his hand again and led him to the table, kissing his forehead.

Her lips were smooth and full, the warmth of their touch against his skin causing the tension to drain from his body. Maybe she was right. After all, if they wouldn't follow up on his findings, it was nothing more than a waste of time. He wouldn't think about that now, though.

It was nearly midnight when Daniel hurried up the steps to his parents' elegant brownstone. He'd lived here since his mother died when he was six years old. His uncle Timothy couldn't keep him, not with the hours he worked, and his father . . . well, he had a few choice words for that man. One thing was certain: Daniel's life was better without him in it. Richard and Sarah Adams had taken him into their home and made him part of their family—no, more than that, they'd made him their son.

A warmth washed over his heart like the gentle waves that lapped at Coney Island's beach. He'd spent many a Sunday there with his family. Out of nowhere, the thought of moving out filled him with melancholy. If he'd had his way, he would have bought the house next door when it was for sale, but Pru thought it best they didn't live too close to their families. *After all*, she'd said, *we are going to be starting one of our own.*

But were they? Their wedding was still two years away—Pru had to have time for all the proper formalities. He sighed and opened the front door. Maybe he should remain a bachelor like his uncle Timothy.

The vestibule door swung open before he could even get his key in the lock. "Really, sir," their butler, Byron, said. "Did you think I wouldn't be watching for you?"

A broad grin broke out on Daniel's lips. Byron was always there. "I truly am sorry for keeping you up so late. I didn't get to Pru's till after nine, and—"

"There's no need for an explanation, sir. In fact, I've been reading an excellent book: *The Hound of the Baskervilles.*"

"Sir Arthur Conan Doyle, yes. I heard he'd revived the old detective."

"You did so love him when you were at school."

Daniel smiled again. "I did, didn't I? Perhaps you can lend it to me when you're finished."

"Of course, sir, just like old times. Well, if you don't need anything else . . ."

"No, I'm just heading up to bed. You go on ahead." Daniel watched Byron shuffle toward the back of the house and up the servants' stairs. He was more than their butler; he was family. Releasing a sigh of contentment, Daniel waited a moment before sneaking into the kitchen, intent on snagging a few of Hattie's delicious cookies.

"You'll be wanting some milk with those, I suppose."

The woman had an uncanny knack of appearing out of nowhere, as did his mother, who joined them moments later, her long, golden hair braided over her shoulder, though specks of silver were now mixed in the deep yellow.

"Hard day?" His mother wrapped her arm around his shoulders and gave him a peck on the forehead.

"A long one." He beamed up at her, letting a big smile break out once more. After the day he'd had, it felt good.

"I don't suppose you'll want to talk about it."

"I really shouldn't. Besides, I'd rather hear about your day. You and Izzy were off to Oyster Bay, were you not? To a luncheon with the Roosevelts, no less."

"Oh, stop teasing." Sarah pretended to slap Daniel's arm. "Your father's known Teddy since he was in the assembly. You remember us visiting Sagamore Hill, now, don't you? You must have been sixteen or seventeen at the time."

"I do, yes. It was lovely. They had two little boys and a girl, if I remember right. The little girl kept following Frankie around. He wasn't pleased."

Sarah laughed, her hazel eyes flashing with gold and emerald sparks. "No, your brother wasn't pleased at all."

"So how was luncheon with the First Lady?"

"Delicious, as I knew it would be, though we barely saw Edith. It was a fundraiser for the Outdoor Recreation League."

"To which I'm sure you contributed generously."

"Of course! All children should have a place to run and play, rich and poor alike. They're hoping to open the first park next October." She stood when he could no longer restrain the yawn that had been threatening to erupt for the last fifteen minutes. "But that's enough talk for now. You have work in the morning. Up to bed with you."

"Yes, Mother." He got up, leaning over to kiss the top of her head before bidding her and Hattie good night.

Coming home always made everything right again. And yet, he couldn't help but wonder who would make things right for Cornelius Desmond.

CHAPTER 1

Two Years Later

Sunday, May 8, 1904 – 7:00 a.m.

Daniel O'Halleran pulled the covers up over his head, hoping to block out the memories: a church full of friends and family, his brother Neil checking for the ring in his pocket, the scent of flowers wafting through the air. It was supposed to be the happiest day of his life . . . until it wasn't. Pru had sent a message. She wouldn't be coming.

Another knock on the door, his mother this time. "Daniel, you must get ready for church. I won't allow that hussy to drive you into sin."

There was no use in arguing. His mother always won out in the end. The thought caused him to groan, and he threw off the covers. "Yes, Mother. I'll meet you there."

He sat on the edge of the bed, contemplating the day before. He'd walked out to take his place before the altar, anticipating the arrival of his bride. Instead, it was his brother Joe that had come hurrying down the aisle. He'd grabbed Daniel by the arm and led him back to the sacristy, handing him a note that had been hastily written on the back of an envelope.

Reaching over, Daniel lifted his jacket from the back of his desk chair and pulled the now crumpled paper from its pocket.

> *Daniel,*
>
> *You, sir, are nothing more than an unscrupulous cad, who thought to win my affection through lies and deceit. How dare you pretend to be born into wealth and status when in fact you are nothing more than the baseborn bastard of a cheap Irish whore. No amount of well-bred rearing can alter your coarse lineage, and I will have nothing further to do with you. Consider our courtship at an end.*
>
> Yours,
> Prudence

"Pretending to be born into wealth and status!" He crumbled the note up and tossed it on the floor before grabbing his robe and walking down the hall to the bathroom. He'd never pretended to be anything, never hid the fact that he was adopted. *Didn't exactly tell her the whole story either, did you?*

He pulled the chain to flush the toilet. And why would he? His parents always told him it wasn't important. Obviously, it was to Prudence, but then maybe he should have realized that. All she talked about was having dinner with important people and being seen in the right circles. And his family never had liked her, but he'd let her beauty blind him to her faults, convinced himself she just wanted what was best for him.

"Fool!" he hissed under his breath.

21

Someone knocked on the bathroom door. "Come on, Danny," his younger brother, Frank, said. "I need to use the toilet."

Deciding he could use his washbasin to shave, he washed his hands, opened the door, and ruffled his brother's hair before heading back to his room. But instead of shaving, he flopped down on his bed. What was he going to do now? He'd left the coroner's office two weeks ago with the intention of joining Pru's father in his practice. *Shit!* He rubbed his hands up and down his face. He didn't even have a job, for he was sure that position was no longer a possibility.

"Daniel, are you almost ready?" His mother knocked on the door again, causing him to smile.

"Yes, Mother. I told you. Go on ahead, and I'll meet you there."

"Daniel?" He could hear the suspicion in her voice.

"I'll be there, Mother. I promise."

Well, now you really do have to go. Groaning, he shuffled over to his washstand. How he wished he could crawl back under his covers and never have to face anyone again. He could still hear his father telling a church full of people that the wedding was off. Even from his relative obscurity in the sacristy, he could hear the curious whispers and imagine the sympathetic glances that were coming his way. His brothers had managed to hustle him out the side door without having to encounter anyone, but now he'd have to face them all head on at Mass.

Can't avoid them forever, Danny. They mean well. Might as well get it over with. Fastening his collar, he gave one more longing look toward his bed before brushing his hair. If he hadn't promised his mother . . . *But you did!*

Maybe what he needed was a change of scenery. He'd heard Queens County was nice, and it had quite a few hospitals. A friend worked at St. John's in Elmhurst, and St. Joseph's in Far Rockaway, which was to open next year, was already looking for doctors. Of course, neither would involve the police work he loved so much. Then again, joining Pru's father in his practice wouldn't have allowed him to do that either.

The old grandfather clock in the hall struck the hour. *Shit!* He was going to be late. Grabbing his jacket, he took the stairs two at a time and darted out the door, stopping only long enough for Byron to hand him his hat. A carriage was waiting outside, no doubt called for by the butler. Lord, he did love that man. Still, they were well into the mass when he arrived at church.

The priest was just ascending the pulpit to read the gospel, but all eyes turned toward him, the look his mother gave him as he slipped into the pew the most piercing of all. His cheeks burned, but he opened his missal, not daring to step out of line for the rest of the mass. After it was over, though, as most of the parishioners headed down the aisle toward the back of the church, he made a beeline for the alley door, choosing to walk home rather than wait for the carriage. He just couldn't face any more sympathy at the moment. At least Prudence had deigned to go to a later mass. Thank heavens for small blessings.

It was a half hour later when he walked into the breakfast nook. Aside from his mother's scolding glance at church, nothing more had been said. Now, however, he knew the discussion would begin, so he decided to preempt the foremost question certain to be on everyone's mind.

"I'm sorry I was late, Mother, but I'm fine."

"Of course you are," his mother said. "You're made of good, sturdy stock, both by birth and by your upbringing."

Daniel smiled and let her kiss him on the cheek while his brothers cringed. Now that the initial shock was over, having one's mother kiss your cheek was embarrassing, though he knew secretly it made them all feel safe and loved.

"What do you plan on doing now?" his father asked, ever the practical man. "I don't imagine Pru's father will be wanting you to take him up on his offer any longer."

"I wouldn't be too sure about that," his mother said. "Word is he's weary of the demand his practice makes on his time. I can't imagine you accepting it, though."

"That *would* be awkward," his sister, Isabell, or Izzy, as they all called her, said. She flittered into the room as usual, a ball of sunshine and bubbles, and sat next to him. "Not that you have anything to feel uncomfortable about, Danny. Everyone knows she's an ill-mannered cow."

"Isabell!" their mother said, more than a touch of annoyance in her voice. Daniel wouldn't want to be his sister when she caught up with her later.

"No," Daniel said. "She's right. I suppose I always knew it, but . . ." He shrugged.

"I am sorry though, Danny," Isabell said, reaching over to put her hand on his. "I just always thought you deserved better."

"Then I'd say my guardian angel was working overtime," Daniel said, forcing a smile to his lips. Though he'd lost his appetite, he managed to shove some eggs in his mouth and swallow them without gagging.

"You're absolutely right," his mother said. "Richard will call the mayor and see if he can't get your job with the coroner's office back. After all, he appointed your replacement."

"Oh no, I will not," their father said. "Daniel was advised against giving up the position, and he made his decision. He has to live with the consequences."

His father was right, though Daniel was a little taken aback at the resolve with which he had made the pronouncement. A look sparked in his mother's eyes, one he knew all too well, but before he could say anything to divert her attention from his father, she pulled the napkin from her lap, pressing her lips together.

"Don't give me that look, Sarah," his father said. "The decision is not up for discussion. Daniel is no longer your brown-eyed little boy. He's a grown man."

"So you don't intend to help him in any way?"

Determined not to be the cause of a disagreement between his parents, Daniel tossed his own napkin on the table. His hunger had completely deserted him anyway. "Stop! Father is right. I made my decision without any help, and I stand by it. Most of the time there was little effort to follow up on my findings anyway. Why would I want to return to that?"

"What are you going to do, then?" Joe asked.

His mother put a hankie to her nose and rose from the table. "Sit down, Sarah," his father said, his moustache twitching ever so slightly. "There's no need for hysterics. I do have a proposition to offer Daniel, though I doubt you're going to like that either."

His mother sank back in her chair, the corner of her mouth quivering, no doubt her attempt to stifle a grin, though her eyes still viewed him with a certain wariness. Daniel had to admit he was intrigued himself. From the look on the faces of his brothers and sister, they were as well.

"Now that I have everyone's attention," his father said, "I have made a phone call. I was speaking to an old college friend last week. He happened to be in town on business of some sort, and he stopped by to see if I could join him for lunch. Nice chap. I always liked him."

"Richard!" His mother rolled her eyes. "Have you not punished us all enough? What did you speak to this gentleman about?"

His father chuckled. "All right, Sarah. That was cruel of me. Samuel Tennyson is a physician out on Long Island—a town called Patchogue. In addition to his private practice, he's also a Suffolk County coroner. Though the position is only part-time, he's kept quite busy between that and his medical office, and he's in need of an assistant." He looked to Daniel before continuing. "It is a private practice, but as coroner, he is required to handle a modicum of police work from time to time."

Daniel didn't need to hear any more. A break from the city would be a nice change, and the position would give him time to decide what he really wanted to do with his life. Before he could voice his decision, however, his father held up his hand.

"Let me finish. You won't be dealing with the same amount of crime as you did in the city, but according to Sam, you won't face the same resistance when a case does arise either. The coroner's word is highly respected, and he works in conjunction with the local constables and county officials. The thing is, as much as he enjoys the work, both as a coroner and as a physician, he's hoping to retire in the next few years, at least partially. He says it's a lovely town on the Great South Bay, and he's looking forward to having some time to enjoy it. Though the coroner's position is elected, his endorsement would go a long way with the townspeople; however, he is looking for someone to take over his practice as well, so it's both or nothing. Of course, he wouldn't expect a decision right away. His retirement is a few years down the road, but he is willing to give you a try."

"I'll take the positions." The added information had only made him more determined. His mother, however, didn't seem at all pleased.

"Patchogue? What sort of a name is that for a town? It must be out at the ends of the earth. Is that what you want for your son, to be stuck in some one-horse town? Daniel is a brilliant doctor. He'll be bored to tears." Only it looked as though his mother was the one on the verge of tears.

As much as he hated to upset his mother, this was something he wanted to do. More than that, he needed an adventure right now, and this might just be it.

"Oh, for heaven's sake, Sarah." His father got up and walked around the table, pulling her up into his arms and kissing her forehead. "The railroad will get you there in an hour and a half. And it's far from a one-horse town. From what I understand, it's quite sophisticated and up-to-date. They even have a theater."

"Mother, please," Daniel said. "I need this, if only to clear my head and decide what it is I truly want to do."

Daniel knew she would never put her own feelings over his needs, and he was right. So two days later, he said goodbye to his family and boarded the Long Island Railroad, heading east.

CHAPTER 2

Thursday, June 9, 1904 – 10:00 a.m.

Kathleen Brissedon paced back and forth across the spacious hall, stopping only when she noticed Doctor Samuel Tennyson making his way slowly down the large central staircase. On a usual morning, servants would have been flitting around from one room to another, going about their usual tasks, but this day was far too somber for such joviality. On the contrary, even the staircase itself was quite devoid of the usual household traffic, save for the doctor and the huddled figure of her stepbrother, who sat crouched on its lower steps.

Dr. Tennyson paused a moment, clearing his throat, and Patrick jerked around, standing as he turned to gaze up the stairs, his turquoise eyes pleading for the news Kathleen feared the doctor could not give. Casting a sympathetic glance in her direction, the doctor continued down the staircase until he stood just two steps above the troubled young man.

"I am sorry, lad," he said, resting a hand on Patrick's shoulder. "We did everything we could. It just wasn't enough."

"No! It can't be." Her stepbrother's chin quivered, tears welling in his eyes, though he blinked to keep them from escaping. "How? She was fine! He did something to her, didn't he?" Patrick shook his head. "She promised not to leave me."

Sadly, Brigid Desmond Brissedon had made a vow she couldn't keep. Kathleen reached out to comfort him, but Patrick darted into the parlor, leaving her standing before the doctor. "She's gone, then," she said, more a statement than a question.

Dr. Tennyson scrubbed a hand across his well-kept beard and nodded before following Kathleen to the parlor doorway. Patrick stood gazing out the window, holding a photograph, an image of his mother and father, no doubt. The doctor sighed. "Bridie had a hard time of it, bringing him into this world. She could never have any other children, but they were happy to have Patrick."

Kathleen smiled, so the physician continued. "His father's . . . mysterious demise shook his life to the core. I'm afraid his mother's death will shatter him completely."

"She and Father had barely been married a year," Kathleen said. "I wish I'd had more time to know her better. Maybe if I had, I'd be able to help Patrick adjust better. You were their friend. What was she really like?"

The doctor chuckled, a warm, sentimental laugh. "This parlor," he said. "She decorated it with the same tasteful elegance that filled her life. I can almost feel her here amongst the stately chairs and polished tables. There was a warmth about her that people were drawn to. It's no wonder Patrick sought refuge in here."

"And his father?" Kathleen asked. "I've heard the rumors about how he died, that he was a drunkard and a gambler who raped and murdered a girl in some New York City tenement, but I've also heard the whispers of those who discount those rumors as vicious lies. I know Patrick refuses to believe them."

"As do I," Dr. Tennyson said. "Cornelius Desmond was a kind and gentle man. He'd been born in poverty, but through hard work, perseverance, and a bit of Irish luck, he was able to build a sizeable fortune with his lumber business. Yet he never forgot where he came from and was generous to a fault."

"You think that's why he was at the tenement that afternoon?" Kathleen said.

"I do, but he never told anyone what he was doing, so I've no proof to offer in his defense. He used to say you'd get no credit at heaven's door if you advertised your good works. Then he'd laugh and be off on another adventure." The doctor chuckled at the memory. "No matter where he went, he dressed impeccably. It didn't matter if it was a grand ballroom on the Gold Coast or a dingy beer hall. There was never any doubt he was a man of means, in spite of the spark of mischief that always lit his eyes. He was a gentleman in every sense of the word, and yet there was a rugged worldliness about him that endeared him to all he met. Patrick is much the same as his father."

A melancholy smile caught the doctor's lips, and he continued. "He even looks like Cornelius, tall and straight, with deep turquoise eyes and auburn hair, not to mention the face of an angel with a disposition to match. Or at least he did have until recently. I understand that's changed over the last year or so."

Kathleen frowned. "I'm afraid he's taken to following my older brother's example. Though I can't say why. He doesn't really get on with Colin, or my father, for that matter." A smile tugged on her lips in spite of the somber moment. "They can be difficult as well, but I'd hoped with

Brigid's influence . . ." She trailed off, sadness filling her voice once more. "They'd hired a detective, you know, Patrick and his mother, to look into his father's death. No one else knew about it. Perhaps if he'd been able to clear his father's name, things might have been different." She shrugged. "Without Bridie, though, I fear his heart may not be in it."

"Fear his heart may not be in what, darlin'?" Her father came to stand in the hallway beside her and the doctor. "I presume 'tis Patrick ye're speaking o'?"

A large, distinguished-looking man in his late fifties, with graying hair along his temples and an unmistakable Irish brogue, Thomas Brissedon had owned a prosperous Connecticut lumber company, similar to the one Cornelius owned, before selling out and making the move to Long Island. In fact, he had been in the process of moving the location of his mill when Cornelius died, and he volunteered to assist Brigid with her husband's faltering estate. There were no romantic overtures at first, just a generous offer of help concerning business matters. A close friendship soon developed between the two, however, and they were married in a small ceremony just a little over a year later.

"Yes, Daddy." Kathleen kissed her father on the cheek. "I fear he may never get over this."

"Hmm, let's move across to me study, shall we? Give the lad some time alone."

The study was still very much to Cornelius's taste, but then it had been barely a year since Brigid and her father had married. Dr. Tennyson sat down in one of the large leather chairs by the fire, looking as though it was something he'd done many time before, and accepted the glass of whiskey her father offered him.

"I don't know what to do about the lad," her father said. "'Tis as if he blames me for his father's death. I met Cornelius Desmond a time or two, 'tis true, but I knew little about the man except he was a fellow Irishman and in the same business as meself."

"You never bid on the same projects?" the doctor asked.

"Not that I'm aware o', though me nephew Jeremy takes care of the financial aspects o' the business. I did it all in me younger days, but not so much o' late."

"You're an immigrant as well, I gather?"

"I am that." Her father laughed and took a sip of his drink.

Kathleen tried not to roll her eyes, sure she was about to hear the same story she'd heard so many times before.

"Seems like ages ago now," he said. "I was no more than thirteen when me family arrived. Lived down round the Five Points for a bit, but then didn't the war come, and off I went. After seeing the rest o' the country, I was determined to get me folks out o' that hellhole, so I moved us up to the country, worked hard, and invested wisely till I was able to buy a wee sawmill o' me own. And the rest, as they say, is history. Me Ellie was alive then, God rest her soul." He blessed himself and wiped his nose with a handkerchief he pulled from his pocket. "I don't know where the years went, and that's the God's honest truth."

The doctor nodded, clearly identifying with the sentiment.

"Bridie and I," her father continued, "we were like two lost souls looking for a buoy to hang on to in troubled seas. When we found each other . . . Well, I suppose we felt safe again. Patrick, though, he never could accept that. I do try, but . . ." He shook his head and took another sip of his drink. "He's become quite disagreeable. Perhaps things will improve when he returns to school this fall."

"Perhaps." The doctor hesitated for a moment before continuing to speak. "Please forgive me if this is inappropriate, but the Desmonds and I have been close for so many years. Is it true that Cornelius was in financial trouble?"

"I wouldn't call it trouble, exactly," her father said, "but he was not as well off as he led everyone to believe, his wife included." He reached over, patting Kathleen's hand before continuing. "'Tis why she asked me to start handling her affairs in the first place. She feared there'd be nothing left for Patrick and hoped what little assets there were would best be handled by someone more knowledgeable in the field. At first, I agreed out o' kindness to the widow, but then Bridie and I grew close, and, well... Unfortunately, they were in far worse condition than even I had suspected. I bought the house to pay off their debts and so Bridie and Patrick could continue living here. The lad knows nothing o' his father's financial straits. I prefer to keep it that way, at least until he's finished his degree and established himself. O' course, he'll always have an executive position at me firm, should he want it."

"I'm certain Bridie will rest easy knowing that." Dr. Tennyson rose. "Now I must get home. I'll just say goodbye to the lad, if you don't mind."

"O' course. I'm sure he'd like that." Her father led the way to the parlor, stopping before the door to take a breath. Kathleen knew this would not be easy for him.

"I'm so sorry, Son." He walked to Patrick's side and rested a hand on the young man's shoulder, but Patrick pulled away without uttering a word. Still, her grief-stricken father persisted. "Would ye like to see her one last time?"

"No! Just leave me alone!" Patrick spat the words, a tear trickling down his cheek as he turned to face the man who would now be his only parent.

The vehemence with which he spoke startled Kathleen. Patrick must have noticed how it upset her, for after a quick glance in her direction, he softened his tone a bit. "I don't wish to see her that way. If I do, I'll have to admit she's gone, and God help me if you're all I have left."

Her father stiffened his jaw, taking a deep breath before speaking again. Patrick's words had been sharp and clearly cut him deeply, but he too must have realized how distraught the young man was and chose his words carefully.

"I'm sorry ye feel that way, lad, but we must all move on, no matter how painful it might be. Now come and bid yer ma a proper goodbye. She'd want it that way."

Gently taking the boy's arm, he began to lead the way, but once more Patrick tore himself away, his eyes glaring with a hatred Kathleen had never seen in him. "No! I won't! What does it matter to you anyway? You never loved her. Did you think me so naive I wouldn't see the game you were playing?"

Kathleen could see her father struggling to maintain his patience, and while she understood her stepbrother was grieving, she couldn't quite comprehend his apparent loathing for the man. After all, hadn't he tried to do right by both Patrick and his mother, providing for all their needs and wants, shielding them from the vicious rumors that surrounded Cornelius Desmond's death? And Patrick had certainly not made it easy for him of late.

"That's quite enough!" her father said. "I loved yer mother in ways ye'll never know, and I'll not have ye or anyone else suggesting otherwise. As to games, I think ye'll find 'tis yerself who's guilty o' that, doing all ye can to shame me and yer blessed mother. Now get yerself upstairs this minute and bid yer last respects to yer dear departed mother, or I'll drag ye up there meself by the scruff of yer neck. Is that understood?"

"I'd like to see you try!" Patrick said, a bitter sneer on his face, though it was clear Thomas was more than capable of carrying out the threat. "You can't force me to do anything. You're not my father! You're nothing to me, and I don't care what any stupid piece of paper says. I'm over eighteen and can do as I will."

That was more than her father's frazzled nerves could take. He reached out and grabbed Patrick by the arm, forcing him toward the open parlor door. "I'm the only father ye're likely to have for a while, laddie, so ye'd best be getting used to doing as ye're told. Now get yerself up those stairs and give yer ma the respect she deserves."

"Daddy, please." Kathleen placed her hand on her father's forearm, her voice a soothing salve. "He's just upset. Aren't you, Paddy? I'm sure all he needs is a little time. You've both said things you don't mean."

"O' course, darlin'." Her father let go of Patrick's arm, patting it gently. "I'm sorry, lad. Ye do as ye wish. I just don't want ye to be regretting not saying goodbye to her."

"Patrick!" Kathleen said when her stepbrother didn't answer. She lifted her fingers to his face, brushing them against his flushed cheek. It worked better than any of the doctor's tonics.

Her stepbrother hung his head, shame written on his face. "I'm sorry, sir. I'm sure you have my best interests at heart, but I've already said my goodbyes."

If her father had only left it at that. "Still, I think it best ye see her one last time, out o' respect."

Patrick had started up the stairs, but with those word, he turned. Anger flashed in his eyes anew. "And as I've said, I prefer to remember her the way she was . . . before you weaseled your way into our lives." He charged down the stairs and pushed past them, storming out the front door.

At least he had tried, she supposed, though he had failed miserably. Kathleen sighed and started after the boy, but her father touched her arm. "'Tis best ye let the lad work it through himself, Katie, darlin'. I understand what he's going through and don't take any offense."

Seven-year-old Ryan came down the hall, and Kathleen knelt to embrace her half-brother.

"I tried to keep him and his sister in the garden, miss," the nursemaid, Moira, said, "but . . ."

"Is it true we've lost our new mama?" her half-sister, Charlotte, asked. She wasn't quite ten years old, and try as she might, she couldn't keep her lip from quivering.

"She was very ill, darlin'," her father said. "I spoke to ye about it, now, didn't I?"

The girl nodded, a tear trickling down her cheek. Kathleen kissed her on the forehead. "Go back outside with Nurse, and I'll try to join you in a few minutes."

"What will happen to Patrick?" Ryan asked.

"He'll stay here with us, o' course," her father said. "Now off with ye. I'll have Mrs. Quinn bring ye some cookies." He watched the nurse escort the children down the hallway, then turned back to the doctor. "And now if ye'll excuse me, Samuel, I must see to me wife's funeral arrangements." Giving a nod, he entered his study, and Dr. Tennyson picked up his medical bag and headed for the front door.

"Do you have a moment for a lemonade?" Kathleen asked the doctor, though she wasn't exactly sure why she felt the need to burden him with her troubles.

"Yes, of course," Dr. Tennyson said.

Kathleen asked the maid to bring some refreshments before sitting in one of the fireside sofas. The smell of the doctor's pipe tobacco filled the air, and somehow it relaxed her. "I'm worried about Patrick," she said without preamble. "As you noted, his behavior is becoming increasingly difficult, but it's more than that. These crimes his father was accused of . . . As I mentioned, Brigid had engaged a private detective to investigate his death. She never believed he was guilty of the accusations. Now that she's gone, though . . ." She got up and paced before the hearth. "I fear Patrick's allowance won't be sufficient to retain the services of this private detective and that he might take matters into his own hands."

"Start investigating himself, you mean?" the doctor said.

She hadn't thought about that, but now that the doctor had mentioned it, she wasn't sure which scenario was worse. "Actually, I'm afraid he might attempt to acquire enough money to engage an investigator by any means available, even those that might be seen as illegal."

"Such as?" The doctor seemed concerned, and she almost regretted mentioning it.

Kathleen bit her lip. "A pair of my father's cuff links went missing last week. He'd taken them off and rolled his sleeves up to work on that newfangled automobile he's bought. Patrick seemed to take an interest at first, but after an hour or so, he wandered off. When Daddy went to retrieve his cuff links, they were gone. I fear Patrick may have taken them."

"Oh dear, that is troublesome. Would you like me to have a word with the boy?"

"I thought perhaps . . ." She frowned again. It was terribly forward of her and might mean risking her own reputation. No! This was to help her stepbrother. "I know you do some investigating of sorts in your capacity as coroner."

"That's not exactly the type of crime I investigate, my dear."

"I realize that, but word is your new assistant used to work for the city police department."

The doctor chuckled. "Word does travel fast."

"Yes, it certainly does, and not always in a good way." She frowned, thinking of Patrick and her own brother, Colin. "Well, in any case, I was hoping he might consider looking into things for me—in his spare time. Of course, it would be inappropriate for me to ask him."

"You'd like me to ask him if he'd look into the theft of your father's cuff links?"

"Oh, heavens no! I'd like you to ask him if he'd look into Cornelius Desmond's death. Do you think perhaps he might have heard something of the case while he was working in Manhattan? I know it's a big city, but . . ."

"I'm afraid I have no idea, my dear."

"Well, be that as it may, I thought perhaps if we were working on it, Patrick wouldn't feel so desperate."

The doctor laughed again, resting his hand on hers. "Yes, of course. Nell's invited my assistant to dinner this evening. I'll speak to him about it and see if we can arrange a meeting after the funeral."

Kathleen breathed a sigh of relief. She could tell her stepbrother their plan later and pray it would help. The anger between Patrick and her father had been growing steadily with each passing day, and now that his mother was gone, she feared it would only deepen. She wished it wasn't so, but she knew it was inevitable, especially since the rest of the family seemed to view the brooding twenty-year-old as being spoiled beyond all toleration.

She, on the contrary, felt incredibly sorry for the young man, who had essentially been left alone in the world. She and her family were the only ones he had to turn to, and she was sure, in his mind, that meant he had no one at all.

"He's pouting again, I see!" Colin sauntered into the parlor just as the maid brought the refreshments. "I passed His Lordship on the way in. What is it now? Too much starch in his shirt?"

Sometimes Kathleen wondered how her brother could be so oblivious to the feelings of others. "Brigid has passed away. Have you no heart at all?"

"Oh . . . I am sorry. But it's not as if we didn't expect it. For God's sake, she's been ill for the last two months."

"She was his mother!"

"And, as I have so often been reminded, ours as well, but you don't see me sulking about like it was the end of the world. Life does go on, after all."

"You're incorrigible!" His insensitivity never ceased to amaze her. "Sometimes I doubt there's any kindness in you at all."

Colin just shrugged and headed for the small sideboard that stood on the far side of the parlor. Brother or not, Kathleen saw him for what he was: a selfish young man whose thick black hair would have made him handsome if not for the snide look that seemed to be permanently affixed to his face. His pale blue eyes lacked the sparkle of his stepbrother's, but as the eldest son of an extremely wealthy man, the local females found the twenty-five-year-old attractive nevertheless, and he used his assets well, much to his father's chagrin.

"'Tis not kindness yer brother lacks, darlin'." Her father had returned to the parlor and frowned at his eldest son. "But sobriety. He drinks so he does not feel, and then because he feels nothing, he drinks some more. 'Tis a vicious cycle and me own fault for being so lax with him."

"Perhaps we could all use a drink right now." Their cousin, Jeremy Radcliffe, hesitated at the parlor door, sputtering the words before following Colin across the room and pouring himself a large glass of brandy as well. "Would anyone care to join me?"

"No, thank you, Jeremy," Kathleen said, "but I think I will send someone after Patrick. A small glass might be just what he needs—to calm his nerves, of course."

"Yes, of course, mustn't forget His Lordship," Colin said when Kathleen rang for the butler. He poured himself another drink, then flopped down in the upholstered chair by his side, one leg hanging over the arm. "I doubt you'd be so quick to send anyone looking for me."

"And since when did you ever want to be found?" Jeremy said, earning a sneer from Colin.

Kathleen had to conceal a smile. Her cousin was an odd-looking man of thirty-five, with a long, thin face and drooping eyelids. His thin, wavy locks hung down over his forehead, seeming more like some sort of strange hat than a head of hair, quite the opposite of his handsome younger cousin, who saw him only as a buffoon. They made quite a pair.

"Kathleen is a gentle soul," her father said, "who worries entirely too much about everyone, much like yer sainted mother, God rest her soul." He stopped to bless himself before continuing. "I fear she'll be hurt by it one day."

"Come now, Uncle!" Jeremy said. "Patrick may be an insolent, sniveling little brat, but I seriously doubt he'd do anything to hurt our Kathleen. I truly believe she's the only one in this family he has any regard for at all."

"It wasn't me stepson I was referring to, ye witless—" On seeing the doctor was still amongst them, he held his tongue. "'Tis Brighton Templeton I'm referring to."

"What has Brighton ever done?" Colin perked up at the mention of his friend's name, as usual, speaking in his defense. "Aside from befriending me, that is."

Kathleen had to give Colin that. He was loyal to his friend.

"If he is indeed yer friend," her father said, "he would do well to keep away from yer sister. She deserves better than that rounder."

"In whose eyes, Father?" Colin stood up and slammed his glass on the sideboard.

"In me own eyes, and they're the only ones ye need be worrying about, boyo, for may I remind ye, without me intervention ye'd more than likely be dead or in jail . . . or worse, if me memory serves me right!"

"Then why take it out on Kathleen? She's never caused you any distress, nor will she now, even though she'd gladly welcome Brighton's affections."

"Colin, please!" Kathleen shook her head, though she knew it would do little good.

Her father glanced in her direction, a spark of warning in his eyes, and a sickening warmth spread across her cheeks. How could he possibly know about their midnight trysts down by the lake? "And she'd best continue to tread carefully," he said. "There'll be no dowry should her reputation become tarnished, especially by a guttersnipe like Brighton Templeton."

"Oh dear." Dr. Tennyson stood up, checking the time on his pocket watch. "I really must be going. Mrs. Albright wasn't feeling at all well this morning. If you need anything, please don't hesitate to call."

"O' course." Her father frowned at her brother. "Please forgive our rudeness. I'm afraid Bridie's death has been a terrible strain on us all."

"How can you stand there and lie like that!" Patrick stood by the parlor's pocket doors, his eyes full of fury. He'd come back just in time to catch the end of the conversation. "You know it's not true. She was nothing more to you than a way to gain respectability."

"You little bastard!" Colin said. "I ought to give you a good thrashing."

"Enough, Colin!" her father said. "The lad's just lost his mother."

"And what do you care?" Patrick said. "The only thing that ever interested you was my father's money. You're nothing more than a common thief, but you've lost your meal ticket now, haven't you?"

"That's quite enough, young man," her father said. "As I've told ye before, I loved yer mother dearly, and whether ye believe it or not, I was in need o' neither her money nor her respectability. Now I think 'twould be best for all concerned if ye went to yer room until yer manners return."

"At least I have manners." He cast a sneer in Colin's direction, then, without saying another word, turned and headed for the staircase, stopping only long enough to deposit his boots by the foot of the stairs.

"I'll walk you to the door, Doctor," Kathleen said.

"Perhaps I could give him something to help him rest," Dr. Tennyson suggested, concern clear on his face.

"Perhaps ye should." Her father watched his stepson head up the stairs. "I'm terribly worried about him, Samuel. So much pain in such a short time, and he blames me for it all."

"That's not unusual," the doctor said. "Give him some time, and I'm sure he'll come around. We all have to deal with grief in our own way."

"I'm sure ye're right. 'Tis just that he's become such a handful o' late. He's grown quite wild, as I'm sure ye've heard."

"Time and patience, Thomas. He was very close to his mother. It's only natural that he lashes out at the person he feels took her from him, no matter how misguided that accusation is. He barely had a chance to get used to your marriage, and now you're all he has left."

"I really have tried to be patient with the lad, but . . ."

Dr. Tennyson nodded and followed Kathleen out into the hallway. "Here, put a few drops of this in a cup of tea, and he should sleep comfortably." He handed Kathleen a small brown bottle of elixir and patted her on the shoulder. "It's only a temporary solution, I know, like a small plaster on a gaping wound, but at least it will let him get some rest. There's little else I can do. Broken hearts are well beyond my purview."

"Yes, have Kathleen do it," Colin said from the parlor doorway. "He gets on well with her. As for the rest of us, I'm sure he'd think we were trying to poison him."

"I think in his heart he knows better," the doctor said, "but for now, it might be for the best. Try to get some rest, all of you. And please don't hesitate to call if you need me."

Kathleen walked out on the large wraparound porch, closing the door behind her. "You won't forget about your assistant."

"Of course not. I'll be in touch soon."

CHAPTER 3

Friday, June 10, 1904 – 7:15 a.m.

Patrick rubbed his forehead as he walked down to breakfast. If he hadn't known better, he would have sworn he had consumed an exorbitant amount of liquor the night before, for his knees felt like jelly and he had an incessant pounding in his head. Stopping on the third step, he grasped the handrail in a vain attempt to steady himself and gain his bearings. For a moment, the entire room seemed to be spinning, and a wave of nausea washed over him. He even contemplated returning to bed and hiding deep beneath the covers. It certainly was a tempting thought, but it was already quarter past seven, and he was certain to receive a good tongue-lashing from Thomas as it was. Perhaps all he needed was something to eat. Taking a deep breath, he continued down the stairs.

"It's about time!" Colin rolled his eyes, grumbling when Patrick walked into the dining room.

Under ordinary circumstances, Patrick would have put him in his place at once, trading jibe for jibe, but this morning was different. His entire world had changed. In his heart, he'd been left an orphan, and the thought only added to the nausea that seemed to be consuming him. Without a word, he slid into his seat at the table and waited for Thomas to unleash his fury, but for some unknown reason, the man simply sat there smugly and nodded for breakfast to be served.

Patrick was grateful for the reprieve, even if it was only temporary, but when the meal finally arrived, he could do little but pick at it, much to his stepfather's annoyance. And yet Thomas continued to hold his tongue for the most part, grunting to himself now and then about wasted food. Kathleen, on the other hand, was more concerned, but in spite of her gentle coaxing, the thought of his mother's lifeless body lying in the parlor somehow took away any appetite he might have had.

The next three days weren't any better, though he somehow managed to function well enough, letting the anger he felt toward the Brissedons keep him going. He cringed every time someone offered their condolences to Thomas, finding it easier to walk away than to remain and watch his stepfather's theatrical performance. After all, he knew in his heart that it was little more, though he said nothing, keeping his anger in check, for he didn't want to disgrace his mother's memory. It was for her that he would carry on. For her and the dignity of his family.

Only when he stood beside his mother's open grave did his fragile façade break down.

Daniel O'Halleran stood next to Dr. Tennyson while they laid Cornelius Desmond's widow in the ground. His heart went out to her son, memories of his own mother's death clear in his memory, even though he'd only been six at the time. The scar on his forehead tingled, like tiny pins were being pressed into his skin, and another image flared across his memory.

So this is my misbegotten little by-blow. His father's words had been cold and painful, and Daniel's reaction had prompted the man to smack him so hard he went skidding across the room into the corner of a coffee table. In spite of the anger, a smile touched his lips. Richard Adams had grabbed the man by the collar, fury rising in his eyes. He hadn't seen such a fierce expression on his adoptive father's face in all the years since, even when he and Joe had stolen that package of gum from the five-and-dime.

"We should pay the family our condolences," Sam Tennyson whispered in Daniel's ear, bringing him back to the present.

"Yes, of course." Burying the memories of the past, he followed the doctor across the dew-covered grass, turning his attention to the beautiful young woman who stood off to the side, her arms around two small children. Sam had asked him to meet with her the following Thursday with the intent of looking into Cornelius Desmond's death. Since it was something he'd wanted to do for the last two years, he jumped at the chance, though if the truth be told, he would have agreed regardless.

"My condolences, Miss Brissedon," he said.

A subdued smile flashed across her soft pink lips. "Mr. O'Halleran? I wasn't aware you were acquainted with Dr. Tennyson."

"You two know each other?" Sam said.

"I've made a visit or two to the library, and Miss Brissedon has been kind enough to assist me." A hint of warmth touched Daniel's cheeks. He should have mentioned it.

"Ah, yes, of course." Sam's eyes twinkled. "Nell's mentioned you volunteer. Well, let me formally introduce you. Miss Kathleen Brissedon, this is Dr. Daniel O'Halleran. He'll be assisting me, both in my practice and in my duties as coroner."

"I'm pleased to meet you officially, Doctor." A hint of pink colored the apples of Kathleen's cheeks, though Daniel was certain the color looked far more attractive on her than it did on his own ruddy complexion. "I understand you have experience with the New York City coroner's office. What on earth brings you all the way out to our little town?" The woman clearly noticed his hesitation, for she quickly continued. "Forgive me. That was incredibly rude."

"Not at all," he said, though in fact he had no intention of revealing the real reason at the moment. "I was just in need of a change in scenery. When my father informed me Dr. Tennyson was looking for an assistant, I applied at once." Close enough to the truth for now.

"Well, we're happy to have you. Perhaps you and Dr. Tennyson could come to dinner in a few weeks, when everything has calmed down, along with your families, of course."

Did she just ask if I have a wife?

"Nell will be delighted," Samuel said, "though I'm afraid Daniel is a bachelor. Perhaps you could introduce him to a few of your friends."

Daniel wanted to punch the man, figuratively speaking. *Mother must have gotten ahold of him.* "Dinner will be quite sufficient, thank you. And again, my sincere condolences." Daniel gave a small nod and moved away, replacing his hat as he trod over the grass-covered ground.

"Really, Sam! My mother's put a bee in your bonnet, hasn't she?"

"Actually, she's put it in Nell's, which of course means I've been instructed to encourage you to develop a social life."

"I have a social life."

"Yes, so I've heard. The library, is it?" A smirk crossed the older doctor's lips. "Well, the best way to get over being thrown from a horse is to get right back on one."

"That's a rude analogy."

"Oh, don't take it so literally. It's your own fault. You could have mentioned you knew Kathleen when we spoke the other night."

"I suppose I should have, but it didn't seem important. Nothing will come of it."

"The investigation or your relationship with the young lady?"

"Either, I'm afraid." He jumped into the doctor's buggy, casting a glance in her direction. She certainly was an attractive young lady, though not in the same way Pru was. No, Kathleen's allure went deeper than mere appearance, all the way to her soul. He could sense it.

"You'll never know unless you give it a try." Sam climbed in beside him and took the reins.

"Once burned, twice shy." But even as the words passed his lips, he couldn't help but hope. *No, stop it, Danny. She's way above your class.* After all, as Pru had so dramatically pointed out in the message she'd sent to the church, in spite of his elegant rearing, he was nothing more than a baseborn bastard. Granted, he probably should have mentioned it to her at some point, but he didn't see what difference it made. Clearly, Pru did. He cast one more glance in Kathleen's direction. A tall, well-dressed fellow put his arm around her waist. *Definitely not in her league.*

Kathleen frowned. Despite her best efforts, she couldn't get her stepbrother to take more than a few bites. Nor would he even take a sip of the tea she'd brewed for him. She feared it wouldn't be long before he joined his mother if he continued along these lines.

"Please, Patrick, at least try one of the custard tarts. Mrs. Quinn made them especially for you. She knows how much you love them."

"I'm just not hungry, Kate," he said before sighing and pulling one onto his plate.

"Dr. Tennyson to see you, miss," Forbes said.

"Yes, I'll be right there. Show him into the parlor, please." She turned her attention back to Patrick. "I need to go speak to Dr. Tennyson. Promise me you'll at least eat that while I'm gone."

His shoulders slumped, but he nodded. "I'll try, but I'm not making any promises." The corner of his mouth quivered as he tried to smile. She kissed his forehead, grateful that he'd at least made an attempt, before moving away to greet the doctor.

"I just thought I'd check to see how you were all doing," Sam said.

"As well as can be expected, I suppose," she said, eyeing the liquor cabinet. "Colin and Jeremy are self-medicating. It's Patrick that has me worried. He doesn't seem to want to eat, which isn't like him at all."

"Give him a few days. I'm sure he'll be fine. He knows his parents would want him to take care of himself."

"I'm sure you're right." Without thinking, she gazed around the parlor. "Has Dr. O'Halleran accompanied you?"

"I'm afraid he's making my rounds for me." A twinkle lit his eye, telling her that she had been far too obvious in her inquiry. "But as promised, I did speak to him at dinner the other night. I hesitated to mention anything at the funeral since you seem to want to keep the inquiry between us; however, Daniel will be happy to meet you on Thursday at twelve noon if that's agreeable. Will Emma Newins's restaurant suit you?

"Yes, of course. That would be wonderful."

"I know it's quite soon after the funeral, but considering your sense of urgency in the matter . . ."

"No, not at all. I was planning to have Trevor take me to the library that morning anyway. It will raise more than a few eyebrows, no doubt, but I feel it will do me good. I believe Brigid would approve."

"I think you're quite right, my dear. In my opinion, the mourning restrictions are a hindrance to healing, and I'm glad to see they are being eased for the most part. I'm sure Dr. O'Halleran would agree."

"Did you mention why I wished to speak to him?"

"I gave him the general idea, and as it happens, he remembers the incident well. In fact, it was his first case. Though he was only privy to the information the autopsy revealed, he knows a detective who did try to investigate it further. It may not help, but it's a start."

"Thank you so much. If I could at least give Patrick hope that his father's death was being investigated once more, perhaps it would help him through this difficult time."

Patrick stared down at the plate before him. He did love those tarts, but all they did now was remind him of his mother. She'd given the receipt to Mrs. Quinn when he was no more than five or six. They'd been so happy then. Where had it all gone wrong? With Thomas Brissedon, that's where.

Throwing a gaze in Thomas's direction, Patrick watched the man check his pocket watch, the one with the three little shamrocks on the lid set in Connemara marble. Only it wasn't his watch.

The memory of that afternoon just over two years before, the last time he'd seen his father alive, was etched into Patrick's memory. His father had been heading to the city to see to the construction of a playroom in one of the orphanages. As he always had when he headed out for the city, he'd checked his watch, then tucked it in his waistcoat and patted the pocket. He'd done it that day, just as he had every day before, but no watch had been found on his body. At least that's what they had been told. Yet here was Thomas Brissedon, flipping open the lid with an air of importance to look at the time.

Patrick had confronted Thomas about it the first time he'd seen the man with it. Little good it had done. As usual, the old man had laughed it off with a condescending tone, telling Patrick he must have misunderstood. The watch had been with the rest of Cornelius Desmond's effects. Heat rushed into Patrick's face. Just seeing Thomas's filthy hands on something that meant so much to his father made him want to beat the living daylights out of the old bastard. But no, not now. He'd bide his time until he could get more evidence, then see the man hanged.

CHAPTER 4

Thursday, June 16, 1904 – 8:00 a.m.

A few days later, Thomas summoned Patrick into his study right after breakfast and bid him stand before the large mahogany desk at which he was seated. What did the old man want now? Best to get it over with, he supposed, though his first inclination had been to ignore the man completely. As the clock ticked away the minutes, and Thomas kept him waiting, he began to think perhaps he should have. At last, the man slammed his ledger shut and leaned back in his chair. Without any of the usual niceties of social behavior, he lit his cigar and got right to the matter at hand.

"Now that yer dear mother's laid to rest, 'tis time we come to an understanding, lad." He pointed to the hard ladder-back chair before his desk and indicated that Patrick was to sit down. When he did, the man continued. "First o' all, ye'll take all yer belongings and remove them to the small room closest to the west wing."

"I beg your pardon, but why would I want to do that?"

"Because ye're no longer the favored son, as it were. Colin will be moving into yer former rooms, and I expect him to find them quite devoid o' yer belongings. Is that understood?"

Patrick's temper flared. "No, sir, it's not! My father designed those rooms for me, and I see no reason why I should vacate them now!"

"Might I remind ye, lad, that yer father is long dead. 'Tis me care ye're under now, and ye'll do as I say or find yerself out in the cold."

Heat rose in Patrick's cheeks. Who did this charlatan think he was? "No, sir! It's you who'll find yourself destitute. This is my home now. For my mother's sake, I had thought to allow you to remain, but I'll not be bullied by you."

"Yer home! Is that what ye think?" Thomas laughed, a cold, vicious cackle that sent a chill through Patrick. "This house hasn't belonged to ye for over a year now. Yer dear mother, God rest her soul, was forced to sell it in order to pay yer father's debts. Fortunately for ye, I was in a position to buy it, and so, because o' me generosity, ye've been able to continue living here."

"But that's impossible! My father's business was quite prosperous."

"That's what Desmond wanted everyone to think, all right. But the truth o' the matter is he was over his head in debt. He spent more than he made on whiskey and whores, then gave the rest away."

"No, I don't believe you, and even if it were true, there's still my mother's inheritance. I know my father put a sizeable endowment aside for her. Surely she's left me something."

"As I told ye, lad, most o' yer father's estate had to be liquidated to satisfy his debts. Yer mother wanted everyone paid, even if it meant dipping into her own funds. It's the kind o' woman she was. She offered her fine jewelry, o' course, but I'm afraid it wasn't even worth the paste it was made o'. Caring for her as I did, I didn't have the heart to break such bleak news to her, especially in those final days, so I've used me own money to supplement yer mother's legacy to ye, including yer allowance. Sure, who did ye think had been paying it?"

Patrick opened his mouth to protest, but Thomas raised his hand. "Perhaps ye should be reading this before ye make any more foolish statements."

Thomas handed him a thin leather packet that was tied with a ribbon. Patrick took the package, trying to keep his hands from shaking as he opened it. His gazed drifted back to his stepfather's smug expression for a moment before he focused on the words written on the crisp ivory parchment. A wave of despair clutched his heart, causing the breath to catch in his throat.

~~~~~~~~~~~~~~~~~~~~~~~~~~~~~~~~~~~~~

LAST WILL AND TESTAMENT

In the name of God. Amen. I, Brigid Desmond Brissedon, of the County of Suffolk, and the State of New York, being of sound mind, but frail in body, do on this 24th day of May 1904 hereby make this my last will and testament in the manner and form following to wit:

First: It is my will that my executor, hereafter named, shall pay all my just debts and funeral expenses as soon as possible after my demise.

Item. I give and bequeath to my beloved son, Patrick Desmond, the entirety of my estate with the conditions and exceptions listed herewith, which consists of . . .

Item. I give and bequeath to my dear son, Patrick Desmond, an annual endowment of five thousand dollars, which he is to receive only so long as he remains a good and loving son to my husband, Thomas Brissedon. Said endowment is to be portioned out at said husband's discretion as he sees fit, but not before said son has achieved his twenty-fifth birthday unless otherwise deemed acceptable by said husband.

Item. Until such time as he receives his endowment, said son Patrick shall receive a weekly stipend of fifteen dollars to be delivered at the discretion of aforesaid husband.

Item. I place my loving son, Patrick Desmond, under the care and guardianship of my husband, Thomas Brissedon.

Finally, I do nominate and appoint my husband, Thomas Brissedon, to be the sole executor and administrator of this my last will and testament. In witness where I have hereunto set my hand and seal this 24th day of May 1904.

Brigid Desmond Brissedon

Witness: *Jeremy Radcliffe*
Trevor Kilpatrick

May 24, 1904

~~~~~~

"Feeling a little peaked, are we?" Thomas asked with a sardonic grin.

"You tricked her, you bastard! You stole my father's business for yourself, then told her it was your own. I won't let you get away with this."

"Don't be ridiculous. And even if it were true, just what do ye think ye could do about it? Everyone knows how ye resent me, in spite of me kindness to both ye and yer mother. It was her wish that I be yer guardian, however, and so I shall be. There were witnesses to it, lad, and Dr. Tennyson will testify that she was quite cognizant at the time. But then, perhaps ye suspect the good doctor as well."

"I'm twenty. I don't need a guardian."

"True enough, lad, and I'll not hold ye here, but keep in mind the conditions of yer inheritance. Ye'll not get one red cent o' it unless I decide ye should, nor will ye continue to receive a weekly stipend from me."

Patrick could hardly speak, but he wouldn't allow himself to give in to childish tears. "You tricked them both, and you've fooled everyone else as well, but I know it's all an act. One day you'll let down your guard, and that's when I'll catch you."

"My God, is that a threat, or are ye simply delusional? I could have ye put away for that, ye know. Ye are in me care, after all, or have ye decided ye're old enough to be on yer own?"

Patrick felt as if the air itself was smothering him. He wanted to run, as fast and as far as he could, but where would he go, and who could he go to? His father had been well liked, it was true, but after his mysterious death, word had begun to circulate about his drinking and late-night excursions to the city. No one actually came out and said anything, but he could see the men talking behind his mother's back and hear the women whispering as they passed.

Thomas, on the other hand, was seen as Patrick's savior. Oh, there were many who didn't like him, to be sure, but they all agreed he must have loved Brigid Desmond a great deal. After all, did he not attend her in her illness? Patrick felt weak and grabbed on to the desk before him.

"So, it's all sinking in now, is it? Well then, 'tis time to hear the rest o' it."

Patrick looked at his stepfather, bile rising in his throat. "Rest of it? What do you mean?"

"Ye don't think I'll be letting ye live here without contributing yer fair share, now, do ye?"

"But I was to continue my schooling."

"And so ye shall. I did promise yer mother I would see to yer education, but then ye have to hold up yer end o' the bargain as well."

"I made no bargain with you."

"But yer darling mother did, and so, if ye don't want to land on the streets or in an asylum, ye'll be a good and obedient son."

"You bastard!"

"Ye'd best watch yer mouth, lad, or I'll cut ye off without a cent and not ever look back. Now to the matter at hand. Ye'll have certain duties to perform, and if done properly, I'll allow ye to continue in residence here. As to yer inheritance, it shall be put in trust for ye, and ye'll receive it on yer twenty-fifth birthday or on the day of yer marriage to a suitable and wealthy young lady o' me choosing, whichever shall be the last to occur."

"But that means I'll have to achieve both before I'm able to access my own money."

"Nothing is yer own, lad. Has that not yet penetrated yer thick skull? All but a meager portion o' it is mine, to do with as I like."

"But my mother left me—"

"A decent endowment, which I had to supplement. D'ye truly think she had enough left to leave ye five thousand dollars a year for the rest o' yer life? Don't be such a fool. If I choose to give ye nothing but what she had, ye'd be through it in five years' time. But she also left yer welfare in me hands, and as such, I control yer assets. Under me skillful management, those resources could grow into a sizeable estate, so it would be in yer own best interest to do as I instruct."

Patrick wanted to scream, but he held his temper. After all, according to the law, he had little recourse. "And just what are your instructions, sir?"

"I would prefer if ye called me Father." A wicked sneer crossed the man's face, calling to mind the wolf in an old fairy tale. "It sounds much more dignified."

Thomas was tormenting him. Patrick could see the pleasure in his eyes. "But you're not my father!"

"According to yer mother's wishes, I am, and I'll be addressed as such, or I'll feel no need to see to yer trust or a weekly allowance. Is that clear?"

"Yes, sir." He balled his hands at his side to keep them from shaking and to control the rage that was seething deep within his bowels.

"Now, as to yer duties. There is a gentleman coming to dinner tomorrow night, a Mr. Benjamin Langston. He has a substantial building concern and is in the process o' looking for a supplier to provide quality lumber for his latest project. As he has plans to begin a number o' those projects in the near future, 'tis me opinion that he'll soon be in need o' material for them as well. I intend to acquire not only this first contract, but any subsequent ones as well."

"What does that have to do with me? I know little of my father's business."

"Elizabeth Langston is yer business. She'll be accompanying her husband tomorrow night, and word has it that she's a terribly unhappy woman. Her husband spends a great deal o' time in the city, and she's in desperate need o' some companionship. Ye, me dear boy, will give her the attention she seeks."

"I beg your pardon?" The man couldn't possibly be suggesting what he thought. "I'm not sure I understand what it is you want me to do."

"Oh, I think ye do, lad. Ye don't seem to have any problem charming the local help. Surely ye can handle an attractive, if over-the-hill, matron."

Patrick stood before his stepfather, spellbound, unable to believe what he was hearing. Once more, a wave of nausea overcame him, and his heart hammered against his ribs. He must have misunderstood. There was no other explanation. Finally, he managed to speak.

"You want me to . . . to bed the woman?" Though the words came from his mouth, they sounded strange, almost like they belonged to someone else.

Thomas leaned back in his chair, a frown crossing his brow. "Well, I hadn't thought o' it going that far, no, but perhaps . . . Let's just start slowly, shall we? I don't want her husband to be catching me stepson diddling his wife, now, do I?" He shrugged. "Well, not yet, anyway."

"But she's Lydia's mother!"

Thomas lifted an eyebrow, a sly grin crossing his lips. "One o' yer conquests?"

"I should say not! I'd hoped to court her, but . . ."

"Ah, yer reputation precedes ye, does it?" Thomas chuckled. "Well, ye can forget it, boyo. Lizzie's got her eye on ye for herself, and I need her for me plans to work. Ye're part o' our agreement."

"What agreement?"

"Never ye mind that. Ye just do as ye're told and tickle the lady's fancy as she likes, eh?"

Patrick wanted to vomit.

"Don't look so appalled by the idea. It's not like ye're a virgin, and when Lizzie's through with ye, maybe she won't mind ye courting her daughter. Right now, though, ye're to use yer considerable charms on her, make her feel giddy, like a young girl again. The way ye do with that lass in the general store. Sure, ye must have bedded her by now."

"No, I haven't!"

"No? Too bad, it might have worked to me advantage. For now, just concentrate on Lizzie, then, eh, and make sure she's happy. Whether that requires ye to become her lover or simply stroke her ego, I couldn't care less. Ye'll do the same for anyone I need ye to. I intend to have the lion's portion o' business, both across the island and in the city, and ye'll see to it that the ladies involved help me achieve that."

"But I don't understand. How can they help you?"

"Secrets, me lad. Everyone has them, and most will pay a king's ransom to see they remain hidden. Even if it means giving me their business. Lizzie knows things, but she'll only share them if ye're part o' the bargain, so . . ." He shrugged again. This was all nothing more than a game to him.

"You're insane!" Patrick glared at his stepfather. "I'll have no part in your depraved scheme."

"Oh, ye'll do exactly as I say, lad, or I'll teach ye what depravity really is. The streets o' New York have a way o'

I.M. FOSTER

educating a young man to the seamier side o' life. D'ye have any idea what they'd do to a lad as fine as yerself?"

"I don't care how many threats you make. I won't do it! You have secrets as well. Perhaps Kathleen would like to know how you do business."

"Don't even try to beat me at me own game, ye ungrateful little bastard. I'm her flesh and blood. Her beloved father. D'ye truly think she'll take your word over mine? Maybe ye're needing a taste o' what life on the streets is like, eh?" Thomas jumped up from his desk, the vein in his neck throbbing. He grabbed Patrick by the arm and hauled him down the back hallway.

Patrick tried to resist, kicking and yelling, but the brawny Irishman's hand was like a steel vise. Cursing, Thomas shoved a rag in Patrick's mouth. "No one's going to come to yer aid, boyo, so save yer strength. Ye're going to need it."

Swearing once more, Thomas dragged Patrick out the hallway door and down to the stables, nearly dislocating his arm more than once and making Patrick wonder if there would indeed be anything left of him by the time they arrived at their destination. He stumbled along, falling occasionally, only to be dragged up again by the scruff of his neck, until at last, they entered the stables. Thomas tossed him at the feet of his two stable hands, instructing the slovenly ratbags to hold Patrick up against one of the stalls.

"Now, ye spoiled little brat, I'll show ye what 'tis like out in the real world, far away from the security o' a loving home." His huge fist connected with Patrick's face, causing blood and spittle to run from his mouth. "Think ye can outsmart me, do ye?" Thomas swung the back of his hand across Patrick's cheek, then landed another punch.

"Ye don't know what poverty is, ye sniveling little ingrate, but I'll give ye a taste o' it." He grabbed Patrick's hair, yanking his head back against the coarse wood and viciously slamming his iron-like fist into his stomach, over and over again, until Patrick could barely stand. Even as he slumped to the ground, on the verge of unconsciousness, the old man pounded his thick leather boot into his side. Patrick doubled over, groaning in pain, wishing the man would just kill him and get it over with.

Thomas bent down and whispered in his ear before dragging him up to his feet yet again. "Perhaps ye're beginning to see things me way now, eh?"

Though he was in tremendous pain, coughing and spitting up blood and vomit, Patrick continued to shake his head in defiance. He wouldn't give in to his stepfather's depraved plot. Gathering up all the strength he could muster, he turned to face his assailant and spit in his face.

Thomas wiped the spittle away, his expression belying the fury clear in his eyes. He grabbed Patrick by the neck once more, nearly choking him this time, and drove his knee into Patrick's groin again and again. "Laying with the old girl disgusts ye, does it?"

Patrick gasped for air, hovering somewhere on the fringes of consciousness, the bile rising in his throat, until at last, Thomas tossed him down at the feet of the stable hands once again. "Finish the job for us, eh, lads, but try not to go too hard on his face." Taking ahold of Patrick's hair, the Irishman lifted his head and patted him on the cheek. "He needs those boyish good looks to hold the old floozy's attention."

CHAPTER 5

Patrick was broken and despondent when Willie Duggan and Mickey Sutton dragged him into the house that afternoon. They'd used him as a punching bag, laughing with each blow, until he'd barely known whether he was alive or dead. Only the pain told him which it was, but though blood ran from his nose and mouth and mud and manure covered his clothes, it was that deeper, hidden ache that caused the most agony.

His heart was shattered, stomped on just as surely and thoroughly as his body. All he had known and loved, all he had cherished, had been whisked away in the space of a few days. How he wished they had killed him, for at least then he would be with those who cared for him.

"Dear Lord!" Kathleen stood at the foot of the sweeping staircase, her face pale and her dusty blue eyes filled with horror. "What on earth happened?"

"He fell from his horse, miss," Mickey stated, a sly spark in his eye. "I ain't never seen anything like it. That mare just bolted up for no reason at all. Why, the way it went on, the lad's lucky to be alive at all."

"Forbes!" Kathleen took charge at once, just like his mother would have. "Send Trevor for the doctor and have Mrs. Quinn bring a basin of warm water. Mickey, you bring Patrick in here on the sofa and then call for my father."

The man hesitated. "Yer da ain't going to be too happy about us tramping in there, miss, getting dirt all over his rugs."

"You let me worry about my father. Now bring him in here before he collapses right there on the floor."

"All right, miss. Long as ye make sure yer da knows it wasn't our idea." He and Willie dragged Patrick along, one on each side, and laid him down on the silk damask sofa.

For a moment, he could have sworn his mother was bending over him, her tender hand caressing his cheek, but then his vision cleared. It was Kathleen whose gentle touch sought to soothe him.

"Now go to the sideboard," she said, "and bring me that decanter of brandy and one of the small glasses." She placed a velvet cushion beneath his head, then, raising him ever so slightly, she lifted the glass of anesthetizing elixir to his lips.

"I don't want any," he said, determined to keep his senses as clear as possible.

"But you must, darling. It will help ease the pain."

Patrick pushed it away again, but Kathleen persisted until she managed to get some of the sweet liquor past his lips. "Where is Mrs. Quinn with that water?" she said.

"Right here, ma'am."

One of his eyes was swelling closed, but he didn't care. Maybe they'd just let him die. Cool water on his face revived him. He opened his one good eye to see tears running down Kathleen's cheeks, and a warmth suffused his mangled heart.

"What in the blazes!" Thomas stopped short, visibly cringing when he saw Patrick's battered form lying on the fashionable sofa.

Didn't think about me bleeding on the furniture, did you? If he hadn't felt so ill, he might have laughed.

Kathleen placed her hand on his chest, glaring at her father, daring him to complain, and the man cleared his throat, throwing a quick glance at his stable hands. "If you two imbeciles had anything to do with this . . ." He bent down beside his daughter, placing his hand over hers.

"Now, Father," Kathleen said, her voice a soothing salve to Patrick's wounded spirit, "calm yourself. It will do Patrick no good to be besieged by your rantings. I'm sure it was no one's fault."

"Ye're right, o' course, darlin'. Are ye in any pain, Son?"

Patrick turned his head away in disgust, unable to abide even looking at the wicked bastard. Kathleen must have taken it to mean that he was, and after wringing out the rag and returning it to his forehead, she took his hand in hers. That small gesture, performed solely out of love, gave him the strength he needed to go on. He knew, at that moment, his mother had not left him alone.

He squeezed his stepsister's hand. "I'll be all right, Katie." Though he made an attempt to smile, the effort caused him to groan again. It was almost worth it, though, for it prompted Kathleen to caress his battered cheek, her cool fingers easing the sting.

"What's happened?" Dr. Tennyson's calming voice echoed from the hallway. Moments later, he was kneeling by Patrick's side. "I want all of you outside. Yes, Kathleen, that means you as well. He's a grown man. I don't imagine he wants his sister watching while I examine him."

As soon as they'd all left, he looked down at Patrick, a frown marring his pleasant face. "I want the truth, son. Did you do this deliberately?"

Patrick's good eye widened. "No, sir. Mama taught me that would be a sin."

A smile brightened the doctor's face, and he nodded. "I didn't think so; still, I had to ask. So what did happen?"

"I went for a ride, and the horse threw me." Might as well go with the standard story. No one would believe the truth, and it would only give credence to Thomas's argument should he decide to see him locked away in an asylum somewhere.

Putting a compress of some sort on Patrick's eye, the doctor frowned, pressing a bit harder than was necessary. "No fall from a horse caused this. So, do you want to tell me what really happened, or should I call Kathleen back in here and let her grill you?"

Oh, what the heck. His reputation wasn't exactly in danger of being sullied any more than it already was. "I got caught with one of the local young ladies. Her brothers weren't too happy."

The doctor shook his head but seemed to accept that explanation. "Good Lord, boy! What's gotten into you? I won't ask who, but I hope maybe this will teach you a lesson. I suppose it's best we continue with the thrown-from-the-horse scenario regarding your father, however."

"He's not my father," Patrick said. "My father's dead, killed when he fell in a drunken stupor while out whoring. Why not tell the whole town? They'll just shake their heads and say, 'like father, like son.'"

"You know better than that. Your father wasn't a drunkard, and there's certainly no way he was unfaithful to your mother."

"Then why won't anyone help me prove it?"

"Sit up while I take a look at those ribs. I don't think they're broken, but one or two may be cracked. Several are definitely bruised. Now, as to proving your father's innocence . . .You aren't alone in your suspicions. Other channels are being pursued."

"What channels?" Patrick winced as the doctor wrapped a cotton bandage around his midsection.

"I'll leave something with Kathleen for the pain."

"No more of your tea!"

The doctor lifted an eyebrow, a suppressed laugh causing his lips to quiver. "Figured it out, did you?"

"I saw what you gave Mama after Papa died. And Kathleen had that little brown bottle in her pocket. She tried to keep it hidden but kept pulling it out to retrieve her handkerchief."

"I'll tell her to reduce the dosage, but if it hurts to breathe, I want you to take it. Do you understand?"

"Yes, sir, but you still haven't told me who—"

"I've pledged my silence, and a gentleman keeps his word. Now I want to get you upstairs to bed." He looked toward the door and frowned again. "Perhaps Colin and Forbes can give you a hand. I doubt Thomas will allow those stable hands to tread that deeply into the house."

"I thought he was going to swallow his teeth when he saw them in here." Patrick laughed briefly before moaning, but the gesture made the doctor smile.

"It's good to see your humor returning." He squeezed Patrick's arm. "Have faith, lad. Things will get better. For now, though, I want you in bed. Since you're so averse to my special blend of tea, I'll leave some tablets with Kathleen. But if you don't take them as needed, I have a syringe that won't be quite so pleasant."

"I'll take them, I promise."

Kathleen saw that Patrick was settled in, making sure he took the tablets Dr. Tennyson had left, then kissed him on the forehead and joined the doctor in the parlor.

"He's a very lucky young man." Tennyson sat with a weary sigh and took a sip of brandy. "It's amazing there wasn't more damage done. Horses that bolt like that have been known to trample their riders to death. A cracked rib or two and a few cuts and bruises is nothing compared to what could have happened."

Colin had joined them in the parlor, retrieving a large glass of brandy before sinking in an armchair next to the sideboard, a smug smile plastered on his face. "I guess we should all be grateful, then. How ironic if he should have been killed just a few days after his mother's funeral. Do you think perhaps he planned it? He has been brooding terribly since she died."

"What a terrible thing to say!" Kathleen stood by the mantel. Now that the crisis was over, her nerves were playing havoc with her stomach. "Honestly, Colin, sometimes I wonder if you ever think before you speak."

"And sometimes I wonder, dear sister, if you wouldn't rather have him for a brother."

"Is that why you despise him so? Well, rest easy, Brother, my affection for Patrick in no way lessens my love for you. I am capable of caring for you both, you know."

Colin's expression softened for a moment. He rose and walked over to her, leaning down to kiss the top of her head. "Yes, Kate, I know that. I don't think I've ever known anyone capable of so much love. Forgive me, please."

"Of course, we've all been under a lot of pressure the last few weeks. Just try and be patient with Patrick. He needs us now more than ever."

Dr. Tennyson finished his drink and got up to leave, turning to Kathleen. "I'd best be going. Just keep an eye on him tonight and continue that cool compress on his head. If he should wake before morning, give him another one of those tablets, then see he gets one each night for the next week or so."

"Not the laudanum?" Kathleen asked.

"No, he's caught on to that, and he might give you trouble over it. The pills won't work as well, but they'll help him sleep and not leave him feeling so groggy."

"Thank you, Doctor," Kathleen said. "I'll see you out."

"And call me at once if he develops a fever or shows any signs of internal bleeding: difficulty breathing, vomiting, blood in his urine. No, I don't expect you to follow him into the toilet. He's a grown man. But have Forbes ask him about it from time to time. I swear that man can smell a lie from hundred paces."

Kathleen laughed, feeling a bit more relaxed. "Yes, of course. He will be all right, though, won't he?"

Tennyson smiled. "Yes, I'm sure he will. Just see he takes it easy for the next few days, and no horseback riding. What he needs now is rest, mental and physical. He's had quite a lot to deal with these last two years. I sometimes wonder if he ever recovered from the loss of his father, and now his mother's gone as well."

"Humph! I wouldn't mind if ours took the count tomorrow," Colin said, just loud enough for Kathleen to hear, but when she threw an angry glance in his direction, he simply shrugged and poured himself another drink.

Daniel O'Halleran sneered down into the cup of coffee that sat before him. An hour ago, he'd been overjoyed, waiting in eager anticipation for his meeting with the lovely Miss Brissedon.

He'd made it a point to visit the library every Tuesday and Thursday during his lunch hour for the past month, hoping to summon the courage to ask the pretty librarian if she would consent to having dinner with him. So when Dr. Tennyson had proposed he look into the death of her stepbrother's father, it seemed like fate had intervened.

What a complete dolt he'd been to hope there might have been more to the lady's request. Had he not already learned his lesson? Still, he remembered the Cornelius Desmond case all too well, and it continued to stick in his craw that the district attorney had discarded his findings without so much as a second glance. He welcomed the chance to prove those bureaucratic nincompoops wrong, even if he didn't stand a chance with Kathleen Brissedon.

He sighed and leaned back against the chair, his large form causing it to creak. He checked his watch again before scrubbing a hand across his face. What was he thinking? Even if she had come, the meeting never would have ended as he'd hoped, for either of them. His uncle had looked into the case at the time, and he was as thorough as they came. Truth be told, there was little chance he'd uncover anything to alter the official report, especially after two years. Was he just giving her false hope, agreeing to take the case to bolster his own ego? No, the evidence was there. He just needed a reason to dig into it a bit more.

The bells from the nearby church struck one. He stood and threw two bits on the table, then, with a nod to the bald-headed waiter, he walked outside, heading north on Ocean Avenue. As he walked, his annoyance grew. She could have at least sent him a note and not left him sitting there like a complete fool. Not that it was the first time he'd been stood up, but somehow this stung a bit sharper. *Sharper than being left at the altar?* He turned onto East Main Street, still mulling the question over in his head.

At least something good had come out of that. Too humiliated to stay in Brooklyn, he'd taken the job on Long Island. Breathing in the clean, fresh ocean air, he recalled his mother's words when they'd realized his bride wasn't coming.

Everything happens for the best, darling. She'd stood on her toes and kissed his forehead, soothing his wounded pride.

Perhaps this was for the best as well. Stopping short, he turned around and headed back to Ocean Avenue, where the library temporarily sublet a room in the George M. Ackerly Block. What if she was ill? Would she have left a message for him there? A sudden surge of fear hastened his feet to the door. What if she'd been injured? Swallowing his pride, he walked up to the desk and bid the fastidious young woman a good afternoon.

She smiled pleasantly enough, though it was clear she thought he was a bit of a rogue. "Good day. How may I help you?"

"I was looking for Miss Brissedon." The prim librarian lifted an eyebrow, so he hastened to continue. "Dr. Tennyson recommended I ask her to help me locate a book."

"Oh, perhaps I can help you with that."

Idiot! Of course she'd say that. He had to think of an answer. "I'm sure you could, but Dr. Tennyson couldn't remember the title, you see. However, Miss Brissedon helped him with it, and he feels sure she'll remember."

"What was it about?"

Good Lord, this one is relentless. "I'm afraid I don't know that either. Samuel couldn't recall the title, but he thought it was something I might enjoy."

"Well, there's likely a record of what he took out. We should be able to tell from that." He was about to give up and suggest he simply leave a note when the woman frowned. "Oh dear. The doctor is quite an avid reader. Do you think you'd recognize the title if you saw it?"

"I'm afraid not."

The woman screwed her face up into a disgruntled expression but seemed satisfied with his explanation. "Miss Brissedon wasn't in today. It seems there was an emergency at home."

"Oh, I'm sorry. Nothing serious, I hope?"

She narrowed her eyes in obvious annoyance. "I wouldn't know. Their butler phoned, but he didn't elaborate. I was assured she'd be in next Tuesday as usual. Not that it helped me today."

"I'm sure it was unavoidable," he said, finding himself defending the young woman.

"Yes, well, to be perfectly honest, I was shocked that she was coming in at all, given the funeral was just held on Monday. But then she telephoned last night to say she had decided to come in. I know mourning restrictions have been eased somewhat in the last few years, and that it was only a stepmother, but still, a certain period of mourning should be observed. Don't you agree? Perhaps she thought better of it."

"Most likely. I'll try back again on Tuesday." He gave a polite nod to the young woman and hurried out the door.

Much as he hated to admit it, the news lifted his spirits. Still, she'd managed to notify the librarian. Why not take a moment to send word to him as well?

Out of nowhere, a red-faced young man ran up to him. "Sorry, Doc. Miss Kathleen just said you were to meet for lunch, but she didn't say where. She was that worried about Mr. Patrick."

"Her stepbrother?"

"Yes, sir. He's taken a terrible fall from a horse." The boy gave a sarcastic huff, though he tried to cover it with a cough.

"And what exactly do *you* think happened?" Daniel straightened his back, as if a ramrod had been stuck up it, for he knew it made his six-foot-two frame look even more intimidating. Then, turning his face slightly so the lad could catch a glimpse of the pearly white scar that ran across the left side of his forehead, he narrowed his eyes. "I'll be expecting the truth."

The boy looked to the ground. "'Tis not for me to say, is it? I don't want to lose my job."

Daniel lifted his eyebrow. "I can be discreet. Now tell me what you think really happened."

The boy kicked at a pebble. "Mr. Patrick's a bit of a rapscallion, isn't he? At least, that's what Ma says. I figure he got caught diddling someone's sister and got the shit beat out of him."

"Ah, I see." A smile tugged at the corner of Daniel's mouth, and he handed the boy a coin. "Could you make sure Miss Kathleen gets this message? It is to go into her hands and no one else's. If any ask, say it is a request from the library."

"Yes, sir," the boy said with a wink as Daniel wrote out a quick note.

"And it's nothing untoward," he said, his eyes staring deep into the boy's. "So don't be jumping to conclusions that could damage Miss Kathleen's reputation."

"No, sir! I would never do that." The boy's expression turned serious. "She looks the other way when Mrs. Quinn smuggles us lads some cookies late of a night."

"And just what are you doing there *late of a night?*"

The boy's shoulders slumped. "I'm apprentice to the groom."

"Don't you like horses?" Daniel thought it might be a rather nice position.

"I like the horses right enough. 'Tis the other beasts that tend the stables I'm not right fond of." Giving a shrug, the boy slipped the note in his pocket and scurried away.

After seeing Dr. Tennyson out, Kathleen headed up the stairs to check on her stepbrother. "Will you take another one of these tablets?" she asked, not wanting to upset him any more than he already was. "I promise it won't have the same effect as the laudanum."

He nodded and pushed himself up in bed, grunting as he did so. She handed him a glass of water and one of the tablets, and though he made a face, he popped the pill in his mouth and swallowed without any comment. Sighing, he sank back down under his blankets. His eyes drifted shut even before he hit the pillow.

She stood to walk away, but the sound of his voice stopped her. "Thank you," he said, his words a bit slurred, "for caring."

"Always, darling." She slipped out the door and headed back downstairs, hoping to steal a moment alone. A sigh of relief escaped from her lips when she entered the parlor to find it empty, and she relaxed against the gold damask love seat.

She'd had such high hopes when her father married Brigid. After losing her mother at such a young age, she'd seen it as a chance to have a real family again. Almost as far back as she could remember, she'd always been away at boarding school. Colin had too. Even when her father had remarried, he'd insisted it was necessary, as he had business to tend to and their new mother had her hands full with the little ones. So, they'd continued to spend their vacations with Mrs. Cole, a sweet old lady who'd lived out in the country. But then he'd he met Brigid, and they'd all moved in together. Now she was gone, leaving a gaping tear in the fabric of their family.

Forbes entered the room, and she shook her head to rouse herself from contemplation. "A note came for you, Miss Brissedon."

"Thank you." She took the folded piece of paper, an unbidden thrill causing her toes to tingle, for her name had been written in a decidedly masculine hand, one that she didn't recognize. Could it be from Dr. O'Halleran?

She took a deep breath to compose herself. *Stop it, Kathleen! As handsome as he is, he probably has a sweetheart back in the city. Besides, you're still allowing Brighton to call on you, albeit in secret. Your meeting with the doctor was purely of a business nature. Nothing more.* In fact, with all the commotion that had been going on earlier that afternoon, she hadn't even remembered it until the clock in the hall chimed the hour. It was only a matter of courtesy that had prompted her to scribble a message and send it off with one of the young stable boys.

She gazed down at the piece of paper. No doubt it was nothing more than a reprimand for her lack of manners, though it did trouble her that it wasn't sealed. Any number of people could have simply unfolded it and gazed upon the contents before it reached her hands. Swallowing the knot that seemed to have lodged itself in her throat, she scanned the short message.

> *My dear Miss Brissedon,*
> *So sorry to hear of your brother's mishap. Perhaps you could meet with me Friday around noon at Mrs. Newins's restaurant to discuss the book you recommended? I know it is not your usual day, but I am anxious to get started.*
>
> *Your humble servant,*
> *Doctor Daniel O'Halleran*

Relaxing against the sofa's comfortable cushions once more, she let out a pent-up sigh of relief. Or was it disappointment? Just a patron asking for help with a book. He certainly was clever. A renewed twinge of guilt tightened her chest. She shouldn't be feeling such excitement over the thought of spending time with another man. Even if they weren't officially courting as yet, she had consented to their biweekly assignations, hoping to get to know Brighton better. And in fact she had. Perhaps her father was right, and she should stop seeing him altogether. After all, what did it say about their relationship if the thought of this handsome doctor released a flutter of butterflies into her stomach?

She jumped as Colin spoke up. He was leaning against the open doorway, studying her expression, no doubt.

"You're not stringing Brighton along, are you? He deserves better."

A flare of anger erupted in her stomach. "That would hardly be possible, considering he's yet to obtain father's permission to pay me court, nor have I said I would welcome it if he did."

"It's because of this doctor, isn't it?" Colin frowned and came to sit beside her. "Father won't approve of him any more than he does Brighton. Though I daresay Brighton has more to offer."

"The note was addressed to me. You had no business reading it."

He reached over and took her hand. "I'm sorry, Kate. I just worry for you sometimes. It was wrong of me, and I apologize."

She should have been furious, but when he looked at her that way, with those pale powder-blue eyes, he always reminded her of a lost waif. She scowled at him but couldn't keep the smile from tickling her mouth. "He's just a patron. I told him I had some book recommendations for him. I am usually at the library on Thursdays, if you recall."

He had the good sense to blush, a warm pink that colored his cheeks and reminded her of the summer afternoons they'd spent together at Mrs. Cole's. "Ah, of course. Do you forgive me?"

"I suppose, but you need to speak to Brighton. I don't appreciate being pressured."

"Then perhaps I should have a word with Father. It's because of his objections that you haven't pressed the issue and insisted Brighton be allowed to court you. This is the twentieth century. You do have a say in the matter."

"Exactly, it's my decision." Colin frowned, and she continued. "Father will come around in time. Brighton just needs to be patient."

"I'll have a word with him, though loving you as he does, that will not be any easy task."

"I understand that, but his incessant badgering isn't helping his case. Father sees my annoyance and takes it to mean he might be making headway." She stood and stuffed the note in her pocket. "So speak to Brighton, please."

CHAPTER 6

Friday, June 17, 1904 – 6:00 a.m.

After dinner, Kathleen stopped by to check on Patrick once more. Though he was sleeping peacefully, she grabbed a blanket and curled up in the Morris chair by the fire, determined to keep watch over him that night.

"Kate, Kate." She sat up in the chair, the sun hitting her in the eyes and causing her to blink. "Did you sleep there all night?" Patrick asked.

She smiled. "How are you feeling this morning?" Standing up, she stretched her stiff muscles before folding the blanket and placing it back on the chair.

"A bit sore, that's all. Perhaps a warm bath will help."

She walked over and touched her lips to his forehead. No fever. That was a good sign.

"Really, Kate, I'm more embarrassed than anything. I'm a better rider than that. So about that bath . . ."

"Very well, then," she said. "I'll call Dr. Tennyson, and if he thinks it will be all right, I'll have Forbes draw one for you." She frowned down at him, hesitating a moment before continuing. "Are you sure there's nothing else you want to tell me?"

"I was angry and spurred the mare harder than I should have," he said. "I didn't try to kill myself."

Kathleen ruffled his hair. "I didn't think you did."

"But I did want to die after . . . it happened."

"You were in a lot of pain, but it's going to get better now."

"Is it, Kate, or is it just beginning?"

"I don't want to hear you talk like that." She invoked her most serious voice, hoping to drive such thoughts from his head. "I know it's hard, losing your father and then your mother, but I'll always be here for you."

"My mother told me that, and now she's gone."

She brushed back her stepbrother's hair and kissed his bruised cheek. She didn't know what to say, how to explain what she didn't understand herself.

He laughed, moaning a bit as the movement pulled at his wounds. "It's all right, Kate. I don't expect you to explain it. Just knowing you care makes it better somehow. I don't feel so alone."

"You're not. Always remember that." She released a contented sigh. "Right then, I'd best call Dr. Tennyson and see about that bath. Do you want me to send some breakfast up?"

"If you like, though I doubt your father will allow it."

She lifted an eyebrow. "Oh, he'll allow it, or I won't talk to him for the rest of the day. He can't stand when I'm angry with him."

"I wish I could just ignore him."

"I know he's not your father, Paddy, but give him a chance. Maybe he'll surprise you. I love you, you know that, but you haven't exactly been behaving like a gentleman. This, for example. Who do you think you're fooling with that story? You said it yourself. You're too good a rider to be thrown that badly."

"I told you. I spurred her too hard. She just reacted, and I was so angry I wasn't paying attention."

"A fall, yes. I could accept that, but your wounds aren't consistent with those a fall would have caused . . . except perhaps for the ribs."

Patrick opened his mouth, but she raised her hand to stop him from saying anything.

"Whoever they were, they gave you a good beating. I'm not going to ask why, but maybe you need to be more careful. Destroying your reputation isn't going to hurt my father, but it could destroy your chances at happiness."

Patrick settled into the cast iron tub his father had installed four years earlier. In keeping with the instructions Dr. Tennyson had relayed to Kathleen, Forbes insisted he didn't remove the bandages around his ribs until he was out of the bath. He supposed he could have argued the issue, but what would be the point? The warm water felt good on them nonetheless.

"I'll be down the hall, sir," the butler said. "Just ring when you're ready to get out."

"Thank you, I will." Patrick leaned back against the enameled tub and sighed. He could almost feel the filth being flushed away. The door opened, and he was about to tell Forbes he wasn't finished yet when Thomas walked in.

A chill ran through Patrick's body, as if the water had gone ice cold. "What do you want?" If he'd come to give him another beating, Patrick would make sure the whole house knew. "I don't need any help. In fact, I'd rather fall and crack another rib than have you help me . . . Father."

"If ye're sure ye're not needing me to wash yer back," Thomas said, his lip turning up in a sinister smirk. "I'll just be stepping outside, then. I'll be back in a minute to see how ye're faring. Wouldn't want ye to be slipping and hurting yerself, now would we?"

Patrick no longer found the bath relaxing. He scrubbed himself as quickly as he could, but it wasn't fast enough. His stepfather returned before he could get out and put on his robe. The man sat himself on the end of the tub and chuckled. He pulled out a cigar, spitting the tip into the bathwater before lighting it and blowing the smoke in Patrick's face.

"Now, Son, do we understand each other, or will ye be needing another lesson today?"

Patrick sank down in the soapy water, hoping its now cloudy surface would conceal his more private parts. "And how will you explain that accident? No one really believes I fell from a horse, you know."

Thomas chuckled again. "No, they think ye got caught diddling one of the local *cailíns*. But no matter. There are ways to cause pain without leaving any mark at all. I'm sure Mickey knows them well. And if not, I'm acquainted with a few gentlemen down on the Bowery who are quite adept at it. So, boyo, I'll ask ye again. Do we have an understanding?"

"I want your assurances—"

Thomas barked a laugh. "Oh, I don't think ye have a clear picture of the situation, me lad. Ye've no bargaining power here. I'll instruct ye in what needs to be done, and ye'll do it, no questions asked. If ye don't, ye'll regret it. 'Tis as simple as that."

"And if I do as you ask?"

"Well then, there'll be less need for punishment. Ye'll have a home here, finish yer schooling as planned, and then marry the young lady o' me choice, one who can be of use to us."

Patrick bit his tongue. He had no intention of remaining once he got his degree. He'd apply to a firm far away from Thomas and marry who he wanted.

"For the last time, boyo, do we have an understanding?"

Patrick closed his eyes and swallowed hard.

"Yes, sir . . . I understand."

Thomas sighed with satisfaction, pulling down on his vest as he rose to leave. "There, that's better, now isn't it?" He reached over and tapped Patrick's sore cheek. "I'll send Forbes in to help ye out, but first things first. Concerning the delightful Mrs. Langston, ye'd best be preparing yerself to spend Tuesday afternoons with the lovely lady, as I've arranged for ye to take piano lessons at her home."

"But I already know how to play." A wave of nausea settled in his gut.

"Then perhaps ye'll be needing a refresher course." Thomas frowned down at him. "See if Kathleen's face cream and powder can hide the worst o' them bruises. Then again, this may work to me advantage. With any luck, Lizzie will take pity on ye. And I'll be expecting ye to be attentive to her in return. Don't be forgetting that."

"What's the piano lesson for, then?"

"Ye can't very well be stopping by for afternoon tea, now, can ye? That'd really set the tongues wagging."

"And what will these *piano lessons* entail?"

Thomas crushed his cigar stub on the side of the tub, the motion causing Patrick to jump and eliciting another snicker from Thomas. "Whatever she likes, boyo. After all, 'tis not the first time ye've entertained an attractive lady, now, is it?" He bent down close, his face inches from Patrick's, his tobacco-laced breath making Patrick want to gag. "Did ye think I didn't notice ye in the stables last month? What was the lovely lady's name . . . Meg McKeon, I believe."

Patrick hung his head in shame. He hadn't expected anyone to see them. If word got out, her reputation would be ruined. "That was different," he said.

"Really, and why is that? Sure, ye weren't in love with the lass. More in lust, I'd say, the way you were going at it. 'Twould be a shame if word o' yer tryst were to get round. Not only would she lose her position at the Wilsons', but she'd get no recommendation either. And ye know what that means, don't ye?"

Thomas got up, chuckling to himself. "Just don't get caught at it, not if ye know what's good for ye." He strode out of the room, still snickering to himself, and closed the door behind him.

Patrick slid farther down in the tub and let the warmth caress his bruised body. There was indeed no way out. The rippling water cover his lips, and he contemplated submerging his nose as well. But no, his mother had warned him how awful a sin that would be, one where there'd be almost no chance of forgiveness. He could hear his father's words after a neighbor had taken their own life. *No matter how tough things seem, me boy, as long as ye live, there's always hope. Cling to that.* And yet he couldn't help but wonder what his father would think of him.

He did have a choice, after all, a wicked one, but a choice nevertheless. Either he said no and ended up on the streets without a cent to his name, committing all sorts of atrocities to survive—for it was certain Thomas would see to it he'd never find employment—or worse yet, he'd be locked up in some sanitarium, where he'd be subjected to tests and experiments aimed at curing his perceived insanity. Not to mention poor Meg being thrown out onto the streets as well, even if he hadn't gotten any more than a good feel. Or he said yes and spent his time flattering randy-arsed older women. Maybe it wouldn't be so bad. They were society ladies. Surely they had some sense of decorum.

The thought of Mrs. Langston snuggling up against him still made him ill, despite his optimistic pep talk. Aside from the fact that Thomas was using him as a cheap whore, she was Lydia's mother, for God's sake. He took a deep breath and ducked below the water, cool now that he'd been sitting in it for so long. Just as he came back up, Forbes opened the door.

"I'm sorry to disturb you, sir, but your stepfather indicated you were finished."

Patrick nodded. "I suppose I am, any way you look at it." Then he gritted his teeth and let the man help him out of the tub.

With his ribs wrapped anew, Patrick headed down for breakfast. Kathleen had apparently decided it was best that he didn't languish in his room all day, so instead of breakfast in bed, Thomas had agreed to hold the meal until he could join them.

"Ah, at last!" Thomas said when Patrick entered the dining room. "Now let's be getting this meal started before 'tis time for luncheon." He stuffed a spoonful of eggs in his mouth, washing it down with coffee before he continued. "And Patrick, I permitted breakfast to be held today at yer sister's behest and because o' yer infirmity, but I'll not allow it again. D'ye understand?"

"Yes, sir," he said. "I understand everything perfectly."

CHAPTER 7

Kathleen arrived early at Newins, not wanting to chance being late and having the doctor suspect she wasn't coming yet again. She was staring down at the menu when someone cleared their throat.

"Good afternoon, Miss Brissedon." The doctor tipped his hat before removing it and sat down in the chair across from her.

"Good afternoon, Doctor. I must apologize for yesterday. My brother was in a terrible accident, and—"

"No need to explain, miss. I hope he's all right."

"Yes, aside from a few cracked ribs and nasty bruises, he seems much better this morning." She fiddled with the white cloth napkin on the table before her and sat up a bit straighter, trying to squelch the pleasant dip in her stomach at the sound of his rich tenor. "I assume Dr. Tennyson has informed you of the general nature of my inquiry."

A smile nudged the corner of his mouth, causing a dimple to appear in his right cheek. "He's actually explained the situation in detail. I was with the department at the time of the investigation. When I mentioned it, he seemed quite excited, but of course—"

"Of course, you don't believe Mr. Desmond was murdered." She let a curt smile touch her lips and began to gather her things, feeling as if not only her hopes were dashed, but something else as well.

"I was hoping you might join me for lunch," he said, standing as she did. "There are a few questions I'll need to ask if you wish me to investigate the matter further."

Her breath caught. "But you said . . ."

He lifted an eyebrow, the dimple returning to his cheek. "I said nothing, Miss Brissedon. You simply assumed what I was going to say."

She released a sigh of annoyance and sat back down. That half-smile she'd first found so endearing was really quite smug and irritating. "Well, it certainly did sound like an enormous *but.*"

"Shall we order lunch? Do you like clam chowder?"

"That will be fine, thank you." Yes, definitely smug—and self-assured. She gave an inward sigh of relief. Perhaps that would quell the annoying flock of butterflies that seemed determined to weigh in on the subject.

He gave the waiter the order. "And two teas," he added before turning back to her. "Where were we?"

"Surely a man like yourself will need more than a bowl of soup for lunch. I assure you, I intend to pay for the meal. After all, you are here at my request."

"But I haven't taken the job yet." His dark brown eyes sparkled with specks of gold, the irises being the darkest at their edges, where they were almost black.

Blast those butterflies. They'd commenced flicking their wings again, more furious than ever. "Still, if you do investigate the matter, I will expect you to attach this luncheon to the bill."

He turned the corners of his mouth down, shrugging one shoulder in a noncommittal way. "We'll reassess that point when I've made my decision. Do you think your brother's assault had anything to do with your inquiry?"

"I didn't say anything about Patrick being assaulted." A pang of guilt ran through her. Hadn't she thought the same thing when he'd claimed his horse had thrown him?

"Come now, Miss Brissedon, even you can't be that naive. I've seen the boy ride, and while there is a slim possibility he was thrown, the injuries Dr. Tennyson described were more akin to a good thrashing."

Kathleen's shoulders drooped. "One he most likely deserved."

He tilted his head to the side, the corners of his mouth momentarily dipping once more. "Possibly, but there are always two sides to every story. To my knowledge, I don't believe the young man has ever forced anyone behind a barn or lured them there under false pretenses."

"Even so, as a gentleman—"

He held his hands up before him, chuckling as he spoke. "Put down your weapons. I didn't say I agreed with what he was doing, only that he wasn't a complete cad."

Her head had started to throb, and she rubbed her temples. "It's why I want to find out what happened to his father, you see. He was such a sweet boy when I first met him. It's only since our parents married that he's exhibited this crude behavior."

"Perhaps his father took a stern hand with the lad?"

For the first time since she'd sat down, Kathleen couldn't keep from laughing. "I doubt anyone could take a sterner hand than my father."

A flash of sadness dulled his eyes for a moment. "Perhaps that's the problem, then. He's not Patrick's father, is he? And yet by law, he is. So let's see what we can find out."

The jovial Irishman sitting across from her had been transformed into a serious physician and officer of the law. He sat with a small pad and pencil, his arms on the table as he gazed at her over the soup the waiter had just delivered. It dawned on her that he expected her to give him some information about Cornelius Desmond's death.

"Oh, I know hardly anything about his father's death. It had already happened when I met Patrick. In fact, my father only made Mr. Desmond's acquaintance a few months before his demise. Father had sold his business in Connecticut, you see, and was in the process of relocating either here or in Brooklyn when it all took place."

The doctor scribbled a few notes on his pad, then looked up and smiled, a soft, gentle smile this time, though it accented his dimples just as distinctly. "I'll see what I can find out, though after all this time . . ."

"I'm aware of that, but I have to try, for Patrick's sake."

The doctor shoved the pad and pencil back in his pocket and lifted a spoonful of soup to his mouth. "I may find out things your brother doesn't want to hear." He reached across the table and rested his hand on hers but must have thought better of it, for he pulled back almost at once and took a sip of tea. Yet even that momentary touch loosed the flurry of butterflies that had inexplicably taken up residence in her stomach.

"I know that as well, which is why I've decided not to say anything about it to Patrick, or anyone else, for that matter. My father would not be pleased that I was spending money on such nonsense."

"I take it your father thinks it's all true . . . about Cornelius Desmond, I mean."

She sighed. "I'm afraid, from everything my father said, it may well be true, at least partially. It appears the man left his widow in dire straits. If not for my father's investments, Patrick would have no inheritance at all. I can't imagine what would have happened to him." A cold chill caused her to shiver, and she picked up her tea, taking a drink in the hope the doctor didn't notice, which was, of course, a foolish expectation.

"Are you all right, Miss Brissedon?" He frowned for the first time since she'd met him, likely concerned about her shivering in the warm June weather. There wasn't even a cloud in the sky.

"It was just the thought of Patrick and his mother being left all alone, penniless. They surely would have ended up in the Yaphank Alms House."

He smiled again, but this time the light didn't brighten his eyes. "They're lucky your father came along when he did, then." After taking one last sip of his tea, he stood and picked up his hat. "What is the best way to contact you should I discover anything?"

"Perhaps it would be wise to contact me at the library. Or you could give a message to Nell Tennyson. She comes in quite often. My brother Colin tends to be overprotective when it comes to me. He has a habit of intercepting my messages."

The golden specks were back in his eyes. "If you were my sister, I might do the same." With that, he tipped his hat and was on his way.

She couldn't explain why, but a sort of emptiness engulfed her. His presence had been so powerful, so uplifting. Shaking her head, she stood. How could she miss him when she hardly even knew him? She picked up her gloves and realized he hadn't paid. The thought made her laugh. Well, she did tell him she would take care of it. As she reached into her handbag, the waiter held up his hand.

"Dr. O'Halleran has already taken care of it, Miss Brissedon. Have a good day."

Kathleen frowned, a bit disgruntled. When had he done that?

Daniel headed down Ocean Avenue toward the bay, unable to keep the grin from breaking out on his face. In spite of his attraction for the lady, he thought he'd managed to conduct himself in a professional manner without being too stuffy, or worse, behaving like a schoolboy. Confident but congenial, his mother would say. He'd even brought a smile to Miss Brissedon's lips once or twice.

A warm breeze caressed his cheeks, filled with the hint of salt air. For the first time since he'd arrived in the village, the muscles in his chest relinquished any sign of tension; even the nagging tingling along his scar had disappeared. He thought again of the lovely chestnut-haired beauty he'd just shared lunch with. Could his sudden lack of angst be attributed to her presence?

He sighed. What did it matter whether it could or not? That tall gentleman he'd seen at the funeral with his arm around her waist was clearly courting her, and to be sure, *he* wasn't born out of wedlock. Reaching in his pocket, Daniel drew out the small piece of Connemara marble his mama had given him just before she died.

Keep this with ye, Danny, mo storín, *and every time ye touch it, 'twill remind ye how much ye're loved.*

He put the stone to his lips and kissed it before burying it safely back in his pocket. Kathleen Brissedon wasn't Prudence Davis. He'd wait and see what developed, if indeed anything did. And if not, so be it. The Lord had sent him a loving family and guided him to this cozy village. Granted, he'd garnered a few wounds along the way, but nothing he couldn't survive. For the moment, he had a case to look into, and the idea invigorated him.

He took a deep breath of the summer air, fragrant with lilacs and the crisp scent of the sea, a sure sign rain was on the way. A colony of seagulls squawked overhead, confirming his suspicions, but not even the threat of a summer storm could dampen his spirits.

Sitting on a bench, he looked out over the bay toward Fire Island and stretched his legs. Even with the storm clouds forming off to the east, the sun was warm and comforting. His mama had loved the sea. She'd kiss his forehead and tell him how watching it always put things in perspective. Daniel closed his eyes and let the gentle lapping of the waves caress his weary soul.

His sister planned on coming out for the day on Saturday. Maybe he'd ask her to bring his notes from the case with her. It had been two years since he'd done the autopsy, so he needed to refresh his memory, but from what he recalled, the whole thing had smelled fishier than the Fulton Fish Market.

He threw a crust of bread he'd brought from the restaurant on the ground and watched the seagulls gather. Imagine coming all the way out here, only to find someone who wanted to open up that case again. Coincidence? Or was it?

"I know you're upset about it now, Daniel," his mother would say when things didn't go right, "but it's only because God has something better in mind for you." He'd always frown, but she'd give him a hug and say, "You'll see." Come to think of it, she never had been wrong.

Maybe there was hope for him and Kathleen Brissedon after all.

He looked out over the bay again, taking another breath of the fresh sea air. Maybe he wouldn't mention any of that to Izzy just yet, though, at least not until he saw where it went.

CHAPTER 8

Wednesday, June 22, 1904 – 6:30 a.m.

Patrick bent over the floral washbasin in his new room and took long, deep breaths. Yesterday's piano lesson with Mrs. Langston had accelerated far quicker than he'd expected. She'd wrapped her arm around his shoulders before he'd even finished the first set of scales, and by the end of "Für Elise," she was running her hand up his inner thigh, pretending not to realize what she was doing. It was clear the concerto that particular society matron wanted to hear was not one played on the piano.

Under ordinary circumstances, he might have shrugged and taken her up on the offer. After all, she was a beautiful woman. One who didn't look anywhere near as old as he knew her to be, almost as lovely as Lydia. And therein lay the problem. She was Lydia's mother, and try as he might, he couldn't purge that fact from his brain. He'd been so disgusted with himself by the time he arrived home, he'd deposited most of his lunch in the new Kohler toilet his stepfather had just had installed.

And he had another lesson Saturday afternoon. He flopped down on his bed and put his head in his hands. For shit's sake! She had a husband. Why did she have to have him as well? He got up, opened the bottom drawer of his bureau, and pulled out a bottle of whiskey, taking a long drink before looking at himself in the mirror over his washstand.

Two more years and it would all be over. He'd have his degree in business and finance and could make his own way. After taking another swig, he slid the bottle back in the drawer and splashed some water on his face. It was almost seven, and he didn't dare be late for breakfast, even if he did feel like death warmed over. He'd drunken himself into oblivion after dinner last night, too ashamed to be in his own company, and this morning he planned on taking a long ride through the countryside to clear his head and try not to think of Lydia.

His initial instinct had been to seek out a local housemaid or perhaps the daughter of a newly arrived summer resident. After all, his reputation for debauchery was already well established, and yet, if he rode down along the river or the bay on his bicycle, he never failed to encounter some agreeable maiden ready for the adventure.

He clenched his fist around his shaving brush and lathered up his face. How could he even think of doing such a thing? Was he not already doing enough to hurt Lydia? True, he had no alternative where her mother was concerned, but rolling in the hay with the local fauna was his choice and only deepened the betrayal he felt toward their love.

Letting out a sigh, he finished shaving and scrubbed a hand across his stubble-free face before grabbing a clean shirt from his top drawer. He looked in the mirror to straighten his collar and tie. *Shit! Shit! Shit!* He leaned on the washstand once more, thoughts of the fair-haired Lydia flashing through his mind. Though he'd only known her a few weeks, he was never happier than when he was in her company. They'd met on an excursion to Fire Island at the beginning of May. With his mother being so ill, he hadn't wanted to go, but she had insisted, and once on the ferry, he was glad he had.

He'd never seen a more lovely young lady. She was new to the area, or so his friends said, so news of his licentious behavior had yet to reach her ears. They agreed to introduce him, with the caveat that he kept his dingus in his pants. Enchanted as he had been by the young woman, he'd agreed at once, and since that marvelous day, he'd sought out her company wherever he could, on church picnics and the like, always under the watchful eye of Monsignor Cronin or one of the local spinsters, for he had no intention of sullying her reputation.

Walking over to his bed, he flopped down on the tangled sheets, a new wave of nausea churning in his stomach. What was he thinking? Her brother had already declared he would never allow him to court his sister.

After all, Edward had seen him at his worst. Two weeks before, Patrick had made a spectacle of himself at a soiree they'd both been attending, depositing the contents of his stomach on the host's prized orchids. How was he to know the flowers were so valuable or that Edward was a special friend of their owner? To be fair, they were the oddest-looking flowers he'd ever seen.

Edward wasn't a bad chap, though, and Patrick had held out hope that he might eventually win him over. He shook his head and buried his face in his hands. But now, he could hear his dreams crashing around his feet like a thousand tiny liquor glasses. Edward might have forgiven a drunken spree, even his wild past with the ladies, but sleeping with his mother . . . Dear God!

A knock on the door drew his attention, and Molly, the upstairs maid, inched it open a crack. "Excuse me, Mr. Desmond, but it is nearly seven."

Blast! He was going to be late again. Wiping his mouth, he brushed back a few unruly strands of hair, groaning when they fell back down across his forehead. Giving a shrug, he flew down the stairs, his jacket hanging off one arm like a cape. "Is he in there yet?"

"O' course he is, sir," Lizzie Maguire, the downstairs maid and laundress, said. "Ye should know better than to ask such a question."

He was still struggling into his jacket as the clock sounded and he stumbled into the dining room, a disheveled mass.

"How nice o' ye to join us." Thomas's eyes flashed a warning, his voice harsh and cold. "Sleeping in again this morning? Perhaps ye need a lesson in courtesy."

"No, sir. It's just gone seven."

"True enough, but look at the state o' ye. Yer tie's crooked, yer shirttail's hanging out, and good God, did ye even bother running a comb through yer hair? Forbes, make me stepson an appointment at the barber this afternoon. I'll not have such a slovenly appearance at me table."

"I didn't want to be late," Patrick said, trying to keep the sneer from his lips.

"Humph! A great deal o' good that did, for now we'll have to be waiting even longer while ye tidy yerself up."

Patrick looked at those seated around the table, but no one said a word. They all knew better than to press their father on that particular issue. So did he, and so, after excusing himself from the table, he hurried upstairs to do as he'd been told. Moments later, he returned, looking much neater, and on a nod from Thomas, Forbes finally began serving breakfast.

Though he wasn't sure he really wanted to eat anything, he thought he might feel better if he managed to get some food into his stomach. It seemed to work, and after eating a healthy portion of sausage and scrambled eggs, he wiped his mouth and looked up. "May I be excused now? I'd like to get a ride in before it gets too hot."

Thomas frowned. "If you must, though I daresay ye're referring to that confounded bone-shaker yer mother bought for ye. Ye'd serve yerself better to take yer horse for a run." When Patrick didn't answer, Thomas stuffed a sausage in his mouth and groaned. "Very well, but don't go far. Mrs. Langston sent word ye're to have a piano lesson this afternoon. At one, I believe."

"A lesson!" Patrick moaned, dreading another round with the horny old nymph so soon, even if it did satisfy his baser sexual needs. "But it's Wednesday. Must I?"

"Ye'd rather be drinking, I suppose?" Thomas said, his lip curled in disgust.

"No, sir! I'll do as you wish, of course. I only thought my next lesson wasn't to be until Saturday. Isn't twice a week sufficient?"

"The lady's decided ye might be in need o' more practice. I'd best not be wasting me money." He narrowed his eyes, his meaning beaming brighter than a lighthouse beacon.

"No, sir. I'm sure the lady will be pleased with my improvement."

"What of the barber?" Forbes interjected, causing Patrick to wonder if the man suspected what might be going on.

Thomas looked Patrick up and down. "I suppose it will have to wait until tomorrow."

"Yes, sir." Forbes nodded and took Patrick's plate.

"May I be excused then, sir?"

"Do as ye will, but be at Mrs. Langston's well before one. D' ye understand?"

"Yes, sir. Perfectly."

CHAPTER 9

Wednesday, June 22, 1904 – 1:00 p.m.

The Langstons hailed from Brooklyn, where they spent most of the year, and had only recently purchased the house on Grove Street as a summer retreat. Mr. Langston continued to stay in the city much of the time, leaving his wife and children to enjoy the country air. Patrick couldn't help but wonder if he realized how his wife was passing the time while she was here. Maybe he should inform him. *And end up in the stables again?* Patrick leaned his bicycle against the porch banister and dragged himself up the steps.

The butler, Standish, answered the door and showed him to the parlor, where the piano sat against the far wall. "Would you like some brandy while you wait, sir?"

Patrick promptly accepted. It was truly incredible how much a jigger or two of fine liquor helped dull the sting of what he was about to do. Downing the golden liquid, he flopped down on the large, uncomfortable sofa, but when the pocket doors opened a few moments later, he was delighted to see it wasn't Elizabeth who entered.

"Are you surprised?" Lydia Langston's eyes sparkled with laughter as she came to sit beside him.

"Yes, pleasantly," he said, his breath catching in his throat. "But you should go. Your mother will be here shortly, and it wouldn't be proper for her to find us together like this."

"My mother, dear Paddy, is out for the day. She's not expected back until late this afternoon, and so I sent for you in her name. You're not angry with me, are you?"

"Angry?" Patrick stood up and strode to the window, trying to settle his warring emotions. "Surely by now your mother's informed you of the reputation I've managed to gain for myself. Do you want to be seen as just another of my conquests?"

"Standish is right outside the door, so calm yourself." She sat up straighter on the sofa, her hands resting in her lap. "I summoned you because I wish to know why you never call upon me." She took a deep breath, clearly nervous. "You always seem to enjoy my company at church socials and such, so I was curious as to why you hadn't asked about courting me." Her cheeks turned the most delicate shade of pink. "It's very forward of me to ask, but I just wish to know if my impressions are misguided. Perhaps you find your tarts more interesting than me? Or is it simply that they satisfy your carnal needs?"

"No! It's because I care for you that I've stayed away. I'll not bring you down with me."

Lydia got up and walked to his side, placing her hand on his shoulder. "Then why do it to yourself?"

It's the only way I have to fight back. The more I embarrass him . . ." He bowed his head and blinked away a tear. "Besides, I don't deserve you." She touched his cheek, and he pushed her hand aside. "Don't! You have no idea what my stepfather asks of me." He pulled away, turning to pick his cap off the sofa.

"No, I don't suppose I do." She hurried to the doors, standing before them to block his way. "But your behavior is hurting no one but yourself . . . and me. I wish my father had decided to buy a summer house years ago. We could have been courting all this time."

"It wouldn't have made any difference. Thomas would still have found a way to get what he wanted, even if it destroyed us both. Don't you see? He takes away everything I love."

"What do you mean?"

"I believe he killed my father to marry my mother and steal our fortune." She opened her mouth to speak, but he placed a finger over her soft, silken lips. "I don't know how, nor do I have any proof, but I know it, deep in my heart. And now he's killed my mother as well."

"Have you spoken to the authorities about your suspicions?"

"Yes, and they think I'm nothing more than a bitter stepson, looking for someone to blame my father's bad choices on. But I haven't given up hope. One day I'll show him for what he is. Until then, though . . ."

He frowned and stared down at the rug, debating how he was to accomplish what he knew he must without causing her any pain. Her slender fingers lifted his chin, and her autumn-brown eyes gazed into his.

"Don't let him destroy us before we've even had a chance to get to know one another." She brushed her lips against his, and though he feigned resistance at first, her persistence was to win out.

He wrapped his arms around her, his heart exploding with joy. Dear God, what was he doing? He tore himself away, returning to gaze out the window once more. "Do you really think your father will allow me to court you after all I've done? Edward's already assured me that will never happen."

"So you did ask," she said, hope brewing anew in the rustic depths of her eyes.

"Lydia!" He crushed his cap in his hand. "Yes, I asked, and it was foolish of me. Edward knows I can never be the man you want me to be, and he was right to turn me away. I wouldn't want my sister's reputation soiled by the likes of me either. It's not even as if I'll be inheriting a fortune. I'll be lucky if I see two bits from the old bastard."

"Well, it's not up to Edward, and Daddy just wants me to be happy. After the day we spent on Fire Island, some of the *ladies* did warn him about you. He laughed and said every lad should be allowed to sow his wild oats before he settled down on the farm and that his daughter knew how to handle herself."

He had to stop this. "Do you? Well, you should believe everything those *ladies* said. It's all true, and if they continue to see us together, they will assume the worst."

"I don't care what women like them say. They've all got dark little secrets of their own, far worse than anything they could say about us."

"What about your brother, then? He's seen me at my worst and will certainly have some input on the subject. Where is he, anyway? I'm surprised he hasn't already burst through the doors and threatened me with bodily harm."

"Off to see the horses run, I believe." She moved closer, pushing his jacket off his shoulders. "So sit down, and I'll have Maddy bring us some lemonade. We need to talk about us."

"There is no us, Lydia. There can't be."

She brushed her hand along his cheek, searching his eyes. "So you don't enjoy our time together? Look at me and say the words. Tell me the touch of my hand doesn't send shivers of delight down your spine, and I won't say another word."

Pressing his lips together, he fiddled with the crumpled cap he still held tight in his hands. He should never have given her any hope in the first place, but being with her was like an island of joy in a sea of anguish. And now, because of Thomas Brissedon, he'd have to relinquish even that glimmer of hope.

"What of Standish?"

"Discreetly polishing the silver, I believe. It was only a kiss, Patrick. I don't want you to diddle me like you do the others." She pulled him down to the sofa. "You will stop seeing them though, won't you?"

He swallowed to dislodge the lump that had caught in his throat. "I can't. Don't you understand? It's who I am, Lydia."

She sighed and brushed the hair from his eyes. "Then do what you must. I can't say I'm pleased about it, but I suppose Father is right, so I'll wait while you sow your oats and be here on the farm when you've finished. Do try not to take too long, though."

"No," he said, his voice stern and unwavering, for he was sure now there was no other way. "I'm done with you, Lydia. You were a pleasant diversion, nothing more. I could never spend my life with someone like you."

Her eyes filled with tears, causing the knife in his chest to twist as it dug even deeper. "But you said . . ."

"I've never bedded a virgin before. I just wanted to see what it was like."

"No. If that was true, you would have already done it. You're only doing this because you want to spare my reputation."

"All right, then, but don't say I didn't warn you." As if to emphasize his point, he pressed his lips against hers once more, engulfing her in his arms. He gave a tug or two at her skirts, determined to let her push him away in a moment or two, after he'd put the fear of God in her. He wished he could cradle her gently in his arms, protecting her from all the wickedness the world held. Sadly, this was the best he could do to shield her from the truth.

The sound of the pocket doors sliding open drew his attention, and Patrick pulled back, the tingle of Lydia's kiss still on his mouth. Edward stood in the doorway, his lips a thin white line, the red coloring his face running down his neck and out to the tips of his ears.

"I beg your pardon, sir." The effort of controlling his temper caused his voice to come out in a raspy baritone. "Kindly release my sister."

"Edward, it's not what you think," Lydia tried to explain, but he ignored her pleas.

He'd taken a few steps into the parlor, his eyes never leaving Patrick. "Go to your room!" he said. "I'll deal with you later."

Lydia moved behind the sofa, her caramel eyes sparkling with tears. "Not until you let me explain. He was just trying to scare me off."

Edward rubbed his fingertips across his forehead. "Just go to your room while you still have a shred of decency left. Please, Lydia."

Lydia opened her mouth to protest further, but Patrick moved to her side. Cupping her chin in his hand and kissing her cheek, he whispered in her ear. "You may as well go. Unless you plan on lifting your skirts in front of your brother, we're done here."

She narrowed her eyes. "I don't know why you're saying such vulgar things, Patrick Desmond, but you're a terrible liar." Her hand flew across his cheek, and she headed for the door, stopping momentarily by her brother's side. "As for you, Eddie, you'd better watch your step too. You have far more to hide than I do."

Edward's hands curled into fists at his sides, and his face, so red just a moment before, blanched a pearly white. "Just do as I've asked. Please, Lydia."

Patrick frowned after her. What little tidbit did Lydia have on her brother that caused the blood to drain from his face? *No!* She couldn't know about his sexual preferences, could she? The man was usually quite discreet. Patrick had only suspected it after Edward had been so attentive to the orchid owner a few weeks before. After Patrick had been escorted from the premises, he'd spied the two men out behind the hothouse in an embrace that was far more than a consolatory hug. Then again, maybe Lydia really wasn't the ingénue everyone thought.

For a moment, Edward didn't move. He stood as still as a bronze park statue, his eyes fixed on Patrick, flashing with fury, until they heard Lydia's bedroom door close. Patrick didn't even see Edward's fist coming, but he felt the sting as it smashed into his face, causing blood to gush from his nose and dribble down across his lips and chin. He blinked away the tears that flooded his eyes, the pain radiating out across his cheeks. He supposed he deserved it, though did Edward have to hit so hard? At least it didn't feel like his nose was broken.

"Speak of this to anyone," Edward said, "and a bloody nose will be the least of your worries. Now get out."

Patrick sometimes wondered about his own intelligence, for instead of heading for the door, he yanked the handkerchief from Edward's jacket and blew his nose in it before speaking. "I was summoned by your mother for a piano lesson."

Edward grabbed him by the collar, throwing him up against the wall. "Do you think I don't know what her classes consist of? I happened upon one of her so-called *lessons* a few years ago, and while I may not be able to keep my mother from diddling your keys, I can certainly keep you from playing my sister's spinet. Now get out before I decide you need another *boxing* lesson."

"If you harm Lydia . . ."

Edward opened the door. "While I would gladly wipe the gutter with you, I'd never touch so much as a hair on my sister's head. That's because I'm a gentleman, which is more than I can say for you, sir."

The door slammed in Patrick's face with such force he nearly stumbled down the steps. He looked up to Lydia's window, but she pulled the curtains closed. It was better this way. Wiping his nose on his sleeve, he mounted his bicycle and headed down the street. In spite of the pain that tore at his heart, there was a seed of joy there as well, a memory he could treasure through everything that lay ahead. His thoughts had drifted away, but a horn from one of those newfangled automobiles blasted, jolting him back to reality and causing him to swerve.

"Watch where you're going, you young fool," a man called out.

He shrugged and continued down the road, blocking out the pain the afternoon had brought and holding the memory of Lydia's kiss in his heart.

"Mrs. Langston?" Thomas Brissedon tipped his hat as he caught up to the woman in front of Swezey & Newins Department Store.

"Oh, good day, Mr. Brissedon. It's a lovely one, isn't it?"

"Yes, it is, but I thought ye'd asked Patrick round for a *piano lesson* this afternoon."

"No, his next lesson isn't until Saturday. Whatever gave you the idea we had another today?"

Thomas tried to keep his breathing even. What was that little prig up to? "I received a note this morning saying as much."

Though Elizabeth Langston smiled genially, Thomas could see the tension in the small lines at the corner of her mouth and eyes. "I'm sorry, sir, but you're mistaken. I sent no missive. Why on earth would I when I intended to come to town today?"

"Why indeed?" He'd thrash the little ratbag when he got home if this was his doing. "I must have misunderstood."

Elizabeth closed her eyes for a moment, seemingly to compose herself, then opened them again. "Possibly, but I fear we'll discover it more likely to be my daughter's doing."

"Yer daughter? But why on earth . . . ?" Before he could continue, Elizabeth raised her hand to still him. Sighing again, she rubbed her hand across her forehead, no doubt to quell an oncoming headache.

"I assume you are unaware that Patrick and my daughter met recently on an excursion to Fire Island. Lydia was quite taken with him."

"Ah yes, he did mention something about her." Thomas didn't need to hear any more. He could already imagine what had transpired. The lady, however, was intent on continuing her tale.

"Of course, with Patrick having the reputation of being quite a rapscallion, I forbid her to associate with him. And who could blame me?"

"Certainly not I," Thomas said. "But are ye suggesting yer daughter sent the note without yer knowledge?"

Elizabeth's forest-green eyes flashed with emotion, but was it anger or admiration? "Please, Thomas, let us dispense with the niceties. Do you truly think I have any intention of sharing Patrick with my daughter? Not only am I suggesting the little minx sent the note behind my back, I am quite certain she did."

"But surely she's not alone in the house."

Mrs. Langston hurried down the sidewalk, waving for a carriage. "I'm afraid she is, except for the servants, but they would never presume to interfere."

"Oh dear!" He was going to thrash that boy within an inch of his life if he scuttled his plans. "Please, I have me carriage. Allow me to take ye home." He helped Elizabeth up into the two-seated buggy before climbing in himself and setting off for her house.

"Did the note say what time he was to arrive?"

If he wasn't so angry, he might just laugh. The nerve of the old floozy. Afraid her daughter might get a bit of what she'd yet to receive, no doubt. "If I recall, he was to go round at one."

"Oh dear," she said, fanning herself. "They've been together for an hour and a half already. What will become of her reputation?"

Like mother, like daughter. Thomas had to clear his throat to keep from snorting. "Let's not be jumping to conclusions. The servants are home, so that might deter them a bit. And as for her reputation, there's no need for anyone to know they were alone or that any intimate . . . contact took place."

Elizabeth practically leapt from the carriage when they pulled in front of her three-story board and batten home. In spite of her perceived refinement, the old girl certainly could move when she wanted to. Thomas hopped down as well, leaning back to grab the whip before following the woman up the wide steps.

"Lydia! Lydia Jane, you come out here this minute." Elizabeth slid open the pocket doors to the parlor with such force; Thomas was amazed they didn't bounce back and slam closed again.

"Yes, Mother?" the girl said. She was sitting on the couch, curled up with a book.

"Where is that lecherous little scoundrel?" Elizabeth stomped across the room, throwing open the doors to what appeared to be her husband's office.

"What's going on, Mother?" Edward looked up from the desk, rising and walking around it to come and stand in the doorway.

Elizabeth turned to her daughter, anger pulsing in her eyes. "Why did you send Patrick Desmond a note saying he had a piano lesson today?"

Edward cleared his throat. "I'm afraid that was me, Mother. Lydia knew nothing of it."

Thomas clutched the whip in his fist and cast a glance in Elizabeth's direction. Was Patrick playing them both for fools?

"Why would you have sent such a message to Patrick?" Elizabeth said.

He had the decency to blush. "There's a certain young lady I was interested in approaching, and, since Paddy seems to be able to charm the ladies, I thought . . ." He shrugged. "I wanted a little advice, but as I doubted he'd come at my summons, I used the excuse of a piano lesson."

"Well, I never . . ." Elizabeth fanned herself once more. Thomas was sure she was about to keel over, but Edward sat her down on the sofa.

"He left almost an hour ago, however. Lydia, could you ask Standish to bring Mother a cup of tea while I see Mr. Brissedon out?"

"Yes, of course." Lydia hurried off toward the kitchen while Thomas allowed himself to be ushered out. The front door had no sooner closed than he turned on Edward.

"Just what exactly was that all about? Unless ye're planning to take up whoring, please don't insult me intelligence by repeating that story about asking Patrick for advice. I'm not a fool."

"I have no idea what you're implying, sir. Now if you'll excuse me, I must attend my mother."

"She's no fool either," Thomas said. "I'd wager she's already guessed what went on."

"Good day, sir," Edward said before slamming the door in his face.

Thomas headed down the steps, chuckling to himself. This was better than he could have hoped. It was only a matter of time till Lizzie came whining to him about Patrick. Yes, sir, he'd have that contract from Benjamin Langston one way or another, and a bit more if all went well.

CHAPTER 10

Patrick was too troubled to go straight home when he left the Langstons'. The visit had reminded him how much he'd lost over the last two years. He walked his bicycle along the curb in town, more determined than ever to find out what had truly happened to his father. Months before, he and his mother had hired a detective named Alexander Morton to investigate, and Patrick had added an additional request of his own.

Curious about his stepfather's background, he'd asked the man to investigate Thomas Brissedon's past as well. He'd managed to keep the entire affair quiet, fearing his stepfather's reaction to his inquiries, even those about his father. Without his mother's financial support, however, he would be unable to keep the man on retainer.

Seeing this as a perfect opportunity to make a final check on Morton's progress, he stopped by the detective's office on his way home. The man was out when he arrived, so he sat on the curb in front of his office. Resting his arms on his knees, he placed his head in his hands. How had his life taken such a turn for the worse? He was lost in his thoughts when someone kicked his leg, and he looked up to see the haggard detective smiling down at him.

"Mr. Desmond, I'm glad you're here. I have some information for you."

"On my father's death?" Patrick jumped up from his perch on the curb.

"Yes, as a matter of fact. Come in, please."

Patrick leaned his bicycle against the building before following Morton into the dimly lit office. It was only a small room, with a plain wooden desk to one side and a moldy-looking sofa pushed up against the wall. There had been no attempt to file any of the dusty folders that sat on the desk or to repair the damaged shades that hung precariously from the window. The detective shrugged, obviously used to the dubious looks on the faces of his clients, then motioned for Patrick to take a seat in the rickety ladder-back chair that sat on the other side of his desk.

"Redecorating," he offered as some halfhearted kind of explanation.

Patrick couldn't help but smile. The detective had been *redecorating* for the last six months. Then again, his fees fit their resources, so he couldn't complain.

"Let's get down to business, then, shall we?" Morton dug out one of the dusty folders. "As to your father's death. It seems a tall man was seen talking to him just hours before, down around Fourteenth Street. An odd-looking fella, by all accounts. Right after talking to him, your father told Mary O'Neill, a flower-seller, that the man had given him a certain address and asked if he'd go there to help a relative who was ill. It was in a terrible neighborhood, down on the Bowery, but of course your father couldn't refuse to aid a dying man. Now here's the curious part: it was at that exact address he was found dead only hours later."

"So someone knew he would be there?"

"It looks to me like someone wanted him to be there, son. That's all I have for now. I'll be in touch should I find out anything else."

"Thank you, Mr. Morton, but I'm afraid I can no longer afford your fee. My mother recently passed away, you see, and . . ."

The detective frowned. "Your mother paid me well in advance, lad, a sizeable sum. I fully intend on seeing this investigation to an end."

Patrick's breath caught in his throat. "You don't know how much this means to me, sir." He wrote the information down on a piece of Morton's stationery and shoved it in his pocket.

"From what I understand, Cornelius Desmond was a gentleman. There aren't many of us around these days," he said. "Besides, you're not the only one who feels he was framed. It would be quite a feather in my cap if I could help clear his name."

"Thank you again, sir." Patrick jumped up and shook the man's hand so vigorously that it caused Morton to chuckle. He was just about to turn and leave when the detective spoke again.

"Oh, by the way, you asked me to look into the affairs of Thomas Brissedon. He's your stepfather, I gather?"

"Yes, did you find out anything about him that would be of interest?"

"Not a trace, I'm afraid, here or in Connecticut, at least not until a few months before your father's death. I found that a bit too coincidental, so I began asking around in the lower circles. Seems a man named Tommy Breslin used to work on the docks years ago, but then he disappeared about '87 or so, after his wife passed on. Rumor on the street is he turned up again a few months before your father's death. What really caught my interest was that this Breslin was seen talking to your father down around Fourteenth Street, only the few people that saw him said he looked like he'd done all right for himself, all gussied up with fine clothes and such, a real dapper. Now here's the kicker. He denied knowing them, said his name was Thomas Brissedon. Makes you wonder what his business was down in that part of town, though."

"So this Tommy Breslin is my stepfather?"

"I believe he may well be, though I've no proof as yet. Those few that remember Tommy Breslin . . . Well, let's just say their memories aren't what they used to be, but they're fairly sure he and this swell they saw hanging around were one and the same. The man certainly fit the description, and up till a few years ago, no one had even heard of a Thomas Brissedon."

Patrick sat back down, trying not to let himself get too excited. "Thomas did admit he'd met my father a time or two. How do you know this swell really was Tommy Breslin?"

"As I said, I don't really. It all just seems too convenient. I have some hunches I still have to look into, but I feel certain they're going to pan out."

"I see. So he may actually be the self-made Irish immigrant he professes to be. He owned a large mill somewhere in Massachusetts or Connecticut, I think?"

"Yes and no. I did finally locate a Brissedon Mills in Groton, Connecticut, but even that didn't exist until a few weeks before your father's death. According to the records, he relocated there from Boston, but I don't see any sign that it actually opened. I haven't been able to check out Boston yet."

"What about this Tommy Breslin?"

"He was fairly well known around the Lower East Side back in the day. Never in trouble with the law or anything, as far as I could see, but not the type you'd want to turn your back on either, and dead poor. Things were so bad he couldn't even get his wife the medical care she needed."

"Wait . . . his wife? He was married when he wed my mother?"

Morton shook his head and leaned back in his chair. "No, this was back before '87. His wife died while their children were still small. Consumption, you know."

"And his children?"

"Two of them, I think." He took out a notebook and read off the names. "Yes, Colm and Catriona. They weren't with him when he reappeared. Of course, they would have been full grown by then. "

"My stepbrother and stepsister are Colin and Kathleen!" Patrick said. Could it really be nothing more than a coincidence? "But what of the other two—Charlotte and Ryan? They're quite a bit younger."

"I'm afraid that's all the information I have at the moment. Like I said, Breslin disappeared soon after his wife died, and that would have been somewhere around the mid-eighties."

"Before the younger ones were born," Patrick said. But what did it all mean? Could it be his stepfather truly had built up his own fortune, just as his father had? "Thank you, sir. You've been very informative. I hope to hear from you again soon."

He jotted down this new information and headed home, his thoughts and his stomach churning. But if Thomas had pulled himself out of poverty with hard work and perseverance, why lie about who he was? And if he'd lied about who he was, what else had he lied about? Maybe he hadn't built his fortune at all, but stolen it, just as Patrick suspected.

A wave of nausea inched up his throat. Had Kathleen been part of it as well? He'd never asked her about her past the way he had Thomas. Surely she wouldn't have been old enough to know what was going on at first, but it would have been another story by the time his father died. He almost hesitated to ask. What if she denied knowing anything about it? Would it be the truth, or would it mean her affection for him was a mere façade? And worse yet, how would he know?

"I'll not have it, I tell ye," Thomas yelled as Colin stormed out of his study, nearly knocking Patrick down. "This will be the end o' it!"

The end of what? Patrick closed the front door behind him and peeked toward his stepfather's study. He'd barely had time to turn around, however, when Colin strode back across the entrance hall and grabbed him by the arm.

"I'll deal with you later," his stepbrother said before he swung the front door open and stormed out, leaving Patrick momentarily stunned.

Thomas's harsh voice brought him back to his senses, and he looked up to see his stepfather standing in the doorway of his study, the vein in his neck bulging through his skin.

"I want to see ye as well. In here! Now!"

Could word of his tryst with Lydia have reached him so soon? He would have to pay the piper dearly for this. Still, he would do it all again in the breath of an instant. The love he'd felt in those brief moments would last in his heart for an eternity. Nothing Thomas did to him could take that away.

Having resigned himself to the inevitable reprisal, he took a deep breath and answered his stepfather's summons. Thomas had already returned to sit in the large leather chair behind his desk, and so, as usual, Patrick took up his position in front of it, trying desperately to stifle a sigh. In truth, he thought he may as well simply head out to the stables and brace himself for a beating. The thought of it sickened him, but he convinced himself that it would probably be no more than the strap this time and breathed a bit easier.

"And where have ye been this afternoon?" Thomas asked, the sarcasm in his voice palpable.

Patrick suppressed a moan. Did they really have to play this game? They both knew where he'd been. Why bother with the formalities? Still, there was a chance, however faint, that his stepfather had not heard the entire story, and so Patrick went along with it.

"I went to Mrs. Langston's, for my piano lesson. You instructed me to do so, if you recall, Father. She sent a message, I believe."

"And ye had yer lesson, then, did ye?"

"Yes, of course." Thomas's hand flung through the air with such speed, Patrick never saw it coming, and he staggered with the force of the blow when it smacked into his face. *Wrong answer,* he thought to himself. The old reprobate did already know.

"D'ye think me a complete fool?" Thomas said, his watery gray eyes bulging with anger. "I came across the lady in town earlier today, and she knew nothing of yer appointment."

Patrick was not sure what to say. If Thomas somehow didn't know about Lydia yet, the chances were slim that he would remain in the dark about that little detail forever, but for the moment he decided to risk another blow and plead innocent.

"Nor did I, sir, not until I arrived. When I found she wasn't at home, I simply assumed there'd been a misunderstanding and decided to ride my bicycle for a bit, being it was such a lovely day and all."

"Ye took a ride, did ye? For the entire afternoon? And where did this leisurely ride lead ye? To some gambling den, no doubt, so ye could spend more of me hard-earned money, or maybe past a neighbor's stable to satisfy yer more visceral instincts?"

Patrick hung his head as if he were ashamed, hoping that his stepfather would take it as an affirmation of his whereabouts.

"O' course!" Thomas grumbled. "What else could I expect? Well, which was it? Shall I feel it in me pocket, or should I expect a visit from an infuriated summer resident whose daughter has just become acquainted with your charms?"

"It was my own money, sir." Might as well go with that for a change, though he rarely visited the gambling hells.

"Was it, now? And how much did ye lose?"

"No more than fifteen dollars or so, I think."

"Fifteen dollars! Well, seeing as ye have such an abundance o' money to throw away, I guess ye won't be needing yer allowance for the next three weeks. It will be donated instead to a local charity."

"But Father . . ." Patrick gritted his teeth. Calling this charlatan that still grated on his nerves.

"Ye've an objection to donating yer money to the orphanage? What would yer dear mother think?"

"No, sir!" Patrick said. *Let it go. You're getting off easy. Don't give him any reason to rethink this.*

"Very well, then, ye're dismissed, but the next time ye come across such a situation, ye're to come directly home. Is that understood?" Patrick gave a polite nod and began to leave, but Thomas was not quite through with him. "Oh, and by the way, lad, since ye chose to feign this morning's liaison with Mrs. Langston, perhaps ye should make it up to her by taking an extra piano lesson next week. 'Tis yer punishment for being so deceitful. Lord help me, ye're as big a liar as Colin, but always remember one thing. Colin is me son, and that fact alone warrants a certain degree of leniency. One that ye do not require."

Once more, Patrick bobbed his head in understanding, keeping his hatred well hidden, then proceeded out to the carriage house. It was late afternoon, and though the sun was low, he thought he might have time for a short bicycle ride before having to head back and get ready for dinner. It helped him think, to put things in perspective and clear away the clouds of anger and frustration that filled his mind.

Anticipating a pleasant ride, he walked into the carriage house and headed for his bicycle, jumping when Colin slipped out of the shadows and leaned up against the forest-green landau carriage. Though his breath caught, he grabbed his bicycle bars, determined not to let his stepbrother intimidate him. "What do you want?"

He'd barely gotten the words out when Colin grabbed him by the collar and slapped him across the face. Pressing him up against the weathered boards, his stepbrother held a knife to his throat.

"You little bastard!" Colin pressed his forearm hard against Patrick's chest. "Did you think you could ingratiate yourself with my father by telling him about the small loan I helped myself to?"

"What are you talking about?" Patrick tried to wiggle free, but it only caused Colin to bang his head hard against the wooden planks.

"You told him about my being in his study yesterday afternoon, didn't you?" He grabbed Patrick by the hair, slamming his head against the dark wood once more. "Didn't you?"

"So what? He was just wondering if I'd seen you there. What does that matter?"

"You told him I took that money!" His lips turned up in a snarl, and he tossed Patrick on the dirt-covered floor, kicking him in the stomach.

"I didn't! I swear! I knew nothing about any money. He simply asked if I'd seen you yesterday afternoon, and I told him that I'd seen you in the study. I didn't know why you were there. I just thought you were looking for him."

"Liar!" Colin dragged him up and slammed his fist into Patrick's stomach before shoving a knee into his groin. "Next time I won't let you off so easily, so you'd best learn to keep your mouth shut. Are we in agreement?"

Patrick slumped on the ground and nodded as he tried to catch his breath, sure another rib must be cracked.

"Good!" He reached down to pull Patrick up, the smirk still on his lips. "Go to your room and clean yourself up. You're a disgrace!"

Patrick practically crawled to his room, using the back stair so no one would notice him. Yep, that was definitely another bruised rib; maybe even cracked. At least there was no blood to speak of this time. Sliding down beside his bed, he reached under the down-filled mattress. It was still there—the knife his father had given him so many years before. Maybe he should take to carrying it around. Grimacing, he laid his head against the heavy quilted bed covering.

He wanted to cry, to let all the anger and sorrow out, though the best he could muster was a single tear. They never seemed to come anymore. Whatever happened, he would hold it in, as if crying would somehow acknowledge they'd won, and he wasn't about to let that happen. Not when he was coming so close to uncovering their secrets. Shoving the knife back under the mattress, he pulled himself up and limped over to the washbasin, throwing some water on his face. Dinner would be soon, and he had no intention of being late. So much for the afternoon's pleasant bike ride.

CHAPTER 11

"Mrs. Langston to see you, sir." Forbes stood aside to show the woman in, then closed the door behind her.

Thomas groaned inwardly. Regardless of her beauty, she had proven to be quite an annoying little tick. He had no doubt why she was there this time, though, and he had every intention of turning the situation to his advantage. He didn't just want Benjamin Langston's custom, as he'd let the lady believe. He wanted the man's entire business, and if all played out the way he intended, he would have it within the next year or two.

"Elizabeth, is something wrong?" He walked around his desk and invited her to sit on the small sofa to its left.

"Yes, terribly," she said. "It seems my initial instincts were correct. I'm afraid Edward wasn't entirely truthful with us today, his loyalty to his sister clouding his good sense."

Good God! She didn't beat about the bush, did she? Of course, disclosing Lydia's little indiscretion to proper society would be another issue altogether. Thomas had no doubt she would be far less forthcoming there, and that played right into his hands.

"I'm not sure what ye mean." He sat behind his desk and did his best to look attentive.

"It was Lydia who sent the note asking for Patrick to call around. In spite of her brother's attempt to persuade me otherwise, she didn't even deny it. She seemed almost defiant. Can you imagine? Of course, she told me I needn't worry, that he had no use for her, but I think we'd both agree that was nothing more than a ruse on his part to get what he wants."

Thomas had to fight to keep the smirk from his lips. "Which is?"

"Oh, come now, Thomas! You know very well what he wants. The boy makes no secret of his sexual prowess."

He leaned back in his seat, his brows furrowed. "Hmm, true enough, but I'll not allow ye to be laying all the blame at Patrick's feet. If what ye say is true, yer daughter must accept some responsibility for it as well. After all, 'twas she who sent the note."

"Because you can't seem to keep a leash on the lecherous little scoundrel." Elizabeth's ivory complexion had taken on a pink tinge, and Thomas was certain her blood pressure must be rising. "I've seen how he encourages the young ladies after Mass, drawing them to himself like moths to a porch light despite their mothers' best efforts. I thought I'd succeeded in shielding Lydia from his debauchery, but clearly I too failed."

Thomas almost laughed. She had no objection to his debauchery when it was directed at her, the arrogant tart.

"You need to rein him in," she continued, "or it's only a matter of time before he gets one of them with child. I have no intention of allowing Lydia to be just another of his conquests, regardless of her reckless behavior."

"'Tis true, the lad has been a bit wild o' late, but what would ye have me do, Elizabeth? From what I understand, he's yet to coerce any young lady into his embrace. In fact, he's quite aboveboard about his intentions."

"Aboveboard!" If her eyes got any wider, they were certain to pop out of her head. "Are you completely blind to the game he's playing? I was under the impression we had an agreement."

"Has he not been attentive at yer lessons?"

"Yes, very much so, but I want your assurances that you'll keep him away from my daughter. She has a reputation to protect, and I'll not stand by and permit that young rapscallion of yours to tarnish it. A girl in her position must look for a husband with breeding, not a common rogue who has nothing more in his favor than an agreeable . . . disposition, shall we say."

"A common rogue!" Thomas chuckled to himself. This woman had no idea what a common rogue looked like. He leaned forward, resting his arms on his desk, and nodded. "Ye want her to marry well, o' course. 'Tis what all parents want for their children, meself included. And I'll be happy to see me stepson refrains from making advances toward yer daughter, though I have to say it might be a tad bit difficult, what with him continuing *piano lessons* and all."

"Don't be ridiculous. I always make sure we're quite alone during his lessons."

I'll bet ye do! "Still, he'll become familiar with the comings and goings o' yer household, begin to feel comfortable making arrangements to meet her behind the stables and such. O' course, if she were engaged to me son Colin, well . . . even Patrick has some scruples." He sat back and took a cigar from the box on his desk, feeling quite pleased with himself.

"You can't be serious?" The red on Elizabeth's cheeks had crept down her neck, highlighting its slender lines. "I have no intention of promising my daughter to either of your rakish sons. Both have reputations for indulging in heavy liquor and wanton women, not to mention an excessive penchant for gambling. I'll not condemn my daughter to a life with either of them."

"Unless, o' course, she should find herself in a family way. Ye can't be with the girl every moment o' the day, now, can ye, Lizzie? Today's a perfect case in point, I daresay."

"Should that be the case, I'll expect you to pay all the boy's debts and induce him to reform."

"Which I would gladly do, if it was indeed Colin who was found to be the father. Alas, as the girl seems more taken with Patrick . . ." He shrugged. "'Tis not likely to be the case, now, is it? And I assure ye, I've no intention o' taking responsibility for me stepson's debts, in or out o' the bedroom."

"You're a fiend, Tommy!"

He rested back in his chair and lit his cigar, all pretext of formality gone. "Oh, come on now, Lizzie darlin', don't speak so hastily. After all, it may be in yer own best interest. The lad seems quite taken with ye. The experience o' lying with someone who knows her way beneath the sheets, no doubt, but still . . ."

From the sour expression on the woman's face, his barb regarding her promiscuity had hit its mark, but she pushed it aside. "I have no idea what you're referring to, Tommy." She patted her hair as if making sure nothing was out of place. Her words may deny it, but her actions were that of an infatuated young lady.

Thomas had all he could do to keep from chuckling. "As I haven't heard any complaints, I'm assuming yer *piano lessons* are moving along nicely."

"They were until the little scoundrel decided to turn his attentions to my daughter." She reached over the desk and touched Thomas's cheek. "You know I don't share well, especially when it's my daughter's reputation that's on the line. So if you ever want to know Benjamin's secret, you'd best rein Patrick in where Lydia's concerned."

Thomas kissed her hand and laughed out loud. "Touché, Lizzie, but ye're forgetting one thing. If I unleash the little miscreant on yer daughter, she'll be carrying his child in no time, and I assure ye, I'll cut him off without a cent. What will become o' her reputation then?"

"You wouldn't!"

"Lizzie, darlin'! Surely ye know better than that. We've been plotting to blackmail yer husband into giving me all his business. Ye can't imagine I'd have any reservations in seeing Lydia listed among Patrick's conquests."

"You, sir, are a vile cad!"

"Yes, well, I wonder what yer husband would say if he knew what ye were about?"

A broad grin crossed her face, her eyes sparkling with mischief. "Benjamin is well aware how I occupy myself. As long as I leave him to his mistress, he couldn't care less."

Thomas nodded. "But does he know ye're willing to sell his secrets?"

Elizabeth's smile dropped away. "Tell him about that, and you won't get what you want either."

Thomas reached into his drawer and pulled out a folder. "I started thinking, what is it a nice little rich lad would want to keep hidden? A child, perhaps, or maybe a stint at the penitentiary? 'Tis amazing the amount o' information a few dollars can buy. Manslaughter, was it?"

"He was only sixteen. It was an accident, and he served his sentence."

"True enough, but there are those who would shun him just the same. Business would drop off, and ye know how people can gossip. What sort o' husband do ye think Lydia would be winning then? Needless to say, I won't be needing yer assistance anymore, unless o' course . . ."

"You truly are a fiend."

"Look on the bright side, Lizzie, dear. If Lydia was engaged to Colin, it wouldn't be unheard o' for ye to be spending a night here from time to time, to discuss the wedding arrangements and all. The guest room is right next to Patrick's, as is the back stairs, should ye desire an unannounced visit."

Elizabeth got up and walked to the window. After gazing out for a moment, she spun back around, apparently having come to a decision. "If I agree to this union, you must see to it Patrick is never again alone with Lydia. To allow such an indiscretion would surely bring scandal down upon us all. And I insist certain moneys be placed in Lydia's name alone to ensure your wastrel of a son can never access them. Should he bring ruin down upon himself with his wanton ways, I want to ensure Lydia and her children will continue to have the life they're accustomed to."

"'Tis agreed, madam, but there is one more condition I must be exacting from ye."

Elizabeth sighed as she slipped back down into the chair, her eyes wary. "Go on, then, Tommy. What else has your devious little mind concocted?"

"I, too, have a daughter who a certain young man is attempting to court. He's a rogue, much like me own sons, I fear, but there's no money involved and no chance of an acceptable agreement being reached. I propose a marriage between me daughter Kathleen and yer son, Edward. O' course, I would provide a suitable dowry, but in return I would expect her to be well taken care o' by her new husband."

"Really, Tommy! Promising both my children to your offspring is far more than any woman could tolerate."

"And how well will ye tolerate yer son's disgrace?"

"I beg your pardon. I've no idea to what disgrace you could possibly be referring. Edward is a respectable businessman, well liked by all his associates."

"Well loved by some, no doubt. Sure, ye can't be telling me ye haven't noticed the lad's preference for the company o' gents over that o' the fairer sex, if ye get me meaning. 'Twould be interesting to discover what yer high-society friends think o' that."

Elizabeth's eyes darkened. "You have sunk low, indeed, when you'll invent such lies to get what you desire."

"Ah, now, Lizzie, ye know better than that." Thomas was enjoying this. Could it be that the old windbag didn't know about her son's deviant behavior? "Has he never mentioned meeting friends at Columbia Hall, or should I say Paresis Hall?"

The woman grinned, looking as though she'd captured the brass ring on the Central Park Carousel. "Yes, of course. It's a gentlemen's club he attends when he's in the city."

"D'ye truly not know what goes on there?" He opened a folder, revealing an extremely unflattering photograph of Edward.

He watched as the air slowly deflated her overblown ego. Tears filled her eyes, and she struggled to swallow. "He would never agree to marry your daughter."

"And why not? Such a marriage would furnish a perfect cover for his preferred lifestyle. All he would need do is provide me daughter with two or three children. Not much to ask in exchange for the advantages the marriage would offer."

"And what of your daughter? She will not appreciate being so badly done."

"She can take a lover on the side if she so wishes, much like yerself." He could see her temper rising again but forestalled any denial. "The guest room is directly next to Patrick's, and when I win yer husband's contracts, I'll see to it a considerable amount is placed in a private account under yer name." Though her eyes still flared with anger, there was something else there as well. "Are we in agreement, then?"

She lifted a gloved hand to her throat and gave a curt nod. "What choice have I? To refuse your demands would bring disgrace upon my entire family."

"That's grand, then. I'll inform the children tomorrow evening. If ye exert the same authority over yers as I do mine, the nuptials will be forthcoming."

"But if Edward protests . . ."

"Then ye'd best be convincing him o' the benefits, or he may find his reputation destroyed. As to Lydia, Patrick will do whatever I tell him, and he's not very discreet."

"Then why not just tell him to stay away from Lydia?" she said, lifting her chin in defiance.

Thomas took a few puffs on his cigar before answering. "Now, Lizzie, darlin', what benefit would there be for me in doing that? I care not about her reputation."

Elizabeth stood, clenching her fists at her sides, but hesitated a moment before turning to storm out the door. Thomas marveled at how she'd managed to retain her composure through their entire discussion, and though the anger in her eyes was palpable, a small smile caught the corner of her mouth. "Very well, then; I do believe I'll be over tomorrow evening to discuss the wedding plans. And I've no intention of spending one moment of it alone. Please see to it Patrick's informed of my needs."

Thomas bowed his head. "Consider it done."

He watched her exit the room, quite pleased with himself. A year or two after the weddings, the Langston men would meet with unfortunate accidents, and Elizabeth's reputation would be ruined. Leaning back, he blew out another puff of smoke. He almost hated to do it to her, but he couldn't leave any loose ends. As Lydia's husband and Kathleen's brother, Colin would be left in control of Langston's business. From there, it would be easy enough for Thomas to transfer all the proceeds into his name, making it look like Colin had gambled away the profits. Even if Edward had managed to leave an heir, there would be little remaining of Langston's estate by the time he was old enough to claim it.

He walked over to the sideboard and poured himself a drink. "*Sláinte,*" he said to himself. It had been a very promising afternoon.

CHAPTER 12

Thursday, June 23, 1904 – 7:00 p.m.

Thomas never should have allowed Patrick to head out on that confounded bicycle of his that morning, but he'd been running to catch a train and had warned the little prig, in no uncertain terms, not to be late for dinner. He should have known better. The sun was already low in the sky when his stepson finally came running up the front steps.

"Move yerself, Patrick!" Thomas growled, his words short and gruff. "Or I'll take the strap to ye here and now. I'll not have me guests kept waiting."

"Yes, sir." Patrick nodded, removing his shoes before scurrying up the stairs, but it did little good. He still managed to keep everyone waiting for twenty minutes.

Thomas took a deep breath to calm himself. He would deal with the little ratbag later. For now, he had guests to enjoy. The dinner was supposed to be celebrating a business deal he'd just finalized with Phillip Stockbridge, but Thomas had an additional reason to raise his glass. He'd negotiated another deal as well, one that would nearly bankrupt Stockbridge. What made it even more delightful was the thrill of knowing a message breaking the news awaited the man on his return home.

The dinner was magnificent, as usual, and they were just moving into the parlor for coffee when a thunderous knock sounded on the front door. Forbes went to answer it and was nearly bowled over when Edward Langston came barreling in.

"I need to speak to you, Thomas!" he said, his eyes flashing with anger.

"As ye can see, Edward, I have guests. Perhaps if ye came back tomorrow . . ."

"I need to speak to you now!" He headed for Thomas's study, throwing the doors wide.

"I suppose I'd best be seeing what this is about," Thomas said. "If ye'll excuse me for a moment, me daughter will tend to yer needs." He gave a gracious bow and followed Edward into the study, closing the doors behind him.

"How dare you try to blackmail my mother," Edward said, his voice no more than a hiss.

"Now, Eddie," Thomas said, "calm yerself." He sat back in his chair, enjoying the moment. "If ye stop and think about this, it could well work out for everyone involved. For one thing, it would provide a certain cover for ye to pursue yer deviant activities."

"What kind of a father condemns his daughter to such a marriage?"

"She'll never know, now, will she? Ye're too much o' a gentleman to cause her heartache. No, ye'll be an attentive husband and see she's happy, provide her with a few children, all the while keeping yer wicked indiscretions well hidden. And if ye don't, well . . . How much encouragement do you think Patrick would need to run off with Lydia? I doubt the little harlot would take much persuading either. After all, she summoned Patrick."

"And he rejected her, left her in tears. Not that she believed the filthy miscreant."

"Did he?" Thomas chuckled. "I assure ye, all it would take to spike his interest is a few dollars in his bank account. In no time, he'd have her believing it was all an act to spare her from his depravity, and then what would become o' her when he truly was finished with her?"

"You keep your promiscuous little bastard away from my sister, Brissedon. I'll marry your daughter to save my reputation, but I'll not sacrifice Lydia as well. I won't allow a marriage between her and Colin."

Thomas barked a laugh. "So noble, but ye misunderstand. I don't need to disgrace ye to see yer sister's reputation destroyed. Lydia's done quite an adequate job o' that herself. D'ye truly think no one noticed Patrick arrive at yer home yesterday? There are people with nothing better to do than watch the comings and goings o' their neighbors. How long were they alone before ye arrived, eh? Even without physical proof, a whisper o' impropriety in the right ears can do a great deal o' damage, I assure ye. O' course, reputations can be ruined in more than one way. A father's jail record becoming public, for instance."

"You, sir, are a fiend. I'll have nothing further to do with you, and neither will my future wife. I'll see to that."

"Oh, I think ye will, sir, or I'll see me daughter sues for divorce on the grounds o' yer deviant behavior." He threw a compromising photograph of Edward down on the desk. "Ye really should be more careful at the clubs ye frequent. But let's not have such unpleasantness between us."

Thomas reached out to shake hands, but Edward pushed his arm aside. "This is far from over, Brissedon." With that, he strode into the parlor and forcefully grabbed Patrick by the arm. "You stay away from my sister, or I'll permanently end your libertine existence! Do I make myself clear?"

Thomas stood just outside the parlor doors, finding the entire spectacle amusing. The outburst must have stunned the maid, for she jumped, letting out a squeal and spilling a cup of coffee down the front of his nephew Jeremy's trousers. "Oh, I'm so sorry."

"It's quite all right," his nephew said, taking a moment to touch the girl's cheek.

So it wasn't Patrick that was keeping her sheets warm, after all. No matter, he was having none of that under his roof. "Wait in me study," he ordered the girl.

Edward must have caught the exchange between Jeremy and the maid as well. "You truly are a wicked man," he said before storming out the front entrance and slamming the door behind him.

Thomas could barely keep from bursting out in laughter. After all, everything was going according to plan. He turned to his guests, apologizing once more for having to attend to such unpleasant matters before excusing himself once more.

Colin shook his head, frowning at the closed study door before returning to the parlor. What was the old man up to now? Sighing, he reached for his empty brandy glass. "Would you care for another?" he asked Phillip Stockbridge, who sat on one of the sofa next to his wife, his back rigid with tension.

"No, thank you, sir. I think we've all had quite enough."

"Speak for yourself," Colin said before grabbing the decanter from Patrick's hand.

The study doors opened, and Molly came running out, sobbing hysterically. Jeremy rose from his seat as if to follow her up the stairs but reseated himself when Colin raised a questioning eyebrow. Now what was that about? Perhaps Jeremy was made of sturdier stuff than he thought.

There was no time to investigate further, however, for almost at once Thomas came to the parlor door and asked to speak to Colin in private. Tarnation! Did his father think he was the one diddling the maid? Colin threw a wary glance in Patrick's direction, but his stepbrother just shook his head and stormed past the old man, slamming the outside door behind him. He'd have to speak to him about Edward's little outburst later. Taking one last drink, he put down his glass and followed his father across the hall. Might as well just get it over with.

Colin had no sooner closed the study doors than Thomas pointed to the chair on the other side of his desk. "Sit down."

"I had nothing to do with that little tart, so don't even think of accusing me."

"What?" Thomas waved the thought away. "No, Jeremy's the one who's been tickling her fancy. I'll deal with him later. I don't care how many o' me neighbors' maids the lot o' ye screw, but I'll not have it in me own home. Now sit down. I have something much more important to discuss with ye."

Colin took a seat, his eyes wary. "Discuss? You never discuss anything with me. You simply issue edicts and expect me to follow them without question."

Thomas shrugged. Perhaps his son was more astute than he thought. "Elizabeth Langston and I have come to an understanding o' sorts," he said. "As part o' the arrangement, I have agreed to a marriage between yerself and Lydia Langston."

"You what!" Colin shot out of his chair, his anger rising so swiftly Thomas feared the man would need to remove his starched collar to let out the steam. "How dare you make such an arrangement? You've no right to choose who I'm to marry."

"Haven't I?" Thomas chuckled, lifting a cigar from the box on his desk and gripping it between his teeth. "I pay yer debts and clean up after yer indiscretions, time after time. Ye didn't think that strumpet o' yers went quietly into the night, did ye? She costs me a pretty penny every month in return for keeping her mouth shut about yer wee by-blow. I have proof o' the birth, though, and the lass has sent a wee letter along with it, swearing to the bastard's identity. But ye're right, 'tis yer decision to make. O' course, should ye choose to defy me in this, ye'll be on yer own. Never again will I feel the need to intercede on yer behalf. If ye want me to stay out o' yer life, boyo, then I'll be doing so in every way, starting with these!"

He held up a handful of gambling notes, then opened his top drawer and threw them in, locking it afterward. Colin stood quietly for a moment, but Thomas could see the hatred seething just below the surface.

"Come now, lad. I've already taken care o' them. Ye're in the clear once again."

"As long as I marry that loathsome virgin, Lydia, you mean. Good God, she's probably frigid."

"I can assure ye, lad, she's certainly not that."

"You filthy old reprobate! You've been with her yourself, haven't you?" Colin looked as though he wanted to vomit.

"Don't be an arse. Let's just say she's been caught in an amorous situation, one her mother's determined to see goes no further. Now, as to yer marriage . . ."

Colin's face lit up, the light dawning just as surely as if the morning's first rays were peeking over the horizon. The lad was putting two and two together. Well, at least Thomas hadn't wasted money on his schooling.

"No, not you!" Colin said with a hint of amusement. "Edward was furious with Patrick. It's him who's had her, isn't it? There may be hope for that boy yet."

"Ye'll keep that information to yerself." Thomas tilted his head back to let out some cigar smoke. "Is that understood? Unless ye want yer wife to be looked on as nothing more than a common whore."

"Wait a minute! That little bastard. It's because of him I've been condemned to this match, isn't it?"

Thomas gave a half shrug. "I'll admit, I used the circumstances to me own advantage. And why shouldn't I? They have wealth and prestige, a combination ye'd do well to associate yerself with. Once the match is made, ye can do as ye please, as long as ye're discreet about it. Ye can even let her go to Patrick's bed for all I care. Plus, ye'll have a sizeable fortune at yer disposal. Now, send yer sister in. I have some news for her as well."

"Katie? You didn't! Condemning me to a loveless marriage is one thing, but locking my sister into a union with that fop is quite another. I'll not stand for it."

Thomas rose, placing his hands before him on the desk, like a tiger ready to pounce. "Ye'll do as ye're told, else the lot o' ye will find yerselves begging on the streets."

"You might do that to me and Patrick, but you'll never see Katie turned out."

Thomas straightened up, nodding. "Perhaps ye're right, but I would make certain she never married. I control who comes into this house, as I've demonstrated with yer friend Brighton." He held up his hand when Colin opened his mouth to contest the scope of his authority. "Oh, I'm well aware she's been meeting the rounder in the copse o' trees down by the lake, under yer watchful eye, no less, and for all I care she can continue to do so once she's wed Edward. Though I do insist she too be discreet. But should he should try to make an issue o' it, he'll rue the day he ever set foot on me land . . . and they'll never find the body." Thomas chuckled and sat back, puffing contentedly on his cigar. "Now get out o' me sight and send yer sister in here."

"I remember things, you know, from before you sent us off to boarding school."

"Do ye now? Then ye'll recall I don't make me threats lightly. Though how ye remember much o' anything is beyond me. Ye were barely six when I sent ye off, ye lying sod. Now get out there and send me yer sister."

Colin came storming into the parlor and headed straight for the sideboard, as usual, taking a long drink before informing Kathleen that their father wanted to see her as well. Though she was surprised, she graciously excused herself and started across the entrance hall, but just before she reached the study, there was a knock on the front door, and Forbes quickly went to answer it. A light-haired man with a strange scar running down the side of his nose stood in the darkness. He introduced himself as Alexander

Morton and explained he had a note that was intended for Patrick Desmond, stressing that it was to be given to him and him alone. Forbes nodded agreeably, then placed the note in his inside jacket pocket.

The butler cast a troubled look in Kathleen's direction. He no doubt suspected the worst. Just that morning, he'd shared his concerns with her over the possibility that Patrick had taken to gambling. Quite by accident, he'd heard the young man tell her father as much the day before. She could only hope that any trouble might be settled without her father hearing of it.

Unfortunately, Colin had been watching as well and swept back into the hallway, putting his hand out for the note. "I'll just keep it for safekeeping." Forbes looked to Kathleen, distress filling his eyes, but Colin caught that as well. "Oh, don't worry, Sister, I'll not give the little prig's secrets away to Father." He lifted his eyebrow at Forbes and nodded to his hand. The poor man had no choice, though he did stress the fact that it was specifically addressed to Mr. Desmond.

"Don't you trust me to see he gets it?" Colin said, daring the man to say he didn't.

"It's all right, Forbes," Kathleen said. "I'll make sure Patrick knows of its existence, just in case you forget, Colin."

The tension was broken when Phillip Stockbridge appeared in the entrance hall, demanding to know what was going on. "I fail to understand why your father asked us here tonight. Perhaps we should just be on our way."

"Oh no, please stay," Colin said. "I'm sure he'll be with you in a moment. He's going to want to brag about his conquests to someone. Do you know what he's gone and done now? He's arranged a marriage between myself and the ever so naive Lydia Langston." He downed the glass of brandy he'd been holding in his hand. "Can you imagine that? Matching me up with that inexperienced little virgin."

"He what?" Patrick stood in the open doorway. He'd returned from his walk just in time to hear Colin's shocking announcement and wasn't at all happy about it. There was no time to ask the particulars, however, for just then, almost on cue, the study door opened. Her father glared at her brothers for a moment, then spoke to Kathleen.

"Well then, from the look on everyone's faces, I suppose yer brother has informed ye. I've made arrangements for ye to be married to Edward Langston."

"To Edward? But . . ." Unable to contain the anger and pain that was welling inside her, she grabbed onto the banister, loath to say something that she'd regret later. Surely she'd heard him wrong, but no . . . she'd seen that look of satisfaction on his face before. Spots started to dance before her eyes, the world fading into a surreal haze.

She turned to Mr. Stockbridge, who still stood in the doorway of the parlor. "I'm so sorry, but will you all excuse me? I'm not feeling very well at all." As she hurried up the stairs to her bedroom, she heard Patrick calling to her, but when she stopped on the landing to answer, her father was already ordering him to wait in the study.

Though Patrick looked around for an explanation, none seemed forthcoming, so he headed toward the infamous desk. He had some idea what was on his stepfather's mind, but why handle such a matter when he had guests waiting? He listened as Thomas apologized to the Stockbridges, excusing himself for a few moments more. Finally, the old man closed the study doors and came to sit in his leather chair.

"If this is all because of the note Lydia sent—" Patrick began, but Thomas stopped him almost immediately.

"Ye're not to go near that girl again, d'ye understand me? If ye do, I swear I'll turn ye out of this house with nothing more than the clothes on yer back. Or worse yet, I'll see ye locked in an asylum so far away no one will ever remember ye exist. Lydia's to be yer brother's wife, and I'll not be allowing anything to interfere with their union, especially the likes o' yerself."

"And whose decision was that? Surely not Lydia's. She doesn't love Colin, and I doubt very much he cares anything for her."

"D'ye think that's all that matters in life? Love, how grand. Well, there are more important things to be considered here, and both Elizabeth Langston and I agree that such a union would be most advantageous to all parties concerned."

"You *agreed*! You have no right to make such a decision, and I won't tolerate it. It's not your life!"

"But it is me home, and as long as ye live in it, ye'll be abiding by me decisions." Thomas rose from his seat, coming to rest his hands on the arms of Patrick's chair, looming over him like some sort of well-dressed vulture. "Ye've nothing that's yer own, boyo, and I tell ye now, if yer behavior continues in this vein, ye'll not even be entitled to yer inheritance. I'll see to it that ye never get one red cent of it."

"You can't do that!"

"I can do anything I like. If ye remember, the will states that ye're to receive yer trust if, and only if, ye remain a good and loving son. Should ye not behave in such a way, ye're entitled to nothing." A wicked spark flashed in his stepfather's eyes. "And I'll back it up by seeing ye committed to a lunatic asylum."

"You'd have to prove it first, and do you truly think Dr. Tennyson is going to claim I'm insane?"

Thomas hissed a wicked laugh. "Ye can't be thinking I'd be so foolish as to consult the good doctor when I could simply buy such a verdict from a corrupt judge? Money speaks, boyo, and the sooner ye realize that, the sooner ye'll come to heel."

"You bastard! Keep your money. I'll not let you condemn Lydia to a loveless marriage. I'd walked away, told her it was over between us, but now I think the only way to protect her might be to tell her the truth and take her away from the lot of you."

"And ye think she'll be going with ye when ye tell her ye've been sleeping with her sainted mother? Good God, man. Ye'll be the last person she'll want to be with, and that's assuming she even believes ye."

"Then I won't tell her. We'll run away and be married, and you'll never find us. We may have to struggle, but we will survive."

"Will ye now!" Thomas bent down farther, his sour breath almost causing Patrick to gag. "How sweet! And how d'ye think she'll feel about ye when ye've dragged her to some dilapidated building on the Lower East Side, when rats and vermin share her bed and her husband is out thieving and murdering, or worse, just to pay the rent on the filthy hovel? She'll have to start bestowing her favors on others because what ye bring in isn't enough to buy a decent meal, but she won't be able to go home. Her reputation will be destroyed, now, won't it, and she'll not even know if the wee brats she drags along behind her are yers or one o' her lovers'. If she didn't hate ye before, she will then."

"Why would we go to the city? We'll find another small town, where I can get a job clerking in a local store or helping in the stables."

"Will ye? And how are ye planning to get there, ye wee fool? Trains cost money, and where will ye stay while ye're looking for a job? Ye've not got a penny to yer name. Ye don't think her family will be providing ye with any, now, do ye?" Thomas was nearly spitting his words. "Edward hates yer guts; he'd see ye rot in the street before he'd lend a hand, and Lydia as well if that's what it takes to free her from ye. As for Elizabeth, she wants ye for herself. Ye can't imagine she'll just be turning ye over to her daughter. As ye've heard, she has other plans for Lydia, and ye're not included."

"Nor was Colin, I'd wager." Patrick gripped the arms of the chair, trying desperately to refrain from strangling the man. "What did you say that made Elizabeth agree to such a marriage?"

"I simply explained the alternatives, and being the wise woman she is, she immediately saw the merit in me proposal."

"You truly are a monster! You can't really think you've won. Edward will never allow Lydia to marry Colin. He hates all of you as much as he does me—more, perhaps."

"So he said, not moments ago, and yet the marriage will proceed in spite o' it. Should ye decide to interfere, just think o' the rats running through her beautiful hair. Edward has, I assure ye. Now get out o' me sight! I'm sick o' looking at ye."

Patrick stood to leave, but Thomas reached out, grabbing his arm to restrain him a moment more. "There was a third point to our agreement. Elizabeth will be staying with us from time to time to discuss the wedding plans. In fact, I believe she may arrive later this evening. She'll be staying in the room next to yers, and she despises sleeping alone. See that she doesn't."

Patrick yanked his arm away and shoved the doors open. Before he left, though, he swung back around, a wave of nausea attacking his stomach. "This isn't over, old man. I swear I'll see you dead for this!" He stormed into the entrance hall and began to head upstairs, but Colin grabbed his arm, stopping him momentarily.

"You'd best watch what you say," he said, his tone baring no malice for once. "Words have a way of coming back and haunting people."

CHAPTER 13

Friday, June 24, 1904 – 12:00 a.m.

Patrick sat on the floor, leaning back against his bed until he heard Thomas close his bedroom door. He wasn't sure how much time had passed. There'd been some arguing outside after he'd come up—the Stockbridges taking their leave, more than likely, though he was sure he'd recognized Jeremy's voice as well. Kathleen was in her room, but he supposed Colin and Jeremy were still downstairs in their cups, or at least on the way there.

A knock sounded on the front door, and his stomach clenched. Elizabeth's nasal tones carried up the staircase, annoyed that Thomas had not been there to meet her. Moments later, he heard Forbes showing her to the adjacent bedroom. Perhaps he could slip down the back staircase and disappear into the night before she even knew he was gone.

This was all Thomas Brissedon's doing. How could he be so blatantly cruel to the people he professed to love? Patrick could understand the man's vindictiveness toward him, though he may hate him for it, but why toward Kathleen and Colin? They were his own flesh and blood. The bed in the next room creaked, and Patrick grabbed his stomach. Did she really expect him to slip into her bedroom? Of course she did, and he knew better than to think it would be for nothing more than a bit of heavy petting.

Reaching under his mattress, he withdrew the pearl-handled knife his father had given him. Its blade sparkled in the dim light of the lamp. One quick thrust, and it would all be over. But no, it was the coward's way out.

Hope always springs eternal, lad, his father's words echoed in his memory. *To end it like that takes away all hope.*

Heaving a weary sigh, he placed the handsome weapon back in its sheath. He could never disgrace his family that way. Of course, using it on Thomas might actually do the world a service, but no, his parents would have frowned on that as well. Not to mention what Kathleen would think of him if she found out. He could risk the wrath of the entire world, but not hers. And yet . . .

He got up to check his jacket pocket for the note he'd written at Alexander Morton's office the day before, but it wasn't there. Rubbing his forehead, he slumped down on the bed, panic clutching at his chest. What if he'd dropped it somewhere? It tied Tommy Breslin to Thomas Brissedon and mentioned Mary O'Neill's name. What if Thomas found it? Would the poor woman be in danger? No, there had to be hundreds of Mary O'Neills in the city. Besides, that and that had been two years ago. Who knew where she was now?

Besides, if Thomas had found it, he surely would have recognized Patrick's handwriting and confronted him with it by now. Colin would have as well. Even if the names meant nothing to him, he'd want to taunt him with it, demand to know who the man was and how much money he owed him or something to that effect.

What about Kathleen? Would she bring it to his attention as well, or just destroy it? He supposed it all depended on how much she knew about her father's past. A tear trickled across his bruised cheek, and he wiped it away. He had to speak to her, to look her in the eye and ask her about her life before her father had married his mother, and it had to be now, before the bitch in the next room demanded his attentions.

Standing up, he brushed aside his tousled hair and walked to the window, trying to summon the nerve to call upon his stepsister. Two figures hurried across the lawn to meet a third. Kathleen and Molly meeting Brighton. He thought she'd stopped welcoming his biweekly visits.

Molly left them by the small copse of trees and headed down to the lake, but there was no hand-holding this time. In fact, her gestures made it seem as if Kathleen was arguing with Brighton. Now what was that all about? Her upcoming nuptials, perhaps?

A thump sounded down the hallway, and he walked over to the door, cracking it to take a peek. Jeremy, already half up the pole. Heading to the toilet, no doubt. Shaking his head, he walked back to the window, but only Brighton remained, sitting hunched over down by the lake. There'd be no asking Kathleen about her past now. He cursed himself for hesitating, though deep down, he couldn't help but release a small sigh of relief as well. At least for the moment, he could hold on to his fantasy, believe she truly was the sister he'd always longed for.

The bed next door creaked again, followed by the patter of feet across the carpet and the creak of a door. He drew in a deep breath, exhaling it slowly. If he didn't act quickly, she'd be in his room, and he certainly didn't want that.

He'd never get the lingering smell of bergamot out of his sheets.

He looked in the mirror and held his stomach. Every time he thought of what he was about to do, his stomach churned in disgust. It was the ultimate betrayal, far more treacherous than diddling one of the local young ladies. God, he couldn't even pretend she was Lydia without reminding himself what a vile creature he was. Doubtless, death would be a preferable fate. Alas, it wasn't an option. Not unless the good Lord saw fit to strike him down on the spot, and his mother had assured him God didn't work that way. Gazing out his window one last time, he checked his pocket for the key to the back door, just in case he managed to find a moment to slip away.

How like the darkened night his own life seemed of late. An endless void without the hope of any light filtering through, but then, even the night embraced its stars, just as he had embraced Lydia. Now even she had been snatched away from him. Just then, he saw another figure dart across the yard toward the house, and he grinned with satisfaction. It seemed Kathleen was not the only one afoot that night, for out of the shadows came the groomsman, Trevor Kilpatrick, with a small bouquet of flowers clutched in his hand.

A warmth caressed Patrick's heart, knowing how much the groom and Lizzie, the downstairs maid, loved each other. The fact that Thomas Brissedon virtually forbid any relationships from developing between his help only made their clandestine trysts all the more enjoyable.

The clock in the hall struck the quarter hour, and he was jolted from his reverie. Almost one. Taking a deep breath, he turned off his lamp and headed for the room next door and Elizabeth Langston.

Kathleen sat on the porch swing, trying to calm herself before heading upstairs. It wasn't her intent to hurt Brighton, but he hadn't taken any of her subtle hints, and her father's announcement of her proposed marriage seemed like the perfect excuse to tell him not to come around anymore. If she hadn't been such a coward, she would have done it weeks ago, but . . . Releasing a sigh, she went inside and headed up to her room.

All she wanted to do right now was get into bed. With any luck there would be a cool breeze blowing through her window. She opened her bedroom door but stopped short.

"Jeremy! What are you doing here? Is everyone all right?"

"Oh yes. Everyone is fine."

She frowned, looking him up and down. "Well, what is so urgent that it couldn't wait until tomorrow?"

"Did you enjoy your stroll with Brighton?"

She left the door open but walked over to lay a flower on her dresser. "You're drunk, Jeremy. I suggest you find your way back to your own room and sleep it off."

"Do you, now?" He staggered to his feet. "That's not a bad idea, but I think you might want to hear what I have to say first."

"Really? And what could that possibly be?"

"I know how we can get your father to cancel your marriage to Edward Langston."

"You do? Well, that's certainly something I'd love to hear, but why don't you go off to bed now, and you can tell me in the morning. You can barely stand up."

151

He hushed her. "No, it has to be done tonight." He walked past her, flashing a smile, but just before entering the hallway, he grabbed her, swinging her around and pinning her against the open door. "It's very simple, really." Brushing his lips against hers, he whispered in her ear. "We lie together tonight, then in the morning we shamefully confess our small indiscretion to all present. Edward will surely demand that the entire affair be called off, and thus we will be free to marry."

"Are you mad?" She struggled beneath him, but it only seemed to arouse him all the more. His heart was pounding against her as he kissed her lips and clawed at her skirts, trying to lift them. She felt as though she were going to pass out. But no, he would surely have his way with her then.

Reaching around his neck, she dug her nails into the tender skin, and he pulled back with a squeal. This might be her only chance. With all the strength she could muster, she shoved him over the ladder-back chair standing beside the door. She darted out into the hall and headed for the west wing, not even stopping to see if he was injured.

Turning the knob on Patrick's door, she raced inside and slammed it behind her. She felt for the key, her hands still trembling, but it seemed to be missing.

"Patrick!" She hurried over to his bed, but as her eyes adjusted to the darkness, she could see it hadn't even been slept in. Where on earth had he gone? Jeremy jiggled the knob, whispering her name, and panic surged through her body. She knew it was just the drink, that he'd regret his actions in the morning, but that didn't help her now.

"Katie, darling." The knob turned. "Don't be like that. I just want to save you from that miscreant my uncle wants you to marry."

If she screamed, would anyone really hear? Colin was probably out as well, and the staff was all the way up on the third floor. And if her father came, he'd kill Jeremy, no questions asked.

As the door opened, she remembered it. Patrick's knife! She dove to the floor by his bed, just seconds ahead of her alcohol-depraved cousin. Jeremy must have thought she'd decided to give in, for he wrapped his arms around her, only to stop short when the cold, sharp steel pricked against his groin. It never ceased to amaze her how quickly a man could regain some semblance of sobriety when faced with the possibility of his family jewels being damaged.

"Now, Katie, darling, I was just teasing. Surely you know I would never do anything to hurt you."

"Get out!" She held the knife tight. "Patrick will be returning any minute, and when I tell him what you've done . . ."

"But I've done nothing, Cousin." Slowly, he pushed himself up and began backing toward the door, wobbling now and then.

"Get out!" she repeated, and so he did, with the utmost haste.

Kathleen collapsed on the floor. She could contain herself no longer and sobbed softly into her brother's quilt. Gradually, she regained her composure, and taking a few deep breaths, she gazed around the moonlit room. Where could he have gone at such an hour?

"Out drinking again, I suppose," she said to herself. "Or with some prostitute." She hated seeing him degrade himself so, but over the last year his moral character had steadily declined until his reputation for depravity rivaled Colin's. Still, he had not lost his tenderness, and for this she loved him dearly. Probably even more so than Colin, whom she sometimes feared was beyond all hope. Of course, if anyone suggested it, she'd adamantly deny feeling closer to one than the other.

She sat a bit longer, then, having calmed herself sufficiently, she replaced the knife and stood to look out the window. Jeremy was pacing back and forth across the yard, mumbling to himself. Feeling secure for the moment, she quickly returned to her room and locked the door behind her, angling the ladder-back chair beneath the doorknob just in case. In the morning, she would speak to her father of it, ask that Jeremy be kept from the liquor cabinet at the very least, but she knew better than to disturb him at this hour.

She had just laid her head on the pillow when she heard Jeremy stumble through the hallway, still mumbling to himself. No doubt he was heading upstairs to find solace in the arms of Molly, the upstairs maid. Breathing a bit easier, she let the tension drain from her body. At least she knew Molly would welcome his advances, though she feared the girl believed he truly cared for her. Perhaps she should have a word with her in the morning as well.

Patrick rolled over on his back, exhausted. God! For an older woman, she certainly had a lot of energy. At least she was asleep now. He gazed over at her shapely body, wondering if Lydia would be that good in bed. The thought reminded him who he was lying next to, and a wave of guilt overtook him. Lord help him! She was Lydia's mother, for God's sake.

In a frantic attempt to purge the thought from his mind, he took a few deep breaths, hoping it would quell his intense impulse to gag. Instead the sweet-tart scent of her bergamot perfume assailed his nostrils, only intensifying the need. It reminded him of Earl Grey tea, and he wondered if he'd ever be able to stomach a cup again.

Grabbing his shirt from the floor, he covered his nose and tried taking shallow breaths in a futile attempt to block out the smell and calm his growing sense of shame. True, he'd told Lydia he'd only wanted to bed her, but it had been nothing more than an effort to spare her any pain, and the truth cut like a knife. He gazed up at the ceiling, praying sleep would free him from this nightmare, and that he'd wake to find himself in Lydia's arms, not her oversexed mother's.

He'd just started to doze off when he heard some voices in the hallway outside the door. Odd, since no one but the servants used the back staircase as a rule, and they would all be asleep by now. Besides, even if they weren't, they'd have no reason to be in the hallway at this hour. After a moment, all went quiet again, so he chanced rolling over, but a few minutes later, he heard more movement in the hallway.

Curiosity getting the better of him, he held his pocket watch next to the small bedside lamp, its dim light barely enough to illuminate the table on which it stood. One forty-five! Who could it be? He sat up, resting his elbows on his knees to quell the deep sense of regret that had brought him to the precipice of tears. When he felt stable enough, the tears imprisoned precariously behind their rickety barrier of denial, he slipped out of bed, being ever so careful not to disturb the snoring beauty beside him. He could definitely see where Lydia got her looks, but another round with her that night, and he was sure his guilt and shame would bring him to his knees in a waterfall of tears that rivaled Niagara Falls. Not that it would necessarily be a bad thing. Perhaps the sight of his sobbing form would make her think twice before asking for his services again.

Scrubbing his hands over his face, he tiptoed to the bedroom door, cracking it slightly. His fanciful comparison of himself to the famous water feature was interrupted at once when he caught a glimpse of Kathleen flitting down the hallway toward the main part of the house. Smiling with affection for his stepsister, he roused himself and returned to bed. A whiff of Elizabeth's perfume touched his nostrils once again, and he considered grabbing his clothes and returning to his own room, but he was too exhausted to get up again, so he pinched his nose and buried his face in the pillow.

Sleep had just begun to overtake him again when a sudden thought caused his eyes to open. Where had Kathleen been all this time? Brighton had been alone down by the lake. Had Thomas sent her to make sure he was with Elizabeth? Was that why she'd been in the hall?

His heart pounded in his throat and throbbed in his temples. Now he was letting his imagination get the better of him, though it had become more imperative than ever that he speak to her. Resolving to do it first thing in the morning, he blew out a long breath. *Hope springs eternal.* The words floated through his mind, calming his nerves and easing his fears. Now if sleep would only come.

Patrick turned over on his side once more. He'd been lying awake for what seemed hours, debating whether or not he could get up and return to his own bed without waking his overeager companion. Checking his pocket watch once more, he cursed. Only forty-five minutes. He threw a glance in her direction. Surely she wouldn't notice him leaving now. He was just about to chance making his escape when he heard the rustling of footsteps in the hallway once again.

Wondering who it could be this time, he pulled on his pants and returned to the door, cracking it just enough to see his stepbrother slither down the back staircase. Common sense warned him to stay put, but as usual, curiosity got the better of him. After waiting a few minutes, he followed Colin to the hidden panel that led to his stepfather's study, though he did retain enough prudence to remain outside. He was all too aware of the price he'd pay if he got caught spying. Then again, if he was found in the hallway, it wouldn't go much better for him. Shrugging, he peeked around the opening and watched as Colin ruffled through the desk for some unknown item.

He must have been there for about ten minutes or so when he shifted his weight, and the old wooden floor creaked beneath him. Pulling back, he pressed himself against the wall, his heart pounding in his throat. *Shit! Shit! Shit!* Why didn't he just go back upstairs right away? Hardly able to breath, he listened for a moment, until finally, he heard movement in the study again—the ruffling of papers and sliding of drawers.

Relieved to have avoided another visit to the stables, Patrick took that as his cue and quietly crept back upstairs, retrieving the rest of his clothes and returning to his own room. His stomach was still a mass of knots, so he took one of the sleeping pills Dr. Tennyson had given him when he'd bruised his ribs. Discarding everything but his drawers, he laid down on his bed, the warm summer air washing over him. Though a third set of footsteps roused him a while later, Dr. Tennyson's pills had already begun to work their magic, and he just shrugged and rolled over. *Probably just Colin heading back.* The bed in the adjoining room creaked, and he held his breath, waiting for a tap on the door. When none came, he let out a grateful sigh and closed his eyes. If anyone else used the hallway after that, they did so undetected, for he didn't wake again until morning.

CHAPTER 14

Kathleen rose early, determined to advise Molly not to believe a thing her cousin had to say. Deciding to take the back stairs, she passed by Patrick's door, wondering what time he'd come home, or if he even had. Maybe she should tell him Daniel was looking into his father's death. Perhaps that would help him get his life back on the right path.

She hurried up the staircase and was just coming to Molly's door when it opened, and Jeremy ran into her.

"Kathleen?" He rubbed his forehead and groaned, sitting down on one of the beds. "I was just leaving."

"Here, drink this," Molly said. "It will help with the headache."

Jeremy smiled up at the young woman he'd spent the night with, clearly ashamed of himself, but Kathleen could feel little pity for him.

"Good morning, Miss Kathleen." Lizzie made a show of straightening the blankets on her bed, though Kathleen knew she hadn't spent the night there. "Is there something ye're needing?"

"Just a word with Molly."

Jeremy groaned again and got up. "I'd best be going, then." He turned to Molly. "I did mean everything I said. Forgive me."

Molly crinkled her brow, but Lizzie stood with her arms folded across her chest. "It's his fault she's been dismissed, ye know," she said when Jeremy had gone.

"Dismissed?" Kathleen said. "What on earth are you talking about? Who's dismissed her?"

"Yer father, miss," Molly said, struggling to subdue a sob. "But 'tis not Jerry's fault his uncle's such a tyrant, begging yer pardon, miss. Any more than 'tis Trevor's fault . . ." Lizzie's eyes widened, and Molly gasped. "I mean any more than 'tis Trevor's or Mr. Colin's or anyone's fault."

"Do as ye will, then," Lizzie said, "but ye can't really think he's planning to marry someone like yerself." She plumped her pillow and threw it back on the bed. "Ye're daft if ye do. He's just using ye for a bit of fluff, and when ye're gone, he'll find another. Well, it won't be me, I'll tell ye that."

"I should hope not," Kathleen said, unable to keep from teasing the girl just a bit. "Trevor wouldn't be at all pleased about that, now, would he?"

"Why would Trevor be upset?" Lizzie said, a slight tremble in her voice.

"I know he comes to visit you at least once or twice a week."

Lizzie slumped down on her bed, tears bursting from her eyes. "I suppose ye'll be letting us go as well now."

Kathleen felt awful. She'd forgotten how serious a threat being let go could be. "Oh no, Lizzie. I think it's sweet, though I do have to talk to both of you. Trevor's a lovely young man, but . . ."

Before she could finish her thought, Lizzie leaned over her basin and retched.

"Oh dear, I'm so sorry. I didn't mean to upset you so."

"'Tis not that, miss," Molly said, "but the babe. The wee thing's been playing havoc with her insides the past few nights."

"Oh, Lizzie, it's Trevor's, isn't it?" She held a damp rag to the girl's head and laid her back on the bed.

"'Tis not what ye think, though, miss," the girl said. "Trev and me, we got married at me cousin's parish a few months ago. We didn't want to say nothing, though, not until we had to." She started to cry again. "He'll let Trev go too, won't he?"

"Don't you worry about anything. I'll talk to my father, and if he won't listen to reason, then I'll see to it you have excellent references. I may even be able to find him another position."

"Ye'd do that, Miss?"

"Of course I would. Love is a wonderful thing, and it should be helped along, not hampered by stupid rules."

"But what o' Molly?"

"I'll talk to my father about her as well." She turned to address Molly. "Though I feel I must warn you, Jeremy likely has no intention of marrying you."

"I know that now." The girl looked down, wringing the damp handkerchief in her hands. "I was a fool to believe anything he said. He told me what he did last night."

"He did? Well, he was drunk, but... I'm so sorry, Molly."

"'Tis all right, miss. If I could just keep me place here, I'll be fine."

Kathleen put her arm around the girl and sat her down on her cot. "I can't guarantee that, but there are always ladies coming in the library asking to let them know if we hear of any good help, so I can promise you won't go without a good job."

Once again, Patrick bolted down the stairs, his hair disheveled and his shirttail hanging out over his pants. Fifteen minutes late! Thomas was going to have his hide, literally! He dashed through the parlor, but as he entered the dining room, he discovered that by some miracle his stepfather had not yet arrived—or had he?

"He's gone for me, hasn't he?" he said with a certain degree of trepidation.

"Calm yourself, Patrick." A snide smile quirked the corner of Colin's mouth. "This time he's keeping us waiting. Quite an interesting turn of events, don't you think?"

Patrick scowled at his stepbrother but took his seat with a sigh of relief.

"How did you sleep?" Colin's lips quivered in an obvious attempt to restrain a laugh, but Patrick was ready for him this time.

"Pleasant enough once I dozed off, though not everyone did. It seems the halls saw quite a lot of traffic last night. It kept waking me up."

It was almost humorous how all vestiges of self-satisfaction drained from Colin's face. Direct hit! But he wasn't the only one to react. Jeremy's cheeks turned an odd shade of red, and he hung his head when Kathleen shot a glance in his direction. *Now, what was that all about?*

Colin must have sensed the tension between them as well, for he changed the subject. "Well, I was out till the wee hours. Ask the stable lads, the younger ones. Mickey and Willie were nowhere to be found, as usual."

"I don't know why we continue to employ them," Kathleen said.

Patrick knew why, but it was Jeremy who answered. "Because they do your father's bidding when it comes to the more unsavory bits of business, the sort he doesn't want you to know anything about."

"What kinds of unsavory business?"

Something flashed in Colin's eyes. Was it panic? "Things like carting away refuse and the like. It can be a filthy job. Most don't want anything to do with it, but they don't seem to mind."

"Oh yes, I suppose it does need to be done." Kathleen smiled, but Patrick could still see the doubt in her expression.

Colin groaned. "For God's sake, where is he? I'm famished."

"I'm beginning to worry." Kathleen walked over to Patrick and brushed back his hair. "It's not like him to be late. Tuck your shirt in, Paddy," she added matter-of-factly, "and for heaven's sake, button your collar."

Patrick stood up and did as she asked, for he valued Kathleen's opinion more than any other.

"I truly am worried," she said when Colin didn't respond.

"Oh, all right, Kate." He got up and kissed her on the forehead. "I'll call for Molly and have her go see about him." When he did, however, it was Lizzie who came in her place.

"She's been let go, Mr. Brissedon. Yer father informed her last night."

"He did? Ah, that's why she was so upset. Well, never mind that. Is she still here?"

"She is," Kathleen said. "Getting her things together. I thought perhaps we could talk to Father about it."

"Yes, of course!" He turned back to Lizzie. "Tell her to go check on my father immediately, and I'll have a talk with him later. I'm sure it can all be worked out."

A subtle smile broke out on Jeremy's lips, and Colin nodded in his direction. So it was true, then. Jeremy was diddling the upstairs maid. Patrick shook his head. What on earth that sweet little thing saw in the tall, gangly, droopy-eyed man, he didn't know.

"I will at once, sir!" Lizzie said. "Thank ye, Mr. Colin."

Lizzie headed back upstairs to get Molly, and Colin returned to his seat with a weary sigh.

"Too much physical exertion last night?" Patrick knew he shouldn't poke the bull, but he couldn't resist.

"Were you exercising last night?" Elizabeth asked. "I do enjoy a good brisk walk just before dusk myself."

Jeremy nearly choked on his coffee, spraying the liquid across the tablecloth. "I'm so sorry," he gasped as Forbes stepped forward to clean up the mess. "It went down the wrong pipe."

"Lift your arms above your head," Elizabeth said. "It does help."

Colin looked at Patrick, his eyes watering with laughter. It was the first time he'd ever shared what Patrick would call a brotherly glance.

"Thank you," Jeremy said. "I'm fine now, really."

The words had no sooner left his lips than a harsh scream echoed down the staircase. For a moment, everyone just sat, glancing at one another, but then they all went running toward the stairs. Colin was nearest the door and so led the way, but Patrick was immediately behind, followed by Kathleen. If Thomas had hurt that poor girl,

Patrick was determined to throttle him, no matter how big he was. But when he rounded the upstairs railing, he soon realized she was quite safe.

They had barely stepped into Thomas's small sitting room when Patrick swung around and stopped his stepsister from going any farther. Though he'd only gotten a peek over Colin's shoulder, he'd seen enough to know it wasn't a sight Kathleen should be subjected to. Forcefully, he gripped her by the shoulders and led her back out to the hallway.

"Patrick!" she said, terror flashing in her eyes. "What is it? You're hurting me."

He eased his hold a bit but didn't dare release her, certain she'd head back for the bedroom, especially with Molly sobbing just outside the door. Jeremy had his arm wrapped around the distraught maid's shoulders, and she buried her face in his shirt.

"He's gone, Kate," Patrick said. "I'm sorry."

"Gone!" She shook her head, tiny lines crinkling her forehead. "Where? He wouldn't have left without saying goodbye."

The words caught in Patrick's throat, physically painful. "Katie, he's dead. There's nothing you can do. Nothing any of us can do."

She tried to pull away from him, but he continued to hold her. "No," she said, "it can't be. I want to see him."

She pushed Patrick back with such force it almost knocked him off his feet, but he tightened his grip. The truth must have shone in his eyes because she collapsed against him, tears streaming down her cheeks. At last, he released his grip, for restraint was no longer necessary. He comforted her instead, holding her sobbing form against his chest. There was no need for words, just soft whispers to soothe her.

"Forbes!" Colin wandered out of the silent rooms, and for a moment his eyes met Patrick's, stunned and tearful.

"I've got her," Patrick said, and his stepbrother nodded, turning his attention to the matter at hand.

"Forbes!" he repeated, and the agile man hurried up the staircase. Lizzie and Elizabeth were standing at the bottom with Moira, the nursemaid, helping to restrain the two smaller children.

Patrick looked down at them, an ache filling his heart. He glanced over toward Colin and saw him staring over the banister as well. He could almost hear his thoughts. How was he going to tell them?

"Take them to the garden, please, Moira." Colin took a shaky breath, and then shifted his gaze to the butler. "Forbes, would you be so kind as to send Trevor for Dr. Tennyson ... No, wait." He stammered, hesitating a moment before continuing. "What use could he be now? No, you must send Trevor for the authorities at once. My father's been murdered."

The older man gasped in horror. Patrick knew he'd never been fond of his new employer, having served Patrick's father for years, but still ... murder! For a split second, it seemed as if he couldn't speak, but then, as always, he quickly composed himself and took charge of the situation.

"Yes, sir, at once, but might I suggest sending for Dr. Tennyson as well. The authorities are surely going to want to ascertain the cause of death, and as he is the coroner ..."

Colin nodded. "Yes, of course. Send one of the stable boys for him."

"Yes, sir. Shall I take Molly downstairs as well, sir? Perhaps Mrs. Quinn could give her something to soothe her nerves."

Patrick threw a glance down toward the parlor entrance and saw the housekeeper standing with her hand over her mouth. On hearing her name, she hurried down the hall to the kitchen, to prepare a tonic of some sort, no doubt.

"Yes, thank you." Colin threw another desperate look in Patrick's direction. "In fact, I think perhaps it would be best if we all retired to the parlor. I could certainly use a good stiff drink."

"How could you!" Kathleen pulled away from Patrick, her hands fisted at her sides. "Our father is lying dead, and you can think of nothing but drowning yourself in alcohol."

"Come downstairs." Patrick wrapped his arm around her shoulders once more. "For once, I have to agree with Colin."

She looked up at him, and he nodded, guiding her shaking body to the parlor below. The pain in her eyes revealed a moment of understanding, but she continued to hold on to him, almost as if letting go would trap her in this endless nightmare.

It was, however, no ghostly dream, for upstairs in the bedroom her father's lifeless body lay saturated in a pool of his own blood. From what Patrick saw, a deep gash cut across his throat had unquestionably been the cause of his death. Quick and immediate! Yet the look of terror on his face suggested a struggle. If that was the case, why had he not yelled out? Or perhaps he had, and no one had heard his frenzied cries.

Jeremy brought a glass of sherry over to Kathleen and knelt by her side, bidding her to drink. At first, she refused, choosing instead to bury her head in Patrick's shoulder.

"To calm your nerves," Patrick said, gently coaxing her to take a few sips.

"This is it, sir." Caleb Croser, the young stable boy, tugged on Daniel's coat and hopped out of the buggy, leading him up the path to the large house set amongst enormous maple and oak trees. Well kept, it's blue siding and gray roof stood out against the leafy backdrop that surrounded it. So this was where Kathleen Brissedon lived? It seemed to fit her perfectly, the color almost matching the shade of her eyes.

Letting out a sigh, he knocked on the wooden frame of the etched-glass door. Too bad he had to visit under such sinister circumstances. He would much rather be coming to call with a bouquet of flowers for the lovely librarian. He scrubbed a hand across his face and was just about to knock again when the door opened.

"Good morning, sir." A tall man wearing a tailored black suit stood gazing at him, clearly distraught and most certainly the butler. "May I help you?"

"He's Doc Sam's assistant," Caleb said, sticking his head out from behind Daniel. "The doc's out on calls, so he came instead."

"Thank you, Caleb," the butler said. "You'd best return to the stables. Mrs. Quinn is too upset for cookies today."

The boy fiddled with his hat a moment. "I was sorry to hear, sir." Without another word, he slapped the cap back on his head and ran off toward the stables.

"Thank you for coming, sir," the butler said. "I do remember seeing you with Dr. Tennyson at Mrs. Brissedon's funeral. I'm the butler, Forbes. Do come in. The younger Mr. Brissedon is awaiting your arrival. It's a terrible state of affairs, I'm afraid."

Daniel followed the butler into a well-appointed parlor, much like his parents'. Whoever had decorated it had impeccable taste, and he couldn't help but wonder if it had been Miss Brissedon.

Colin looked up from the sideboard and frowned. "Where is Dr. Tennyson?"

"He's making his rounds, I'm afraid, but I'm his assistant."

"Assistant?" Colin looked over to Kathleen. "Perhaps we should wait for the doctor. We need someone who knows what they're doing."

"Colin." Kathleen took a moment to blow her nose before continuing. "Dr. O'Halleran is a physician and more than qualified. He used to work for the coroner's office in the city before coming to assist Dr. Tennyson."

"Oh, I'm terribly sorry," Colin said. "Yes, I do remember seeing you at the funeral now. Thank you for coming so quickly. My father appears to have been murdered. Cut down in his sleep, it would seem. Why, or by whom, I'm afraid I have no idea."

"He's upstairs, then, I gather?" Daniel shot a look at Miss Brissedon, who sat staring at the floor, another, younger man's arm around her shoulders. Patrick, if he remembered correctly. Her beautiful eyes were puffy and red, and it was all he could do to keep from going to comfort her himself.

Forbes cleared his throat, and Daniel looked over to see the butler standing with Sergeant Owens from the local constabulary.

"Glad you're here, Doc," the man said. "I've never had to deal with anything like this before." He tilted his head before adding, "From what Doc Tennyson says, you have, though, right?"

"Sadly, on a number of occasions."

Colin put his glass down and wiped the back of his hand across his mouth. "Yes, well, if you and the sergeant will follow me, I'll take you up." The others remained in the parlor while Colin led the way to his father's rooms. "In there," he said, clearing his throat, "just beyond the sitting room. If you don't mind, I'll wait out here. It's quite a gruesome sight."

Daniel nodded, then suggested Sergeant Owens stay with the man while he went into the bedroom. Colin had been right: the ashen corpse that lay before him was a grisly sight indeed. Rigor mortis had already begun to set in around the neck and jaw muscles, though the rest of the body remained flaccid. His skin, however, was still warm, and his wide eyes had already completely clouded over, telling Daniel that he could not have been dead more than four or five hours at the most.

"Dear God!" Sam Tennyson stopped short as he came to stand beside Daniel. "I got your message and came straightaway."

"I'm glad you did. This is clearly a murder." Daniel hesitated for a moment, reluctant to say what was on his mind but feeling he must. "But then I don't suppose we'll need to know any more than that."

"This isn't the city, Danny. We don't have many murders out here, but when we do, we find out who's responsible—rich or poor. I've sent word to District Attorney Smith. I told him you were investigating and that we'll give him a progress report in a few days."

"Will the sergeant and his men . . . ?"

"I've also contacted the new chief. The sergeant and his men are at our disposal. Though from what your uncle Timothy says, you're quite an investigator yourself."

"You know Uncle Timothy as well as my father?"

Sam smiled. "One of these days, lad, you'll learn the world's a much smaller place than you think it is. Now, tell me how Mr. Brissedon died."

"Obviously, the knife to the neck would have been quite sufficient."

Sam crossed his arms over his chest, lifting an eyebrow as he tilted his head to the side. "If I wanted obvious, son, I could have asked the sergeant out there. I expect more from you."

"The amount of blood not only indicates it was antemortem, but that he would have bled out almost immediately, thus resulting in his death. I'd venture to say he saw it coming as well."

Sam nodded. "And why's that?"

Daniel had the feeling Sam was testing him, but if he was to take over for the man one day, he supposed he had every right. "His eyes are wide open, for one thing. If he was sleeping, they would have been closed. Not only that, but the muscles of his face are contorted, not relaxed, and the bedclothes around his feet are twisted. There also appears to be skin under his fingernails. I would bet the murderer has a series of scratches or gashes somewhere on his body."

"And then there's the muddy boots." Sergeant Owens stood in the doorway, pointing down at the floor.

Daniel knelt down for a closer look at footprints pressed into the fancy Persian rug. Though most had only left a trace of mud, one or two were full prints.

"I've called in a few more men," the sergeant said. "Just let us know what you want us to look for."

Daniel was expecting Sam to answer, but instead the doctor nodded to Daniel. "You'll be reporting your findings to Dr. O'Halleran. He'll be heading up the investigation."

Despite the somber situation, a shiver of excitement surged through Daniel's body. "Right then, Sergeant, let's see where these muddy prints lead, shall we?"

Daniel instructed the newly arrived officers to check the room for anything else that looked out of place, then he and Sam followed the sergeant out into the hallway, curious to see where the footprints led.

"Whoever was wearing those boots is our murderer," Daniel said.

"And how can you be sure of that?" Sam asked, a hint of curiosity sparking in his eyes.

"The position of the indentation in the rug. There's a print right next to the bed, facing the headboard, but only one, as if the other leg was on the bed. And though it's only the front portion of the boot, it's more distinct than any of the others, showing more pressure was exerted there."

Sam chuckled. "Looks like I'm going to owe both your father and uncle a round of beer."

"You bet on me?"

"That's the only kind of gambling my Nell will allow. Good thing, too, considering I'm about to lose."

Colin was still standing outside his father's rooms, leaning against the banister and chewing on his nails. "Mr.

Brissedon?" Daniel nodded down the hall to his left. "May I ask where the door at the end of this hall leads?"

"It's basically the servants' staircase. It goes up to their third-floor rooms and down to a hallway that takes you to the kitchen. Oh, and there's a door leading outside, though it's kept locked at night."

"And what about the inside door? Is it kept locked as well?" Daniel knew it wouldn't be, but he wanted to hear Colin's response.

"No, of course not. The help needs access for various reasons."

Daniel almost laughed. He got the impression Colin Brissedon was a condescending prig. "What about the outside door? You said it's locked at night. Who has the keys?"

"As far as I know, just my father and Forbes. Though he may have lent it to some of the other help from time to time. I'm afraid I can't help you there. Would you like me to summon Forbes?"

"That won't be necessary right now, thank you. I'll need to speak with everyone in the household, both family and staff, as soon as we're finished here, though. Is there somewhere I can conduct the questioning in private?"

"You mean individually? But why? You can't believe any of us did this?"

"Of course not, sir, but someone may have seen something they'd feel uncomfortable mentioning in front of others. So is there somewhere I can meet with everyone . . . individually?"

Colin seemed quite put out, but the look of disgust that crossed his face told Daniel he'd resigned himself to the inevitable. "Yes, of course. My father's study should suffice."

Daniel headed down the hallway. "May I ask whose rooms these are?"

"The first is Patrick's, my stepbrother, and the one closest to the stairs is a guest room. Mrs. Langston stayed there last night."

Daniel rubbed the back of his neck and pulled a small brown notebook from his jacket pocket, along with a pencil. Then, in a change of tack designed to throw Colin off guard, he asked, "Who discovered the body?"

"What?" Colin looked like he needed to sit down, but he managed to rouse himself. "Oh yes. That would be our upstairs maid, Molly. My father was late for breakfast, which is completely unheard of, so after about twenty minutes I asked Molly to see what was keeping him. She had a key, so I suppose when he didn't answer, she thought to walk into the sitting room and knock on the bedroom door." Colin shook his head. "I've never seen such terror in anyone's eyes before. The poor girl was horrified."

"I imagine she would be. Where may I find the young lady now?"

"Downstairs . . . in the kitchen, I presume. Mrs. Quinn, our housekeeper, is trying to calm her down. She's so young. The whole experience has been upsetting for us all. I can't imagine how hard it's been for her, finding him the way she did."

Daniel shifted his hat from one hand to the other. "Unfortunately, I do still have to question her. She may have seen more than she knows. I will try to be gentle."

"Yes, of course." Colin sniffed and rubbed a hand over his clean-shaven face, as if he were waking from a dream. "We can go down the back stairs if you'd like. That will take us directly into the kitchen, and I can show you the back door."

"And the constables can see where those footprints lead," Daniel said to the sergeant before following his host.

CHAPTER 15

Daniel walked into a clean, bright kitchen to find a young woman sitting at the table, sobbing softly while an older woman tried to get her to drink some tea. Hattie and his mother did that as well. Why did women always think tea solved everything? A man knelt on the floor beside her, holding her hand, attempting to calm her.

"Never in all me twenty years have I seen anything so brutal, Jerry." She blew her nose and continued. "Even an animal deserved better than that."

"It's all right, darling," the man said. "My cousin has called for the authorities. I'm sure they'll get to the bottom of it."

"They'll think I did it, won't they?" She started to sob all the harder.

Colin knelt down before her. "Of course they won't, Molly. Why would they?"

"On account of him letting me go last night."

"But you weren't alone last night, darling," the man she'd called Jerry said. "I was with you."

Though he couldn't be sure, Daniel thought he'd seen him at the funeral as well. Since he'd referred to his cousin calling the authorities, he must be a member of the family.

Sam must have noticed his confusion, for he leaned over to whisper in his ear. "Jeremy Radcliffe, a cousin."

"But it wasn't the whole night," Molly said, "and I can't be speaking o' that anyway, now, can I? What will they think o' me? Yet if I say naught, they're sure to suspect . . ." She picked up her hankie and sobbed into it again. "They're not going to take me away, are they, Mr. Colin?"

"Now, Molly," Colin said, his tone kind but firm. "I want you to stop this. We know you didn't kill my father, and so will Dr. O'Halleran here. But he does need to ask you some questions." He stood up and turned to the other woman.

"Mrs. Quinn, I know my father and Forbes have keys to the door by the back stairs, but do you know if anyone else has one?"

"I'm afraid not, sir," she said, "though I'd be flabbergasted if they did. Your father only gave Forbes one out of absolute necessity. I kept telling him it would be so much easier if he gave me one as well, but he refused. I'd have to ask every time we'd have a late delivery or some such thing."

"Did that happen often?" Daniel asked.

"Not really. Most of the deliveries come right to the kitchen door. It was only if they needed to work on the plumbing or electric—something like that mostly. Mr. Desmond . . . I mean, Mr. Brissedon, he liked all the modern conveniences."

Daniel flashed her what his mother referred to as his *boyish* smile and noted her slip of the tongue. "You indicated Mr. Brissedon kept more than one key?"

"I don't recall that I did," she said, a twinkle in her eye. "But yes, he had two for himself."

"Would you happen to know where he kept them?"

"'Course I do. He'd didn't make no attempt to hide where they were if I asked for them. One's in his study, in the upper right-hand drawer of his desk, and the other is in the small table by his bed."

"Thank you, Mrs. Quinn, is it?"

"It is, sir, chief cook and bottle washer." The woman laughed, a hearty sound that reminded him of his parents' housekeeper, Hattie. "Can I get you a cup of tea, then?"

"Yes, that would be greatly appreciated. Milk and one sugar, please." Mrs. Quinn went about getting his cup of tea, and Daniel sat down by the maid's side. "Now, Molly, I'm not accusing you of anything, but I do have some questions. You may have seen something that can help us catch the killer. Will you help me?"

"O' course I will. Like I said to Jer . . . Mr. Radcliffe, no one deserves to die like that."

"No, they don't. Did you hear or see anything suspicious as you went upstairs, someone darting around a corner, something dropped?"

"Just them muddy boot prints. Lord, if Mr. Brissedon had seen them. No one's to wear their outside shoes upstairs. Even when Mr. Patrick was so poorly, he stopped to take them off. And us just finishing cleaning up Mr. Colin's and all."

Colin seemed to pale a little, and Daniel made a note in his book to ask him about it later. "Thank you, Molly. You've been a great help." He produced his most sympathetic smile while Sam gave Mrs. Quinn something to calm the girl's nerves.

Daniel downed his tea and fought to keep the grimace from his face. She must have emptied the sugar jar in it. "Thank you, that's all for now, but I may have more questions later."

They headed down the hallway toward the outside door. Colin and the sergeant strode ahead while Sam walked behind with Daniel.

"What do you think?" Sam said.

"That there's more between Molly and Mr. Radcliffe than either of them is willing to let on."

"You know how that goes. It's just not done."

"Oh, it's done," Daniel said. "Only it's meant to be hidden beneath the sheets."

Sam frowned. "True enough, but I was talking about a member of the family marrying the help. Suppose the parties involved wanted it to be more and Thomas forbid it."

"It's possible. Jeremy doesn't seem to be hiding his feelings for her. Or maybe he's just using her as an alibi, though Molly scuttled that when she said it hadn't been the whole night."

"I can't believe she even admitted it at all," Sam said.

An ache pricked Daniel's heart as he recalled how innocent his mama must have been when her employer's son spoke to her of love and marriage. "Regardless of what his true feelings are, she believes they're honorable. Besides, she was afraid we were going to accuse her of murder. I don't think a woman did it, though."

Sam grunted. "As deep as that cut goes, the assailant would have had to have some strength behind him."

"Or be so angry they found the strength." By the time they returned to the dead man's suite, the constables were waiting just outside the bedroom door.

"We didn't find much, sir," one of them said. "Nothing looked disturbed, aside from the bed, of course, though we did stumble across this. It was lying on the floor by the bureau."

Sam took the gold cuff link and indicated for Daniel to step over to the side with him. "The other day, Kathleen Brissedon mentioned a pair of her father's cuff links had gone missing. She feared her stepbrother might have stolen them. I even thought that's what she wanted you to investigate at first. Of course, it is possible the old man simply dropped them himself, and to be honest, I can't say for sure this is the pair she was speaking of, but it might be something you want to look into."

"That's my father's." Colin grabbed the piece from Sam, causing Daniel to unleash his most intimidating stare. It had the desired effect, for Colin almost shoved the piece back in Sam's hand. "It's just that the pair went missing a few weeks ago. I'm afraid I might have accused Patrick of stealing them, but I suppose Father just lost them."

"Most likely," Daniel said, though he took Sam's advice and made a note to keep it in mind before turning back to the constables. "Did you come across anything that might have been used as a murder weapon?"

"Afraid not, sir," one of the men said, but then Daniel never really expected they would. The fact that the room had been left undisturbed, however, seemed to rule out the possibility that robbery was the motive.

He walked back into the bedroom and stared down at the man's body. No, this was not a mere theft gone wrong. Someone had entered his room, gone straight to his bed, and slit his throat. Deliberate and calculated. He slipped open the small drawer by the bed and removed the silver key.

"And you said that staircase is only used by the help?" he asked Colin, who was standing uncomfortably outside the bedroom door.

Colin shrugged, a tinge of pink touching his cheeks. "Well, it leads to their quarters, but just about everyone has employed them at one time or another. I've used them quite a few times myself when I wanted to sneak down and get a snack without anyone knowing. I'm sure Jeremy and Patrick have done the same from time to time."

Daniel flashed him a polite smile, the statement prompting memories of his own shenanigans and Hattie's mock scowl when she'd catch him. He cleared his throat, bringing his thoughts back to the situation at hand. "Patrick . . . that would be your stepbrother?"

"Yes, Patrick Desmond. My father married his mother after her husband . . . died."

"He was the other gentleman in the parlor, I presume?"

"Yes, the younger one sitting with my sister Kathleen. I believe you might know her . . . from the library." It was more of a statement than a question, and there was a glint of something else—was it suspicion?—in Colin's eyes. Could he be aware of their meeting? Daniel was under the impression she hadn't wanted anyone else to know about it.

"Tuesday and Thursday mornings," he said with a carefree laugh. "She's been very helpful in locating some reading material for me." He checked his notebook again. "What about the outside door? Do you or your family utilize that?"

"No, not really. Why would we? We're old enough to come and go as we please."

"But it is used by the staff and for certain deliveries."

"On occasion, I suppose; at least, that is what Mrs. Quinn said. As she told you, there is a door that leads directly into the kitchen, so I don't imagine the other is used that often."

"Have you had any servicing done lately?" Daniel asked. Colin's head popped up, his eyes wide, though it was all too obvious he was trying to contain a laugh. "On your home's plumbing or such?" Daniel added in annoyance. Even his youngest brother, Frankie, was beyond such childish innuendos.

"Ah, of course, but no, not that I'm aware of. I'm sure Mrs. Quinn could tell you more about that. I don't usually concern myself with such mundane affairs."

"Dr. O'Halleran." Sergeant Owens pushed his way past Colin, sparing Daniel from dignifying the young Mr. Brissedon's statement with an answer. "Those footprints seem to lead outside, but we lose them after that. Too much traffic, I'm afraid. Strange, that, don't ye think?"

"Yes, I do," Daniel said, for if no one used that particular entrance all that much, why was there such an abundance of footprints just outside its door?

"There's another door down there as well, sir," the sergeant continued. "I think you should see it."

Once again, Colin's face seemed to go a shade lighter. Daniel looked to him, raising his eyebrow. He hadn't noticed another door.

"That would be Father's study," Colin said, leading the way. "Though it's more of a hidden panel than a door. I would imagine he used these stairs to get to his room from time to time, or maybe even one of the unoccupied rooms. He was, in some ways, an extremely eccentric man. One who tended to go to great lengths to protect his privacy. It wouldn't surprise me in the least to find he slept in a guest room occasionally rather than returning to his own."

"Maybe so, but it was his own bed he slept in last night. There's no question about that." They stopped short as they entered the study. Papers were thrown asunder and drawers emptied out onto the floor. This did not seem to be in keeping with a man who placed so much emphasis on a quality such as punctuality. "Is the room usually in such a state?"

Colin's voice cracked as he surveyed the room. "I should say not, but then, I didn't spend much time in here."

"Yet you did know there was a panel leading to his office, so it wasn't exactly a secret, now, was it?" Daniel tugged on the top right drawer, which had somehow been left unscathed. Locked. Colin knew more than he was sharing, but he'd let it go for now.

"No, I don't suppose it was, but I doubt it would have mattered. The window's wide open. Clearly, the thief came in that way."

Daniel shrugged. "Do you know where the key to this drawer is?"

"No, why would I?"

"You are his eldest son. I thought perhaps he might have mentioned it."

"My father shared very little with me, Doctor, except what was absolutely necessary. As I told you, he was a private man."

"You won't mind if we jimmy this drawer open, then. We need to see if the additional key is missing."

"But why? It's clear the assailant came in the window."

"And just happened to know about the secret panel and leave by way of a locked door, a key for which should be in this drawer."

"Yes, I see your point. No, I have no objection."

Daniel nodded to one of the constables, and they broke the drawer open. Aside from a box of cigars—very expensive ones—and some stationery, the drawer appeared empty. "It looks like the key is missing, and yet this drawer was locked, which means the assailant likely found that key as well. Can you see anything else that might have been taken?"

Colin swallowed hard and wiped a hand across his mouth. "Not that I can tell, but then as I told you, I wouldn't really know. The truth is, we were all forbidden to cross the threshold, unless of course he wanted to see us. Then it was almost a command appearance."

"Was that a bit of resentment I heard in your voice, Mr. Brissedon?"

Colin let a smile crack the corner of his mouth. "He was my father, sir. I loved him dearly, but we did have our disagreements. Do you find that unusual?"

"No, not at all. In fact, I may have found the opposite a bit suspect." Daniel let a smile escape himself. No sense in putting the man too much on edge just yet.

"So it was a robbery, then." Colin frowned, shaking his head at the sight before him.

"No, Mr. Brissedon. I doubt that very much. What thief would risk discovery by walking to the far side of the house to murder its occupant, only to leave behind a cigar box full of money?"

"Money!" Colin exclaimed, his eyes widening as the constable tipped out the cigars to reveal at least three thousand dollars in large bills. "Dear Lord, I told you he was a bit eccentric. He should have known better than to leave it lying around like that."

"Maybe so, but I doubt this is what got him killed. No, it was something far more personal." Daniel rubbed his forehead. This was going to be a long case, for if Colin Brissedon was any indication, there was a lot more going on here than met the eye. "I think we've seen enough here.

Shall we go back upstairs? I'll need to know where everyone sleeps. Was Patrick the only one in this wing?"

"Yes, just his and the guest room." Colin fiddled with the lid on the cigar box. It was clear he was itching to pocket the money. Didn't the fool realize it would be his now anyway? "Father gave him that room because he snores so," he continued. "He was keeping everyone else awake. It's the drink, you see."

"Is it, now?" Daniel had to fight to keep the amusement from his voice. "Well, nevertheless, I'll need to speak with him."

"Yes, certainly, but there's no need to go back upstairs. We can go out that door and be right across from the parlor."

"That would be perfect." Daniel motioned for Colin to lead the way. He'd return upstairs to see where everyone else slept later. For now, he wanted to start asking some uncomfortable questions.

CHAPTER 16

"I'd best be getting back to my rounds," Sam said on entering the large entrance hall, though there was a tinge of regret in his voice.

"I'll fill you in later." Daniel understood the man's reluctance to leave. They would have had to drag him away in chains.

After seeing the older doctor out, Colin shoved opened the doors to the parlor and returned to the place where they'd begun their enlightening journey. Jeremy was in the midst of pouring himself a drink, though he looked up momentarily before replacing the top of the decanter and taking a seat on the large sofa directly across from Kathleen.

"Can I get you anything?" he asked her, but she turned her head away without a word and rested it on her stepbrother's shoulder. As for Patrick, he frowned down at the rug as if he would find the answer to everything hidden in its Persian weave.

A shapely woman rose from her seat by the fireplace. "At last! How long do you propose to ask that I remain in this . . ." She shivered, for dramatic effect, no doubt. "I could have been killed myself."

"You are?" Daniel asked.

"This is Mrs. Elizabeth Langston." Colin turned up his nose in disgust and went to the sideboard to pour himself a glass of golden liquid, most likely whiskey.

"I doubt you had any fear of that, ma'am," Daniel said. "It seems likely Mr. Brissedon was the killer's intended target."

"Still, I'm very uncomfortable here and would like a carriage so that I may return home."

"And I will call one for you as soon as I've finished my questioning. Perhaps I can ask Mrs. Quinn to bring you some tea." She opened her mouth to argue, but Daniel cut her off, his voice stern. "If you continue to protest, ma'am, I'll have no choice but to assume you are involved."

Her hand flew up to her chest, her mouth open as she flopped back down in the chair. "Well, I've never . . ."

"Yes, you have, Elizabeth," Patrick said. "Now sit down and shut your mouth before I open mine."

Daniel frowned at Patrick, not sure what he was talking about. Only Colin reacted. His eyebrows lifted, and he turned his back to the room, his shoulders shaking. Daniel made a note to find out what that was all about. First, however, he needed to speak with the help.

"Would you like me to ask Mrs. Quinn to bring you some tea as well, Miss Brissedon?" Though tears still slid down her cheeks, it seemed that Patrick had managed to calm her down considerably, a feat for which he was grateful.

"Yes, that would be lovely, thank you," she said.

"Just please don't make it Earl Grey." Patrick threw a dismissive look in Elizabeth's direction. "The smell makes me ill."

Kathleen frowned, but before she could say anything, Colin spun around, clearly trying his best to stifle a laugh.

"You said you needed to ask us some questions?" He walked over and sat down on the sofa next to his cousin, Jeremy.

"I'd like to talk to you all separately, of course, but while I have you together, I must ask, do you know if your father had any enemies, anyone who would profit by his death?"

"My father was a ruthless businessman," Colin said. "It would be odd indeed if there weren't at least half a dozen of his associates who would have loved to see him come to this sort of end. Why, only last night he snatched a huge account right from under the nose of Phillip Stockbridge, even as the man himself dined at our table."

"Would this Phillip Stockbridge have known about the back staircase?"

"The back staircase?" Patrick asked. "Is that how they got in?"

"No!" Colin interjected before Daniel had a chance to speak. "It seems the murderer got in through a window in my father's study but then used the back stairs to get to his room. He likely used the back door to escape, though, as the key is missing."

"The key?" Patrick said.

"So it would seem," Daniel interrupted, not even attempting to keep the annoyance from his voice. "But if you don't mind, Mr. Brissedon, I would prefer you left the leaking of information to me in the future."

"Yes, of course. Forgive me."

Daniel gave a curt nod and continued. "Did anyone hear or see any unusual movement around the house last night, a shadow, an unusual sound?"

Everyone in the room seemed to stiffen, as if they were all holding their breaths, waiting to see if anyone revealed their secret. But no one did. They all just shook their heads or mumbled some negative response, after which he could almost hear a collective sigh of relief. This was not going to be easy.

He curled his left hand into a fist, trying to remember all his uncle had told him. *Ye get more rats with cheese, lad, and once they start nibbling, they're yers for the taking.*

"Of course, Patrick was late for breakfast," Colin said, "but that's hardly unusual."

"And you practically stumbled to the table," Patrick said in retort, his eyes glaring.

"And how would you know when you hadn't even rolled out of bed yet?"

"Stop it! Both of you!" With one disapproving glance, Kathleen stilled them both. Daniel almost wanted to kiss her for stepping in. He had enough to figure out without corralling two antagonistic stepbrothers. He nodded at her respectfully, then walked over to the window. After allowing himself a moment to gather his thoughts, he turned around and took a deep breath.

"This is a rather awkward question, and I apologize to the ladies if they take offense, but I'm afraid I must ask. Is it possible your father used one of the guest rooms to entertain a female companion?"

Patrick couldn't conceal a snort, and within moments Colin had grabbed him by the collar and dragged him up off the sofa. The older man's eyes were seething with hate, but his young stepbrother stood his ground and stared back with contempt.

"No, please!" Kathleen stood up, her hands clutched at her sides, tears still trickling down her lovely cheeks. "Can't you two put your differences aside, even at a time like this? Our father is dead, step or otherwise, murdered by some villain who places little or no value on human life."

The two men looked at each other contritely and stepped apart. For all their differences, it appeared they did have one thing in common—an unwavering respect for Kathleen. Daniel, too, was rapidly forming a favorable opinion of the young woman who managed to conduct herself with such grace, and he quickly spoke from the heart.

"I am truly sorry, Miss Brissedon. I assure you, I never intended my questioning to bring any unnecessary grief to your family."

"It's quite all right, Doctor," she said with a quivering sigh. "My brothers see eye to eye on very little, I fear, but I'm sure they'll be able to get beyond that, at least until our father's murderer is found." She threw them each a look that would have frozen Niagara Falls in the middle of August. "Now, you asked about Father entertaining any female companions. As far as I know, there were none. If you recall, we recently lost my stepmother, and he was still in mourning. He loved her deeply, you see."

"Yes, I'm sure." Daniel graced her with his most sincere smile, hoping he didn't have to burst her bubble when he was finished with his investigation.

A sudden pounding on the door drew their attention, and Forbes barely had time to open it before Phillip Stockbridge came barging in. Though Daniel had only been in town a little over a month, he had made a point of identifying the most prominent members of this and the surrounding communities. It wouldn't do to be asking them who they were should he be put in a position where he was required to question them or tend to their infirmities.

The man stopped in front of Colin with hate flashing in his eyes, so much so that his hands were shaking. As he spoke, his face grew dark red and the veins in his neck began to protrude.

"Where is the lying scoundrel? I'll boil him in oil if I get my hands on him. He deserves no less than hanging. I'll do it myself if given half the chance!"

Though Colin tried to calm him down, the man continued ranting and demanded to see Thomas. Finally, Daniel stepped forward, identifying himself, and ordered the man to sit down and be quiet. Phillip began to object, but when the sergeant slammed his nightstick against his hand, the pompous man obliged.

"Just what is your relationship to Thomas Brissedon?" Daniel said, his voice brooking no nonsense. Being raised in wealth by a prominent attorney had served him well, especially when combined with the street-smart presence acquired at the hands of his uncle Timothy.

"He's the man I was telling you about," Colin said. "The one who came to dinner last night."

"You had a disagreement over business with Mr. Brissedon?" Daniel asked.

"Disagreement! A business agreement was what it was supposed to be, but the rogue may just as well have robbed me blind. He outbid me on a construction project he'd sworn he had no interest in. He deserves to be dragged through the streets and exposed for the lying charlatan he really is."

"I'm afraid that won't be possible, sir. Mr. Brissedon was murdered last night, quite brutally."

"Murdered!" Though Stockbridge did appear shocked, he must have seen the irony of the situation, for a smirk of satisfaction crossed his rugged face. "Well, I guess we all truly do get what we deserve in the end. May I ask who was kind enough to perform such a service?"

"Unfortunately, we don't have the answer to that yet," Daniel said, "which, I'm afraid, brings up the question as to your whereabouts early this morning."

"My whereabouts! Surely you don't think I . . ." The seriousness of the situation hit him all at once, and his face grew pale and drawn. "Why, I was at home, of course. Where any respectable man would be, unlike certain members of this family, who carry on till all hours of the morning. They're quite a disgrace. Everyone knows about their wanton behavior. Most respectable families won't even allow their daughters to be seen in their presence. They were a constant embarrassment to Thomas."

Colin rolled his eyes and went back to the sideboard for another drink. Daniel couldn't help but wonder if the man was right, but then again, he knew how many of these pompous men had secret lives of their own. To the public, they were the epitome of virtue. Honest, hardworking, and, above all, morally upright. But in reality, it was these very men who kept clandestine meetings with their mistresses and shunned their bastard children. At least Colin's and Patrick's promiscuity was an acknowledged fact, though he was certain Thomas Brissedon had done everything he could to conceal it.

"Nevertheless," Daniel continued, "I will need to question you further, so please keep yourself available."

"And where would I go?" Stockbridge said, his voice ripe with bitterness. "I'm ruined! Even from his deathbed, Thomas Brissedon has seen to that! If you have no other questions for me at the moment, I must go break the news to my wife."

Daniel nodded. "Yes, of course. Thank you for your cooperation."

Stockbridge made a disgruntled sound, then strode out the door.

"It could have been Stockbridge, you know," Jeremy said, a little too eagerly. "After all, he was here last night, wasn't he? What if he never went home at all, but snuck back in after we'd all gone to bed and murdered my dear uncle?"

"Through the west wing?" Colin shook his head in disgust. "And what could he have hoped to gain? Nothing has changed. Business will continue as usual."

"Perhaps, but at least he'd have the satisfaction of seeing to it Uncle Thomas didn't share in the profits. To a man like Stockbridge, honor is everything."

"That's exactly why he didn't do it," Patrick said. "It wouldn't have been honorable. Not that this family knows anything about that virtue."

"I think that's quite enough, Mr. Desmond." Once more, Daniel employed his well-honed tone of authority. He had heard more than enough of their sibling bickering, though he suspected the emotions went far deeper than a bit of brotherly rivalry. "Now, back to the case," he continued on a more congenial note. "I must agree that Mr. Stockbridge does have an excellent motive. I've seen honorable men kill for much less. Still, the evidence is far from conclusive, and at the moment I can list him as no more than a suspect. Now, if it would be convenient, I'd like to speak to the help. I'll expect you all to be here when I return."

Colin took another swig of his drink, then, after leading Daniel and the sergeant to the kitchen, sat down at the large rectangular table in the center of the room. Daniel waited while Forbes gathered the indoor staff, hoping

Colin would take the hint, but then finally turned around sharply.

"Alone, if you don't mind, Mr. Brissedon."

"Oh! No, not at all. I wasn't sure if you'd find your way back."

"I think we'll manage." That was all he needed—Colin Brissedon hanging over his shoulder while he questioned his help. If they were like other loyal staff, they'd already be reluctant to speak.

"Yes, of course." Colin bowed politely before heading back toward the parlor, and Daniel turned to the four faces looking up at him, filled with dread. "Is this all of you?"

"All except Moira," the butler said. "She's upstairs with the children."

Daniel blew out a long breath. "Right, then."

Patrick looked up as Colin entered the parlor. His stepbrother's face was pinched in annoyance, his lips pressed so tight they could barely be seen. At first, he assumed something had happened in the kitchen, but the hate in Colin's eyes as they exchanged glances told him otherwise. Not a word needed to be spoken. The jealousy, the fury, that Kathleen had turned to Patrick in her grief instead of him, was undeniable.

Kathleen must have sensed it too, for her body tensed. But just as Patrick steeled himself for another confrontation, Colin turned and headed for the front door, clearly deciding to get a bit of fresh air instead.

Jeremy seemed to brace himself as well, but as soon as Colin left, he continued his pacing from one side of the room to the other, stopping only long enough to refill his glass. At last, he put his drink down. "I'm going for a walk as well," he said. "I feel as if the walls are closing in on me. Would anyone care to join?"

He held out his hand to Kathleen, but she declined rather abruptly. Standing up, she brushed down her skirts. "I think I'd best go up and check on the children. Perhaps Mrs. Langston would care to join you."

"Actually, I thought I might go upstairs to take a nap," Elizabeth said, "since it appears I'm not permitted to leave. Would you walk me up, Patrick? I can't seem to remember the way."

"I think I should stay here in case the doctor needs anything, but I'm sure Kathleen will be happy to show you."

"Of course," Kathleen said. "It's on my way."

Elizabeth cast him a look that promised he'd pay dearly, but Patrick didn't care. He'd rather die than go another round with her, and now that Thomas was dead, maybe he wouldn't have to. Letting out a sigh, he got up to pour himself a brandy, grateful for the moment's solitude.

"Must you, even now?" Kathleen said, tears welling in her eyes.

He turned to see his stepsister still standing in the doorway. Apparently, Elizabeth had gone on ahead. "Just one, Kate, I promise. To calm my nerves."

Kathleen smiled, the tenderness returning to her eyes, before she turned and headed for the staircase. Patrick listened as she hurried up the stairs, then he downed the numbing elixir in one swallow. A twinge of guilt tugged at his conscience as he poured a second, but it didn't stop him. It was going to take far more than one to calm his nerves today. He downed the second glass in one gulp as well, though after pouring the third, he put the stopper back in the bottle. Weary to the bone, he sat on the sofa and took a sip, closing his eyes to help drown out the guilt and shame. A man was dead, and he couldn't help but rejoice. God help him.

CHAPTER 17

Colin had no sooner left the kitchen than a heated debate erupted between Mrs. Quinn and Forbes, though as yet Daniel had not made any inquiries of them.

"It's none of our business!" Forbes said, his brows drawing together. "Best leave family matters to the family."

"It's not family matters when a man is dead!" Mrs. Quinn said.

"Still, it's not for us to say!" Forbes persisted.

Mrs. Quinn pressed her lips together. "They've done what they've done, and we've no need to be lying for any of them."

"Enough!" Daniel rubbed the bridge of his nose. It wasn't even noon, and already he had a pounding headache. "Might I remind you all, it is a crime to conceal anything that might be construed as evidence."

Molly began to whimper, and Mrs. Quinn knelt by her side. "Now, now, darling. You've done nothing wrong. Just tell the good doctor the truth, and no one can fault you for that, least of all one of them Brissedons."

"Please, Miss Buchanan." Daniel pulled one of the kitchen chairs over. He sat down across from the girl, leaning his arms on his knees, and softened his tone. "Did you hear or see anything unusual in the last few days?"

"That's just it, sir," she said with a sniffle. "There's nothing unusual about it, not in this house. They're arguing all the time about one thing or the other. Nobody got along with Mr. Brissedon, God rest his soul."

"So there were arguments recently, then."

"There were, sir, more than one; ye can be sure o' that."

"And who were involved in these arguments?"

"They all were, weren't they, except for Master Ryan and Miss Charlotte, and that only because he saw little o' them."

"All right, let's start with Wednesday, then. Who did you hear Mr. Brissedon argue with first?"

"That would have to be Mr. Colin. I was bringing some laundry down to Lizzie, wasn't I, after I'd finished up all the rooms in the east wing. She's our laundress." She pointed toward a rather buxom young lady sitting in a chair on the other side of the table.

"And the downstairs maid," the woman added with pride.

"Yes, thank you," Daniel said before returning his attention to Molly. "Did you hear what the argument was about?"

"Oh no, sir. Only Mr. Colin comes storming out, and doesn't he grab Mr. Patrick by the arm, saying 'twas his fault and all. And him just coming in himself."

"What happened then?"

"Mr. Brissedon calls Mr. Patrick into the study and slams the door, but I couldn't hear anything else as Lizzie came along and asked me to help her carry the laundry into the washroom."

"Well, go on," Mrs. Quinn said, giving Forbes a slight nudge. "You heard what the doctor said. It's a crime holding things back."

"Yes, well, all right. I'd just come into the entry hall. Ethel . . ." He cleared his throat. "Mrs. Quinn had seen Mr. Patrick down at the carriage house, and I wanted to be there to see to his needs when he came in."

Daniel had to suppress a grin. Byron was always at the door to greet him when he arrived home. "And what did you hear while you were there?"

"They argued over money, as usual. Mr. Brissedon seemed to think Mr. Colin had stolen some."

"And he hadn't?"

"I'm sure I wouldn't know, sir, but it wouldn't surprise me if he had."

"What time did this take place?"

"Sometime around four, I believe."

"And what was the argument with Patrick Desmond about?"

Forbes frowned. "Apparently, Mr. Patrick had feigned a piano lesson with Mrs. Langston, and his stepfather was suspicious as to his whereabouts."

"Where did he think he was?"

"I'm sure I couldn't say, sir, but Mr. Patrick is fond of the lady's daughter, Miss Lydia. As it turned out, however, the boy had gone to a gambling den."

"And his stepfather believed him."

"Yes, sir, he seemed to. Sad to say, it's not completely out of character for the young man."

"I see." Daniel made a few notes, then asked, "Were there any other arguments that day?"

Forbes sighed. "You'd best go on and tell the doctor everything, Miss Buchanan."

"I suppose that would have to be Mrs. Langston. I was up straightening Mr. Patrick's room, like I always do o' an afternoon. Being in the west wing, 'tis the last one I get to, ye see, and with him rarely coming back for dinner, 'tis no trouble. And even if he does come in, he never complains about it not being done yet, not like some—"

"Get to the matter at hand," Forbes said from his position behind her. "I'm sure the doctor doesn't care to hear the logistics behind your daily routine."

The young woman scrunched up her nose, clearly annoyed, but she moved on. "Well, as I said, I was straightening up Mr. Patrick's room, and I had the window and door open. I always like to air it out a bit while I'm working, ye see, especially on such a nice summer's day. I wasn't listening on purpose, mind ye, but 'twas hard to miss, the study being right at the bottom of the back stairs and all. And Mrs. Langston all but screaming at Mr. Brissedon, saying she wouldn't have it."

Daniel ran a hand across his forehead, wishing the girl *would* get to the point. "What wouldn't she have?"

"Sure, I couldn't say exactly, sir, it being muffled and all."

Leaning in closer, Daniel let his mouth quirk up at the corner, knowing it would reveal a dimple, and softened his tone. "But surely you must have snuck down the stairs to hear better. It's certainly what I would have done."

The girl's cheeks flushed a soft pink. "Well, maybe, just a bit. 'Twas still muffled some, but I could tell Mrs. Langston wasn't none too happy. She said she'd not allow her daughter to be married off to the likes o' Mr. Colin."

"That's true enough," Mrs. Quinn said. "I couldn't believe it when I heard. It wasn't like her at all . . ." Daniel looked up at her and lifted his brows. "Oh, I guess I'm getting ahead of the story, aren't I? You go ahead, Molly."

"Thank you," Daniel said before turning back to Molly and trying not to laugh. Mrs. Quinn sounded just like

Hattie. He wondered if there was a training manual. "Go on, Miss Buchanan, you were saying."

"Well, Mrs. Langston wasn't having it none o' it, was she, but then Mr. Brissedon said something I couldn't catch, and all o' a sudden like she was agreeing to it, though she said Mr. Brissedon had best be keeping Mr. Patrick away from the girl."

Mrs. Quinn's eyes narrowed. "That would be just like the vicious old fiend, trying to secure a good marriage for that no-account son of his by throwing poor Mr. Desmond to the wolves."

Forbes nodded and lifted the older woman from the floor, where she'd been kneeling next to Molly. "No one ever had to worry about keeping young Mr. Desmond away from anyone until he began following in his stepbrother's footsteps."

"In what way?" Daniel asked.

Mrs. Quinn flattened her lips into a long, white line, clearly annoyed at Forbes. "He's been a bit of a handful since his ma and Mr. Brissedon wed." She sat in one of the kitchen chairs and fiddled with a napkin in her lap.

"Even from a bit before, if truth be told," Forbes said. "He was never happy about the way Mr. Brissedon seemed to ingratiate himself into their lives so soon after his father's death."

Daniel looked from one to the other, waiting for the pair to say exactly what Patrick had been up to. Kathleen had alluded to it, but he wanted to get the staff's take on it.

Mrs. Quinn scowled at Forbes once more before continuing. "He's been drinking quite a bit, and gambling, but more than that, he's won himself a reputation as a bit of a rogue with the ladies."

Lizzie and Molly both snorted at the description, though it was Lizzie who spoke. "More than a reputation, from what I hear."

The look Mrs. Quinn gave them sent chills through Daniel. His mother had a look like that, and it never boded well for whomever she turned it on.

"And that's not the worst of it," Lizzie said, almost in defiance. "Go on, Molly, tell them what else ye heard."

Much to her credit, Molly looked to Mrs. Quinn for approval. Though the woman's face was pinched with annoyance, she nodded. "I told you to tell the truth, Molly, and I meant it."

"Mr. Brissedon also mentioned Mrs. Langston's son, Edward, was to wed Miss Kathleen."

Daniel's stomach clenched, though he knew he was being ridiculous. Any chance that a woman like Kathleen Brissedon might be attracted to someone like him was about as likely as a pig taking flight. He cleared his throat. "I'm sorry, I thought I'd heard a rumor she was already being courted by someone else?"

"Brighton Templeton." Forbes virtually hissed the man's name. "I would hardly call it courting, though he no doubt sees it as such. That is one point on which Mr. Brissedon and I agreed. The man's nothing but a rounder who's managed to charm his way into Miss Kathleen's affections. He's been banned from the house, of course, though I daresay betrothing her to Edward Langston is going a bit far."

"Are Colin and Kathleen Brissedon aware of these marriage arrangements?"

Forbes frowned. "Yes, sir, I believe they are. Though I didn't hear what transpired exactly, being busy with Mr.

Brissedon's guests in the parlor, they both seemed out of sorts by the end of the evening."

"'Course they were," Mrs. Quinn said. "I've not known them long, but I can't see Mr. Colin being ready to settle down, especially with a sweet, innocent thing like Miss Langston. And Miss Kathleen, she seems a bit of a romantic to me. She'll be wanting to marry for love, that one. And good for her, I say."

"Yes, I agree, but are you saying Mr. Brissedon spoke to them while he had guests?" Daniel was flummoxed by such behavior. His mother would have slapped him six ways from Sunday if he had tried anything like that.

"Yes, I'm afraid so," Forbes said. "Though to be fair, I suppose Mr. Langston bursting in and demanding to see him did precipitate the audiences."

"So Edward Langston wasn't happy about the arrangements either?"

Forbes frowned. "Again, sir, I can only assume he wasn't, though it was Master Patrick he threatened after coming out of the study."

"Threatened how?" Daniel asked.

"Told him to stay away from his sister, he did." Molly blew her nose again, her lip trembling. "'Twas why I spilled the coffee all over Jer . . . Mr. Radcliffe. Scared the daylights out o' me, but Mr. Brissedon didn't care. Let me go just the same."

Daniel frowned. "You must have been terribly upset."

"I was that, sir, but Miss Kathleen, she said not to worry about it. And then Mr. Colin said he'd have a word with his father as well. But now . . ." She started to cry again, and Forbes patted her shoulder.

Daniel cast a glance in the sergeant's direction. The man had been sitting quietly, taking notes, but on hearing

Molly's lament, he looked up, a hint of disbelief in his eyes. Apparently, he and the sergeant were the only ones who had processed what Brissedon's death truly meant.

Daniel cleared his throat, trying not to sound condescending. "You do realize Colin Brissedon will likely be your employer now?"

Molly's face lit up. "So I won't have to be leaving, then?"

"You'll have to speak to the younger Mr. Brissedon, but given what you've told me, I would have to say no."

The two younger girls started laughing, while the older help smiled. Though they clearly weren't mourning Thomas Brissedon's death, somehow he didn't think any of them were responsible for it either, but his uncle always said not to jump to conclusions. *Killers can be canny buggers.* Guilty or not, however, they may be able to help him decipher who was.

"Mrs. Quinn," Daniel said. "You mentioned Mrs. Langston never would have agreed to let her daughter marry Colin. Why is that?"

"Well, his reputation's worse than Mr. Desmond's, isn't it? I'll be surprised if that boy ever gets himself a decent young lady. It's no wonder Mrs. Langston wanted nothing to do with him. I just don't understand what that old goat had over her to make her change her mind."

"You think he was blackmailing her?"

"Now, Ethel, we know nothing of the sort." Forbes frowned down at her. "I did manage to hear Mr. Brissedon mention monies being set aside in Miss Lydia's name and his assurance that Mr. Desmond would stay away from her. It might have been nothing more than a mutually advantageous business arrangement. Mr. Langston is a successful builder, so it would make sense to form such an alliance with a man in the lumber business. It wouldn't be the first time I've heard of such an agreement."

"No, it certainly wouldn't. Back to Thursday night, though. From what you've indicated, everyone knew of the marriage arrangements by then. How did they react? Did they go for a walk, head up to bed, drink themselves into oblivion?"

"Well, we did have guests, of course," Forbes said, "but after warning off Mr. Desmond, Mr. Langston stormed out of the house. The younger Mr. Brissedon did go straight to the liquor cabinet in the parlor, as is his habit, but Miss Kathleen excused herself and headed up to bed almost at once."

"Even while the Stockbridges were still here?"

"Yes, it was quite unlike her. Mr. and Mrs. Stockbridge remained, however, at Mr. Colin's request, while Mr. Patrick was summoned in to speak with his stepfather. I couldn't hear what was said, but when he came out . . ."

Forbes hesitated a moment, and Mrs. Quinn spoke up. "It was just said in the heat of the moment. The boy didn't mean anything by it."

"What was said, Mrs. Quinn? I understand your inclination to protect Mr. Desmond, but someone else will tell me if you don't. Perhaps someone not quite so understanding."

The woman looked over to Forbes, her eyes pleading, and the man nodded. "You're right, of course, Doctor. Mr. Patrick was terribly upset. So much so, he almost forgot to take his shoes off before heading upstairs. I'm sure he didn't mean a word of it."

"What did he say?"

"He told Mr. Brissedon that he would see him dead."

Daniel frowned, but he knew well threats said in anger, shouted in the spur of the moment, were not usually carried out. Still. "What about the others?"

"The Stockbridges truly had put up with enough by then. They left a few moments later. Then around eleven thirty or so, Mr. Brissedon headed up to bed himself, as did Mr. Colin, but Mr. Radcliffe was rather upset. He stayed up a bit longer. Till around midnight, I believe, right before Mrs. Langston arrived."

"Mrs. Langston arrived that late?" Once again, Daniel was taken aback. Even when he'd lived with his uncle Timothy, guests didn't just show up at that hour.

"Yes," Forbes said, clearly trying to restrain his distaste, but was it for the breach of etiquette or the woman herself? Perhaps both. "I showed her to the guest room, then proceeded to bed."

"And I'll assume all you ladies had already retired."

"Oh yes, sir," Mrs. Quinn said. "We're up by five. That's how I know Mr. Colin was out. Heard him stumbling up the main stair."

"Left his boots on and all," Lizzie said. "We had a right time cleaning it up."

"When did you clean them up?" Had they unknowingly disturbed some evidence?

"About five thirty or so, we got started. Molly helped, even though she didn't have a job here no more. Didn't it take us near an hour, but himself would have raised the roof if he came down to breakfast and noticed them." She seemed to realize what she'd just said, and her cheeks blushed a becoming pink.

"Where did the footprints lead?"

"Straight to Mr. Colin's room, and him snoring like a wild boar inside."

"You didn't notice the other set of footprints leading to Mr. Brissedon's room?"

Molly and Lizzie both shrugged, though it was Molly who answered this time. "No, sir, why would we? Mr. Colin's room is off the other way. And we'd already got started on them when Mr. Patrick mentioned the others."

"Patrick knew about the other footprints?"

"He did, sir," Lizzie said. "They went right past his door, didn't they? We were hoping Mr. Brissedon wouldn't notice them straight off, being they were over toward the back stairs and all, and that we'd be able to clean them up while he was at breakfast. But then . . ." She trailed off, swallowing hard. "I reckon it's good we didn't."

"Yes, it is. I think that will be all for now, but please keep yourselves available. I'd like to speak to you all again later, but as it's nearly lunchtime, why don't we take a break?"

"Of course, sir," Forbes said with a polite nod. "We shan't go very far."

Mrs. Quinn rose right away. "Will you and the lads be joining us, then?"

"No, I'm afraid I have to head back to town for a bit. But thank you for the tea, Mrs. Quinn. You make as fine a cup as my grandmother used to, and that's saying a lot." It certainly was, since he'd never known his grandmothers.

The woman blushed and waved him away. "Oh, go on with you. I'll have some muffins to go with it next time."

Daniel smiled, and he and Sergeant Owens headed back out to the parlor. "There's one thing my uncle always told me, Sergeant."

"Only one, Doc?" the man said with a grin. "What's that?"

Daniel chuckled. It seemed like his uncle had advice for every situation, but he was never wrong. "Speak to the help first, and you'll never be short of suspects."

"Sounds to me like any one of the family and beyond would have had reason enough to do away with the old man."

"I got the same impression. Now all we have to do is figure out which one."

When they arrived in the parlor, Daniel's grin turned into a scowl. Only Patrick remained, sitting in a chair by the fire, his arms on his knees and a half-empty glass held between his hands. He was staring at the cold fireplace and jumped when Daniel cleared his throat.

"Oh, I'm sorry, Doctor. I didn't hear you come in."

"Where is everyone else? If I'm not mistaken, I indicated no one was to leave."

"They haven't, not really. Colin and Jeremy are out for some fresh air, Mrs. Langston went up for a nap, and Kathleen . . ."

"Is right here," the young woman said as she entered the parlor.

Once more, Daniel was struck by how beautiful she was, with long, sun-kissed chestnut hair, neatly styled into a fashionable coiffure, and deep blue eyes, the color of the sky just before dusk. Eyes that could easily intoxicate a man if he wasn't on his guard. But this was neither the time nor the place for such thoughts.

"I'm sorry, Doctor," she said, her smile somehow brightening the already sun-drenched room. "I wanted to check on my younger brother and sister. You won't need to be questioning them, will you? They're already taking this quite hard."

"No, I don't see any reason that would be necessary—unless they were wandering around the hallways between two and six this morning?"

She laughed, as sweet and warm as an early summer morn. "I hardly think so. Would it be all right if I asked Mrs. Quinn to fix some lunch? You see, we never did get breakfast, and the children especially are starting to get irritable."

"That would be fine, Miss Brissedon. I was just coming to tell you that I'd like to start questioning the family on an individual basis this afternoon. I have to return to town, but I'll be back around two."

"You'll not be joining us for lunch, then?"

"I'm afraid not today. Dr. Tennyson will need my signature on the death certificate since I was the first one on the scene."

Daniel could see the cloud of pain and disbelief dull her eyes for a moment, but she fought through and composed herself, just the way his mother or sister would. "How about you and your men, Sergeant?"

"Thank you for the offer, ma'am, but I do need to get back to the village and check on things."

"Could you please see that everyone is assembled when I return?" Daniel said. "Barring the children and their nursemaid, of course. I know it's a trying time, but I really must insist."

"Of course. I'll see you then." She showed him to the door, then stepped outside, pulling it closed behind her. "If I could have a moment alone, Doctor."

Daniel nodded for the sergeant and his men to go on ahead. "What is it, ma'am?"

"I know this may be a lot to ask, but if possible, could you continue investigating the case we discussed? Now more than ever, I feel it's important."

"Do you think the events may be connected?"

She frowned, taking a deep breath before speaking again. "I hope not, but whether they are or not, I believe we need to know."

He nodded. "I completely agree. Rest assured I haven't put that investigation aside."

She smiled, and he dashed down the steps, climbing into his buggy and heading back toward Main Street. Try as he might, he couldn't forget the impulse he'd had to take her in his arms and comfort her that morning. He pulled up in front of Dr. Tennyson's home and shook his head. *Forget it, O'Halleran. It would never have worked out anyway.*

Kathleen picked at her food and excused herself after only a few minutes, saying she really needed to rest a bit before the doctor returned. In truth, a nap was the last thing on her mind. Hurrying up the stairs, she stopped outside her father's rooms and scanned the hallway before entering. She closed the door behind her, pressing up against it, willing herself not to be ill, even as the tears drizzled down her cheeks. *Why are you doing this? The sergeant's men already completed a thorough search. Because you have to be sure they didn't miss anything, that's why.*

Thankfully, someone had thrown a clean white sheet over her father's body. She said a quick prayer, then bent to the floor, studying the boot prints. Her hands shook as she took the measuring tape from her pocket and noted the length and width, both at the toe and heel. There was a small chip out of the right heel, and the print seemed to indicate the person leaned heavier on the inside of that boot as well. Recording it all on a piece of stationery, she stood and studied the rest of the room. A matchbox lay on the floor at the back of his nightstand, wedged in between it and the bed. Squeezing her arm through the crack, she pulled it out, then brushed the hair out of her eyes to read what was written on the cover. *Columbia Hall, 392 Bowery, Manhattan.* She frowned. Her father did go into the city for business, sometimes staying overnight, so perhaps it might be his.

Shoving it and her notes in her pocket, she walked back out into the hallway and followed the footprints downstairs. They seemed to begin beneath the window in her father's study, before making their way upstairs and ultimately leaving through the back door. Interesting. The ground outside the door was a mass of footprints. It would be hard to distinguish one from the other.

Instead, she headed back through the panel and tiptoed into her father's study. Gently lifting the window, she examined the chipped frame, but something caught her eye on the floor right below it. Three white slivers of wood lay against the wainscoting, one partially hidden by the Persian rug. *Now, that was odd. Why would they be inside the room if someone forced it open from outside?* Grabbing a piece of paper from her father's desk, she made a makeshift envelope and placed them inside, shoving the paper and its contents in her pocket. Still musing over the meaning of her latest discovery, she stood back up and surveyed the room.

A pen lay on his desk, poised to write, a half-smoked cigar rested in an ashtray, and an old sweater hung over the arm of his chair. Tears streamed down her cheeks. She'd been so angry with him last night. He'd just been looking out for her best interest. She knew that, but . . . she always dreamed she'd marry for love, not for power or money. Unbidden, the image of Dr. O'Halleran swam into her head. *Stop it, Kathleen! As handsome and accomplished as he is, you stand no chance.*

A wave of guilt washed over her. Poor Brighton. She'd used her father as an excuse for ending any hope he had of courting her, when in truth, she wasn't in love with him. Why didn't she have the courage to admit it? Maybe if she had, her father wouldn't have felt the need to pair her with Edward Langston. He was a nice enough man, but he just didn't make her heart race, not the way the handsome doctor did.

She rolled her eyes and wiped the tears from her cheeks, checking the watch pinned to her pale blue bodice. Almost two. Looking around again, she pulled out each drawer, bending to pick up an ivory envelope wedged against the partition in a bottom drawer. It was addressed to Mr. Patrick Desmond, and the seal had been broken. Questions raced through her mind.

Was this the note the rough-looking man had dropped off the previous night? And if so, had Colin given it to her father? Opening the envelope, she slipped out the folded sheet of paper to read the short message.

Dear Mr. Desmond,

We need to speak at your earliest convenience. I have discovered some interesting information that I would rather not divulge through the post. I do believe we have a break in the case.

Yours,
Alexander Morton

Alexander Morton, so that was the name of the detective Patrick and his mother had hired. She sat down in her father's chair and sighed. If only she could find out what he'd discovered, but the man would probably tell her it was confidential. Perhaps she should ask Patrick, see if he'd ever received it. A horrible thought occurred to her, one that sent a chill through her bones. What if Colin *had* given the note to Patrick, and he'd dropped it while he was in here, ransacking her father's office? Or what if it was Colin who had dropped it?

A knock sounded on the front door. Two o'clock! Running up the back stairs to her bedroom, she quickly tidied her hair and straightened her clothing before heading downstairs to greet the doctor, her discoveries tucked safely away in her pocket. She hadn't decided just yet what she would do with them. For now, they were safe enough.

CHAPTER 18

Daniel nodded to Forbes and headed straight for the parlor, where he found everyone in much the same position they'd been in that morning, except for Kathleen, who was just coming down the stairs.

"I know this is a difficult time for you," Daniel said, using his most sympathetic tone, a talent he'd learned from his uncle. "But as I mentioned earlier, I'd like to question you all separately." He directed his next words to Colin. "Is there anywhere we can speak without being disturbed?"

"Yes, certainly," Colin said. "I suppose Father's study is out of the question under the circumstances. Would the library be suitable for your needs? It's at the back of the house, so it's much quieter than the study, at any rate."

"Yes, I believe that would suit my purposes. Mr. Desmond, I'll speak to you first, given the proximity of your room to both your father's and the back staircase."

"He was my stepfather!" Patrick said. "My father died two years ago."

"Yes, of course," Daniel said. The young man certainly had a bone to pick, but that didn't mean he'd murdered his stepfather.

Patrick nodded, casting an uneasy glance in Kathleen's direction. A stern look from Colin intercepted it, which caused the already anxious young man to become even more troubled as he led the way to the library. Once there, he sat on the edge of a stiff damask-covered armchair, as if he didn't want to make himself too comfortable.

Daniel couldn't help but wonder what all the eye contact in the parlor had been about, but his uncle had taught him the best way to start was to put the suspect at ease. And as much as he hated to admit it, Patrick Desmond was definitely a suspect.

"There's nothing to be nervous about, Mr. Desmond." Daniel flashed his well-practiced smile of sincerity. Only his mother recognized it for what it was, though it did seem to relax others.

Patrick returned an uneasy smile, then cleared his throat. "I've never had to do anything like this before."

"I should hope not," Daniel said. "Just relax and answer my questions honestly, and you'll have nothing to worry about." Patrick gave a quick bob of his head, and so Daniel began. "I gather you didn't get along with your stepfather?"

"No, sir, we tolerated each other. That's about all. But I didn't want to see him dead."

"No, I'm sure. You did argue with him quite a bit, though. Wednesday, for instance?"

"Yes, pretty much on a regular basis, but Wednesday . . . I believe we may have had words."

"You don't remember?"

"As I said, we argued a lot. It's hard to recall exactly when and where."

"I can imagine, but please, just relax and try to remember what you argued about that day?"

"Wednesday?" Patrick's right leg began to twitch up and down. "Um, yes, I was to have a piano lesson, but when I got there, Mrs. Langston wasn't at home. He wanted to know why I hadn't returned immediately."

"Are you always required to inform him of your movements?"

"What? No. It's not that. I presume he thought I'd arranged to meet Lydia instead . . . Mrs. Langston's daughter."

"And had you?"

Patrick's face turned a blotchy red. "She'd sent the note, but it was completely innocent. Please, I have no desire to tarnish her reputation. She was just concerned I hadn't called round. Besides, nothing happened. Her brother came home and threw me out."

"And why hadn't you called round like a proper gentleman?"

This time Patrick barked a laugh. "As if I'd be allowed. I have quite a reputation, you see. Having arrived in Patchogue more than a month ago, I'm sure you've heard the rumors by now." Patrick stopped speaking for a moment, then got up to stare out the large French doors that opened onto the garden.

Daniel nodded. "You argued about that very lady last night, didn't you?"

"He warned me to stay away from her, that he'd made an arrangement for her to marry Colin, as if that bastard cared about anybody but himself."

Daniel breathed a sigh of relief. From what he knew, the man seemed to be telling the truth so far. "And your stepfather made such an arrangement knowing you had feelings for her?"

Patrick spun back around. "That's probably why he did it. He didn't care how I felt as long as his son married well, and Lydia was the answer. The joke was on them, though. I had no intention of bringing her reputation into question by being seen with the likes of me."

"Had you told him that?"

"Why would I? It wasn't as if he'd believe anything I said. Besides, when her mother asked him to keep me away from her daughter, I'm sure he saw it as a perfect opportunity. Not only would it grant her request, but it was a way for him to torment me and broker a good marriage for his lecherous son as well."

"What did you do?"

Patrick paused for a minute, as if contemplating whether or not to admit something. He sighed, clearly having made a decision. "I told him I'd see him dead. I was angry." Flopping back in the chair, he put his head in his hands, running his fingers through his hair before looking up once more. "I never really intended to do it. Though I'm not surprised someone did. It's not as if I was the only one who was unhappy with his edicts."

"No, I'm sure you weren't. He argued with your stepbrother a good deal too, didn't he? On Wednesday, for example. Do you know what that was about?"

"No, I stayed away from them when they argued. Colin tended to come out of the study blaming me for whatever issue arose. I presume it was about money, though. That's what they usually argued about. Colin likes to gamble ... heavily. But he rarely wins."

"And their discussion on Thursday evening?"

"I gather that's when the old bastard informed him he was to marry Lydia, but I'd gone for a walk, so I can't be sure."

"It's clear you didn't think much of your stepfather. May I ask why?"

"Because he swindled me out of my inheritance. I can't prove it yet, but I know he did. This was all mine, and then suddenly, after my mother died, I learned that my father had been virtually penniless. All that remained was a small allowance from my mother, which my stepfather controlled. Now Colin will be in charge."

"So you wouldn't really profit by your stepfather's death except, of course, for the satisfaction you'd gain."

"Are you mad? I was better off with Thomas. Colin will go through the money like it was water, and then there'll be nothing left for any of us. At least Thomas was a good businessman, even if he was a thief. What's the old saying? Better the devil you know than the one you don't. I may not have gotten much with Thomas, but as long as I didn't go too far astray, I got what little allowance was due me, and he was paying for my courses at NYU."

"So you hate your stepbrother just as much as you did your stepfather. That must have made them angry at times." Daniel noticed the bluish-purple bruise on Patrick's cheek, just under his eye. "Angry enough to beat you, perhaps."

"My stepfather took the strap to me more times than I care to remember, if that's what you mean, but other than that, no."

"Did he do it in his study?"

Patrick frowned, then shrugged. "Sometimes, but mostly he'd take me out to the stables. He'd whack me a few times with the strap and send me to my room. I guess it wasn't something he wanted to do in the house."

"Did he punch you?"

Patrick touched his cheek. "This? No, I got caught canoodling with a young lady. Her brother didn't like it."

"What about your stepbrother? Did he beat you?"

"We got into fisticuffs a few times. I suppose he got the upper hand now and again, but beat me? No, not in the sense you mean."

Daniel nodded. Time to switch things up and catch him off guard. "Why did you hire a detective?"

Daniel watched as Patrick's Adam's apple bobbed up and down. Finally, he croaked out an answer. "My mother did. She hired him to prove my father, my real father, wasn't a murderer. The police said he raped and beat a young girl to death, then met his own demise when he fell in a drunken stupor. I won't say he didn't like a drink now and then; who doesn't? But he would never hurt anyone, not even when he was in his cups. He was down there to help people, not to hurt them. Thomas said my father built the west wing for his whores, but that's not true." Tears came to Patrick's eyes, but still he went on. "I just want to know the truth, and if I find out something about Thomas Brissedon in the process, all the better."

"Did you? Find out anything about Thomas Brissedon, I mean."

Patrick must have realized his slip of the tongue. "No, I don't think Mother found out anything. Once she died, it all ended. I can't afford a detective."

"What was the man's name, the one your mother hired? Just so I can corroborate your story."

"I'm sorry. She never told me. I went to look for his card after she died, but Thomas must have discovered it and thrown it out."

"And this detective never contacted you?"

"No, why would he? Mother hired him. When he discovered she'd passed, he probably figured he'd made himself a bit of easy money. Is there anything else?"

"Just a bit more, if you don't mind." Daniel could feel the effort it was taking for Patrick Desmond to remain calm. The man was hiding something, but what? "Miss Brissedon, how do you feel about her?"

For the first time, the man's eyes softened, and he seemed to relax a bit. "I care a great deal for Kathleen. I can't imagine any blood sister being closer to me than she is."

"She argued with Thomas yesterday as well, though, didn't she?"

"No, not really. He told her he'd arranged for her to marry Edward Langston, and she just . . . She was upset, I know, but she simply excused herself and went upstairs."

"I can imagine her dismay, being she already has a beau. A Brighton Templeton, I believe."

"I wouldn't say he was her beau, exactly. He likes to think he's courting her, but my stepfather didn't approve of him. Nor do I, for that matter. He's Colin's friend, more like his leech, you might say. Kate knows her own mind, though, so I didn't interfere."

"Thomas Brissedon did interfere, though, didn't he?"

"Yes, blatantly! Not only did he forbid Brighton from entering the house, but he arranged for her to marry Edward. The sad part is he didn't have to. She'd realized she no longer cared for Brighton and was going to tell him to stop coming round, just as soon as she found the right moment. Kate doesn't like hurting anyone's feelings, you see. If you're looking for a reason why I would have wanted my stepfather dead, that alone would be enough. I won't tolerate anyone hurting Kathleen, not even him. I don't care what he does to me; I'll survive, but I'll not stand by and watch him destroy her."

"Well, he won't be harming anyone now, will he?"

Patrick sat back against the chair and shook his head. "No, but that upset her too. She loved the old bastard, in spite of everything."

Interesting, but was it an attempt to explain why he couldn't have killed Thomas Brissedon, or was he simply sorry he had, now that he realized how much grief the old man's demise had caused his stepsister? "Just a few more questions," Daniel said. "Where were you between two and six this morning?"

"I was in bed, asleep. Where else would I have been?"

"And you were alone, of course."

"Yes," Patrick exclaimed with a touch of disdain. "I don't appreciate your insinuations, Doctor. I may like a roll in the hay, but I make sure the hay is not my own."

"Forgive me." Daniel flashed an apologetic smile. "Oh, one more thing. Could you tell me where you got those scratches on your neck? They look rather fresh."

Instinctively, Patrick lifted his hand to the tiny marks. Panic flashed in his eyes, followed by a spark of resignation. "All right, I wasn't alone last night, but please, I'd rather not say who I was with."

"Soiling your own hay, then?"

Patrick cringed. "After all that went on, I took solace in the arms of another. While cavorting amongst the sheets, I'm afraid, she got a bit carried away."

"May I ask how she arrived?"

Patrick hesitated a moment. "I snuck her up the front stairs after everyone had gone to bed. They were all so wrapped up in their own troubles that no one noticed."

"Not through the back door, then?"

"No, it's kept locked."

"Yes, of course. And how did she come to know of your . . . need?"

"There's a phone in my stepfather's study. I used that."

2222222

"After your stepfather retired?" Patrick gave an almost imperceptible nod, so Daniel continued. "Was Miss Langston with you the entire night?"

"Lydia! No, she's a lady and would never consent to that. I'm afraid you misunderstand, sir. My mistress was with me all night, till just before daybreak, but it was not Lydia. My reputation isn't completely unearned, but even I have scruples."

"I'll respect your wishes of confidentiality as far as I am able, Mr. Desmond, but it may become necessary to speak to the lady at some point in the future."

"I'm afraid I can't divulge that. Besides, she'd only deny it, I'm sure. She has her own reputation to think of. I may not be much of a gentleman, but I am in that."

"Not exactly a call girl, then? Regardless, the choice may not be yours. That will be all for now. Could you send your stepbrother in?"

Patrick stood, his face a mask of concern. "Please, it wasn't Lydia. Don't drag her into this. She's done nothing to deserve it, and even the hint of such an accusation could ruin her."

"I'll do my best, Mr. Desmond, but a man is dead. The lady you were with might have heard or seen something you did not."

"She didn't. Once we'd . . . She slept the rest of the night. I know because her snoring kept me awake."

"I'll do my best to keep Miss Langston out of it, but unless you can furnish me with an alternative, I can promise no more." Patrick looked as though he was set to argue the point, so Daniel held up his hand. "That's all for now, Mr. Desmond. Your stepbrother, please."

Though Patrick clearly wasn't happy, he nodded and headed down the hallway, throwing a glance or two over his shoulder as he went. Daniel leaned back in his chair and watched him go. That young man was not being completely truthful with him. The question was, would he be able to figure out what the lies were? He could almost hear his uncle reassuring him.

Of course ye will, lad. Just be patient and watch closely. Even the best liars have some flaw that'll give them away, like a tell in poker.

Daniel looked up when he heard the library door slide closed. "Mr. Brissedon, please have a seat. I just have a few questions for you."

Taking a deep breath, Colin nodded and went to sit in the chair opposite Daniel. "Patrick informed me I was to be interrogated next," he said, attempting a cheery demeanor.

Daniel flashed a polite smile. "I'd hardly class it as an interrogation, Mr. Brissedon."

"Yes, of course. I was just trying to lighten the mood. How can I help you?"

"I'm not quite sure, but I'd like to start with Phillip Stockbridge. You said your father had undermined him in a business deal just last night. Can you tell me the particulars of that deal?"

"Yes, of course, Stockbridge held a small contract with Mr. Talbot, a local builder. This time, however, the consignment was far more than usual, and he'd gotten in over his head. He didn't have the money or the manpower to complete the job on time."

"And your father did, I presume, but why go to him? From what I can tell, he's not the only lumber mill on the South Shore, or even here in Patchogue."

"No, Mr. Bailey's business is quite prosperous, as is Mr. Overton's over in Bellport. There are a number of others as well, but my father was the only one bidding on two small projects in the city that Stockbridge was also interested in. He'd hopes of expanding his business, I believe."

"Why didn't your father just bid on the Talbot project himself?"

"He would have liked to, but Talbot was an old friend of Stockbridge. The man had been working with Phillip for years and believed in a certain degree of loyalty. Besides, I don't think Mr. Talbot cares for my family very much. Something about us being a disgrace." Colin twisted his mouth in an effort to repress a grin.

Daniel lifted his eyebrows, and Colin shrugged. "I suppose he was speaking about Patrick and me, but I'm certain Stockbridge added fuel to the fire. Anyway, Stockbridge knew he'd never make the deadline. He'd had some setbacks last year and had to reduce his staff. Realizing he couldn't do it by himself, he came to my father with a deal. He'd share the Talbot project if my father would overbid on the city projects. That way they'd both get what they wanted."

"I gather your father had other things in mind."

"Once Talbot agreed to the deal, Father underbid Stockbridge with the city firms, effectively ending Phillip's hopes of expansion. He still has a few other out-of-town contracts and some smaller projects hereabouts, but his income will be so curtailed, he'll never be able to fill his portion of the Talbot order. As a result, Talbot will be obliged to award the entire contract to us."

"And you consider this good business."

"I, Doctor, don't consider it anything. It is legal; that's all I know. As my father's attorney, I checked it out well in advance. It's Patrick who will eventually step into the management part of it—if he ever graduates. His grades aren't the best. For now, Father and Jeremy handle it."

"I was speaking more about the ethical side of it."

"I never pretended my father was an ethical man. He was ruthless when it came to business."

"Then I gather Mr. Stockbridge may not be the only man who will find your father's death not altogether tragic."

"No, sir, sad as that may be. He did have his champions, though. Men who appreciated his business acumen, and he was charming with the ladies."

"He saw quite a few, then?"

"I'm afraid I know very little of my father's romantic entanglements. He kept them to himself, and I preferred it that way. Unlike my sister, however, I don't believe he was without them."

"You argued with him on Wednesday. May I ask about what?"

"My trust fund. The way it's set up, I'm not to receive a dime until I reach twenty-five or marry, whichever comes later. So even though I am of age, I can't collect it since I remain single. I find that extremely unfair, and I told him so."

"Your betrothal to Lydia Langston should please you, then."

"There is a limit to what a man will do for money. I enjoy my freedom and have no intention of sacrificing it for a dowdy bore like Lydia Langston. Patrick can have her for all I care."

"Is that what you argued about yesterday?"

"You obviously know it was, sir. So why ask? I'm sure Patrick's told you all about it."

Daniel nodded. "Yes, he mentioned it. Is there a reason he shouldn't have?"

"No, what difference does it make? If arguing with my father was proof that one killed him, Patrick would be a prime suspect. He was constantly at odds with him."

"What did they argue about?"

"It would be easier to ask what they didn't argue about. Patrick was always moaning about one thing or another. Mostly his precious inheritance. He thought this should all be his."

"It was once his father's estate, was it not?" Daniel said.

"There was nothing left of his father's precious estate," Colin said. "He's lucky my father came along when he did, or both he and his mother might have ended up in the Yaphank Alms House. I think Father was extremely generous with them."

"Some people might not see it that way."

"I really don't think that's any of your affair."

"Just making an observation, Mr. Brissedon, one that may very well be my affair if it leads us to the person who killed your father. It must have made Patrick Desmond very angry, knowing this all should have been his, in his eyes, anyway."

Daniel took out his notepad and made a few notes, waiting to see if Colin would react. It was clearly wearing on his nerves, but all he did was scrub his hand across his face and tap his fingers on the arm of his chair. Finally, Daniel looked up from his pad and continued his questioning.

"Was money the root of the arguments Patrick Desmond had with your father over the last few days, or was it something else? A beating, perhaps?"

"I beg your pardon?"

"Did your father beat Patrick Desmond to keep him in line?"

"Is that what Patrick said? If so, he's a liar. My father may have used his belt on him a time or two, but I assure you it was nothing more than he deserved. Far less, in fact, and I'll challenge any man who says otherwise, Patrick included."

"And you, did you ever become physical with him?"

"We've exchanged blows on occasion, but he is quite capable of handling himself. He is, after all, on his college football team. Father encouraged it."

"What was so overwhelming yesterday that would cause your stepbrother to threaten your father's life? Mr. Desmond argued with him on numerous occasions, and it never had that effect before."

"He told you about the threat, did he?" Colin raised his eyebrows. "It was the news about my engagement to Lydia Langston. Patrick fancies her for himself."

"And so Patrick threatened to kill him?"

"He was terribly angry. I don't think I've ever seen him in that state. He swore he would see Father dead. I tried to calm him down, told him how his words could very well come back to haunt him, but it was to no avail. He stormed up the stairs, supposedly to go to bed."

"But you don't think he did?"

Colin shrugged. "It wouldn't be the first time he's snuck out in the middle of the night."

"Everyone heard his threat, of course."

"Yes, I'm afraid so, even Stockbridge and his wife. They hadn't gone home yet."

"Interesting. A perfect opening for anyone who wanted to do away with your father. After Patrick's threat, all eyes would be on him. Then again, Patrick could have realized that and used it to his own advantage as well."

Colin frowned. "I suppose so, on both counts."

"What did you think about your sister's proposed marriage to Edward Langston?"

Colin chuckled, but Daniel didn't crack a smile. "Come now, Doctor," he finally said. "Surely you jest. Edward Langston and my sister? Good God, man! He must hate that idea even more than I do, but not exactly for the same reasons." He held off for a minute, clearly expecting Daniel to ask the reason, but he wasn't about to oblige. Finally, Colin continued. "Edward prefers the company of gentlemen, you see. I have that on very good authority."

"May I ask whose?"

"I would rather not divulge that information. Suffice it to say that the person in question has firsthand knowledge of it, and I do mean in the carnal sense."

"Does Miss Brissedon know of this?"

"No, of course not, but she doesn't want the marriage either. She's being courted by a friend of mine, Brighton Templeton."

"I understood that your father had not given his approval."

Colin's lip turned up in a snarl. "No, Brighton wasn't well-off enough. Never mind that he loves Kathleen. All my father cared about was how well placed he was in society."

"Which, of course, Mr. Templeton wasn't?"

"He's placed well enough," Colin replied. "Just not well enough for my father."

"He must have been furious when he heard the news."

"As it was, I accompanied Kathleen when she went to meet him last night. Since he's not allowed in the house, they meet by the lake, and I chaperone. We both assured him that it would all be straightened out within the week, and he went home satisfied."

"Did you go out then?"

"No, I escorted Kathleen back to the house and went to bed."

Daniel tapped the notepad with his pencil. "You're sure you didn't go out?"

Colin cursed under his breath. "It was that little prig, Patrick, wasn't it? I thought I heard him. Yes, all right, I went out for a bit. The thought of spending the rest of my life as Lydia Langston's husband sickened me. I wanted to feel the touch of a real woman, so I went where I could find one."

"And did you . . . find one?"

"Yes, I did. I can give you the name of the establishment if you'd like."

"That won't be necessary at the moment. What time did you head out for your rendezvous?"

"I don't know. Somewhere between two and three, I imagine. I tried to go to sleep first but found that I was more interested in the bottle on my bureau. I decided to take it with me."

"I see. Just one last question, then. Those scratches on your hand, where did you get them?"

"I wasn't exactly sober when I headed out last night, but I decided to saddle my own horse so as not to alert anyone to my departure. I was a bit clumsier than usual, I'm afraid."

"Thank you, sir. If you could send your sister in, I'd appreciate it."

"She's in the garden, I believe. Right through those doors on your left."

"Thank you again. That will be fine."

CHAPTER 19

Daniel took out his notepad and went over it again, searching for some small contradictory statement or, for that matter, any statement that seemed too well rehearsed. Patrick had gotten a raw deal, there seemed no disputing that fact. A perfect motive for murder. Perhaps too perfect.

Then, of course, there were the ill-fated marriage arrangements. Could someone have killed to escape such a fate? Would Thomas Brissedon's death really make any difference? According to the help, Elizabeth Langston would never, under ordinary circumstances, have allowed such matches to take place. Why, then, did she have such an abrupt change of mind? If, indeed, she'd had any at all.

Once more, Daniel rubbed his eyes. It was turning into quite a long day, and he still had three more inquiries he wanted to conduct before it ended. Stretching his arms, he got up and walked over to join Sergeant Owens, who was occupying himself by looking out over the gardens.

"Beautiful, aren't they, sir?" the officer said.

"She certainly is." A smile touched Daniel's lips as he gazed at Kathleen Brissedon.

The sergeant chuckled. "I meant the gardens, sir."

"As did I," Daniel said hastily, but the look on Owens's face made him smile just the same, for they both knew where his eyes had really been. "Trust me," he said, "it's no more than wishful thinking." Then with a shrug, he opened his notebook again. "We'd best get to it, or your wife will be railing at me for making you late to supper."

"It'll be all right, sir. I may not always be able to tell who did it, but I'm usually pretty good about who didn't, and I can say with assurance that the lady did nothing to be ashamed of."

Daniel squeezed the sergeant's shoulder, then joined Kathleen in the garden. She was talking to her younger brother and sister. On seeing Daniel, however, she asked Moira to take them for a walk down to the lake.

"How do I explain it to them?" she said. "They're so young. Ryan's just turned seven, and Charlotte's not even ten yet."

"Won't your brothers help you?" Daniel sat down by her side and watched the threesome head down toward the small lake.

"Patrick would; he's good that way, but I'm afraid the children despise him, and he has no great love for them either. As for Colin . . . He has a hard enough time facing things like this himself. He would only make matters worse. They both mean well. It's just that . . ."

"That you'll probably end up doing it yourself anyway."

"Something like that." She blinked the tears away and turned to face him. "So how can I help?"

"Yes, right," Daniel said, "let me just check my notes." He fumbled for a moment with his notebook, trying to compose himself. Just being around Kathleen made him feel like a schoolboy again. Not very professional. After a moment, he managed to collect himself and looked back up.

"You argued with your father last night," he said, trying to cover his obvious infatuation with his beautiful suspect.

"It was about your proposed marriage to Edward Langston, I presume. Is that correct?" Kathleen had started to sob softly, so Daniel took his handkerchief out and handed it to her. "I truly am sorry to have to bring this up."

"No, I understand completely." She wiped her cheek and blew her nose before taking a breath. "There wasn't any argument, though. I'm not even sure I said anything. He'd called me into his study, but before I could get there, he came out and simply informed me I was to wed Edward. Clearly, he thought Colin had already told me."

"But he hadn't."

"No. I was stunned. Father never cared for Brighton; I knew that. But to arrange for me to marry a man I hardly knew . . ." She shook her head, dabbing her eye with the hanky. "I won't deny I was angry with him, terribly angry. The next thing I remember is sobbing and running up the stairs. And now it will be the last memory I have of him. I'll never see him alive again. It's a terrible thing to have to live with."

"Your father died quickly, Miss Brissedon, but I'm sure if he'd been given time to think of you, that moment would not have been what he remembered."

"I know you're right, and there's no doubt he would have reconsidered once he realized how unhappy it made me. I believe it's important to love the person you're going to spend your life with. Don't you, Doctor?"

"As a matter of fact, I do. But not everyone feels that way."

"Well, I'm sure you love your wife very much, and my father would have wanted that for me as well."

He frowned down at her. "My wife? What makes you think I have a wife?"

"No, of course, Dr. Tennyson did mention you weren't married when we spoke at Brigid's funeral. You'll have to excuse me. I was a bit preoccupied that day. Surely you must have a fiancée, though. That lovely young lady I saw you walking along the dock with last weekend."

A smile touched his lips, but he didn't want to laugh and hurt her feelings. "That would be my sister, Isabell. She claims Mother wanted her to make sure I was settled in properly, which is likely true to a certain extent, but I think it had more to do with Izzy wanting to see the village."

"Oh, I'm so sorry. It was foolish of me to make such an assumption. You just seemed so comfortable with each other."

"I suppose we are. She is my sister, after all." He could feel the heat radiating out across his cheeks. "But I really do need to concentrate on the case." Had she just been staring at him? How he wished he could open his collar. Though it was a lovely day, the temperature seemed to be rising rapidly.

"Yes, of course. I am sorry."

Turnabout was fair play, and though he chided himself for thinking it, he did have to ask. "You mentioned that your father didn't like this Brighton Templeton, but your brother Colin seemed to imply that he was courting you."

This time it was Kathleen's cheeks that blushed, though she frowned, looking down as she twisted the handkerchief in her hand. "Poor Brighton. I'm afraid I didn't handle it very well, but . . . he wasn't allowed in the house, you see."

"Yes, your brothers mentioned that."

"Of course, but did they mention I would meet him out by the copse of trees just this side of the lake?"

"They made reference to it, yes."

She looked up at him, her cheeks now a deep dusty rose. "Of course, we were never alone. Molly would accompany me most of the time, though Colin was acting as chaperone last night. I suppose Brighton did like to think he was courting me. I should never have encouraged him. I knew Father wouldn't give us his blessing, you see."

"We don't always choose those our families approve of. You were chaperoned, so it's no different than meeting him for a walk in the park."

She looked up through her eyelashes. "At one in the morning?"

"Well, it is noon somewhere in this vast world of ours." He smiled, and it made her laugh, loosening the tightness that had gripped his heart.

"I suppose so, but still . . ."

"Is there any way he could have heard about your father's plans for you to marry Edward Langston?"

"Yes, I told him last night, and it was terribly cowardly of me."

He scratched the back of his head. "Why would you think that?"

"Because I used it as an excuse. I've known I don't really care for Brighton for a few weeks now, but I didn't know how to tell him. So when father announced his plans for me to wed Edward . . ." She shrugged. "I saw it as an opportunity to end it. I'm a terrible coward."

"Ah, I see what you mean." His heart was pounding so hard, he was sure she must hear it. "I don't think you're a coward, though. You were just trying to spare his feelings."

"Would you want someone sparing your feelings that way?"

"Well, no, but . . ." Good Lord, now she had him tongue-tied.

"Exactly. I should have been honest with him. And I mean to be as soon as all this is over. I just can't right now."

"Why don't you let one of your brothers tell him? From what I understand, he's a friend of theirs, and it might be easier coming from them."

"He's Colin's friend, not Patrick's. My stepbrother thinks he's out for my dowry. And I haven't told Colin yet either. How I feel, I mean. The truth is, I think allowing Brighton to call on me might have been a bit of a rebellion on my part. You know, the forbidden fruit."

"Yes, I know it well." *Calm yourself, O'Halleran. She may not have made any commitments, but there's still the issue of your birth.* Then again, Kathleen wasn't Prudence Davis. Was it possible he had a chance? He took a breath, trying to bring his attention back to the matter at hand. Of course, the spurned lover would be a perfect suspect. It would certainly remove the fiend from the picture. And no one but Colin seemed to like him, so it was really for the best. He shook his head. "What are you thinking?" He whispered to himself in disbelief.

"I beg your pardon, Doctor?"

"I'm sorry, I was just going over my notes in my head. So do you think your clandestine meetings with Brighton are why your father arranged the marriage with Edward? Would he have taken such a drastic step?"

"You didn't know my father. He hated Brighton, and I suppose he really did believe promising me to Edward Langston was in my best interest. But as I said, I'm sure he would have come to his senses, once he realized how unhappy it made me."

"What did he have against Mr. Templeton, anyway?"

"He's not of the correct social class. My grandparents came to this country as poor immigrants, you see, and though Father made something of himself, he's never quite felt accepted by others of the same financial standing. Brighton comes from a poor family, and so no matter how hard he works or how promising his future may be, Father can't see beyond his humble beginnings. He wanted me to marry someone well placed in society, with an illustrious pedigree. Perhaps that's why he's so hard on Patrick as well."

"You're very close to Mr. Desmond, aren't you?"

"Sometimes I feel like his surrogate mother." She laughed, and the sound spread a joy through his heart that he hadn't felt in a very long time. "He needs that right now, for I think he feels very alone. I vaguely remember losing my mother, and that was hard enough. I can't imagine the pain of losing both parents so close together the way he did. There was barely two years between their deaths."

"How old were you when you lost your mother?"

"Only about five or six. My father sent Colin and I off to boarding school soon after. He'd always come to see us when he could, of course. I hated it so when he'd have to leave. I vaguely remember crying myself to sleep at night, especially in the first few years."

"Yes, it must have been hard." Daniel swallowed the lump in his throat and forced his mind back to the task at hand. "Did your father have to discipline Mr. Desmond much?"

"Occasionally, he'd take the strap to him, but never more than two or three strikes, then he'd send him to his room. Sometimes I think Patrick is harder on himself, always tripping down the stairs or walking into doors."

"Clumsy, is he?"

"Yes, a bit." She beamed up at him, but then a sadness dulled the sparkle in her eyes. "It was hard for Patrick. Not only having a new family, but learning that your father might have been nothing more than a murdering drunkard and feeling like you'd been cheated out of what was rightfully yours."

"Which, of course, he wasn't."

"No, of course not. At least not the way he thinks, but that's why I want you to investigate his father's death. Maybe if he knows the truth, whatever that may be, he can get on with making something of his own life. His mother understood her circumstances and was grateful to Father for all he did. She realized what it would be like for a boy Patrick's age, being left all alone, and so she named my father as his guardian. Unfortunately, Patrick doesn't understand that yet."

"But Colin will inherit the bulk of your father's estate, am I correct?"

"A good portion of it, yes. Being the eldest son, it's only fitting, I suppose.""

"I can't imagine Mr. Desmond was too happy about that."

"No," she said, her voice tinge with sadness. "I've tried so often to help him understand, but even I have a hard time reaching him when it comes to that. And it's not like Father left any of us destitute. We'll all receive sizeable trusts and a portion of the business"

"Even Patrick?"

Her cheeks blushed a dusty rose once more. "Not quite as sizeable as everyone else, but with his education, he should be able to live comfortably."

"So he'll be able to access it now that your father is deceased."

"Oh no, none of us can, with the exception of Colin and Jeremy, of course. My father's will is very specific. Colin is to have the bulk of the estate as long as he cares for the rest of us. Our trusts, however, are beyond his reach, though they can't be released to us until our twenty-fifth birthdays."

"Or until you marry, whichever comes later."

Kathleen tilted her head. "No, not anymore. It's simply until our twenty-fifth birthdays. All the other stipulations attached to our trusts have been removed."

"Ah, I must have misunderstood. Did Patrick and Colin ever get into fisticuffs over money issues?"

"Oh, constantly, over money and everything else, it seems. Typical sibling rivalry, I suppose, and yet, in a way, I think he almost looks up to Colin—or down to him, as the case may be."

"You mean his gambling and the like?"

"Mostly his drinking, where Patrick is concerned. He's taken to it quite regularly of late."

"Do you think they were out drinking last night?"

"I have no idea," Kathleen stated, her voice wavering for the first time. "As far as I know, they went to bed. If you recall, I did mention I was with Brighton last night."

"But not alone."

"Oh no, of course not. Molly sat by the lake while Brighton and I talked."

Daniel's heart clenched, for she'd contradicted herself more than once. She was lying to him, but why? He wasn't going to challenge her on it just yet, though. "Have you any idea how long that was? What time did you come back in?'

"We were probably together about four hours, so I came back in around four or five. He was very upset last night, and I felt bad leaving him. We sat there looking at the stars and enjoying the breeze off the lake."

"Just a few more questions and I can let you be on your way. Last night, did you see anyone moving about outside? Anything that might have been out of the ordinary?"

"No, I'm afraid not. As I said, I spent most of the night with Brighton. I did see our groomsman, Trevor Kilpatrick, going toward the house right after I met Brighton, but he does that a lot. He's seeing Lizzie, I'm sure of it," she said with a grin, "and if Father knew, he'd be furious. They do make such a lovely couple, though, don't you think?"

"I'm afraid I'm not well enough acquainted with them to judge."

"Thank you for not pretending you could. It shows you've been paying attention."

"It's my job to pay attention, now, isn't it?"

"Yes, I suppose it is." Her voice was playful and sure again, so what about her time with Brighton had made it waver? Was she just embarrassed by it? No, it was more than that.

"Was Trevor the only one you saw about?"

"No . . . I saw Jeremy as well . . . just before I went out. He was inebriated, as usual, and heading up toward Molly's room. Poor girl, she really is a hard worker but a bit naive, I fear. I suppose she believes Jeremy will marry her one day, but I doubt that will ever happen."

She'd contradicted herself again. "He doesn't care for her?"

"I suppose he does in his own way, but it doesn't matter. Father would never permit it."

"Not the right class and all that."

"I'm afraid not," Kathleen said, clearly embarrassed by her father's obvious snobbery. "I didn't say he was a saint, but he did care a great deal for us and worried constantly about our futures. It can't be wrong for a father to feel that way about his children, can it, Doctor?"

"I wouldn't think so, miss. There is one more thing before you go. Please forgive me for asking it, but I feel I must. The scratches on your forearm, how did you come by them?"

"Oh, these? I'm not sure. I suppose I must have brushed up against one of the bushes when I met Brighton. It seems we move farther and farther away from the house each time we meet."

"That explains it, then. Thank you, Miss Brissedon."

"Why is that important?"

"I beg your pardon?"

"Why are the scratches on my arms important?"

Daniel's brain was rushing for an excuse. He hadn't wanted to release that information, and thus far no one had questioned it. "I was just concerned. I wouldn't want to find out they'd gotten infected because you hadn't noticed them."

Kathleen's eyes narrowed, and she crossed her arms over her chest. "Come now, Doctor, I've answered your questions. Now it's your turn. I might have even discovered something that will interest you. If you're willing to share, that is?"

"First of all, you are a suspect in a homicide investigation." Her eyes widened, but before she could voice her indignation, he raised his hand. "I didn't say I believed it. And secondly, it's against the law to withhold information relevant to an ongoing investigation."

Her eyes met his, sparkling like the evening sky at dusk once more. "As you wish, but it is fairly obvious. My father must have scratched his assailant in the struggle. And if you plan to arrest me for withholding information, you'd best be able to prove I am." She stood and started to walk away.

"Why did you lie to me, then?" Daniel asked, causing her to stop short and spin around.

Her eyes blazed, storm clouds rising in the dusky blue skies. "I did not lie!"

"Didn't you?" he said, trying to keep his voice low. "I'm very good at what I do, Miss Brissedon. When you're ready to tell me the truth—about everything—let me know."

Kathleen balled her hands at her sides, the soft pink in her cheeks deepening into a fiery red, but she didn't relent, so Daniel just gave a nod of his head and went back into the library.

"What happened out there, sir? You look madder than a wet cock at dawn."

"Never mind, Sergeant. Just ask Forbes to bring Jeremy Radcliffe, would you?"

Daniel flopped down in the chair and ran his fingers through his hair. He was angry . . . and hurt. Not only that she'd lied to him, and he was certain she had, but that she'd denied it and withheld information that might—or might not—be crucial to the investigation. Why was he such a fool? Just another society chit. Hadn't he learned his lesson? He wasn't one of them. He never would be, and in truth, he was glad of it. Pulling the notebook from his pocket, he flipped it open and turned to a new page. *Jeremy Radcliffe—Cousin.*

Kathleen's fists were still clenched as she reached the copse of trees just this side of the lake. How dare he accuse her of lying? *Well, you did,* the voice inside her head echoed. Oh

God, she had, hadn't she? She'd only meant to conceal Jeremy's bumbling attempt at seduction and Patrick's absence from his room. *And keep him from pointing a finger at Brighton or Colin.* Leaning up against the nearest tree, she closed her eyes, massaging her temples.

As much as she hated to admit it, she knew she couldn't protect them all. Someone had killed her father, and whoever it was didn't deserve her protection. Yet she couldn't bear thinking it was someone she cared about. Worst of all, Daniel O'Halleran had seen right through her. The heat rose in her cheeks once more. Why did she care?

He was handsome. There was no doubt about that, with eyes the color of autumn and hair to complement them, brown with highlights of blond and red mixed in amongst the waves. And those dimples when he smiled, filled with a sincerity that went all the way to his eyes. She had to take a breath to calm herself, for just thinking about him caused her pulse to race. Which was completely ridiculous.

She opened her eyes, flexing her fingers. But he'd just shown he had a dark side as well, hadn't he? Or had he? He'd merely pointed out the truth and remained remarkably calm in doing so. Maybe she'd ask Patrick and Colin about this Columbia Hall. If the matchbox wasn't theirs, she'd give it to Dr. O'Halleran. She groaned. *You're doing it again. You can't protect them. Just give him what you found and let him get to the bottom of it.* If she could only trust him to be fair and do a thorough job.

As she pushed away from the tree, a glint of something shiny caught her eye. She bent down, pushing aside a clump of grass, and her heart froze. How had her father's cuff link gotten all the way out here? Her fingers trembled as she reached down to pick it up. And who could have dropped it? Patrick often rode his bike down this way, and

Colin would pass by with his horse as well. Jeremy liked to walk along the shore too, and this was where she'd met Brighton. She wouldn't be surprised if Lizzie or Molly met their beaus down here from time to time either.

Her little brother laughed, and the sound warmed her heart. She'd forgotten they'd headed for the lake. Taking a breath, she put the single cuff link in her pocket. She would need to tell Dr. O'Halleran what she'd found and trust that he wouldn't jump to conclusions. But not tonight. Tonight she'd spend with her family, and maybe make a few inquiries of her own.

CHAPTER 20

"You wanted to see me, Doctor?" Jeremy Radcliffe strode into the library and lit his pipe. Immediately, the sweet aroma of fine Dutch tobacco filled the air, and Daniel had to fight the urge to light up himself. Instead, he gazed intensely at his notebook, flipping through the pages until Jeremy was well settled.

"All right, Mr. Radcliffe," he finally said. "You were Mr. Brissedon's nephew, I believe?"

"Not exactly, we were more like cousins, but Thomas helped raise me from the time I was eight or so. My mother, God rest her soul, was his cousin, and Thomas came to live with us after my da passed. Then when she died suddenly, he and his wife, Ellie—they were married by then—took me on as their ward."

"And how old were you then?"

"Probably about twelve or so."

"And you've lived with him ever since?"

"That's right," Jeremy said, his eyes narrowing slightly, "but what does any of that have to do with my uncle's death?"

"Just trying to get some background on who everyone is." Daniel smiled, and the man seemed to relax a bit. "You work at your uncle's mill now, is that correct?"

"That I do. I'm in a managerial position, taking care of finances and such." He tapped his fingers on the table to his side, his attention elsewhere. "Excuse me, Doctor, but would you mind if I called for Forbes to bring me a drink? The day's rather warm, after all, and I must say I am a bit parched."

"No, not at all," Daniel said, rubbing his finger under his nose to keep from laughing. "Some lemonade would hit the spot rather nicely about now."

"Lemonade!" Jeremy looked like he was about to protest, but Daniel tilted his head, and the man sighed. "Of course, lemonade it is."

Forbes came at once, a smile tickling his lips when Jeremy asked for lemonade, but he nodded his assent and headed off to fetch their beverages. While he was gone, Daniel resumed his questioning. "What do you know about the arguments that took place here yesterday?"

"Not much, I'm afraid. I try to keep my nose out of family affairs. There were the marriage arrangements, of course, which I'm sure you've been informed of by now. No one save Uncle Thomas was happy about them. I believe Patrick had hoped to claim Lydia Langston for himself, but then he has a bit of a wandering eye; just ask any servant girl from here to Canarsie."

"Mr. Desmond flirts quite a bit, does he?"

"I think it goes a bit further than flirting much of the time, if you get my drift. Uncle Thomas was forced to take the whip to him for it on more than one occasion."

"Beat him, did he?"

"No, not exactly," Jeremy replied a bit too hastily. "He'd take him out to the stables and give him a good thrashing, that's all. Nothing more than any concerned father would do."

"Did you ever hear Mr. Desmond threaten him?"

"Just the once, last night after they'd argued. He was angrier than I'd ever seen him."

"I've been told he could be a handful at times. He must have kept poor Mr. Brissedon busy?"

"He certainly did. I don't know how many times my uncle returned home to face the wrath of some angry gentleman whose sister had just been graced with the pleasure of Patrick's company. Of course, Colin isn't much better, but then, Patrick was only his stepson, so my uncle didn't have as much tolerance there."

"But he did have tolerance with Colin?"

He chuckled. "Yes, far too much if you ask me."

There was something in the man's eyes. Was it jealousy, resentment? "But not with you either?" Daniel said, venturing a guess.

Jeremy heaved a sigh. He scratched the back of his head and peeked up at Daniel from under his heavy lids. "No, not with me either, though I can't say what would have happened to me if Uncle Thomas hadn't taken me in when my ma died."

"He didn't send you off to boarding school?"

"No, Ellie was still alive then. Colin must have only been about two. Besides, I was almost twelve by then and able to help in his business. Don't get me wrong. He always treated me well enough. He just wasn't as lenient with me as he was with his own. Colin even got . . . Oh, I guess that's really not important, not with Uncle Thomas dead and all."

"Why don't you tell me what you were going to say, and I can just discard it if it's of no use?"

"Well," Jeremy stammered, clearly regretting he'd said anything and feeling cornered now that he had. "It's just that Colin got a girl in the family way a little over a year ago, but Uncle Thomas did right by the girl. Short of having Colin marry her, anyway. She had no family except for a maiden aunt, so he gave her a sizeable allowance and sent her and the old woman off to England. She's probably never lived so well in her life. You see, Colin frequents the seedier side of town more often than Patrick."

"It was a local girl?"

"What? No, it was just before we moved out here. Colin wanted one last fling, as it were."

"Do you remember her name? I'd like to check that she's all right."

"Are you insinuating something nefarious became of the girl?" Jeremy seemed indignant. "I never would have allowed that. She was a sweet thing. Her allowance is paid monthly. I can give you the details if you insist."

"I do." Daniel didn't crack a smile, and Jeremy nodded.

"I'll send the information to Dr. Tennyson's office tomorrow morning. I don't have it here with me now."

"Just make sure you do, or I may have to take things into my own hands." Without giving Jeremy a chance to reply, he continued. "Mr. Desmond keeps his amorous encounters closer to home, then."

"I don't know about that. He's taken the automobile out a few times and used a full tank of gas, but he certainly visits the better areas." A silly grin crossed his face that made him look more like he belonged in a Barnum & Bailey sideshow than sitting in a well-furnished library.

Daniel changed the subject. "You said you worked in a managerial capacity for your uncle. Did you know anything about the deal with Phillip Stockbridge?"

"Mr. Stockbridge got greedy. He wanted to expand into some Manhattan projects but keep the local custom as well.

The only problem was he couldn't even handle the jobs he already had scheduled. He expected Uncle Thomas to foot the bill while he kept the contracts for himself. My uncle simply turned the tables on him."

"So your uncle was nothing more than a shrewd businessman. One who didn't want to be taken advantage of."

"That's right. Why, if you look at the number of new accounts we've landed in the last year, you can see he must have been doing something right."

Or something very wrong. Daniel turned the page on his notepad, trying not to show his utter disgust. "Tell me, do you remember anything of importance from last night? Did you see or hear anyone up and about after you went to bed? Forbes said he saw you in the parlor around midnight, and you looked rather upset."

"Upset? No, not at all. Just a bit tired. I'd had a long day at the mill, and then Uncle Thomas had guests for dinner, so I was obliged to stay up later than I normally would have."

"You're speaking of Mr. and Mrs. Stockbridge?"

Jeremy nodded before eagerly turning his attention to the tray of lemonade Forbes had just placed on the low coffee table. "Yes, and then Elizabeth Langston arrived not long after the Stockbridges left. As everyone else had already headed off to bed, I was left to organize the staff in seeing her to her room." Nonchalantly, he took a flask from his jacket pocket and poured some of the contents into one of the glasses. Daniel cringed to think what it would taste like.

"I was under the impression you'd already gone to bed by that time and that Forbes took care of seeing Mrs. Langston settle in."

"Did he? Yes, I suppose you're right. I'd just reached the top of the stairs when her melodious strains echoed through the hallways."

"You don't seem very sure of it."

"I was extremely exhausted, Doctor. I'm lucky I remember the night at all."

Or extremely drunk! "But you are certain you didn't go to bed until after Mr. Brissedon."

"Yes, but it wasn't long after. I believe I had another drink or two first."

Hmm, or three or four. "Before your uncle and cousin went to bed, what did the three of you talk about?"

"Mostly how angry Stockbridge was going to be when he discovered he'd been outsmarted. Uncle Thomas loved to get the upper hand."

"Did he mention why Mrs. Langston would be arriving so late at night? She can't live more than half a mile away."

Jeremy squirmed in his seat. "He didn't say, but I presume she wanted to get an early start on the wedding plans the next morning. I suppose she might have had an engagement earlier and came straight from the affair. She was certainly dressed as if she had."

"Now that your uncle's dead, will anything change as far as the business?"

"No, not really. Colin will take over, of course, but other than that, things should stay much the same. My uncle kept ahead of things, so all the deals he meant to broker have already been struck and should continue as scheduled."

"I'm sorry to have to repeat this, but we seem to have gotten sidetracked. Did you see or hear anyone moving about after you went to bed last night . . . aside from Mrs. Langston, that is?"

His face pinched like he'd eaten something sour. Then again, it could just be his drink. "I saw Kathleen around twelve thirty, maybe a bit later, making her biweekly rendezvous with that bourgeois beau of hers."

"I take it you don't like Mr. Templeton very much?"

"He doesn't love her, not the way she deserves to be loved, and he certainly can't give her the things she's used to."

"But it was my understanding that he was relatively well situated."

Jeremy made a derisive grunt before taking another drink. "It wouldn't matter if he'd inherited a fortune. Not that he did, mind you. He'd just gamble it away. It's all he wants my Katie for. To keep him in gambling money!"

His Katie, now that was interesting. "Did you happen to notice what time she returned from her rendezvous with Mr. Templeton?"

"I'm afraid I would have been asleep by then. I did see one more thing, and this might be extremely important. Our groomsman, Trevor, was heading for the house around the same time. I can't imagine what for. He's not allowed any farther than the kitchen. None of the outside help are. Perhaps Mrs. Quinn was giving him some leftovers. She's very good that way."

"You spent the rest of the night in your room, then?"

His eyes narrowed. "I did, until around five thirty or so. Did someone say otherwise?"

"Not to my knowledge. Is there a reason you might suspect them to?"

"I may have made a visit to the toilet at some time during the night, but I wouldn't have spent more than a few minutes."

"You don't remember?"

"Actually, I don't. I was bound to be half-asleep at the time and, after doing my bit, would have headed straight back to bed without thinking much more about it."

"I don't like being lied to, Mr. Radcliffe. So tell me, why it is that you and Miss Buchanan discussed having spent the night together? And before you deny it, yes, I was present when you were comforting her earlier."

It was almost like watching the man's face melt. The corners of his mouth slid down, and his eyelids dropped lower, if that was even possible. "Well, yes, I did, but please, you mustn't tell anyone. It would ruin the girl's reputation, and even Colin would be hard-pressed to continue her employment if she were known as a loose woman."

"Then why risk it?"

The man's hands balled into fists, but the anger didn't seem to be directed at Daniel. "Because I'm a cad," he said. Then more quietly, he added, "And I truly do care for her."

"Which makes what you do seem even worse," Daniel said.

The man nodded, and for once there seemed to be some honesty in his manner.

"When did you leave her?"

"A little after five, I think. I woke to find her packing her things. My uncle had dismissed her, you see. She was rather distraught and spurned any comfort I sought to offer, so I suspected it best I head back to my own bed. I hoped to confront my uncle about it in the morning, but, of course, he never came down to breakfast."

"Did you see or hear anyone else at that time?"

"I bumped into Kathleen on the way out. She'd come up to speak to Molly, about her dismissal, I suppose. And I spied Paddy down by the lake, though I've no idea what he was doing down there at such an early hour." Jeremy shrugged and relit his pipe. "I do wonder about him sometimes."

"He has a key to the back hallway door?" Jeremy would probably just say he'd used the main stairs, but it was worth a try.

"I would imagine so, no matter what he says about Uncle Tommy taking it back."

Uncle Tommy! A chill ran down Daniel's spine, though he didn't know why. "What makes you think that?"

"Because I've seen him using it to sneak out late at night. My uncle would have had a conniption if he knew. Besides, Patrick is probably well acquainted with it, since it was his father who had the place built."

"Thank you, Mr. Radcliffe, that's all for now, but please don't go far."

Jeremy hurried from the room, and Daniel leaned back in his chair, nibbling the end of his pencil.

"I've seen that look before, Doc," Sergeant Owens said. "What's on your mind?"

"I'm not sure yet, just the way Mr. Radcliffe referred to his uncle at one point. Probably nothing more than a familial slip." He took a deep breath and stood up. "Never mind, we're finished here for today, I think."

"What about Mrs. Langston?"

"Send her home. I'll deal with her and her family tomorrow morning."

"Won't that give them time to close ranks, sir, and organize their stories?"

"It might, but it will also give them a little time to sweat."

Sergeant Owens accompanied Daniel back to the parlor, where Mr. Ruland, a local funeral director, was speaking to

Colin. Kathleen was off to the side, once more weeping softly into Patrick's shoulder, while her cousin talked quietly to Monsignor Cronin about the services that would take place on the following Saturday. As Daniel entered the room, Colin excused himself politely. He looked haggard, as if he hadn't slept for days, and in a way, Daniel almost felt sorry for the young man who stood before him.

"Is there anything else you need, Doctor?" Colin asked in a strained voice.

"Not for today, Mr. Brissedon. I'm sorry to have to bother you at a time like this. My sincere condolences on the death of your father."

"Thank you, sir. I'll have Forbes show you out."

"That's perfectly all right. You have business to attend to, and we can find our own way. I'll be in touch. Try to get some rest over the next few days. If you need to contact me, you can leave word with Dr. Tennyson."

"What do you think, Doc?" the sergeant asked as they headed out toward the carriage.

"I think something incredibly sinister is going on in that house, something that began long before the death of Thomas Brissedon."

"Like what?"

"I'm not sure, but I have every intention of finding out." Daniel climbed into the buggy and indicated for the sergeant to do the same. "Ride with me. I have a favor to ask."

The sergeant obliged, and Daniel continued while they headed toward the center of town. "First thing tomorrow morning, would you see what you can find out about Colin Brissedon's gambling habits, as well as those of Patrick Desmond and Brighton Templeton? Oh, and Mr. Radcliffe is to be sending some information to Dr. Tennyson about a girl Colin Brissedon left in a family way. Supposedly, she's in England and being sent a sizeable amount each month to stay there. See if you can confirm it. I'll pay for any telephone fees incurred."

"Of course, Doc," the sergeant said. "Is there anything else we can help you with?"

"No, I think that'll be all for now." Since the sergeant had taken the reins, Daniel took the opportunity to ruffle through his notes. "I'll go straight to the Langstons' tomorrow morning. It should be interesting to see what they have to say about Thomas Brissedon and these supposed marriage proposals."

"Right you are, Doc! I'll check in with you later in the day, then."

Daniel stared off in the distance for a moment, gathering his thoughts. "I gave my uncle a call this afternoon, asking if he can get his hands on the Cornelius Desmond file. My sister brought out my notes on the autopsy last weekend, but I have no idea what they discovered beyond that. One thing I do know, it was no accident, and I have this nagging feeling in my gut the two cases are connected."

"Find the answer to one, and you'll have the solution to the other?"

Daniel chuckled. "I'm not sure about that, but one may at least shed some light on the other."

Owens nodded. "You know, most folks around here always have suspected there was more to that case than met the eye, myself included."

Daniel couldn't keep a smile from popping out on his lips for his new partner in crime. "What background can you give me on him, Sergeant?"

"Well, let's see. Cornelius Desmond was the son of an Irish immigrant, raised on the Lower East Side, but he had a keen eye for business and loved the smell of sawdust. He worked hard, did without for a number of years, from what I heard, but he managed to do very well for himself." He frowned. "Or so it seemed. Word was everyone on the Lower East Side loved him. He used to go down and help them out, you see, with money and the like. He even found some of them jobs, decent ones so they could move out of the filth."

"So he never forgot where he came from."

"Or how fortunate he'd been. Anyway, one day he's found facedown on the floor of an old wreck of a building. Dead as a doornail, he was, and smelling of whiskey. Looked like he tumbled over the banister, so it was ruled an accident. Then they find this slip of a girl upstairs, beaten and violated beyond all recognition, along with an old fellow who had met his maker the very same day. Stabbed to death, both of them, and where do you think they found the knife? Right next to Desmond's body, and blood covering his hands, no less. But then, you know all that."

Daniel always marveled how a tale could get distorted from the first telling to the last. "Except that's not exactly what happened. First of all, the old man died of natural causes, and there was no blood on Desmond's hands, though the knife was found by his side. As for the young lady, she was stabbed, but not beaten. And Desmond didn't go over that banister of his own free will. I'd stake my reputation on that."

"Then you need to prove that, Doc. Maybe it would give young Patrick some of his dignity back. Lord knows he's lost it in the last year or so."

Daniel nodded, convinced the man was right. "What else do you know about it?"

"Well, the worst thing was those witnesses, saying they saw him with the girl right before she died. Of course, being he was already dead, no one bothered pursuing it any further, but I'll tell you one thing: Patrick wasn't the only one who thought there was something fishy there."

"And what did you think, Sergeant?"

"I never heard a wicked word about Cornelius Desmond before that day; I'll tell you that. In my mind, it was those witnesses of theirs they should have been looking into."

"Do you remember their names?"

"No, but I'm sure you'll find the answers in those files of yours."

"That's what I'm hoping, though I'm not so sure. It seems Brigid Desmond hired a private investigator to look into it. It's hard to believe he didn't stumble across them. Of course, he may have, for all I know."

The sergeant looked at Daniel as if the answer was obvious. "Why don't you just ask him?"

"I would if I knew who he was. Unfortunately, Patrick says he can't recall the man's name."

"And you believe him?"

"Not for a minute, but if Patrick Desmond has some proof that Thomas Brissedon was involved in his father's murder, that may have been all the motive he needed to kill him."

CHAPTER 21

Saturday, June 25, 1904 – 9:30 a.m.

T

he morning sun was shining brightly on the stately three-story home, its gingerbread trim contrasting nicely with the lavender board-and-batten siding. Daniel knocked on the elaborate etched-glass door and then turned his back, listening to a robin that was chirping in a nearby maple tree. A moment later, he heard the door open and swung back around to be greeted by a stocky gentleman in a black jacket and dove-gray pants—the butler, no doubt.

"May I help you, sir?" the man asked, tilting his head ever so slightly.

"I believe Mrs. Langston is expecting me," he said, cognizant of the fact his appearance was well outside of accepted visiting hours. "Doctor Daniel O'Halleran."

"Oh yes, of course, sir, in relation to the demise of Mr. Brissedon. Such tragic news." He led Daniel into a well-furnished parlor, though he had to admit it was a bit overdone for his taste. It was clear Mrs. Langston had opted for the appearance of wealth over style and comfort. "If you'll just wait, here, sir," the butler continued. "I'll tell the family you have arrived."

Daniel thanked him and sat down in one of the heavily brocaded chairs. *Just as uncomfortable as it looks.* He decided to stand, turning instead to look out the bay window, which was framed with elaborately embroidered drapes. He cringed. His mother would hyperventilate just looking at them.

"Dr. O'Halleran, is it?" a voice said from behind.

Daniel turned to face the man. His dark hair was split over his forehead so that it curled slightly at his temples, and he sported a well-groomed handlebar moustache. As he didn't appear to be much younger than Daniel, he assumed this must be the son.

"Edward Langston, sir." He reached out his hand in a firm shake before motioning that Daniel should sit in one of the uncomfortable chairs by the fireplace.

"Thank you, no," Daniel said. "I find I can think much better while standing."

Edward shrugged and sat in one of the chairs. "Mother and Lydia will be down presently."

"And your father?" Daniel asked.

"I'm afraid he has his business in the city and spends much of his time there. He does try to get home on weekends, though that wasn't the case today. Hopefully, he'll grace us with an appearance next weekend. He hates it out here, you know."

"Really, and why is that?"

"He finds it desolate, plus I suppose he prefers his . . . time alone."

Now that was interesting. He may have to make another trip home to interview Mr. Langston. Just because his son didn't think he was here during the week didn't mean he wasn't.

"Before the ladies arrive," Daniel said, "I'd like to speak to you about your relationship with the Brissedons."

"You mean my impending marriage. That, sir, was an arrangement my mother made. Rest assured I have no intention of following through with it."

"You weren't happy about it, then?"

"Happy about it!" Edward barked a laugh. "I couldn't be more furious. They're vulgar creatures, the lot of them."

"Surely Mr. Brissedon would have realized you'd never honor such an arrangement. Unless, of course, there were other, more compelling issues involved."

A muscle twitched in Edward's jaw despite his otherwise calm demeanor. "I can't think what they would be."

"Perhaps to prevent Patrick Desmond from running off with your sister, or worse."

This time the color rose in his cheeks, though he fought to keep his voice even. "My sister is too naive to realize what's good for her."

"But a marriage to Colin Brissedon would certainly end the danger."

He huffed, shaking his head. "Mother thought it would, but all she'd be doing is taking Lydia away from the pup and handing her over to the wolf."

"But Thomas Brissedon saw it as a perfect solution to both problems," Daniel said, more as a statement then a question.

Edward nodded. "It seems he was faced with the same dilemma as my mother. His daughter was seeing someone on the sly, even though the man had been banned from the premises. Though I can certainly understand why he wanted to ensure Brighton Templeton was no longer in the picture, I don't approve of his solution."

"Which was to marry his daughter off to you."

"Exactly, though I doubt the lady is enamored with the arrangement either."

"Why not just see your sister married to someone else, then?" Daniel found the story intriguing, but his gut told him there was more to it than met the eye.

Edward looked as if he was going to be ill. "Patrick came by here the other day while everyone else was out. I arrived home unexpectedly and walked in on him and Lydia in a rather compromising position. I was furious. If word were to get out that Lydia was involved with such a rogue, her reputation would be ruined. Mother insisted on going to Thomas and demanding he keep the little lecher away from my sister."

"And Thomas suggested the mutual marriage agreement was the only way to ensure that."

"Suggested? Thomas out-and-out used his stepson's attempted *intimacy* with Lydia to blackmail my mother into agreeing to those godforsaken marriages. That was his price for keeping the little rake away from my sister." He strode over to the sideboard and poured himself a drink, downing it before speaking again. "But as I stated, I've no intention of going through with it. I very much doubt Kathleen Brissedon will want to see it through either. Her tastes run along much coarser lines."

"You're referring to Brighton Templeton, I presume?"

"Yes, but then the poor girl doesn't know any different, does she? After all, who has she had to compare him with? Certainly not her brothers. One's a blatant philanderer and the other an out-and-out wastrel.

"And yet, blackmail or not, your mother was willing to allow your sister to marry Colin Brissedon, who, as you say, is far worse. In fact, she was there to discuss the wedding plans the night Thomas Brissedon died."

Edward scrubbed his hand across his face. At first, Daniel wasn't sure he would answer, but after cursing under his breath, he did. "My mother doesn't . . . have a need for Colin, at least not at the moment."

"I'm not sure I understand, Mr. Langston."

"It's quite simple, really. She wants Patrick for herself. And that disgusting old reprobate, Thomas Brissedon, was egging the little bastard on. In fact, it wouldn't surprise me if that was the reason my mother was there that night."

"I was told it was to discuss the wedding plans."

Edward let out another laugh before pouring himself a second drink. "Indeed! I fail to see why. She knows I'd never consent. And as for Lydia . . . She defended Patrick's lack of moral fiber, pretending he had no choice in the matter, that he was driven to it by an overbearing stepfather and his stepbrother's poor example. Even knowing her reputation could be destroyed just by being with him, the lovesick fool would have let him court her if I had permitted it."

"What does your father say about all this?"

"My father stays far from the scandal. The truth is, the last I heard he was in Rhode Island. Mind you, I don't suspect he's any better. We're all permitted to do as we please, so long as we keep it discreet."

"Except for your sister, that is?"

"Yes, except for poor Lydia, who knows none of this. I would prefer it was kept that way."

"I see," Daniel remarked in amazement. "So you're saying that your mother and Patrick Desmond were having an affair."

"More of a dalliance, I'd say. After all, Patrick is known for diddling half the young ladies in the county. Why wouldn't Mother have a go?" Edward took a drink and frowned. "Then again, maybe my sister has a point, at least in this case. Thomas may well be have been forcing him into bed with my mother. She's not exactly his type, is she?"

"Why would Thomas Brissedon condone this *dalliance*, let alone demand Patrick take part in it?"

"Were you truly born under a cabbage, Doctor?"

No, only on the wrong side of the sheets. "Just say what you mean, Mr. Langston."

"Thomas wanted my father's custom . . . exclusively. He deluded himself into thinking he could attain it by keeping my mother entertained. Little did he know my mother has no influence over my father's business dealings. I suppose the next step would have been to try and blackmail my father."

Daniel didn't know why he was surprised. People were the same wherever you went, the good and the bad. If what Edward was saying was true, however, Desmond certainly had more than enough reason to want Thomas Brissedon dead. Still, he needed more proof than the word of one angry young man. He cleared his throat before continuing.

"Regardless of the circumstances, I will still have to speak to your mother and sister, though if your father is in Rhode Island, I imagine I can forgo his interview for the time being. Of course, it doesn't completely let him off the hook. He could have hired someone."

"You misunderstand, Doctor. My father has a mistress in Rhode Island. He couldn't care less what my mother does here."

"Unless, of course, she becomes an embarrassment."

Edward flopped down in one of the heavily brocaded chairs, suited more to torture than to comfort, though its current occupant didn't seem to notice. "Yes, I suppose you're right. Though Mother will just deny it all, you know. She's under the delusion that people will believe her word over anyone else's."

"Nevertheless, I will need to question her."

Edward seemed to resolve himself to something. "Yes, of course." He stood abruptly and called for the stout gentleman. "Standish, call for my mother at once. The doctor would like to question her about Thomas Brissedon's untimely death." The butler nodded, then immediately walked back out into the hallway.

"Tell me, Mr. Langston," Daniel said, "just out of curiosity. I understand your dislike of Patrick Desmond, and even Colin Brissedon, for that matter, but what is it you find so abhorrent about Miss Brissedon?"

Edward swallowed hard, as if his Adam's apple had grown too large for his throat. "There is nothing wrong with the lady, but I think we would both rather wed someone we cared for. Too many marry out of duty or because it's the thing to do. I wouldn't have that for Kathleen. Nor, do I think, would you, Doctor."

A spark lit in Edward's eye, and Daniel looked back at his notebook, praying the heat rising in his face was not apparent. "It has nothing to do with your sexual preferences, then?" Daniel asked, effectively countering Edward's pretentious remark.

"I beg your pardon, sir! Why would you even suggest such a thing?"

"Just a rumor I'd heard, obviously erroneous."

"Far worse than that, Doctor! It's dangerous. I would appreciate knowing who's spreading such malicious accounts about my personal life."

"I'm afraid I can't divulge that information, but suffice it to say, I will hold any fallacious information in the strictest confidence."

Edward looked as if he were about to protest further, but Elizabeth Langston came to the door and swept into the room. She was dramatic. Daniel had to give her that.

"My dear Dr. O'Halleran," she said, "how may I be of assistance?"

"It's good to see you more relaxed today, ma'am," Daniel said.

"Yes, thank heavens I was able to escape unscathed." She sat down in another monstrosity of a chair and pressed her hand against her chest. "I don't know if I could have survived one more moment there."

"It was quite safe, ma'am. I feel certain that whoever killed Thomas Brissedon was after him alone."

"I would hope so. To think of those poor children alone in that house."

Edward scrunched his face up in disgust. "They're hardly children or alone, Mother. Don't be so dramatic." He downed the remains of his drink and turned to Daniel. "If you don't need me anymore, I do have some business to attend to."

"Yes, by all means, Mr. Langston. Just one more thing, however. The scratches on your hands, may I ask how you came by them?"

"Pruning the roses, I suppose. The gardener tends to butcher them, so I prefer to care for them myself. Why?"

"Thank you for your time, sir," Daniel said without answering. "You will be available should I need to question you further?"

"Yes, of course. With Father away, the mundane running of the business is left to me. If you'll excuse me."

"Such a serious boy," Elizabeth commented as her son closed the parlor doors behind him, though she didn't say anything else until she heard his footfall on the stairs. "He never seems to bother with anyone outside his small circle of friends."

"Perhaps he enjoys their company?"

"I'm sure he does." Her lips curled into a snarl, the thought clearly revolting her, though the expression lasted no longer than a moment. "Still, he should get out more, sample the finer things in life, especially those bestowed by the ladies who frequent the seedier establishments of the city. A man needs to bring a certain amount of experience to a marriage, don't you agree, Doctor?"

"I don't know about that, ma'am, but perhaps your son prefers the favors of gentlemen."

Her eyes widened, her hand clutching the fine chiffon of her skirts. "I beg your pardon, sir! To suggest such perversions is not only cruel, it's dangerous."

"I meant no disrespect, ma'am. I only thought—"

"Well, you thought wrong, sir! As you doubtless already know, my son is to be wed to Miss Kathleen Brissedon in the very near future." She brought a hanky up to her eyes, though Daniel was sure he didn't see a tear lingering there. "This is all just so horrific. Why, only the day before, Thomas and I had met to discuss our children's futures, and now the poor man is dead, murdered in his own bed. How dreadful!"

"Yes, it is. Can you tell me, though, why did you meet with Mr. Brissedon to discuss wedding plans when your son has no intention of going through with such a marriage?"

"Doesn't he? I suppose it's possible he's smitten by some other lady. He doesn't tell me everything, you know.

I'm sure there are things you keep from your mother, aren't there, Doctor?"

Did she have something in her eye, or was she actually flirting with him? "My mother died when I was six." That always stopped them cold.

"Oh. Well, I'm terribly sorry, but you must know what I mean."

"It's quite possible, I suppose," Daniel said, glad the woman had stopped winking at him or whatever it was she was trying to do. "Why make such arrangements, then, when you haven't even consulted him?"

She sputtered as if she'd just fallen in the lake and was coming up for air. Daniel had to bite his lip to keep from laughing out loud.

"He spent so much time at the Brissedons'," she finally managed to say. "Thomas and I just assumed it was to see Kathleen."

"Did he? He never mentioned it."

"Well, he wouldn't, would he? Oh dear, I hope it wasn't to see one of those maids of theirs. How gauche! More to the taste of Patrick Desmond, I think."

"Really? I had heard Mr. Desmond was seeing your daughter, Lydia. In fact, was that not the reason you agreed to a marriage between her and Colin Brissedon?"

"I agreed to it because Thomas assured me that my daughter's future would be secure. And before you ask, yes, I know Colin is a bit of a rogue, but Thomas promised to see to his son's rehabilitation and make sure my daughter had her own accounts. As for Patrick Desmond, he was nothing more than a passing infatuation that could have been easily dismissed in any case."

"But if she cared for him, why not make the same arrangement between her and Patrick?"

"Thomas would never have agreed to such an arrangement. Patrick is, after all, only his stepson, and a poor one at that!"

"Is that the only reason, or is there another, more personal, perhaps?"

"I have no idea what you're referring to, Doctor!" A twitch appeared in her left cheek, though she covered it by turning her face to the side.

"Then I'm afraid I'll have to be blunt, Mrs. Langston. Are you now, or have you ever been, involved with Patrick Desmond?"

"I beg your pardon, sir!" Elizabeth rose to her feet, the twitch pronounced now as the blood rushed to her face. "I'm a respectable married woman and do not appreciate your implications. If this is to be the tone of your questioning, then I must insist you leave my home at once. I will be notifying your superiors."

"You should certainly do as you feel necessary, ma'am, but I am only following through on an accusation made by your son. It's my job to ascertain if there's any credence to it."

"Edward told you that?" She flopped back down in the chair, grasping on to the heavily carved arm. "How could he imply such a thing?"

"He seems to be very angry with you . . . and your husband, for that matter."

"Yes, I suppose he is. He doesn't understand how quickly things can deteriorate. Our marriage was arranged, but we truly thought we cared for each other. Apparently not. Though Benjamin and I have made sure neither of the children are touched by our . . . little indiscretions. At least we thought we had until recently."

"Children are far more observant than we imagine."

"I suppose they are. Of course, Edward blames me for it all. He has no idea what that man put me through. I don't know what to do." She began to weep, dabbing her eyes with the hanky again. "He says such hateful things."

"Please, ma'am." The sudden onset of the woman's tears flustered him, even if he wasn't sure they were real. Though his mother had taught him to be sympathetic, there was no way he was going to let this display of emotion hinder his questioning. "I didn't mean to cause you any undue sorrow. I'm sure your son will soon realize all you've sacrificed."

Elizabeth blew her nose, sniffling delicately. "I suppose you're right. He's always been close to his father. It's just so trying at times." She cleared her throat, then, after straightening her dress, she continued. "Now, where were we? Oh yes, Patrick Desmond. I don't know what he'll receive from his stepfather's will, but I can't imagine it will be much. He'll never be able to give Lydia the financial security she deserves. Colin, on the other hand, will be quite able."

Daniel frowned. How convenient of Mrs. Langston to forget where they'd actually left off. He hadn't. "Yes, I can see your reasoning; however, it was quite possible that Lydia and Patrick might have decided to ... force the issue."

"What do you mean?"

"Patrick admitted to spending the night of his father's murder at home, but not alone. Though he did refuse to give me the young lady's name, I can only assume it was Lydia."

"That's preposterous! The guest room is right next to Patrick's. Surely I would have heard if something untoward was going on. The walls really are quite thin."

Actually, they're not. "You're probably right. Just one more question, ma'am. You arrived at the Brissedons' rather late that night. May I ask why you didn't wait until the morning?"

"Yes, of course. I wanted to get an early start, and to be truthful, I tired of hearing Edward's complaints about his proposed marriage."

So she did know he didn't approve. "He's a grown man. If he refuses to marry Miss Brissedon, there is little you can do about it."

"My son will do what is needed or pay the consequences, I assure you."

"Consequences?" Daniel asked, though he was afraid she had already realized her slip.

"Yes, of course. His father could cut off his trust fund."

Edward had a bigger worry than that, but as the woman had already denied it, there was no sense returning to it. At least not at the moment. "Thank you for being so candid with me, Mrs. Langston. Now if you would call Miss Langston, I'd like to speak to her as well since she is at least in some way involved with Patrick Desmond and Colin Brissedon."

"Only in passing! She never really had anything to do with Patrick, and her engagement to Colin has not even been announced yet."

"Still, she does know them, and I would like to ask her a few questions."

"Of course." Elizabeth smiled politely as she called for the butler, though Daniel could see she was uncomfortable with it.

Within a few seconds, the young girl had answered her mother's summons. She sat down daintily on the royal blue sofa across from Daniel, and he could immediately understand why Patrick had become so agitated when ordered to stop seeing her. Her long blond hair fell softly over her shoulders, and a shy blush touched her cheeks as she gazed quizzically at her mother.

"The doctor needs to speak to you, dear," Elizabeth said. "It's about Patrick Desmond. I think there may be a question as to the boy's whereabouts on the night his father was murdered. I told him you weren't with the scoundrel, but I guess he needs to hear it from you."

"Something like that," Daniel said, annoyed by Elizabeth Langston's attempt to shade her daughter's answer. "But if you don't mind, I must insist on speaking to Miss Langston alone."

"That's highly improper, Doctor. I must think of my daughter's reputation."

Rather than point out again that he was a doctor, he decided to take another tack. "Have you a lady's maid, Miss Langston?"

"Yes, sir, she's just upstairs."

"Would you go fetch her, please?"

"I'll send her down—" Mrs. Langston began, but Daniel stopped her before she could go any further.

"If you wouldn't mind, I'd prefer Miss Langston to do it." The old woman opened her mouth to protest, but once more Daniel cut her off. "I must insist."

"Very well." Elizabeth twisted her lips in an expression that did nothing to enhance her natural beauty. "Please tell my daughter I'll be in my sitting room if she should need me."

Lydia returned a moment later with her lady's maid, who was even more demure than Lydia. The girl sat quietly in the corner, mending a piece of clothing. Daniel didn't look close enough to see what it was, but as it was white, he assumed it was an undergarment. He turned to face Lydia, who sat on the same sofa she'd vacated not moments before.

They both waited until they heard Elizabeth's bedroom door close, but before Daniel could ask a question, Lydia jumped up, tears shining in her soft brown eyes. "You don't suspect Patrick, do you? I know he didn't get along with his stepfather, but he would never murder anyone. He's not capable of doing such a thing."

"You'd be surprised what people are capable of when pressed, Miss Langston, even the most innocent of young ladies."

"Me?" Her eyes widened, and she flopped back down on the uncomfortable sofa. "But I don't even know Mr. Brissedon. Why would I want to harm him?"

"Perhaps you were angry about his plans to marry you off to his son, Colin, especially if it was Patrick you cared for."

"Oh, that." She let out a weary sigh. "I'm afraid you're wrong on both counts, Doctor. My brother never would have agreed to such a marriage, and as for Patrick . . ." She shrugged and dabbed her hanky to her nose, much as her mother had done, only the tears in her eyes were all too authentic. "I'm afraid he doesn't want to see me anymore, though I suspect it's just to protect my reputation."

"When did he tell you this?"

She had the good manners to blush, a soft hint of pink that accentuated her youthful cheeks. "I'm afraid I summoned him here under false pretenses the other day, pretending the note was from my mother."

"Does your mother send him notes often?"

"No, of course not, but he takes piano lessons with her, so I wrote that she needed to change the day and asked him to come on Wednesday. You see, I knew Mother was going into the village, and Edward had plans to go to the track with some friends."

"Ah, so you would be alone."

She sat up straighter and smoothed her skirt. "No, we weren't alone. I'm not that foolish. Standish, our butler, was across the hall polishing the silver. I just wanted to ask Patrick why he hadn't asked to court me. That is what a gentleman does when he cares for a lady, isn't it?"

"I believe so, yes." He had to suppress a smile. "And what did you find out?"

"He said it was because he didn't want to sully my reputation, but when I insisted it didn't matter, he claimed it was all just a game."

"What sort of a game?"

"One to get me into bed, apparently, but I don't believe it. He just wanted to upset me, so that I'd hate him and never want to see him again."

"Clearly, it didn't work."

"It did at first. I was furious with him, but then I realized he was just doing it to protect me."

"So did you . . . see him again? The night of his father's murder, perhaps?"

"Is that what Patrick said?"

"It really doesn't matter what he said, Miss Langston. I'm asking you. Were you with Patrick the night of his father's death?"

Lydia's face grew pale, and she began fiddling with the bow on her dress. She took a deep breath to calm herself, then closed her eyes momentarily. Finally, she swallowed hard and, opening her eyes, answered Daniel's question, though he knew it would be a lie.

"Yes, sir, but I promised him I would never tell anyone. He worries so about my reputation."

Yep, she's lying, to protect Patrick, no doubt. "Did you see your mother there that morning?"

"My mother!" She swallowed again and returned to worrying the bow on her skirt, unable to look him in the eye. "No, she doesn't even know I was there."

"She stayed at the Brissedons' that night, hoping to get an early start on the wedding plans."

Lydia's eyes darted around the room, no doubt searching for what to say. "I slipped out through the back stairs before dawn."

"How did you get out? That door is locked."

"Yes, but Patrick has the key his father gave him. Not even his stepfather knows about it."

Daniel didn't believe it for a minute. More than likely, Mrs. Langston had been with him herself, but as Lydia seemed to have no idea about her mother's extracurricular activities, he decided to let it be. One thing he was fairly sure of: Lydia could be crossed off his list of suspects.

"Back to the marriage arrangements, then. Your brother was very angry about them, wasn't he? Maybe angry enough to lash out at Thomas."

She sat up straighter in the chair, alarm crossing her innocent face. "Oh no! Not at all. He was angry, yes, but he knew not even Mother could force us to go through with them."

"What if Thomas had some leverage, information your brother might not want to be made public?"

Panic suffused the young girl's face. "No, he couldn't . . . I mean . . . I can't imagine what that could be. Not that it would matter. Edward doesn't have it in him to kill another man."

Lydia might have been in the dark about her mother's sexual proclivities, but she was obviously well aware of her brother's. Questioning her further on that subject, however, would likely cause her undue distress, and since he'd already learned what he wanted, he chose to change the subject.

"What about you? How did you feel about marrying him? Colin, I mean?"

"Awful! I was terribly upset when Mother told us, but then I knew Edward would never allow it. He is, after all, the man of the house when Father's away, which is pretty much always. And even if Father were here, he'd listen to Edward's advice."

"So there was no doubt in your mind he was going to put a stop to it?"

"Oh yes, I'm sure he would have. He was furious when he came home from the Brissedons' that evening. He and Mother had a terrible fight over it."

"Why do you think your mother made such arrangements? She must have realized you'd both be upset."

"I imagine she wanted to keep me away from Patrick, though Colin is far worse. He'll inherit a good portion of his father's estate, however, where Patrick only has a meager trust fund. She was just looking out for us, I suppose."

"What did you think when you heard Edward was to marry Kathleen?"

She thought for a moment, and this time Daniel sensed she would be telling the truth. "I thought they might be happy. Edward would do his duty by her, regardless of his inclinations . . . I mean the circumstances. In spite of what you may think of him, he is an honorable man."

Somehow Daniel believed she was right. "Thank you, Miss Langston," he said, giving her an encouraging smile. "You've been most helpful."

"You don't really believe Patrick could do something like this, do you, Doctor?" Her eyes seemed to be pleading with him, but it wouldn't be fair to give her false hope.

"I'm afraid I haven't ruled anyone out as yet, nor do I pretend to have even the slightest notion of who the guilty party may be. These things take time, you understand."

"Yes, but it couldn't have been Patrick, for I was with him all night. I left right before he went down to breakfast."

She had no idea how she'd just contradicted herself. He didn't remember Izzy ever being that naive, but then she had three older brothers to wizen her up. "That's true," he said, although it wasn't, "and for a lady like yourself to admit such a transgression, you must love him very much. Perhaps even enough to lie for him," he added, not wanting to let her think he'd completely bought her story. Then, with a slight bow, he headed for the door. "Good day, Miss Langston."

Before she could protest, Daniel was out the front door and down the steps. He'd agreed to meet the sergeant at Murdock's, a restaurant situated not far from the law firm of Grayson and Brice, to see what he'd discovered that morning. Then, after speaking to Brighton Templeton and the Stockbridges, he'd head back to the Brissedons', for he'd received a message from Kathleen that morning, asking if he could meet her there around three.

CHAPTER 22

"Over here, Sergeant," Daniel called from a corner table of Murdock's. "Join me in a bite of lunch. If I'm correct, your morning has been far too busy for you to stop and eat."

"That it has, sir!" The officer sat down, placing his hat on the chair beside him, and ordered the crab cakes before taking out his notebook. "Now, where was I. Ah yes, about Colin Brissedon's gambling. He's no small fry. Plays often and heavily. Tends to get himself in quite a bit of trouble, but dear old daddy always makes good on his bets. Brighton Templeton plays just as heavily but far more successfully. Thomas Brissedon does *not* bail him out when the need arises, however. Colin has, though, on more than one occasion."

"But if he had the cash, why not just pay his own debts?"

"I don't suppose he could afford to. As I mentioned, Templeton plays heavily all right, but he's a far better gambler than Brissedon, so his debts, while still substantial, are nowhere near as significant. The amount Colin Brissedon has handed out on Brighton's behalf wouldn't put a dent in his own obligations."

"What about Patrick Desmond?"

"Covers his own debt, what little there is. He goes to the track now and then, but that's about the extent of it. He prefers playing with the ladies, and not the ones who charge for their favors."

"Who, then?"

"Someone here for the summer or perhaps a neighbor's daughter, but mostly their help, like Radcliffe said. He's quite charming, they say, though word is he's received a good beating or two when a lady's brothers discovered him and their sister going at it in the hay."

"What about Colin? Did you find out anything about a child?"

"Yes, sir. Radcliffe sent over the payment information and an address in the Cotswolds. I even spoke to the girl. She refused to say what Brissedon was sending her the money for, said I'd need to ask him about that. When I inquired how her son was doing, though, she said growing like a weed. I pushed it a bit more and hinted at him being three months or so now, and she bubbled with pride, saying he'd be six months in a week, with dark hair just like his daddy, though she hastily added 'God rest his soul' to that bit."

"Ask about a woman's son, and it's amazing how she'll warm up to you. I wish we could be sure it wasn't someone Thomas paid off to pretend to be the girl. Would he really want a kid around that could claim to be his grandson?"

"Well, I thought about that, sir, so last night I called a friend of mine who works with one of the passenger lines. He got back to me first thing this morning. Sure enough, two first-class tickets were indeed purchased by Thomas Brissedon on a ship that departed for London in October of 1903. They were used by a Mrs. Annabell O'Dwyer and her aunt. Pete said the steward remembered her right off because she just didn't seem to fit the fine clothes she wore, plus she looked like she was about ready to give birth there and then. He said she appeared to be surprisingly well off, though."

"Good, I'm glad to hear it. I'd hate to think anyone could be so callous as to contemplate killing his own grandchild. At least he's seen to their care, which is more than some would do." Daniel was reminded of his own mother but quickly put the thought out of his head.

"Yes, sir, I know what you mean." They ate in companionable silence for a few moments before the sergeant spoke again. "Oh, and I did manage to find out the name of that detective Mrs. Desmond hired."

Daniel grinned. If only he'd had this kind of cooperation in the city. "How did you manage that?"

"Seems he's been poking around here and there. Made a few calls from Conklin's Confectionery. Even asked some folks what they thought about this Brissedon fella Mrs. Desmond married. Got an earful back from more than a few about Colin and Patrick, no doubt."

"But they knew who he was?"

"Of course they did, Doc. He has a small office down on Railroad Street. His name's Alexander Morton."

Daniel took another bite of his fried clams, then wiped his mouth before speaking again. "So the chances are fairly good that Patrick did know who his mother hired."

"I hate to say it, but there's no doubt about it. He was seen talking to the man on a number of occasions. The question is, why lie about it? I suppose he might just be scared, especially if Morton found out anything of interest."

Daniel nodded. "Something that linked Thomas Brissedon to his father, for example." He took a sip of tea and wiped his mouth again. "This case gets more and more interesting by the minute. Do you know what I found out this morning? It seems Thomas Brissedon was forcing his

279

stepson to entertain a certain wealthy woman in return for her convincing her husband to send his business Brissedon's way."

"You're joking! He's not much more than a boy. Who could blame the poor lad for feeling a bit resentful?"

"Unfortunately, it gives him yet another strong motive for murder. Still, it's going to take more than that to convince me he's guilty." He took some money out of his pocket and laid it on the table. "Right then, Sergeant, are you finished with your lunch?"

"I am, sir, and a fine one it was. Almost as good as the Missus's."

"Then it's off to see Mr. Templeton, I think. His offices aren't far from here. Tell me, do you think he really loves Kathleen Brissedon?"

The sergeant took a deep breath. "Well, that's hard to say, Doc, not having spent much time with him. One thing I can tell you. There's another lad who does."

"Is there? And who would that be?" Daniel asked with surprise.

"Oh, I think you know him quite well, Doc," the sergeant replied with an impish grin. "I just don't understand why he's so afraid to admit it."

Daniel scowled at the man before taking a deep breath himself. "All right! I do find the lady enchanting, but I've a job to do. I can't have that kind of emotion clouding my judgment."

"You may know all about the body, Doc," Owens said, patting Daniel on the back, "but you've got a lot to learn about love. The heart knows its own mind. But don't fret so about it," he added as he walked on ahead. "Like I said, she's as innocent as the new-fallen snow. Any dolt can see that."

Daniel hoped the sergeant was right, but either way, there could never be anything between them. Daniel had gone that route once, and paying court to a wealthy debutante had brought him nothing but humiliation. Regardless of his sister's advice, he vowed never to subject himself to that again, even for the lovely Miss Brissedon.

The law firm of Grayson and Brice was a prestigious institution indeed. For Brighton Templeton to acquire a position there, he would need to have excellent prospects and be well on his way to establishing himself among the better classes. Why, then, had Thomas Brissedon objected so vehemently to the young man courting his daughter?

"Mr. Templeton, please," Daniel inquired on entering the building.

"Mr. Templeton!" The young man at the reception desk let out a scornful cackle. "Hey, Brighton, get up here."

"Right away, sir," a messenger sitting at a rickety desk in the back corner said. He put down his pencil at once and walked up to the front desk. "What is it you need, Mr. Sanders?"

"There's a gentleman here to see you."

"A messenger!" Daniel said, unable to keep the tinge of amusement from his voice. "You're not even a clerk."

"No, sir. I never claimed to be. Is there something I can help you with?"

"Dr. O'Halleran," Daniel said, once more gaining his composure, though Sergeant Owens still had a look of joviality on his face. Daniel gave the sergeant a firm look, then continued. "I'd like to speak to you about the death of Mr. Thomas Brissedon."

"Oh, I see." Brighton's face seemed to blanch. "I have my lunch break in ten minutes, sir. Could we wait and talk somewhere a bit more private?"

"That should be fine. We'll just wait over there, if that's all right."

"Yes, sir. Thank you."

True to his word, Brighton joined them in exactly ten minutes, and they made their way back to the very restaurant Daniel and the sergeant had left not fifteen minutes before. The waiter gave them a funny look before taking their orders, though only Brighton actually ordered lunch.

"I'll get right to the point, Mr. Templeton. You have by now heard of Mr. Brissedon's death?"

"Yes, sir, I read it in the papers."

"You didn't know before that?"

"No, sir! I'd just seen Kathleen on Thursday night. Not alone, of course. Her maid accompanied her . . . the little one with curly hair . . ."

"Molly?" Daniel said, finding the man more and more disagreeable by the moment.

"Yes, that's the one. Either she or Colin would accompany her and busy themselves with a book or some such thing while we talked. Anyway, we only meet twice a week, so I wasn't to see her again until Monday.

"Didn't Colin Brissedon tell you? He is your friend, I believe."

"Yes, sir, he is, but I hadn't seen him for a few days."

"Was that the day he paid off your gambling debt?"

Brighton hesitated for a moment, but then answered. "Yes, sir." He must have been slightly embarrassed and so tried to explain. "You see, I did get in a bit over my head this time, but Colin understands that. He's a good friend, and so he helped me out. I want you to know I have every intention of paying him back, even though he doesn't expect it."

"What did he want in return?"

"I beg your pardon! He didn't want anything. He's a friend, and out of friendship he came to my aid. There's nothing more to it than that."

"He's helped you before, then?"

"Yes, on occasion." He glanced nervously around the small restaurant, as if gauging whether or not he could make a break for it. "And I've come to his aid just the same. Not with money, perhaps, but with a lady or two who's been, shall we say, a bit too aggressive. Friends do that for one another."

"Did you help him with Annabell O'Dwyer?"

"Annie! You know about her?"

"Did you help him with that?"

"I wasn't going to say it was mine like Thomas wanted, if that's what you mean, but Colin never expected me to. The old man even offered me money to marry her. Of course, it wasn't much more than I'm getting at the law firm. He ended up handing her ten times that!"

"Would you have taken that amount if he'd offered it to you instead?"

"I'm in love with Kathleen, sir. I would never do anything that would keep me from her, not for any amount of money. Thomas thought he'd found the perfect way to separate us, but he was wrong. I may not have a tremendous job at the moment, but it's fair enough, and I'm going to school to improve myself. Mr. Brice has graciously promised to consider me for a position as a law clerk after I earn my degree."

"You hope to be an attorney one day? Where are you attending school?"

"Columbia University. And I've only another year to go. I couldn't afford to finish as quickly as Colin did."

"That's quite a trek every day."

"I stay in the city during the school year. Mr. Brice has an office there."

"And what of Kathleen?"

"I come out occasionally on weekends, and Colin brings her in from time to time. We trust each other, so there's no need for concern, barring the ache our being unable to see each other brings. Besides, it will be worth it. Once I finish my degree, Mr. Brissedon will have no cause to object to my courting his daughter. Though I guess that will no longer be an issue in any event. Colin certainly won't disapprove."

"When you heard of his plans to marry her off to Edward Langston, it must have caused you a bit of concern."

"No, not at all. Thomas could never stand to see Kate unhappy. Whatever else he was, he was a good father, to her at least. He would have done anything to ensure her happiness. Colin would have simply pointed that out to him. He might have protested at first, but eventually he would have seen it was a mistake and changed his mind."

"What if it was too late?"

"There was no fear of that!" Brighton's lip curled into a snide smile, a telling glint in his eye. "Edward Langston would never have gone through with it. Word is, he has no taste for women, you see."

"Word from Colin Brissedon, no doubt."

"Yes, that's right. In fact, if it came down to it, Edward may have even offered to pay me to marry her. An assignment I would have eagerly accepted, I assure you."

"He doesn't like the Brissedons very much, does he? I mean, he won't even allow his sister to see Patrick Desmond."

"Well, first of all, poor Paddy has the same problem I do: a shortage of substantial funds. In other words, not well placed. Everyone knows Thomas has left him practically nothing. Maybe not by my standards or even yours, but to a man like Edward Langston, his meager trust fund leaves Paddy in the undesirable category. More than that, he wouldn't want to give his mother another reason to visit the Brissedon household."

"Why's that?" Daniel asked, though he was fairly sure he knew the answer.

"Aside from the help, I think Jeremy's the only male in that family Elizabeth Langston hasn't bedded."

"Elizabeth was Thomas Brissedon's paramour?"

"Well, she was until her tastes turned to Patrick. I don't suppose Thomas gave a damn, though. She was nothing more than a means to an end for him."

"You mean a way to acquire her husband's business."

Edward shrugged. "That's certainly the impression I got, and it would be just his style."

"And how did you become privy to the intimate goings-on at the Brissedon household, especially being you weren't allowed in the house?"

"I may have been banned from the house, but not from hearing the gossip. As I said, I meet Kathleen twice a week."

"And she was privy to her father's liaisons?"

"No, but Colin was. He'd stay and talk sometimes after Kathleen would go in. Besides, I'd see things while I'd be waiting for her. It wasn't hard to figure out. Thomas thought he was so smart, learning everyone's secrets and using them to get his way. Well, he had a few secrets of his own, and if anyone found out, they could make it very difficult for him."

"What kind of secrets?"

"Let's just say, if anyone's a murderer, it's Thomas himself."

"Go on," Daniel said, his patience wearing thin.

"I was raised on the Lower East Side, Dr. O'Halleran. I remember Cornelius Desmond and don't believe for one second he beat and raped that young woman or murdered the old man, for that matter. Many a family would have starved if not for him, my own included. Then out of nowhere, Thomas Brissedon appears to console his grieving widow. How convenient! There's no way Cornelius Desmond was flat broke either. He always had a pocketful of dough, and everyone knew it. Not the day he was found dead, though. His pockets were empty. The kind of blunt he used to carry could get someone in all the right doors. A grieving widow's, for instance."

"You think Thomas Brissedon murdered Cornelius Desmond, robbed him, then used his money to set himself up as a wealthy immigrant?"

"It wouldn't surprise me. Of course, I have no way of proving it either. People rise and fall around there like a whore's knickers. It's hard to keep track."

"But if everyone knew the kind of money Desmond was used to carrying, maybe someone decided to help himself and things just got ugly."

Brighton shook his head. "No, sir, and why would they? If you found yourself short, all you needed to do was ask, and Neily would help you out. Everybody knew that as well. Killing him would be like killing the goose that laid the golden egg."

Daniel couldn't argue with that. "Did Colin know about his father's past?"

"Colin!" Brighton laughed. "I doubt it. Thomas kept his children hidden away in some boarding school. Colin's all right, though, nothing like his old man."

"You get along quite well with him, then? How did you meet?"

"At Columbia. He wasn't working *his* way through, though, that's for sure."

"You seem to have done all right for yourself—coming from such humble beginnings."

"I worked hard from the time I was eight, saved most of what I earned . . ."

"Not to mention you're a fairly decent gambler, and when you aren't, you can always count on your friend Colin to pay your debts off for you."

He shrugged. "So what? He has plenty of cabbage. His old man might get madder than a wet hen at him from time to time, but ultimately he pays his debts. Lord knows they were ten times worse than mine."

The more he talked, the more the hard Lower East Side tough emerged. "I suppose that's true." Forbes was right. The guy was a rounder. "You said you'd meet Kathleen by the lake twice a week, that you met her Thursday night."

"Yes, of course. Molly accompanied her. As a matter of fact, the girl dozed off and Kathleen and I spent a lovely evening together." Daniel lifted his eyebrows. "Please, Doctor, get your mind out of the gutter. Not the way you think. She's too fine a lady for that. We just talked, discussing what to do about her proposed marriage to Edward."

Daniel nodded. "Murder her father, for instance."

Brighton's eyes opened almost as wide as his mouth, and he looked around, lowering his voice. "No, of course not. I told you. Once Colin pointed out the folly of such an arrangement, he would have called it off."

"Kathleen knew about Edward Langston's preferences, then?"

"Now you are being ridiculous," Brighton said with a scoff. "That's not something a gentleman speaks to a lady about. She simply believed her father would see reason."

"Did you see anyone else that night?"

"Yes, as a matter of fact, I did. Just after Kathleen arrived. That groomsman of theirs, Trevor something or other, he was sneaking over to the main house. He's diddling one of their maids, no doubt about it. Even got a bun in the oven, according to Colin. That's why the old man fired her."

"It was Molly he fired, not Lizzie."

"Really! Are you certain? Perhaps that's why Colin accompanied Kate that night."

Sergeant Owens had to squeeze his nose to keep from snorting. This man was a series of contradictions, but Daniel was sure he'd manage to concoct an explanation for that one as well, so instead of bringing attention to it, he continued his questioning.

"How could you know he'd fired the maid? Kathleen and Colin didn't even know about it until the next day, and the last time you saw either of them was the night before his death."

"That was the last time before I read the news in the paper. I did manage to stop by the house early this morning to pay my respects. Colin mentioned it in passing. His father didn't think it would look very respectable to have an unwed mother for their maid. Besides, Thomas never was too happy about another mouth to feed. He only kept Patrick around because of his . . . *significant* contribution."

Daniel scratched his head, astounded by the amount of skullduggery that went on, for lack of a better word. But then, why did he delude himself into thinking there was anywhere it didn't go on? Still, he couldn't let it slip by this time. "Molly wasn't with child."

"Oh, right, well, Thomas didn't need much of a reason to dismiss someone."

"I suppose not. Did you see anyone else that night? Colin, perhaps?"

Brighton looked at Daniel warily, then answered, though it was obvious he was nervous about his reply. "Yes, as a matter of fact, I did, just a little after Kathleen had gone in." He must have realized the contradiction in this statement, for he corrected himself. "She was chilly and went in to get her shawl."

Brighton tried to cover his tracks, but he wasn't very good at it. It had been sweltering that night. Daniel remembered because he'd slept in the buff with his window open. "You were up at the house, then?"

"Only by the back hallway door. Colin came out and told me not to worry about the marriage plans his father had made. So I didn't."

"You were that sure his father would change his mind?"

"Yes, sir, as I told you, he loved Kathleen and couldn't bear to see her unhappy. Colin was sure of it as well, and I had no reason to doubt him. If there's nothing else,

Doctor, I do have to return to work." He stood, picking up what was left of his lunch and wrapping it in his handkerchief.

"Of course. Thank you for your time. Just one more thing before you leave. Those scratches on your chin, how did you come by them?"

"The other night I reached into the rose bushes to pick Kathleen a flower. I guess the thorns must have grazed me a bit."

With that, Brighton nodded and headed back to work. Sergeant Owens finished the last bit of his ice cream, then sat back with a satisfied sigh and waited for Daniel to speak.

"An ambitious young man, wouldn't you say?" Daniel said.

"Oh yes, sir, but I guess there's nothing wrong with setting your sights and aiming high."

"Perhaps a bit too high."

"I can't rightly say, Doc, but there's one thing I do wonder about."

"What's that?"

"What kind of a *gentleman* confesses to spending the night with his sweetheart, even if it wasn't *doing what you think*? Seems to me he'd be a bit more concerned about preserving her reputation. Perhaps it wasn't only his lack of money, but his lack of honor that worried Thomas Brissedon."

Daniel peered over his cup, taking a sip of tea before responding. "Perhaps, but from what I've heard so far, the money issue would have been quite sufficient."

"I suppose you're right there." Owens scratched his head. "I'm a bit confused, though. Was it Molly or Colin who was chaperoning?"

Daniel shook his head, chuckling. "Your guess is as good as mine, Sergeant."

"Do you think he's just nervous?"

"I think he was trying to establish an alibi. The question is for whom: himself, Colin, or Kathleen."

Owens nodded. "That would explain some of the inconsistencies. I mean, Miss Brissedon going in for her shawl? God in heaven, it was so hot Thursday night I nearly sweat my . . ." He stopped short, clearing his throat. "Well, you know what I mean."

Daniel couldn't help but chuckle at the sergeant's flushed face. "I know exactly what you mean, and if you did what I did, the Missus mustn't have been bothered at all."

Owens rolled his eyes. "That's the thing, Doc, she was hot and bothered, and while the result was more than pleasant, it didn't do a thing to cool me down."

Daniel laughed out loud and smacked the sergeant on the back as they stood and headed for the door. "I don't imagine it did."

"So where to now, Doc?"

"To see Mr. and Mrs. Phillip Stockbridge, I think. Now there's a man with a grudge, even if it is an honorable one."

CHAPTER 23

The Stockbridge home was a humble abode when compared to that of either the Langstons or the Brissedons. A modest two-story, it sat on a pretty tree-lined street amongst others of similar construction, yet Daniel felt it was probably a far happier place to grow up.

Mrs. Stockbridge answered the door herself, and when Daniel introduced himself, she immediately invited him in. Then, after offering him a cup of tea, she excused herself and called for her husband.

"Dr. O'Halleran, wasn't it?" Phillip Stockbridge asked, in a far calmer mood than he'd been at their last meeting. "I would like to apologize for my outburst yesterday. Had I any idea of what had taken place, I would have tempered my tone somewhat, though I must admit I'm not in the least bit troubled by his demise. Still, no man deserves to die the way he did."

"Could you tell me exactly what happened between you and Thomas Brissedon?"

"Yes, for years I've had an exclusive contract with Mr. Talbot, a builder here in town. However, when he expanded his order this year, as did two firms I work with in Manhattan, I realized I'd be unable to fulfill my commitments. It would mean giving up my connections in Manhattan or losing my exclusive agreement with Talbot."

"So rather than lose any," Daniel said, "you offered to share the Talbot contract with Thomas. In return for what, may I ask?"

"With the understanding he wouldn't underbid me on the two Manhattan firms."

"Wouldn't other mills be bidding as well—Mr. Bailey and Mr. Overton, for example?"

"Yes, I suppose some of them would, but their bids would be honest. I felt sure I could underbid any fair price. The bid Thomas would submit, however, would be so low it couldn't possibly be done."

"I don't understand. How did he make any money?"

"A number of ways. In some cases, he'd deliver the first shipment, then announce he'd have to pull out of the contract because his costs had gone up considerably and he'd be unable to fulfill his commitment. In other cases, he'd deliver an inferior product. I think in one instance, he might have even resorted to robbing a company's warehouse and selling them back their own goods."

"Couldn't they sue him, at least in the first two instances?"

"Technically, yes, but by then their projects were well underway. It would cost them far more in lost time and damaged reputations to have to go through the bidding process again."

"So they agreed to Thomas's new terms. But surely they'd never work with him again."

"You would think that, but they did, consistently. Thomas has beautiful lumber, but . . ." Phillip shook his head. "He'd raise the price with every new project, and they still stayed with him."

"Do you think he was blackmailing them?"

"It has crossed my mind, but I've no way to prove it. They certainly aren't going to tell me."

"Then why approach him in the first place?"

"Oh, he wasn't my first choice, but no one else could fit Mr. Talbot's projects in. Business is booming. I just wanted a bit of it. Is that so bad?"

"No, I wouldn't think so. How did Brissedon manage it, though?"

"Probably by paying his employees less and working them harder than anyone else would even consider."

After all he'd heard about Thomas Brissedon, Daniel was beginning to think someone had done the world a favor. But that wasn't the way he was raised. "So Thomas agreed to the proposition."

"Yes, and then invited us to dinner to celebrate the joint venture. When I rose Friday morning, however, two notes arrived from the Manhattan firms. Along with his own high bids, the blackguard had submitted two additional bids under Colin's name through a dummy corporation he'd set up for the boy. He underbid me by thousands of dollars. Needless to say, they couldn't afford to turn it down. They sent their regrets, but business is business, after all."

"How did you know the winning company belonged to Brissedon?"

"A third note arrived as well . . . from Brissedon. He never missed an opportunity to rub salt in a wound."

Stockbridge sat down on the green floral sofa and put his head in his hands. "To make matters worse, I've had to pull out of the Talbot contract altogether. Without the down payment from those Manhattan firms, I don't have the capital to hold up my end of the bargain, let alone the workforce. I certainly can't afford to alienate the other smaller accounts I do have. Talbot understands, but he has no choice. He needs the lumber, so Brissedon's firm will receive the entire contract. It's my own fault, I suppose, for wanting to try and expand."

"And now Brissedon has got his foot in the door both with Talbot and the two Manhattan firms."

Stockbridge just nodded. "As a result, I'm barely holding on. The reputation it took me years to build up is all but ruined. Yes, I was angry enough to kill Thomas Brissedon, but you can be sure that if I did, it would have been a public execution!"

"Now that he's dead, though, surely there'll be some changes."

"Why? Colin Brissedon will just reap the benefits of his father's maneuvering. He'll be set for the next five years at least."

"You said that you received the notes Friday morning?"

"Well, yes, the two from the Manhattan firms, but the one from Brissedon was waiting for me when I arrived home Thursday night. He'd received word of their decisions that afternoon."

"So you knew what he'd done on Thursday night. Did you return to the Brissedons' then?"

"No. I wanted to, but my dear wife convinced me to sleep on it."

"You were home all night?"

"Yes, of course, in the arms of my wife." The woman stood beside him, her hand on his shoulder, and he reached up to clasp it.

"I know this may seem unimportant, but may I ask how you got the mud on your boots? We've not had rain since early Thursday evening."

"Unlike the Brissedons, I have to clean my own boots when I get the time. I have but one part-time maid, and that is not one of her duties. As it turns out, I've been too busy trying to salvage what's left of my business to take time cleaning the mud from my boots. Why is that so important, anyway? Did he die with mud on his boots? How ironic that would have been!"

"How is that?"

"Thomas was a fanatic about their boots being clean. He wouldn't even allow anyone to go upstairs without removing them. Something about expensive Persian rugs. He would have probably preferred that everyone remove their boots at the door, but even he must have realized how ridiculous that would have sounded."

"Yes, it does sound a bit impractical. One last question, Mr. Stockbridge. Do you have any fresh scratches on your person?"

"Scratches!" Stockbridge said, though there was an uncertainty in his voice. "No, none that I know of."

"Thank you, sir." Daniel stood up, nodding to Mrs. Stockbridge before shaking her husband's hand. "If I have any further questions, I'll be in touch."

Frances Stockbridge smiled and led Daniel and his sergeant to the door. She paused for a moment before opening it, then whispered softly, "He was home with me all night, and I'm sure I would have noticed any scratches."

"Thank you, ma'am," Daniel said before nodding again. "Good day."

The sergeant raised an eyebrow as they walked down to the sidewalk. "Now why do you suppose she felt the need to confirm his whereabouts?"

Daniel smirked. "You know very well why."

"Because he wasn't home, most likely. And if she's trying to convince us he didn't have any scratches . . ."

"The ones she's worried about are under his clothing, and highly unlikely they were made by Thomas Brissedon."

"But more likely they were made by a paramour." The sergeant frowned, letting out a sad sigh. "That's too bad. They seemed like a nice couple."

"Maybe it was a one-time thing, after finding out what Brissedon did, and she'll forgive him."

The sergeant grunted. "I know what my Milly would do if she found out I'd cheated on her."

A smile cracked Daniel's mouth. "What's that, Sergeant?"

"Suffice it to say she'd never have to worry about such a thing happening again."

Daniel cringed as he climbed into the buggy. "Let's make sure it doesn't happen, then, eh?"

"No need to worry there, Doc. Where are we off to now?"

"I'm to attend the lovely Miss Brissedon at her home for tea. It seems she's remembered some information I might find relevant to the case. As for you, Sergeant, see what you can find out about this business transaction between Stockbridge and Talbot. Each version is a little different. And then see if you can discover what Phillip Stockbridge was really up to that night. Also, check out Brighton Templeton's assertion that he's in his last year of law school at Columbia. You'll have to wait for Monday morning for that, though. My parents paid a fortune for my brother Neil. I can't see Mr. Templeton managing it on a messenger's pay."

"You think he might have made enough gambling?"

"Possibly, or maybe with a little blackmail. If he knew about Colin's little error in judgment, he might have known other things. I plan to head to my parents' tonight and spend Sunday with them. Hopefully, my uncle will have that file. I'll also ask my father if he has any friends from Columbia that might know about Brighton. I should be back sometime early Monday morning.

"You got it, Doc. Do you think the file might tell you anything?"

"I can only hope."

Daniel walked up the path to the Brissedons' home. Though as large as the Langstons', it seemed more demure and welcoming somehow. Its board-and-batten siding was a soft colonial blue, highlighted by simple lattice work and shutters. Small pots of pink and lavender impatiens hung at various points around the porch, and a pink-and-pale-green-striped porch swing sat off to one side, while white wicker chairs with matching cushions dotted the remainder of the wraparound porch.

He mounted the steps to the porch and, wiping his clammy hands on his pants, knocked on the wood that surrounded the door's finely etched glass. Almost at once, it opened.

"Good afternoon, Dr. O'Halleran," Forbes said. "Miss Brissedon is awaiting your arrival in the parlor."

"Thank you, Forbes. I know the way."

"Very good, sir. I'll fetch the tea."

Even though it was clear she was expecting him, he stopped at the doorway and gazed in. She was standing, facing out the window. A dainty bun sat atop a wave of chestnut hair, done up in the popular fashion of the day. The sun played off the subtle shades of russet and brown, creating a halo effect, and Daniel's breath caught in his throat. She must have sensed him there, for she turned around and smiled, unnerving Daniel even more.

"Dr. O'Halleran, thank you so much for coming."

"You did say it was important." How he was able to keep his voice from shaking, he didn't know, but he'd become well-versed in hiding his emotions over the years, thanks to his father's training. *Always retain your dignity, Daniel. It will serve you well.*

"Yes, I did." She sat down on a sofa of green damask, far more inviting to look at than the furniture in the Langstons' parlor, and far more comfortable, too, he discovered as he sat in the smaller sofa across from her.

"Did you remember something about the night your father was killed?"

She bit her lip and fiddled with a button on her skirt. "Actually, I found something I thought might be relevant . . . in my father's room."

"Your father's room!" Good Lord! He should have insisted they not enter, but he'd really had no cause once the constables had searched it for clues.

"You didn't say we couldn't, and it had to be cleaned."

He sighed a little easier, though the thought of her entering the room where her father had been murdered still troubled him. "After the funeral director had taken your father away, you mean."

She looked back down to her button. "Well, no, not exactly. But Dr. Tennyson had covered him with a sheet," she added quickly.

"What!" Heat flooded his cheeks. Why hadn't her brothers protected her from what must have been a harrowing experience? "I am sorry. I should have insisted no one enter until—"

She reached out and touched his knee. "It's not your fault. It was ... difficult, but I found something. The footprint definitely belonged to a male."

He sat back, his knee still tingling from where she'd touched it. "Yes, Miss Brissedon. I hope you didn't subject yourself to such an ordeal just to determine that."

She straightened her shoulders. "Then why didn't you mention it?"

"With all due respect, miss, I wasn't aware I was to report all my findings to you."

She squiggled up her mouth. "Well, you're not, I suppose, but ... that's not all I discovered. There was a small chip on the right heel, and the sole was worn more on the inside. Surely that should narrow it down even more. My father doesn't allow shoes upstairs, so it will be easy to check our shoes and eliminate the family."

He leaned forward, resting his arms on his knees. "It's possible it could help some, but I'm sure you'll find those features on many a man's soles."

She sat back as Forbes delivered the tea tray. Nothing more was said until he left, and she handed Daniel a cup. "I added milk and one sugar. That is the way you like it, isn't it?"

"Yes, thank you." He took the cup, watching the spark of humor that seemed to glisten in her eyes before she spoke again.

"I found something else in my father's room. It was pushed up against the wall at the back of one of his nightstands." Reaching in her pocket, she pulled out a matchbox. "I haven't been able to discover what Columbia Hall is, however. Do you think it might be associated with the university?"

Daniel nearly choked, spilling some of the tea on his pants. "I'm so sorry." Yanking a handkerchief from his pocket, he wiped his mouth and dabbed at the wet spot on his trousers. "It must have gone down the wrong pipe."

"Can I do anything to help?" she said.

"No, thank you. I'm fine now." What was he going to tell her? But even more to the point, what did that matchbox mean? Had Edward Langston been in the room, or had Thomas picked it up himself to use against him?

"Well? Have you heard of the place?"

"It's a gentlemen's club in the city, I believe."

Her shoulders slumped, and she seemed to deflate before him. "Oh. I suppose it belonged to my father, then."

"Most likely. I am sorry." He blew his nose and tucked his handkerchief back in his pocket before standing up. "If that's all, Miss Brissedon . . ."

"Oh no, there is more." She smiled sweetly again. "Would you like to borrow a pair of my brother's trousers? I'm sure Lizzie would be able to get that stain out."

He sat down again, returning her smile. "No, thank you. It will dry in no time. Now, what else did you come across?"

She reached in her pocket again and drew out a folded piece of notepaper. "I found these on the floor just under the window in my father's study."

"You went in the study as well?"

Kathleen gave a weary sigh. "I thought we'd established that you'd put no restrictions in place as to where we could or could not go, so I would appreciate it if you would refrain from comments along those lines."

Daniel ran a finger under his nose to hide the smile forming on his lips. "Yes, ma'am. I do apologize. What did you find?" Opening the makeshift envelope, he saw three white chips of paint, from the window frame, no doubt. "Well, I did say the window had been jimmied open."

"Yes, and I would expect to find the paint chips on the ground outside, not lying beneath the rug or pushed up against the wainscoting to the right of the window."

"I see what you mean." This was an interesting development, though he doubted she realized the true implications of her discovery. "If that is the case, however, it would indicate someone who was already in the house wanted to make it look like a break-in."

Giving a deep sigh, she sat back against the sofa, though her expression told him she had already considered the matter. "I just don't know who that could be. And please, you don't need to remind me of my father's ability to raise my brothers' hackles. I'm well aware. Still, to think either of them or my cousin had anything to do with this is more than I care to speculate. I am, however, enough of a realist to know this is information you should have."

"Yes, it is, thank you." She never ceased to amaze him. Though she looked as dainty as a violet, there was an inner strength to her, a grit that belied her gentle appearance.

"I do hope it doesn't prevent you from pursuing all avenues of investigation. It is possible someone else did break in and left those paint chips there precisely for the purpose of making my brothers look guilty."

"I promise I will not fail in my due diligence, both in and out of the household."

"Thank you." She gave a nod of satisfaction and took a sip of her tea. "I knew you could be counted on to be fair. There is one last thing, and I hope you will continue to keep an open mind about it as well."

"Of course, as much as I can."

She reached in her pocket again, this time pulling out a single gold cuff link, a diamond shamrock set in the center of a gold-rimmed square of Connemara marble. It was an exact match to the one they'd found in Thomas Brissedon's room, the one she'd been afraid Patrick Desmond had stolen.

As if sensing what he was thinking, she spoke. "I have no proof Patrick stole them, nor do I believe he killed my father. Why would he? He'll gain nothing by his death."

"Perhaps he was simply angry at losing Lydia to Colin?"

"That will never happen, and in his heart he knows it." She closed her eyes for a moment, rubbing her forehead before opening them again. "But you're right, of course—though I still refuse to believe either of my brothers would commit so heinous an act."

"And they may not have," he said, feeling the need to say something to soothe the stress he heard in her voice. "Did you find this in your father's office as well?"

"No, it was down by the copse of trees, but we all use that path on a regular basis."

"May I take it with me?" When she nodded, he rose. "Is there anything else?"

"No, thank you for coming, Doctor. You will keep me informed, won't you?"

"Yes, of course."

CHAPTER 24

Kathleen saw the doctor to the door, watching as he hopped into his buggy and rode away. He certainly was an attractive man, with dark brown eyes that sparked gold in the center when he was angry or found something humorous. And he did have a sense of humor. She could see that in the tiny laugh lines that creased the corners of his eyes and mouth and the deep dimples that appeared whenever he let his guard down and revealed a genuine smile.

Taking a deep breath, she pulled herself back to the present. It was nearly four o'clock. A touch of guilt tugged at her conscience, but the doctor already suspected Patrick. She wasn't about to give his suspicions any more credence. Instead, she called for her butler.

"Could you have Trevor bring the carriage around? I have an errand to run in town."

"Of course, miss."

She knew he must be thinking it was rather late for errands in town, but she wanted to get there before the doctor found out about Mr. Morton. Pulling the piece of paper from her pocket, she read the note from Alexander Morton again. Could this be the note the detective had delivered the night before her father was murdered? And if so, how had it ended up in his study? Surely Colin wouldn't have shown it to him that night. Or would he?

No, this must be from an earlier date. Colin was always intercepting their messages. He'd probably never delivered this one to Patrick either, but she doubted the doctor would see it that way. It made sense, though. How else would it have ended up in her father's desk drawer?

Putting it back in her pocket, she reached for her hat and gloves. Regardless of how it had gotten there, she intended on discovering what this Mr. Morton found so urgent before she passed the note on to Patrick or showed it to Dr. O'Halleran.

Grabbing her bag, she hurried down the steps and told Trevor to take her to Mr. Morton's. Moments later, they stopped before a plain storefront. "Are you sure this is it?"

"It is the address you had me look up this morning, miss." He helped her from the carriage. "Perhaps I should accompany you inside?"

"I'll be fine, Mr. Kilpatrick. He's a businessman, and you can see inside clear enough. Should it look as if anything untoward is about to happen, you can come to my aid."

He tipped his hat and leaned against the lamppost, pulling a newspaper from his pocket, while Kathleen strode forward and opened the door.

"Can I help you, ma'am?" A tall, disheveled-looking man stood up from behind a well-worn wooden desk.

Kathleen recognized him at once. "Alexander Morton?" She moved forward and gazed down at the dusty ladder-back chair at her side.

"Yes, ma'am, at your service." He quickly scooted around the desk, yanking a blue scarf from his pocket and wiping off the chair. "Please have a seat."

Well, she supposed this was all Patrick could afford, and if he was good at what he did . . . She took a seat, placing her hands in her lap before her, while the man hurried back behind his desk, trying desperately to straighten his tie.

"My brother received this message, but he's been unable to come himself. We were hoping you could give me the information instead."

Morton looked down at the note, then up at Kathleen. "You were in the hallway when I gave this note to that butler of yours. How do I know Mr. Desmond ever got the message? Maybe you're just here to find out what he's asked me to do."

"I'm perfectly aware what he's asked you to look into, Mr. Morton. Patrick doesn't believe his father was murdered, nor do I. Now you can either talk to me or to Dr. O'Halleran, the coroner investigating my father's death. It makes no difference to me, but it might to Patrick."

"Mr. Desmond is my client, and as such, I don't have to tell you or the cops anything about him or his case. And with you being a Brissedon, I'm thinking I'll just hold on to my information until I can speak to Mr. Desmond himself."

"I completely understand your hesitance to share the information with me, but at the moment it would be foolish for Patrick to meet with you. He's under suspicion for my father's murder, and while I don't believe it for one moment, I'm hoping you've uncovered something that might help me prove his innocence." Kathleen was gripping her handbag with both hands, desperate to convince the detective of her sincerity. It must have been apparent in her eyes, for the man sat back, causing the rickety chair to squeak, and wiped an ink-stained hand across his face.

"Look, Patrick's a good kid. He wouldn't hurt a fly. All he wants to do is prove his father's innocence. You tell that copper to ask around town. The boy's no murderer. A lover, yes, but a murderer? They're looking at the wrong man."

"I agree, but my word won't be enough."

"You seem like a nice young lady. If you want to help Patrick, just go home, burn that note, and forget you ever heard of me."

She stood, the heat rising in her face. Was he trying to protect her? "What did you find, Mr. Morton? If you insist, I'll go home and return with Patrick, though I'm certain the constables are watching his every move. Or maybe you would prefer I brought Dr. O'Halleran instead?"

The man's temper was rising as well. She could tell by the tinge of red on the tips of his ears and the hard line his jaw had taken on. "You don't want to know what I found out, miss. Now just go home and leave it be."

She turned, walked the few steps to the entrance, and yanked open the door. "Mr. Kilpatrick! Return home and fetch Mr. Patrick here at once, but take care you're not followed. It's urgent!"

"Yes, ma'am! But will you be all right?"

"Now just wait one minute," Morton said. "Tell your man to hold up. I've no desire to see that boy come to harm. But I'm warning you now: you're not going to like what I found."

Trevor looked at her, and she nodded. "Go back to your paper, Mr. Kilpatrick. I should be finished here in a bit." She moved back to the chair and sat down, but Mr. Morton paced back and forth in the small space.

"Last thing I told him was about a man named Tommy Breslin. He lived down around the Bowery back in the day, but then about sixteen years ago he disappeared. At least he did till two years back. Doesn't he show up again, all decked out like a swell."

Kathleen held tight to her handbag, as if doing so would hold her erect. "Go on," she said, somehow managing to keep the tremor she felt inside from echoing in her voice. "What does this Tommy Breslin have to do with my father?"

He frowned at her but continued. "Anyway, I told Paddy, er . . . Mr. Desmond . . . that this Tommy Breslin had taken to calling himself Thomas Brissedon. Guess the fella figured he wanted a new name to go with his new clothes."

Her breathing eased a bit. Her father had always said he was a self-made man. Kathleen nodded, and he continued his story.

"The thing is, I couldn't locate no Brissedon Mills prior to just before this swell showed up. Then again, I didn't find any criminal record for a Tommy Breslin either, so who knows?"

"But you already told Patrick all of this, and none of it sounds too incriminating. My father acknowledged that he wasn't always wealthy. What else have you discovered?"

"I'm getting to it. There was a flower-seller, Mary O'Neill. She works in a millinery shop now over on Madison. Got herself married to a—" He stopped at the desk and checked his notes. "Stephen Brady, that's it. Does up the artificial flowers on ladies' hats now. Anyway, it seems Cornelius Desmond always bought a flower from her on his way past, for far more than it was worth, she said. This one day she sees this fella talking to Neily Desmond. She'd never seen him before but described him as—" He stopped to check his notes again. "Tall and thin, with eyes that made you think he was about to doze off on you."

Kathleen's heart was pounding in her throat, and she felt as if she could hardly get any air in her lungs, but she had to remain calm . . . for Patrick.

"So then Neily walks over to her, like he always does. He buys a flower and tells her he's off to this address down in the Bowery to see the man's sick uncle. A few hours later, they find him at that very address, dead and smelling of booze, with a bloody knife inches from his fingers."

He stopped for a moment, to check her reaction, no doubt, and it was all she could do to smile at him. "Please continue. I don't have all day."

Morton scratched his head, clearly puzzled at her calm acceptance of what he was telling her. Little did he know what was going on inside. Her stomach was tying itself into knots, and every nerve in her body was quivering. She hardly wanted to take a breath for fear it would come out in a sob. So instead she concentrated on Patrick, the look in his eyes when she'd find him sitting on the porch with his head in his hands, the loneliness she sensed in his heart.

"This is where it gets interesting. There was this kid that always hung around with Tommy back in the day, a nephew or cousin or something, or so people said. Would have been about seventeen or eighteen last time anybody saw them, I reckon. Went by the name of Jerry McRady. Now doesn't he show up again right about the same time as old Tommy—older, of course, only he's not dressed so fine. Funny thing is, he fits Mary O'Neill's description to a tee, right down to the droopy eyes."

He sat on the edge of the desk and looked down at her. "I'm sorry, miss, but I did warn you. I need Patrick to bring me photographs of your father and cousin so I can show them to Mary."

She stood, praying her knees would hold firm until she got to the carriage. "And you'll have them, Mr. Morton, as soon as I speak to Patrick."

The sun cast long shadows across the road as they headed home. She stared off into the distance, thoughts racing through her mind. One vision played larger than any other, burned in her memory—a gold watch lying open on her father's bureau the day she searched his room. Though she hadn't thought anything of it at the time, it was all the evidence she needed now. For in the cover were engraved the initials *CD*.

She barely made it to her room before she collapsed on the bed. Her entire body was shaking, but there was still something she had to do. If Patrick got to the watch before she did, Daniel O'Halleran would take it as proof that he'd killed her father. He'd never believe her stepbrother didn't know about everything.

Pushing herself off the bed, she hurried down the hallway, breathing a sigh of relief to find the watch still where she'd last seen it.

"Kate, are you all right?" Patrick said from behind her.

Spinning around, she plunged the watch into her skirt pocket, her cheeks wet with tears. "It's finally all just hitting me."

"You shouldn't be in here." He walked to her side, wrapping his arm around her shoulders so her head rested against his chest.

Like it or not, she'd have to tell Dr. O'Halleran what she'd discovered, but not before she made him understand that Patrick had no knowledge about any of it. There was one more thing she had to do to be certain, though. She could have no lingering doubts when she explained it all to Daniel. Telling Patrick she needed to rest, she waited for him to head for the carriage house before slipping down the stairs to her father's study. Tucked up on one of the bookshelves was a set of three books, only they weren't books at all, but a kind of hollowed-out box. She'd seen her father slipping papers into it one afternoon, but assuming they were business contracts or some such thing, she'd given it no more thought. Until now.

Taking the books down, she opened the box. A birth certificate for a Thomas O'Dwyer, born 6 January 1904 in Bibury, Gloucestershire, England. Mother: Annabell O'Dwyer. Father: unknown. For some reason, Kathleen couldn't stop staring at it. Why would her father have a random birth certificate for a child born earlier that year? Unless . . . the child was named Thomas. Could he have been keeping a mistress?

An envelope dropped to the floor, and she picked it up. It was addressed to Thomas from a Mrs. O'Dwyer in Bibury, England. Closing her eyes for a moment, she took a breath to calm her nerves, then opened them again and slipped the letter from the envelope.

Dear Mr. Brissedon,

As you requested, I've sent wee Tommy's birth certificate, though given you want to keep his father's name a secret, I can't understand to what end. It does pain me that Colin will never know his son, but I suspect it's for the best. Should you ever change your mind and wish to inform him, all you need do is ask.

My sincere thanks for your continued kindness,
Annie O'Dwyer

Unable to support herself any longer, she flopped down in the armchair at her side, trying to catch her breath. Her stomach was churning like a pot of boiling water about to spill over. Colin had a child? Dear God, what else was in this box? And if her father was intent on keeping the child's birth a secret, why did he want the birth certificate? As some sort of insurance? What other secrets did her father have?

She placed her hand over her mouth to stifle a sob. But no, there would be time for that later. Right now, she was searching for one specific document. Something the police would have given to Brigid, an inventory of sorts, her husband's belongings.

She shuffled through the papers, trying to focus, not allowing herself to be sidetracked by anything else. There, New York City—an inquest into the death of Cornelius Desmond. How her father had gotten his hands on it, she didn't know. Maybe Brigid had been given a copy. She didn't care. There was only one thing she wanted to find. A name caught her eye—Doctor Daniel O'Halleran. That's right. He said he'd done the autopsy.

Her hands were trembling now. There it was—a list of the items returned to the widow. Mostly clothing, a set of cuff links and matching tie pin, a white handkerchief. A wave of nausea washed over her. No watch. Patrick said his father never left the house without that watch. That could only mean one thing. She pulled over a wastebasket and vomited until there was nothing left to come up.

CHAPTER 25

Saturday, June 25, 1904 – 7:30 p.m.

Daniel ran up the steps to his parents' brownstone, taking them two at a time. The front doors were still wide open, as was the transom over the vestibule door, letting in the light and fresh air on the balmy summer evening. He fiddled with his key, juggling the cake boxes he'd stopped to get on his way from the station while turning the lock. The door opened, and he reached down to grab his leather satchel.

"Mother, Father, it's just Danny!" As he closed the door behind him, his brother Frankie stuck his head through the crack in the parlor doors before quickly closing them again.

"Good evening, Mr. Daniel." Byron flashed a disapproving frown before taking Daniel's bag and placing it on the portmanteau.

"Yes, I know," Daniel said, trying to stifle a smile. "If everyone used their key, you would be out of a position, but that's not strictly true. We'd still need you to answer the door for guests."

The butler ignored his statement and nodded toward the two white cake boxes Daniel had teetering in the crook of his arm. "Would you like me to take them as well, sir?"

"Oh, right," Daniel said. "The top one is for you and the staff, and the bottom is for Mother."

"Thank you, sir," the man said, a twinkle lighting his eye. "Your parents are waiting in the parlor . . . with a guest." At this last statement, he could sense the butler's change in demeanor.

"She's not set me up with another debutante, has she?" He searched the butler's eyes, but as usual, Byron was the one man whose emotions he couldn't seem to crack.

"I couldn't say, sir. If there's nothing else, I'll finish preparations in the dining room."

"That's it, isn't it?" Daniel cursed under his breath. "It's why she wanted me to wear a good suit. Well, I'm not going to oblige." He started up the stairs. "Tell her I was shattered by the day's work, and I'll see her in the morning."

He'd no sooner started up the stairs than he heard the butler clear his throat, the way he always did when he disapproved of his or one of his siblings' behavior. As a butler, he had no authority to do so, yet not one of them would ignore the man's cautionary advice. Daniel groaned and turned to see Byron glaring at him, his eyebrow lifted in his characteristic arc.

"I suspect you might find the visitor even more disturbing, but it is my sincere belief that you will be severely upsetting your mother if you do not make an appearance."

Daniel scowled. Who was it? He hadn't given anyone stitches lately. Well, except in his capacity as their doctor, and surely they hadn't come to complain.

"I'll have Hattie send up some hot chocolate and your favorite cookies, shall I?"

This made Daniel frown all the more. "I'm not eight years old anymore."

"No, sir, you're not." Byron turned toward the parlor door. "Shall I announce you?"

He couldn't stop the smile from creeping across his lips. Byron always had the most refined way of saying, *Now stop acting like a child and get your backside in there.*

"No, they are expecting me. Besides, I'm sure by now Frankie's mentioned my arrival. You might ask Hattie to prepare something for a headache, though. I have a feeling I might need it."

"As you say, sir." Without blinking an eye, the butler headed down the hallway. "A nice cup of chamomile tea."

"With a good dose of whiskey," Daniel called after him before pushing open the pocket doors to the parlor. "Good evening, Mother. Sorry I'm late, but the train—" He hadn't gone three steps when he stopped in his tracks, his hands instinctively clutching into fists at his sides. "What is he doing here?"

"Now, Daniel," his mother said, "perhaps it's time the two of you talked things over."

Daniel turned around and walked back into the entry hall, his mother on his heels. He grabbed his satchel off the portmanteau and turned to kiss her on the cheek. "I'll be at the Y if you need me."

True to form, Sarah Adams was having none of it. She yanked the bag from his hand and stood glaring up at him. Though she was barely five feet tall, even his father cowered when she got that look in her eyes.

"Enough of this, Daniel!" She pointed a finger at him, her hazel eyes flashing with specks of golden fire. "He is your . . . father, regardless of the circumstances."

"My father is the head of this household, your husband, not some lecher who refers to me as his 'misbegotten little by-blow.'"

Her expression softened, and she touched his cheek. "I know, darling, and no one has brought him to task for it more than I, but you're not a child anymore. Maybe it's time to forgive, even if you can't forget."

"I know he's your brother, and what he did hurt you too, but . . ." He ran his hand back through his hair, trying to quell the storm brewing in his stomach. "How did he even know I was going to be home?"

"I don't think he knows you left. He just showed up at the door, asking to see you. I believe Byron's first instinct was to slam it in his face, but he has too much class for that."

"And so do you." He sighed. "Which explains why he's sitting in our parlor."

She shrugged. "You're my son, and I know how much he hurt you, but maybe we need to hear what he has to say. I'm convinced he's the reason you continue to have such headaches. It's all my fault. I should have realized what he was up to sooner, should have taken your mother with me when I wed. Perhaps if I had . . ."

Daniel couldn't help but chuckle. "All right, Mother." He looked over his shoulder toward the parlor and took a deep breath. "It is just for dinner? And then he's gone."

"Of course," she said, her lips quirking up into dimples. Her manipulative skills never ceased to amaze him. "I may be willing to tolerate him on the chance it may help you, but I'll never forget how he hurt you or your mother. You need to come to terms with him, Daniel. You're no longer six years old. Why, if you wanted to, you could send *him* flying across the room. Not that you should."

"Maybe just a little . . ."

"No, Daniel!" She laid her hand on his chest, looking up into his eyes. "You never deserved any of this."

A tear trickled down her cheek, and he wiped it away, sorrow clutching at his heart. Pinching the bridge of his nose, he tried to stifle the headache that had been growing all day.

"This has all given you one of your headaches, hasn't it?"

"No, it's just a case I'm working on." He cast another look toward the parlor. "I'll try to keep a civil tongue in my mouth, but you'd best advise him to do the same."

"If he doesn't, your father—my husband," she added with a twinkle in her eye, "will show him the door in no uncertain terms."

Daniel chuckled, remembering how Richard Adams had grabbed the man by the arm and practically thrown him bodily down the front stoop twenty-two years before. "Just one question, Mother."

She lifted an eyebrow. "Only one? You're usually good for at least three."

"I've had to ask a lot today, so I'm petering out. I was just wondering. Why is he here?"

"Hmm, aren't we all? He says he wants to express his sorrow for treating you so badly and hopes you can at least have some sort of relationship."

"You don't sound like you believe him."

"He always was a pathological liar, so no, I don't. He wants something, though. You can be sure of that. Just do try and keep your composure."

"He has a family now, doesn't he? Why the sudden interest in building a relationship with me?"

"I don't know." She frowned, taking him by the arm as they headed back into the parlor. "Let's find out."

Arthur Pritchard stood up, and Daniel was six years old again. The words his father had spoken that day twenty-two years ago still resounded in his ears and haunted his dreams.

So this is my misbegotten little by-blow. You don't seriously think I'm going to take responsibility for the filthy bastard, do you? It's only the whore's word against mine anyway. Let her prove it.

The man looked him over, an arrogant sneer on his face. "Is that the best suit you have? If your valet can't do any better than that, perhaps it's time to look for another. I have a few I can recommend."

"I don't need a valet," Daniel replied, his lips tight.

"Oh, that's right. I heard you'd joined the police department." He said the words like he'd tasted something sour. "Well, there's no arguing you look the part. It's the Irish in you, I suppose." He let out a disapproving grunt. "Right then. It will have to do. I've made a reservation at my club, and thanks to your amateur theatrics, we're already running late."

Daniel had the sudden urge to burst out laughing. "I beg your pardon. You want me to go to your club with you? I was under the impression we were to be dining here."

"Yes, well, I thought we could get reacquainted better in the privacy of my club. I have something I want to speak to you about . . . privately."

Reacquainted? They'd barely ever been acquainted. Daniel couldn't believe the audacity of the man. "Thank you for the offer—"

"Yes, I know it's quite sudden, but I suppose it's time we come to an agreement."

Daniel's eyes widened. The man actually thought he was honored by the invitation. "I'm sorry, but you misunderstand. I have no desire to join you at your club or anywhere else, for that matter. I can't even believe you had the nerve to suggest it. And anything you want to speak to me about can be said in front of *my parents.*"

The man's face took on that hard edge he remembered all too well. "Still the same ungrateful little whelp. Your mother played the coquette and got caught. I owe you nothing."

"Go to hell, you bastard!" Though he went to lunge for the man, his brothers grabbed him by the arms, holding him back.

Arthur lifted his hand to smack Daniel, but his father took hold of the man's wrist in midair. "I think it's time you left, Arthur. You clearly misrepresented your reason for coming. I would suggest you don't bother visiting again, or I may unleash him on you. And trust me, you won't like the results."

Arthur yanked his arm down and barked a laugh, pulling on his cuffs to reset his jacket. "Typical low-class Irish ruffian. Even you couldn't purge the bogtrotter out of him, dear sister. I should have known better. He likely wouldn't have been any use to me anyway. I doubt he has the connections." He began to leave but stopped next to Daniel. "You'll never be anything more than the misbegotten bastard of a two-bit Irish whore," he said before storming from the room.

Daniel listened for the door to click shut, then flopped down on the sofa, his head resting in his hands. Why did he let the man get to him so?

His mother sat beside him, calling out a number of directives. "Byron, ask Allie to fetch my headache powders and have Hattie brew a pot of chamomile tea. Richard, darling, could you retrieve that bottle of whiskey you keep hidden in the bottom drawer of your desk?"

Byron stopped to open the front door, and Isabell came rushing in. "What was that brute doing here?"

Danny heard the maid return with the powders. Byron put down the teapot. Isabell was frantically trying to discern what had happened. "Did he hit Danny?" He should look up and calm them all down, but he just felt so drained. What he really wanted to do was hit something. A moment later, his brother Joe was pulling him up and dragging him away, much to his mother's dismay.

"We'll be back in a minute, Mother. He can drink your magical potion then." Tugging him down the cellar stairs, his brother continued. "Frankie and I have been working on this for the last few weeks. We think it's just what you need."

Daniel couldn't keep from breaking into a grin. His brothers had constructed a sort of exercise room in the corner of the cellar, complete with a punching bag.

"I joined the boxing team at school," Frankie said, "and Joe thought I needed to bulk up a bit. Have away at it."

Daniel pulled on a pair of gloves and laced into the innocent bag with every bit of anger and frustration that had been building up since that morning. He heard a muffled voice call down the stairs but didn't stop until Frankie touched his shoulder.

"Mother says the tea's getting cold," Izzy shouted down the stairs. "And if you don't get up here now, she intends on having Hattie mix that ghastly concoction she used to make us drink when we were children."

Recalling the putrid liquid, Daniel gave a final punch and still managed to reach the parlor first, where his mother passed him a cup of tea, liberally doctored with whiskey. Though the warm beverage was certainly relaxing him, he'd no sooner taken three sips than she grabbed it back, her nose scrunched up.

"Byron, see to a bath for Daniel and ask Hattie to hold dinner for a half an hour." Turning her gaze back to Daniel, she frowned. "And you return smelling a bit sweeter. I don't relish the stench of sweat overcoming the delicious aroma of Hattie's roast."

He knew better than to argue.

Having let out his anger on the punching bag below and soaked off the aggravation of the day, Daniel entered the dining room a half hour later in a far better state of mind. A delicious meal of roast beef and mashed potatoes didn't hurt his outlook either. It was good to be home again, even if it was only for a day. And to top it all off, his brother Neil and his wife had been invited for dinner, as well as his uncle Timothy.

"So," his father said as he snatched one of the apple tarts Daniel had brought from the bakery, "how do you like the new job?"

"Very much so. Thank you for putting in a good word for me with Dr. Tennyson."

His father's mouth twisted below his handlebar moustache, but his eyes were sincere. "I wouldn't have recommended you if I didn't think you were the right man for the position."

Daniel nodded and took a sip of coffee to cover the heat that was rising in his cheeks.

"It's not too quiet for you out there?" Joe said, but before he could answer, Isabell chimed in.

"I think it's lovely. When I wed, I'm going to have a summer home out there, just like Mr. Roosevelt, though not as grand, of course."

"I like it as well," Daniel said, "but it's not as quiet as you may think."

"Oh, that reminds me," his uncle said. "Don't let me forget to be giving ye that file ye were on about." He took his napkin to wipe a dab of apple from his lips. "What makes ye think it has something to do with this case ye're working on now?"

"What's this?" his father said. "You're not going to keep it all to yourself, are you?"

Daniel chuckled. He could swear he actually saw his father's ears perk up, and Neil had moved to the edge of his seat.

"You remember that first case I worked on as the coroner's physician?"

"Of course," Neil said. "None of it ever sat right with me. Too many dead ends."

"I recall reading about it in the papers," his father said. "And I have to agree with your brother. But that case has been closed for two years now. This can't be an official inquiry."

"Yes and no," Daniel said. "I've been asked to look into it privately, and I can't help but think there's some connection to a case I am working on officially."

His mother put her cup down, her mouth pursed in disapproval. "If you'd stayed with the city coroner's office, you wouldn't need to work two jobs. No wonder you look so bedraggled."

"Really, Mother!" Isabell said with a laugh. "What a thing to say."

She frowned at her daughter. "You know what I mean."

Daniel reached across the table and squeezed her hand. "I'm fine, Mother, and I like what I'm doing."

"So what about this case?" Neil said. "And more importantly, why do you think it's connected to Cornelius Desmond's death?"

"It's a murder investigation. A man named Thomas Brissedon."

"Yes," his father said. "I read about it this morning in the Eagle."

"I was at Vassar with a Katie Brissedon," Izzy said, "though she was a year or two behind me." She took a bite of apple tart. "It can't be the same family, though. I think they were from Connecticut, or was it Massachusetts?"

"Did you know her?" Daniel asked.

"Not very well. Seemed nice enough, though, from what I remember. Kept to herself."

"Definitely not in your group, then." Joe grinned, but she ignored him.

"I do remember she had an older brother. I heard he was . . . a bit of a rake, shall we say."

"And Danny wasn't?" Neil grinned, earning a frown from his mother.

"Not the way he was." Izzy gave Danny a peck on the cheek. "Is it the same family?"

"I believe so. The stepbrother's at NYU now. Colin's the brother."

"Yes," Izzy said, "I knew it was something like that— Colm or Colin or Connell."

"Well, their father's been murdered."

His mother gasped, raising her hand to her chest as if horrified, though Daniel knew there wasn't much that shocked her. "Must we talk of such unpleasant things at the dinner table?"

His father squeezed her hand. "No, dear, we could speak of them in my study if you'd prefer, but then your neck would grow stiff from listening at the door."

A pink blush touched her cheeks, and she swatted him playfully. "Oh, go on, then. What about these Brissedons? How are they connected to the Desmonds?"

"The father, Thomas, recently married Desmond's widow. But she died barely a year after they exchanged vows."

"Interesting," Neil said. "You think Thomas did it?"

"I've no reason to suspect he did."

"What about his murder, then?" Neil raised his eyebrows expectantly. "Any suspects?"

Daniel shook his head. "A whole houseful! None of which it would be appropriate for you to represent, considering I'm investigating the case."

"True enough." Neil shrugged. "Then why are you looking into the Desmond case?"

"His daughter approached Dr. Tennyson and asked if I might consider it. It seems Desmond's son doesn't believe his father's death was an accident."

"Wait a minute," Frankie said. "Patrick Desmond?"

"That's right. Why?"

"He was in one of my classes last semester."

Daniel held up his cup for Byron to refill. "That's right. I keep forgetting. You're a college man now."

"Really, Danny?" his brother said in mock consternation, causing Daniel to chuckle.

"All right, college boy, so what do you know about Patrick?"

"Nothing much." Frankie dug into his apple tart, a grin breaking out across his face. "Only he must be taking after his stepbrother because he's got a reputation for sleeping around."

"Hmm, the same one he has at home, I imagine. Kathleen hopes my finding the truth will put him back on the straight and narrow."

"Kathleen!" Izzy said. "Of course! That girl we met walking along the dock last weekend, the one I caught you flirting with. I thought she looked familiar."

Daniel frowned. "I wasn't flirting! She's a librarian. I was just asking if a book I'd requested had come in yet."

Isabell let a knowing smile settle over her lips, while his mother and brothers grinned at him like they'd all just seen the lights turn on at Luna Park for the first time.

"You can forget it." Daniel threw his napkin on his plate and glared back at them. "Now that I've seen where she lives, it's out of the question."

Isabell opened her mouth to argue, but the words died on her lips when their father cast a warning glance in her direction.

"Now, Danny boy," his uncle said, coming to his rescue, "I can tell ye what I remember about the Desmond case, but it won't be much. I tried to investigate at the time, but then in September we got involved with that Pulitzer murder, and that was that. As far as Brissedon, I've never heard o' the man, but I could ask around if ye like."

"I'd appreciate that. I can't explain it, but I really do have a feeling the two cases are somehow connected."

His uncle nodded, a proud twinkle in his eye. "Following yer gut, just like I taught ye, eh, boy? Glad ye haven't lost the touch, what with being out in the country and all."

"Yes," his mother said in an obvious attempt to steer the conversation in her desired direction. "Isabell mentioned the place was quite rustic."

"I believe the words I used were 'quite refreshing.'"

"Well, either way, I was concerned to hear you hadn't found more suitable lodgings. Really, Daniel, do you think it's appropriate for a doctor to be living like a traveling salesman?"

"I don't see patients in my rooms, Mother, and it's a very nice hotel."

"Yes, so Isabell said, but still, it must be terribly cramped." She took a sip of tea before continuing, clearly weighing her words. "I was thinking perhaps your father and I could buy a small bungalow. It would be much more convenient when we visit. A pair of rooms in a hotel really isn't adequate, especially if we all decided to visit at once."

Daniel's brow furrowed, a tinge of his headache returning. "I can just imagine what that *small bungalow* would look like. I'm not saying no, just asking you to wait a while."

"The boy had a purpose for moving out there, Sarah," his father said. "Give him some time."

She scrunched up her face disapprovingly but seemed to acquiesce to her husband's suggestion. Daniel realized she liked all her pups close, but he had to build a life for himself and not continue to rely on their generosity. That didn't mean he was too stubborn to ask for their help when the situation called for it.

After enduring a few more hidden inquiries and innuendos about his relationship with Kathleen Brissedon, Daniel excused himself, electing to spend the rest of the evening looking over Cornelius Desmond's file. He settled back against his headboard and opened the coffee stained folder. About half a dozen witnesses admitted to seeing the Irishman enter the building that afternoon. Getting straight answers from any of them, however, was another story. One woman named Annie had proved to be too inebriated to recall much more than his arrival, though a drunken man who called himself General Grant had seen him stop by the girl's rooms. He thought Desmond had given her money, but instead of going in, he'd headed down to the old man's room. Unfortunately, *the General* didn't remember much after that since he'd blacked out. Another man, who was clearly in an opium fog, swore he'd seen two Desmonds.

Daniel shook his head. How could anyone let themselves sink to that level of alcohol and opium? His mama had been poor, struggling from one meal to the next, even with the pay his uncle Timothy managed to bring in as a policeman, but she'd always retained her dignity, in spite of how she'd been used by Arthur Pritchard.

"Then again," he said, a lump forming in his throat, "who knows what's gone on in their lives?" What would his mama have done if not for her brother? As little as his pay had been at the time, Timothy did bring in enough for them to live in a decent apartment, and while they may not have eaten like the Astors, there was food on the table, even if his mama did have to stretch it in every way imaginable. He smiled to himself as he remembered the small roast and potatoes they'd have on Sunday, which would be turned into hash for Monday and Tuesday and what was left mashed with potatoes or cabbage for some form of casserole on Wednesday. It might have been boring and consistent, but it was stable. Many people didn't have that. Cornelius Desmond seemed to want to alleviate their distress. And for that, Daniel wanted to find justice for the man.

Turning the page, he continued reading. One woman, Mary O'Neill, had noticed Desmond talking to a tall, slender young man a half hour before he was seen at the tenement. Desmond told her the man had asked him to go to that very building to tend his sick uncle. Unfortunately, she'd never seen the man before, and all she could remember was that he wasn't very good looking and seemed as if he were ready to fall asleep the whole time he was speaking to Desmond. Some of her friends thought his name might be Jerry McReedy or Ratty, or something to that effect.

Daniel stopped reading for a moment, then quickly turned back to the list of witnesses. Peter MacFarland, Tommy Breslin, Annie Shay, Camille Lenati, Anthony Rizzelli, Jerry McRady. How interesting. Tommy Breslin and Jerry McRady. He needed to know more about these two witnesses, but there was no more to be found. The police had never even identified the gentleman that Mary had seen Desmond with earlier that day. Perhaps a trip to Manhattan was in order, after all.

First, however, he'd have to locate this Mary O'Neill. Closing the file, he stretched over to turn out the light, and, slipping beneath the cotton sheet, he went to sleep.

Sunday, June 26, 1904 – 9:00 a.m.

The next day, after accompanying his family to Mass, he sat down at the breakfast table, though he didn't feel much like eating.

"Was the file any help?" His father piled some scrambled eggs on a piece of toast and shoved it into his mouth, wiping the remnants from his moustache as he chewed.

Daniel nodded. "And if my hunch is right, it gives Patrick Desmond more reason than ever to want Thomas Brissedon dead."

"Oh dear," his mother said. "What will you tell Miss Brissedon?"

"I don't know." He pushed his plate away, his appetite deserting him. "I'm more certain than ever that Cornelius Desmond was murdered, but I can't prove it. I feel it in my gut, though, and I'm fairly sure Thomas Brissedon was behind it."

"That's a serious accusation, Son," his father said. "But I trust your gut. Is there anything I can help you with?"

"There was a witness, a Mary O'Neill. She was a flower-seller at the time. If I could find her and show her a photograph of Brissedon and his nephew, she might recognize them. The problem is, it's been two years."

"I'll pull in a few favors," his father said, "see if we can't locate her. I'll get your uncle Timothy and Neil on it as well."

"There's also a fella named Brighton Templeton, a friend of the family. He claims he's studying law at Columbia. You still have some connections there, don't you?"

"Of course I do. I'll make a few telephone calls this afternoon. See what I can find out."

"Wonderful!" His mother pushed his plate back in front of him and lifted an eyebrow. "Now finish eating. You'll never have the strength to comfort that young lady if you don't eat."

"I'm going to be telling her the father she loved may have murdered the father of the stepbrother she loves. How exactly is that going to comfort her?"

"Good God, Danny!" Joe exclaimed. "Have you truly been living in a tortoise shell? She's going to want someone to turn to after you break the news."

"I doubt it will be the one who breaks it to her." Daniel rolled his eyes and bit off a piece of bacon.

"That will depend on your delivery, little brother." Joe stood up and gave Daniel a pat on the shoulder. "I'm off to visit Irene. Don't worry about it, Dan. If anyone can handle this, it's you."

Daniel hoped his brother was right, and even though he still didn't feel like eating, he finished his plate, knowing his mother wouldn't let it go if he didn't.

After breakfast, he sat outside on the top step of the brownstone's stoop, nodding or having a few amiable words with neighbors as they passed. It was a beautiful summer day, the scent of the roses from the front areaway tickling his scenes and bringing to mind Kathleen Brissedon. Her cheeks were the same soft pink as his mother's blossoms. He shook his head, coming back to himself just as Isabell came to sit beside him.

"So!" Isabell wrapped her arm around his and snuggled up next to him. "Why haven't you asked Katie if you could court her yet? And don't give me that drivel about her being wealthy."

He scowled at her, his pleasant mood shattered. "Let it go, Izzy."

She groaned. "Why, so you can continue to lick your wounds? You do realize you're one of Brooklyn's most eligible bachelors."

"A rumor started by you, no doubt, but it changes nothing. Whether I like it or not, she's a suspect in the case I'm working on, so it wouldn't be professional. Besides, I know my place."

"No, Danny. That's the problem. You don't." Daniel opened his mouth to object, but she raised her hand to cut him off. "I understand the part about not wanting to ask because of a case, but the case isn't going to last forever." She scowled at him. "Get over it, Danny. We all have our crosses to bear. Mine is being so devastatingly gorgeous."

Daniel rolled his eyes at his sister jest, for in fact, she wasn't lying, even if she couldn't see it herself. Any one of his friends would have stumbled over themselves to pay her court. "Stop underestimating yourself, Izzy."

"I'll try if you'll do the same." She jumped up and headed back inside, leaving him speechless, as usual.

He leaned back against the railing and chuckled, closing the file on his lap. The Brissedons and Desmonds could wait until tomorrow. For today, he was just going to sit back and enjoy the warm summer weather and his family.

CHAPTER 26

Monday, June 27, 1904 – 9:00 a.m.

The sergeant was waiting for him at the station when he arrived back in Patchogue Monday morning. "Any luck?"

Daniel explained the situation and watched as the crevices in the man's forehead deepened. "What are you going to tell Miss Brissedon?"

"I can't lie to her. Sooner or later, it's going to come out, and I suppose it's better she heard it from me."

"Well, that might be sooner rather than later, Doc," the sergeant said. "She left a message for you this morning, asking that you meet her at Newins for a late luncheon around two."

Taking a deep breath, Daniel nodded. "Drop me off at my rooms. While I change my shirt, you can send a message saying I'll be happy to meet her. Just put it on my hotel account. After that, I want to head over to the Brissedons' again and speak to the groom and stable boys. There's no need to bother anyone in the house."

"Afraid you might run into her before you can prepare yourself?"

Was that a smile he saw on the sergeant's face? Daniel frowned. "Maybe, but never mind that. What did you find out while I was gone?"

"Well, Stockbridge wasn't at home, but he wasn't with a lady either. Spent the night a few towns over, drowning his sorrows in a glass or two of whiskey."

"A glass or two?"

The sergeant chuckled. "Yes, sir, the tavern keep said that's all he had. Just sat there, nursing those drinks, mumbling to himself. Got there about one and didn't leave till six. The bartender still had to clean up after closing, so he let him stay till he was finished, then sent him on his way. As far as the business deal, it's just like Stockbridge said. Talbot wasn't very happy about the turn of events. Said he thought he was helping Stockbridge out. Worse yet, it's a five-year contract, so there's nothing he can do about it for a good piece anyway."

"From everything I'm finding out, I'd almost like to forget about the entire case. Brissedon seems to have gotten what he deserved."

"Yes, sir, that appears to be the consensus, but I doubt it's in either of us to just let it lie."

Daniel shook his head. "What about Brighton? My father hadn't heard anything back before I left."

"Just got a phone call from him before I came to pick you up. Mr. Templeton is not a student at Columbia, nor has he ever been."

"So what game is he playing?"

"Maybe he's hoping Mr. Brice won't check."

"To what end? He won't get his promotion until he's got that diploma."

"Maybe he's waiting until after he and Miss Brissedon are hitched. She might not like being married to a mere messenger, but there wouldn't be much she could do about it."

"No, but we can make sure she has all the facts before she makes that decision."

Owens rubbed his hands together, a broad grin breaking out on his face. "I just love frying me up a little weasel."

Sergeant Owens had no sooner pulled the buggy up in front of the Brissedons' stables than the two stable hands stumbled out, looking more than a bit put out. They were covered in muck and hay and smelled of horse manure. Daniel heaved a weary sigh, but he had a job to do. He jumped down from the buggy, trying not to breathe too deeply. Considering the fastidious gentleman Thomas Brissedon was purported to be, Daniel marveled at how these two bounders had managed to retain their positions. He'd worked at a stable for a time himself, during his teen years, and he knew better than to think their appearance was a result of the job.

"The house is up that way, Doc," the dark-haired one said. Daniel was sure the man must be using grease from the wagon wheels to slick back his hair and mustache, for it didn't smell like any hair tonic he'd ever come across.

"Yes, I'm well aware, but it's you two fine gentlemen I've come to speak to."

"Does Mr. Colin know you're here?" the lighter-haired one said. Compared to his dark-haired friend, this one didn't even look as if his straw-like hair had ever seen a comb, let alone a dab of hair tonic.

"You can run up and tell him if you like, but it's just drawing out the inevitable, and my mood is likely to deteriorate the longer I have to wait."

"What's he mean?" the light-haired one said.

"He means if we make him wait while we talk to Mr. Colin, he's going to be right testy. Don't ye, Doc?"

"Very good." Daniel flipped open his notepad. "Mickey Duggan, is it?"

"Yes, sir, that's right. So, what can I do for you?" The man wiped his sleeve across his nose, leaving a trail of slime. "I don't know nothing about Mr. Brissedon's murder."

Double negative, perfect. Daniel glanced down at the man's slimy sleeve. His mother would have given him a good slap in the back of the head if he ever did that. "Nevertheless, I'd like to speak to you about that night. Did either of you see anything that seemed unusual?"

"Not really, just the usual goings-on."

"Which would be?"

"Miss Kathleen, of course." The light-haired man snickered with a lewd twinkle in his eye.

Daniel checked his notes again to keep himself from giving the man such a punch he'd end up in Canarsie. "You must be Willie Sutton."

"That's right. She met that Templeton fella of hers twice a week."

"But she always had someone with her." Mickey took a step back, eying Daniel warily.

"And who was with her that night?" he said.

"Can't say I rightly remember. That sweet looking little maid of hers, I think."

Dear God, was the man salivating? "Was she with him long?"

"Nah, twenty minutes, maybe. Not even long enough for a good feel."

Daniel wasn't sure if he wanted to puke or haul off and punch the disgusting little creep. "What about Colin Brissedon? Did you see him go out that night?"

"No, sir," Willie said with a snicker, "but we heard him, sure enough. Stumbling all over the place, he was. Drunk as a sailor on shore leave."

"What time was that?"

"Darned if I know. Must have been about two, I reckon, maybe three. Just a bit after Mr. Kilpatrick headed back from the lake. He didn't go to his quarters, though. He was heading over to the main house. Been playing at thread the needle with one of them maids of theirs, you know. Even knocked her up, from what I heard. That's why Tommy . . . uh, Mr. Brissedon . . . he was going to fire the tart. Don't want that kind of scandal in his household . . . or another mouth to feed. He was a bit tight with his money."

Daniel pinched the bridge of his nose. *It wasn't Lizzie that was fired, you daft fools!* "Two or three, you say? I might ask what you two were doing up at that hour in the first place."

Willie let out a naughty snicker, and Mickey threw him a disapproving glance. "Well, he woke us up, didn't he?" the latter said. "Out rummaging around at that time of night."

Time for a change of subject. "I understand Mr. Brissedon would bring Patrick out here for punishment from time to time. Did it ever go beyond a few stripes with his strap?"

"How would we know? You think we got nothing better to do than stand around watching the little prig get his ass whupped?"

Daniel lifted an eyebrow. "Really, he never asked you to lend a hand?"

"You'd best be telling him, Mickey," Willie said, not finding the conversation so funny anymore. "He knows for sure, and I ain't covering for the old bastard."

"Your friend is right, Mr. Duggan," Daniel said. "I assure you, it will be in your own best interest."

"I don't know what you're talking about. He'd bring the young buck out here all right, for a good ass whupping now and again, but nothing more than the boy deserved."

"And what did he beat him with?"

"His strap, of course." Mickey set his jaw and folded his arms across his chest. "I don't know what you're getting at, Doc, but I think you've got the wrong idea. Mr. Brissedon did right by his stepson. It was the boy who did everything in his power to aggravate the poor man."

"How's that?" Daniel said.

"Sleeping around the way he did, not just with the local help, but with some of them high-class chits that come out for the summer, then leaving Mr. Brissedon to face the wrath of their fathers or brothers. That boy has no self-respect. Why, just a few weeks ago, he took to messing about with Mr. Pratt's girl right in the gentleman's own barn. Got caught at it, too, and Pratt demanded some satisfaction. What else was Mr. Brissedon to do but give the lad a good sound thrashing? Imagine bringing such shame on your own family. If there was trouble between Mr. Brissedon and his stepson, it was Mr. Patrick who brought it on."

"You seem to know a great deal about their relationship. Did you spend a lot of time in the house?"

"Good Lord, no!" Willie grinned, obviously glad to be on safer ground once more. "The old man never let any of the outside help in the house. That's why Trevor would sneak over on the sly, you see. Mr. Brissedon didn't want us leaving our muddy boot prints all over the place. He was a real stickler about that. I'm surprised he even let Mr. Patrick in the house, but then I suppose he'd have to, wouldn't he?"

"I thought you said he had no animosity toward Patrick?"

"Ani—what?" Willie scratched his head.

"Animosity, you fool," Mickey said. "And he didn't, not usually, but like we said, that boy did anything he could to aggravate the poor old man. Things like scraping his muddy boots across the floor and leaving a trail of horse dung, or so Mr. Colin says."

"Just one more question," Daniel said. "Could you tell me where I might find this Trevor Kilpatrick you spoke of?"

"You can't," Mickey said. "Not this morning, anyway. He's taken Miss Kathleen into town for the day. Probably won't be back till dusk."

"It's almost one, sir," the sergeant said. "Should we head on back?"

"Yes, I suppose we should." He turned back to the two stable hands and tipped his hat. "Thank you for being so accommodating, gentlemen."

He rolled his eyes as he started back for the buggy with Sergeant Owens. "You'd best drop me off at my rooms again. After talking to those two, I'll need to get cleaned up before meeting Miss Brissedon at Newins."

"Do you have anything you want me to look into?"

"Yes, check out the local bawdy houses and gambling hells. See if you can find out what Colin Brissedon was up to at two or three in the morning the day his father died and what time he got home."

"Yes, sir. Don't stay out too late, now."

"It's luncheon, and her groom's going to be waiting."

"Unless you send him away and take her home yourself."

"That would be highly inappropriate. I'd never put a lady in such a compromising position."

"Good for you, lad. See you in the morning, then."

Daniel noticed Trevor leaning up against the lamppost reading his newspaper when he arrived at Newins. He was tempted to go talk to the man right then and there, but it wouldn't be very polite to keep the lady waiting. Besides, putting it off another day or so would give him a reason to return to the Brissedons' home again.

"Sorry if I kept you waiting." He slipped into the chair across from Kathleen. She looked paler than usual, her cheeks a faded blush, but she smiled up at him, nonetheless.

"I actually just arrived myself," she said. "How was your visit with your family?"

"My uncle was able to get a copy of the police report," he said. The waiter came over and they ordered, waiting for him to walk away before continuing their conversation. "I was wondering if you might be able to get me photographs of your father and cousin? Just to eliminate them . . ."

"I know what was in the police report, Doctor," she said, stopping him short.

"I'm sorry? How could you know? Did Sergeant Owens—"

"No, I'm afraid I wasn't completely honest with you on Saturday. I withheld a vital piece of information."

Daniel rubbed his forehead, trying to stay the ache forming in his head. "What piece of information?"

"Please understand I didn't intend to keep it from you forever, but you seemed so intent on blaming my father's murder on Patrick. I just wanted to see where it led before I turned it over to you."

All of a sudden, he'd lost his appetite. What he needed was a shot of whiskey. "All right. I assume you've had time to follow it up by now, so would you mind sharing it with me?" It was a struggle to hold his temper, but he had no intention of embarrassing himself or the lady. If they hadn't already ordered, he would have simply suggested they leave.

"When I was searching my father's office, I came across a note that had fallen into one of his drawers. It was addressed to Patrick from an Alexander Morton, who is a private detective."

"And you thought it best to keep this from me?" Daniel could barely contain his anger. Having this information could have saved him a trip to Brooklyn, maybe even answered some of the questions he still had.

"You would have assumed Patrick dropped it while ransacking my father's office, that he knew everything we both know now, but I don't believe Patrick ever received the note. Colin intercepted it. Whether he kept it or gave it to my father, I don't know. But one thing I do know now is that Patrick never went to see Mr. Morton after the note was delivered, so he has no idea . . ." She stifled a sob and held her handkerchief up to her face.

After taking a drink of water, he crumpled up his napkin. Dear God, what kind of a monster was he? Surely she realized who Tommy Breslin was, just as he did. Her heart must be breaking. "Perhaps we should leave. I'll take care of the bill and tell the waiter you're not feeling well."

"No!" She blew out a deep breath and seemed to calm herself. "I'd prefer to speak here, where no one in my family can overhear, and where you're more likely to keep hold of that Irish temper of yours."

"I beg your pardon?"

The touch of a smile crossed her lips, and she looked up at him through her lashes. "Did you know you get golden specks around your iris and a red patch right in the center of your forehead when you're angry?"

He touched his forehead self-consciously. "I don't."

"Oh, but you do, Doctor. However, I'm sure you'll keep a tighter leash on it in a public place than in private."

"I assure you, miss, I'm not prone to do you harm simply because I lose my temper."

"I'm sure you're not, but I suspect you'd give me a hearty lecture, and to be honest, after learning what I have about my father, I'm in no mood for such a scolding."

The waiter placed their plates on the table, then moved away. Daniel looked down at his flounder, not sure whether he should feel angry because of her deception or feel guilty because he'd forgotten how devastating the news must have been for her. She sat quietly, staring down at her salmon, and guilt won out.

"I'm sorry, Kathleen. I don't know how else to interpret the information. I have my uncle trying to locate Miss O'Neill, and if you can lend me photographs of your father and cousin, perhaps I can get some more definitive answers."

She bit her lip. "I know where Miss O'Neill is, but I want to go along on the interview."

Daniel's temper flared again, though he tried to keep his tone steady. "You want to what? This isn't some kind of game, Kathleen. People have been murdered here."

This time her temper flared. "Yes, and my father and perhaps even my cousin might be involved. How can I face Patrick if I haven't verified it all myself?"

"I'm sorry. It's out of the question."

"Then don't expect me to be supplying any photographs. Come to think of it, I'm not sure I have any."

"That's blackmail!" Daniel clasped his hand around the fork and stabbed his fish.

"Call it whatever you like, but you'll not be getting them or Mary O'Neill's address unless I have your word that I can go along."

"I could lock you up for this." His jaw was so tight he was afraid it would never open again.

"Do what you feel you must, but I'll not give in. I need the truth, and I want to judge Miss O'Neill's words for myself."

He brushed his hand back through his hair and massaged his forehead. "It would be completely inappropriate. Think of your reputation."

"And a night spent in that drafty lockup of yours would do more for my reputation?"

"Don't be impertinent. You know very well what I mean."

"Point taken. I'll have my maid, Molly, come along. She'll find it an adventure, and no one can say we were unchaperoned. Or maybe you would rather my brother Patrick join us?"

"You are a conniving little . . ."

"Yes?" She lifted an eyebrow, daring him to finish his thought.

"Fine, just Molly, then. But you are there to observe and nothing more. Is that understood?"

"It is." She blew her nose and proceeded to eat her smoked salmon.

"I am sorry, Kathleen."

"It's all right, Daniel. I have reconciled myself to the fact that the father I loved is nothing more than a cold-blooded murderer. I've shed all the tears I intend to for him. My only goal now is to see that Patrick isn't blamed for his demise. He's had to endure quite enough already."

"And what if he is guilty?"

"Then my father got what he deserved. I'll not help you convict Patrick for his death."

Daniel reached across the table and touched her hand. "You don't mean that."

She closed her eyes for a moment, a tear trickling down her cheek, before blinking and looking up at him. "No, not really, but I don't want to lose Patrick too. I know he's not actually my brother, but . . . it's hard to explain."

"You don't have to. I was adopted, you see, and I feel the same about my brothers and sister." He frowned, not wanting to make her a promise he couldn't keep. "But I have to follow the clues, and if they lead to Patrick . . ."

"I know," she said, wiping the tear from her face. "I would expect no less of you."

CHAPTER 27

Tuesday, June 28, 1904 – 7:00 a.m.

Daniel settled into the seat across from Kathleen while Molly sat next to her, gazing out the window at the passing sights. Though she tried to appear sophisticated, a grin kept breaking out on her pretty face. She had clearly never been on a train before, let alone one heading for New York City.

"Why *are* you so determined to blame Patrick for this?" Kathleen finally said after Molly had dozed off. She sat with her hands atop her small, beaded handbag, worrying a few of the beads with her fingers.

"I'm not determined to blame anyone, but right now the evidence is overwhelmingly pointing in his direction."

"Such as?" Kathleen stilled her fingers, glaring at him pointedly.

Daniel sighed. Aside from his family, he wasn't used to discussing cases with anyone outside his colleagues in the department. "He has the most reason, hasn't he? Your father took possession of everything he thought might one day be his, none of which he's in line to inherit. Then to add insult to injury, he married his mother. Patrick probably felt as if she was being taken away from him too. And then there's Lydia's proposed marriage to Colin."

She winced. "When you put it like that, I suppose it doesn't look good for him. But what real evidence do you have?"

"Those cuff links, for one."

"I told you," she said, trying to keep her voice low. "I don't know that Patrick stole them. It could have been anyone. Father put them on a shelf so he could roll up his sleeves, but any number of people stopped by the carriage house to look at his new automobile that day."

A smile tugged on the corner of Daniel's mouth. "And you know that because . . ."

"That's what I like to see. That sweet little dimple that appears in your cheek when you're relaxed and happy."

"You didn't answer my question."

"It was a beautiful spring day, and I have to admit the contraption is fascinating. Have you ever ridden in one? It's quite liberating."

"Yes, it is. My father has one, though he only uses it when he goes out of the city. But back to the cuff links. If so many people were in and out, why did you suspect Patrick?"

"Because they were his father's, I suppose."

"That's a reasonable assumption. Imagine how he felt, seeing your father wearing them, knowing they should be his. I can't say I wouldn't have been tempted. He did manage to retain one thing from his father, though." Had Kathleen's face just blanched a bit? Probably just the lighting. "He had a key to the back hallway door he didn't tell anyone about."

Her eyes widened. "He did?" But then she shook her head. "But why would that matter? All he'd have to do was walk across the hallway to the main part of the house. My father's room is right there."

345

"Yes, but it would come in handy if he wanted to make it seem like the break-in came from outside. It would also explain those paint chips on the floor and the open window. Patrick cared for Lydia Langston, and your father had just informed him he was going to make sure they would never be together. Perhaps that was the final straw. Patrick even threatened to kill him hours before his body was discovered."

Kathleen was frowning again, and Daniel had to smile at the way her lips curled at the sides when she was annoyed. He looked away, trying to tamp down the desire that had risen in his thighs at the thought of his lips pressing against hers.

"I won't deny he has a bit of a temper," Kathleen said, "but I can't believe he really meant it. Besides, he'd have to be a fool to go through with it after making such a threat."

"Or maybe that temper of his got the better of him."

She gazed out the window, glancing back at him a few times, as if she were considering whether to tell him something or not. Finally, she sighed, her decision apparently made.

"Patrick wasn't even home that night."

"And you know this because . . . ?"

"Because I went to his bedroom after I came in from speaking to Brighton."

Daniel tilted his head, narrowing his eyes. "I thought you spent the night with Brighton? But you meant to spend it with Patrick instead?"

Her eyes widened. "No, of course not! Nor did I spend it with Brighton. I just didn't want . . ." She bit her lip.

"Didn't want me blaming him for the murder either."

"Maybe. But Brighton wouldn't . . ."

"Tell me, then, Kathleen, who did it? I mean, it's not Patrick or Colin or Brighton or Jeremy. Should I go on?" He clamped his mouth shut, breathing through his nose in an attempt to calm his temper. Turning away, he stared down the aisle, debating whether or not just to return home. His uncle would discover Mary O'Neill's address eventually, and perhaps he could contact the photographer in Patchogue to see if they had photographs of Thomas and Jeremy to show her.

"I'm sorry. You're right." When he didn't answer, she pressed her hand against his arm. "Daniel, please."

A lump caught in his throat, his defenses weakening. He closed his eyes for a moment, the silence between them deafening. Taking a deep breath, he opened his eyes and turned to her.

"I need the truth, Kathleen. All the lying does is make everyone look guilty. Trust in the truth and have enough faith in me to sort it out."

"I was only with Brighton about thirty minutes. That's all I ever spent with him."

"And who accompanied you? You couldn't seem to make up your mind the other day."

Kathleen's cheeks blushed a deep pink. "It was Molly. Colin was already well up the pole."

"What else have you lied to me about?"

"Nothing." She let out a groan and looked over to make sure Molly was still dozing. "I may have neglected to mention a thing or two, however."

"Really! You do realize I could arrest you for withholding information?"

This time she rolled her eyes. "Don't be so dramatic. Aside from the fact that the threat is getting old, my information has nothing to do with the case. Jeremy was waiting for me when I came in. He was drunk and tried to get me to sleep with him."

Daniel was sure someone had set his cheeks afire. "He what?"

"I didn't consider it," she said defensively. "He got a bit aggressive, so I ran to Patrick's room for help, but he wasn't there. I knew he kept his father's knife under his mattress, so I threatened Jeremy with it, and he slunk off. He probably went up to Molly to sleep it off."

He threw a glance in Molly's direction. She was so sweet and innocent, much like his mama must have been. All he could do was hope Jeremy had more integrity than Arthur Pritchard had.

"He still could have come back later," he said. "That doesn't give him an alibi." Taking a breath, he tried to focus on Kathleen's words. "Wait. Patrick has a knife? Where is it now?"

"You can't possibly believe I used it to kill my father?"

"Don't think it didn't just cross my mind," he said, gritting his teeth.

She rolled her eyes once more, as if to say now he *was* being ridiculous. "I put it back under his mattress, where it always is. It's the only thing he has from his father."

"And it could very well be the murder weapon."

She smiled, her eyes twinkling. "But if I had it, that means Patrick didn't. Besides, there was no blood on it."

"And what time was that?" He raised his eyebrows as if that was explanation enough.

"Oh. Well, still . . ." She stared down at her handbag for a moment, tapping her finger on its clasp, before gasping and raising her head to glare at him once more, anger shining in her eyes.

"You're just following up on the Cornelius Desmond case to prove Patrick had even more reason to want my father dead, aren't you?"

He huffed a laugh. "You're the one who asked me to look into it, remember? But if it happens to be more evidence against Patrick, then so be it."

She grabbed the handbag with both hands, squeezing it so hard Daniel was glad it wasn't his neck she had ahold of.

"Look, if you really want to prove Patrick innocent, try to think of something in that police report to convince me someone else might be involved."

She gave a nod, though she didn't speak to him for the rest of the ride, even declining to take his arm as they disembarked from the train and boarded the ferry to Manhattan.

"Well, lead the way, m'lady," he said when they arrived. "You're the one with Mary O'Neill's address, but I would suggest both you ladies take an arm. This isn't Patchogue."

"I'm well aware of that. I have been to the city before." Begrudgingly, she took his arm and headed down the street, stopping after a moment. "Here's the address of the millinery shop where she works. It's on Madison Avenue. Oh, and her name is Mary Brady now."

"I thought she sold flowers from a little stall on Fourteenth Street?"

"She did, but she married a trolley car conductor named Stephen Brady, so she lives farther uptown now and was able to secure a job at the milliners. She arranges the artificial flowers on ladies' hats. People can move up, you know. Look at Cornelius Desmond."

"And how did you find all this out?"

"Mr. Morton may look a bit disheveled, but his records are impeccable."

Daniel stifled a smile and called for a carriage. "Unless you'd prefer to take the El."

Kathleen narrowed her eyes and followed Molly into the cab. At least the young maid was excited. Her head was turning so quickly Daniel was amazed she hadn't made herself dizzy.

They finally stopped before a fashionable millinery shop on Madison Avenue. Daniel introduced himself to the owner, explaining the situation, but Mary must have been watching from the back room because she came running out almost at once.

"Is Stephen all right?" Tears welled in her eyes, but Daniel hurried to calm her fears.

"Oh, I'm sure he is, Mrs. Brady. That's not what I've come about. I understand that you were a witness in the death of Cornelius Desmond."

"Neily Desmond! That was over two years ago. I told the police everything I knew back then, though I don't think they paid me a lick of attention, mind you."

"Why do you think that?" He pointed to two sofas in the showroom, indicating they should sit down.

"Well, they never tried to find out who that homely fella I told them about was, did they?"

Daniel cast a glance in Kathleen's direction. "The one who sent him to the address where he died?"

"That's the one. Neily was murdered, that's sure." She looked between the two of them, her eyes pleading. "But they said he'd fallen over the railing, three sheets to the wind. Well, I know better. Neily, he could hold his liquor, not that he drank that much anyway. And I never saw a man more devoted to his family. Not till my Stephen, that is."

Daniel smiled, certain his dimples would appear. "You don't think Cornelius killed that girl and the old man, then?"

"Good Lord, no! Neily was the gentlest man I ever met, next to my Stephen, of course." Love shone in her eyes, causing Daniel's smile to broaden.

"You stated that you saw him talking to a homely fella, that he was a tall, slender young man with drooping eyelids." He nodded to Kathleen, and she handed him the photographs.

"That was it, like he was sleeping the whole time."

"Did you know who he was?"

"I'd never seen him before or after, for that matter. He may just have been passing through. Some friends of mine thought he might go by the name of Jerry Mc-something-or-other—Ready or Ratty. I can't really remember. It all seems so long ago now."

"What about Tommy Breslin?"

"Tommy Breslin," she repeated thoughtfully. "No, I'm afraid not."

"Or Thomas Brissedon," Kathleen said.

"No, but now I think on it, about three months before Neily was killed, a friend of mine pointed out this swell and said his name was Tommy Breslin. Went right up to him, she did, saying it was good to see him and all. Well, didn't he stage a fit, insisting his name was Thomas Brissedon. Said he had no idea who she was, but that she could bugger off if she thought he'd give her a dime."

"Annie was right put out, being he'd been after her to marry him back in the day. 'Twas after his wife died, and he had two little ones to care for. Probably wanted nothing more than a nursemaid. 'Tis one thing to look after your own, but tending to another's child is a whole other story."

Daniel thought of his Aunt Sarah, the woman he now called Mother, and how he'd always felt so loved. A burst of warmth filled his heart, and he had to clear his throat to continue. "What about this McRady fella? Did your friend ever mention him?"

"You know, I do remember Annie mentioning something about him. He was a cousin, or maybe a nephew, of Tommy's. Followed him around like a puppy, she said."

"Where can I find Annie now?" Kathleen asked.

"Oh, you can't, I'm afraid, darling. Poor thing got influenza a few months back and passed on. Probably weak from the beatings her boyfriend gave her."

Daniel handed her one of the cabinet cards. "Do you recognize the man in this photograph?"

Mary put her glasses on and looked closely. "Why, that's the sleepy-eyed fella that was talking to Neily, isn't it? Dressed a mite finer than he was back then, but it's him just the same. I reckon he must have done all right for himself as well."

"And this one?"

"I can't swear to it. I only saw him the once, and he didn't have anything about him you'd remember like the other one. But I'm a monkey's uncle if that's not Tommy Breslin, or Thomas Brissedon, as he'd taken to calling himself. I reckon once he got some money, his Irish name wasn't good enough for him."

"Thank you, Mrs. Brady. You've been more help than you know."

"My pleasure, sir. I'm sorry, I didn't catch your name. You looked like a copper, and I was so worried something had happened to my Stephen."

"It's Dr. O'Halleran. Some of us are still proud of our Irish."

She grinned and slapped him on the arm playfully. "Oh, go on with you, then. There'd be no denying it with a handsome face like that."

Kathleen giggled, and Daniel could feel the heat rushing all the way to the tips of his ears.

"Dr. O'Halleran, then," Mary said, "what are you looking into Neily's death for? I mean, you being a doctor and all."

"I work for the coroner's office out on Long Island."

"Long Island? I guess his widow finally convinced someone out there to take her serious. Good for her. Are you going to be reopening the case, then?"

"I may be, ma'am. Why do you ask?"

"Then you find out who murdered dear sweet Neily Desmond, will you? When they found that knife, they just closed the case, as if he didn't matter at all, but I tell you, sir, there are few men that matter as much. This one detective did try, God bless him, but . . . well, there wasn't much to find, I suppose. Come to think of it, his name was O'Halleran too."

Daniel nodded. "My uncle Timothy."

"I should have seen the resemblance. He was a looker too, a bit old for me, but he must have been a handsome man in his day."

He chuckled, his gaze stopping on Molly, who was eyeing a pretty white picture hat with a brim turned down in the back. It had dainty pink flowers and white tulle on the side and a velvet ribbon of a deeper pink around the crown. "While I'm here, would you be able to help me with a few purchases? I'll think I'll take that one."

"Yes, of course, Doctor," Mary said. "I'll box it right up for you."

"No, I think the young lady might like to wear it. You can put her old hat in the box."

Molly's eyes widened. "Oh, Doctor, I can't afford anything so fine."

"It's a gift," Daniel said, "to thank you for coming along with us today."

Kathleen put her arm through his, the warmth in her eyes palpable. "That was very kind of you, but did you see the price?"

"Should I have?" He turned back to Mary. "And that boater for the lady, I'm thinking. It just has a bit of white on it, so it should keep with your mourning attire."

Kathleen pulled him aside. "Daniel, they must be at least half a week's pay for you, if not more. This is a millinery shop, not the Sears Roebuck catalog."

"Really? Oh, well then . . . which hat do you favor, Mrs. Brady?"

"Oh, I've always liked this pretty little black-and-white picture hat. 'Twould look lovely on the lady."

"It's yours, Mrs. Brady. As a thank-you for all your help."

"Oh, but I couldn't, sir."

"Of course you could, darling," the shop owner said. "Is there anything else I could help you with, Doctor?"

"Yes, as a matter of fact. That boater with the blue-and-white-striped ribbon for my sister and something for my mother."

"This feathered hat is not so bold, but still very fashionable for an older lady."

"Yes, I think she'd like that. Can you box up that and the boater with the striped ribbon and have it delivered to this address?" He took out his pad and wrote down his parents' address.

"Would you like me to include a note?"

"Just say, 'All my love, Danny.' The other two we'll take with us."

"Yes, of course, sir. That will be $24.65."

Kathleen started to open her handbag, obviously planning to cover anything he couldn't, but she stopped short, a look of amazement on her face, when he grinned and paid the bill.

"Thank you," he said, "and please give the change to your favorite charity."

Pleased with himself, as he'd decided to at least let Kathleen into a little of his background, he was surprised to find her scowling at him when they got outside. "You were one of those corrupt officers Mr. Roosevelt tried to eliminate from the police department, weren't you? Is that why you had to come out to Patchogue? To avoid getting caught?"

A spark of anger flared in his chest, but he stamped it down. He supposed it wasn't fair. She knew nothing about him. Still, to think he was corrupt. "No," he said, a touch of frost to his voice, "I happen to have a small trust fund that I rarely dip into."

"And that's why you decided to become a policeman, I suppose. You've so much money you don't know what to do with yourself, and after all, it is fun poking around in people's lives."

"Actually, I have a medical degree, and I chose to become a coroner's physician because I like giving the dead a voice. Their bodies can tell us what happened to them and maybe even who did it. Besides, I suppose I wanted to follow in my uncle Timothy's footsteps. He, by the way, is as honest as the day is long, not that it's any of your business. Do you look into Brighton's background when he buys you a bunch of flowers? Because maybe you should."

"For your information, Brighton is studying to be an attorney."

"He is, is he?" He bit his tongue, trying not to lash out in anger and hurt her.

"Yes, he is, and those hats you just bought are far more expensive than any bouquet of flowers he might bring me."

He stopped, rubbing his hand across his forehead, and made a decision. "Come on, we're taking the El connection."

"We can walk . . ."

"Not to Brooklyn. I'm going to introduce you to my parents. They can confirm my trust fund and assure you I'm not corrupt."

A smile played peek-a-boo on her lips, though she tried to conceal it. "You're introducing me to your family?"

He scowled at her. "I suppose I am, technically. But don't get any ideas. I just don't like the notion of you thinking I was some form of corrupt cop."

"Of course," she said with a demure smile.

Daniel groaned. What had he done now? *Exactly what you wanted to do, and you know it.* But he couldn't reveal everything, not yet. His mother and father had always said his secrets were his to tell, so he knew they'd honor his decision. Memories of Prudence Davis almost made him change his mind, but no. He wanted to get his father's opinion on a few things. Besides, he needed to keep Kathleen's mind occupied so she didn't dwell on the fact that her father had almost certainly murdered Cornelius Desmond. His mother and sister could keep her busy while he spoke with his father.

Molly's eyes were wide as they walked down the tree-lined street, stately brownstones standing along either side, and Daniel was happy the girl was enjoying herself.

"This is where you grew up?" Kathleen gave a tug on his sleeve. "If I'd known that, I wouldn't have volunteered to pay for lunch that first day we met."

"You didn't pay for it." He gave her a quick smile and led her up the next stoop, using his key to open the heavy black vestibule door within its clean white frame.

"Mr. Daniel," the butler said, his voice a study in untiring patience.

"Sorry, Byron," Daniel said. "Would you like me to go out and start again?"

"Don't be impudent," Byron said. "It doesn't become you, sir. Shall I announce you?"

"No, I'll just go in, though I imagine Molly here would enjoy some tea. We missed lunch, I'm afraid. And this is Miss Kathleen Brissedon. She's apparently helping me with a case."

Daniel cast Byron a warning glance as the butler struggled to prevent a smile from breaking out on his face. "Pleased to meet you, Miss Brissedon." Then, turning to the maid, he put out his arm for her to take. "If you would accompany me, Miss Molly, we'll see about getting you some sustenance."

Kathleen was watching him warily from the corner of her eye, but she didn't say a word, taking his arm as he escorted her into the parlor. His mother was the first to look up, dropping her embroidery and coming over to give him a big hug.

"Daniel! We weren't expecting you back so soon. You'll stay for dinner, of course."

"Yes, Mother, but then we must catch the train back to Long Island."

"Well, I suppose if you can't stay longer, I'll have to be grateful for what time I do have with you. And who is this lovely lady?"

"This is Miss Brissedon. We've been chasing down a lead in the Desmond case. You'll love her, Mother. She refused to give me the information I needed until I agreed to let her come along."

"Now that's my kind of girl." Isabell came through the doorway and gave him a peck on the cheek.

Daniel kissed her on the forehead. "Perhaps you could both keep Miss Brissedon entertained while I speak to Father?"

"I'm sure they're more than capable, Daniel, my boy." He'd put his newspaper down and walked over to give Daniel a pat on the back. "Why don't we retire to my study?"

His father had no sooner closed the door than he turned to face Daniel. "Sit down and tell me what's troubling you, Son. Is it something to do with the case or the feelings you have for that young lady?"

Daniel blurted it all out. How she was Thomas Brissedon's daughter and what they'd discovered about the man, how he was afraid Patrick might be her father's murderer, and how he was hesitant to open his heart again. And as usual, the man listened quietly, puffing on his pipe, never mocking or minimalizing Daniel's fears.

Finally, his father laid his pipe aside and sat back in his chair, folding his hands across his waist. "I want you to listen to me, Son. Prudence Davis is a stuck-up little prima donna who thinks her shit doesn't stink."

Daniel's eyes sprang wide, but his father continued undaunted. "There'll never be any man good enough for her. She'll marry that Clermont buck for money and prestige, nothing more. But not every woman is like Pru. I'd wager to say that little lady out there won't care what side of the sheets you were conceived on. Seems to me she was fond of you even when she thought you nothing more than a coroner's assistant, maybe making twelve or thirteen dollars a week."

"But she lied to me."

"Pshaw!!! That's not lying, boy. Do you truly think your mother doesn't have her secrets? The fact is, you're lying to her as well. Have you told her about Arthur, or who your mama was?"

Daniel could feel his cheeks flushing. "No, but that doesn't have anything to do with the case. And what does it matter anyway?"

"It doesn't. You're the only one who seems to think it does. As for the case, she's just trying to protect her family. No different than you would, I imagine." He reached over and clasped Daniel's arm. "The fact that she did eventually tell you says a lot, Danny. And if what you say is true, that girl is going to need a strong shoulder to lean on in the coming days. Don't deny her that because you're afraid of being hurt again."

His father frowned and leaned his forearms on his knees, looking up at Daniel from beneath his graying eyebrows. "Do you truly think we all haven't had pain in our lives, Son? You've had more than your fair share, I'll give you that, but I'm hoping you've had a good bit of happiness as well."

Daniel smiled, tears welling in his eyes. "I love you, Father."

"I know you do, Son." He leaned back and picked up his pipe. "Now what about this Brissedon case? Do you really think the stepson did it?"

"I don't want to, but the evidence just keeps stacking up against him."

"And what does your gut tell you?"

"That it's too much evidence. Almost as if someone is setting him up."

"So maybe let them think you've bought into it. People have a tendency to lower their guard when they think they're in the clear. Try to figure out who has the most to lose, and I'm not just talking money. People have been known to kill for anger, love, revenge. Don't eliminate the other reasons just because money is on the table." He sighed, his forehead crinkling. "Of course, money always does seem to be a part of it all, doesn't it?"

"I suppose it does in one form or another, but you're right, as usual. It may not be that clearcut." Daniel smiled at his father, wondering if he'd ever be that wise.

His father stood and patted him on the back. "Now, according to the grumbling in my stomach and the sound of footsteps on the stairs, I'd say it's almost time for supper." He went to grasp the brass handle of the dark oak pocket door. "As for your secret, it's yours to tell, Son, when you feel the time is right. Just don't fault her if she keeps a few of her own as well."

It was late when they pulled up to the Brissedons' home. He'd phoned from his parents' to let them know where they were, so Forbes was waiting at the door when they arrived. The other men were sitting in the parlor, which had been prepared for Thomas Brissedon's wake on the following day.

Daniel bid them all good night, then had the carriage drop him off at his rooms at Roe's Hotel. After taking off his jacket, he undid his collar and tie and flopped down on the bed to consider all his father had said. He needed to find out more about them all. Except for Kathleen and Lydia Langston, any one of them had enough reason to want Thomas Brissedon dead. He could probably exclude Mrs. Quinn as well. She would have just poisoned him in an effective but undetectable way. He had to chuckle. That was what Hattie would do if she had a bit of wickedness in her. Fortunately, she didn't. Somehow he didn't think Mrs. Quinn did either. Now, Mrs. Langston was another issue. He could see her putting on a man's boots and finding the strength to rip the knife across Thomas Brissedon's neck. He shook his head, purging the image from his brain.

What about Molly or Lizzie? If what he'd been told was true, Trevor was paying court to Lizzie. That wouldn't have lasted long if Thomas Brissedon had found out, and he'd fired Molly for no good reason that Daniel could see, unless the old man knew his nephew was tickling her fancy. But could those sweet young girls muster enough strength to do the deed? Possibly.

He scrubbed his hands over his face. And how did Cornelius Desmond's death fit into it all, if it even did? Would someone wait two years to get revenge? Why not? Maybe they hadn't worked it out until now. One thing he was sure of: it was far more than a coincidence. It had to be, but how?

Thomas Brissedon, or Breslin, had more than likely set the whole thing up with the aid of his nephew, Jerry McRady—who he now knew went by the name of Jeremy Radcliffe—then murdered Cornelius Desmond, took his money, and married his grieving widow.

Though Patrick's life must have been hard after his father died, it clearly took a hard turn for the worse with his mother's demise. Thomas no longer needed to keep up any pretense of being a loving father. He beat his stepson and forced him into a kind of prostitution. Then to add insult to injury, not only did he forbid Patrick from seeing the woman he cared for, but she was to be handed over to his stepbrother in marriage. It must have seemed like a nightmare to Patrick. A nightmare from which he couldn't wake.

Still, something was missing, an integral piece of the puzzle that would tie it all together. Patrick Desmond was the son of the kindest man Mary Brady had ever known. Could a child so born be capable of murder? Why not? Daniel muffled a yawn. Considering all Thomas Brissedon had done to him, the boy had every reason on earth to want the old man dead, and that hate and anger might have been festering for two years. So why didn't Daniel believe it?

Because something was off. It was all too solid. He tried to put himself in Patrick's position. What would he feel like if he found out someone had killed his father and stolen everything he owned? Good Lord, he was ready to beat the shit out of Arthur for calling his mama a whore. But would he have killed him? No . . . and neither would Patrick. Run away with Lydia, perhaps. Gather proof of what Thomas had done, definitely. But kill him, no. Patrick wanted to clear his father's name and regain his fortune. With Thomas dead, that was unlikely to happen.

Besides, according to Kathleen, Morton hadn't spoken to Patrick about the new evidence. Was she lying to him about that too? Maybe he needed to visit this Alexander Morton himself.

It was nearly midnight when he laid his head on his pillow, thoughts of what he'd learned that day colliding into one another. No, he didn't believe Patrick Desmond was guilty. Now all he had to do was prove it. With the mounting evidence against the young man, that would be no easy task. One he'd never accomplish if he didn't get some sleep. Heaving a weary sigh, he rolled over and, plumping his pillow, finally fell off to sleep.

CHAPTER 28

Wednesday, June 29, 1904 – 9:00 a.m.

"Alexander Morton?" Daniel asked as he nearly bumped into the tall, disheveled-looking man who was hurrying out of his Railroad Avenue office.

"Yes?" Morton was rummaging through his pockets in search of something and hardly spared a look in Daniel's direction. "How can I help you? I'm really very late, but if you'd like to make an appointment . . ."

"I'm afraid I must speak to you now, sir." Daniel put his arm across the recessed entry, blocking the man's way. Morton stopped short, scrunching up the paper he held in his hands.

"What is it now?" he said. "I've filed all the proper papers, signed where I was supposed to. What more can you possibly need?"

"I have no idea what you're talking about, sir, nor do I care. I've come on pressing business and need speak to you about Patrick Desmond."

"Mr. Desmond is a client, and as such, I can't tell you much about him or his case."

"I understand completely, but if it turns out that he's murdered his stepfather, you could be charged as an accessory after the fact, having held back knowledge that could perhaps have convicted him."

"Who are you? The cops?"

"My name is Dr. O'Halleran, and I'm investigating the case for the coroner's office."

"Look, he's a nice kid," Morton said with a softened tone. "He just wants to prove his father's innocence. But I told all this to his sister. Ask around town; he's a lover, not a killer. I think you've got the wrong young man, Doctor."

"I agree, but I have to prove it. I've already spoken with Miss Brissedon about the particulars. All I need to do is check on a detail or two."

"Aw, what the heck? You'd best walk with me, then. I just uncovered another possible witness. We can talk to him together." They started to walk, and Morton threw a quick look in Daniel's direction. "What details are you looking for, anyway?"

"Just how much of what you found did Patrick know?"

"Like I told the lady, all I was able to give him was the name Tommy Breslin and that I found no Brissedon Mills prior to a couple of months before Cornelius Desmond died. I hadn't gotten my hands on the police report yet. Though I had a witness identifying Tommy Breslin as Thomas Brissedon, there was nothing connecting him to the murder."

"But you sent Patrick a note."

"Yeah, asking him to meet me, but the kid never came. His sister showed up instead, saying he was a suspect and that you'd be watching him."

Daniel's jaw dropped. He should be angry, but he couldn't. His uncle Timothy would be proud of her. "Yes, well, I suppose he was."

"Not so sure now?" Morton asked.

"The evidence tells me yes, but my gut says no."

"Go with your gut, kid. It never steers me wrong."

They stopped in front of the offices of Grayson and Brice. "Brighton Templeton is your witness?"

"Yeah, how'd you know?"

"I have some questions for him myself. Who gave you his name as a witness?"

"This shoeshine boy who heard I was trying to find Neily Desmond's killer. The kid's not one for cops, but when he heard I was a private detective working for Neily's son, he decided to come forward."

Daniel shook his head and huffed a sarcastic laugh. "And he gave you Templeton's name as being a witness?"

"Well, not a witness so much as someone who seemed real interested in finding out who was responsible for Desmond's death. Everybody liked the man. Seems he was a decent sort, always willing to help out a chap down on their luck. This one fella, though, he took to grilling Mary O'Neill, that's the flower seller I told Miss Brissedon about. He was harassing her so much, she asked the trolley car conductor to step in one day, just so he'd leave her alone."

"Mr. Brady, no doubt."

Morton laughed. "I reckon some good comes out of everything."

They walked up to the front desk, but before Morton could say anything, the clerk turned around and shouted to the back. "Hey, Brighton, that doctor's here to see you again."

Brighton came hurrying up. "Dr. O'Halleran? What can I help you with? I told you everything I know."

It seemed Morton was happy to let him take the lead. "Did you now? Is there somewhere we can speak privately?"

Brighton scratched the back of his head before nodding and leading them to an empty office. "I really can't be away for long."

"This won't take but a moment. Why did you lie about being enrolled at Columbia?"

Morton's eyebrows lifted, but Brighton swallowed and flopped down in an empty chair, running his hand through his hair.

"Did you seriously think we wouldn't check, or that we wouldn't speak to Mary O'Neill?"

"Who?" He looked up, his eyes darting back and forth between Daniel and Morton. "I don't know any Mary O'Neill."

"Do you know a flower seller down around Fourteenth Street?" Brighton closed his eyes and groaned, so Daniel continued. "Why were you harassing Mary O'Neill after Cornelius Desmond died?"

Brighton's head popped up, his eyes wide. "I wasn't harassing her. I was just trying to find out if she knew the name of that fella who sent him to the tenement. Neily Desmond was a good man. He helped my mother and I out after my father drank himself into an early grave. He didn't deserve to be left sprawled on a tenement floor, lying in a pool of blood, his clothes soaked in whiskey."

"He was going to pay your college tuition, wasn't he?" Daniel leaned back against the wall and crossed his arms over his chest. "Is that why you sought out Kathleen Brissedon? Revenge?"

"What? No, why would I think Kathleen had anything to do with what happened to Neily? All that flower girl knew was that some hooligan with droopy eyes sent him to the address. I tried to find the man, but no one ever saw him again. With Neily gone, college was out of the question, but rather than go back to the factory, I started looking for a job in a law firm."

"Why in Patchogue?" Daniel asked.

"It's not, except during the summer. I told you, Mr. Brice has an office in the city. That's where I am most of the time, but in the summer he needs extra help out here."

"And you recognized Jeremy?" Daniel narrowed his eyes, trying to gauge the man's sincerity.

"Jeremy? Why would I recognize him?"

"He's the man Mary saw send Cornelius Desmond to that tenement."

The color seemed to drain from Brighton's face, but was it from shock or fear? "You can't be serious. He's been here all this time? I never saw the man, you see. I'd heard word on the street that Mary had, that's all, and hoped she could supply his name, which she apparently did."

"No, actually, she didn't," Daniel said, still watching Brighton through narrowed eyes. "She identified him from a photograph."

"Ah, of course." Brighton stood, but when Daniel didn't move, he sat down again. "I don't know what else I can help you with."

"You still haven't told me why you lied about going for your degree." Daniel had moved over to one of the desks and sat perched on its edge, his arms folded across his chest—not very comfortable, but it was intimidating.

"Because I haven't mustered up the courage to tell Mr. Brice yet. He thinks it's taking me longer because I'm paying for it myself. You're not going to tell him, are you?"

"No, but I suggest you do," Daniel said. "Things like that have a way of coming out sooner or later, and it will go easier for you if you're straight with him."

"So you think he'll keep me on?"

Daniel frowned. "No, but at least you won't have to lie about it anymore."

Brighton's shoulders slumped. "Look, I need this job, and I love the work. I have been saving up so I can go to school, but college is expensive. That's why I gamble. There's this night school for lawyers, though. It doesn't cost nearly as much."

For a moment, Daniel almost felt sorry for him. "At least tell Kathleen. She deserves to know the truth."

"I will, but after the funeral when things settle down a bit."

"Is Brighton Templeton even your real name?"

"No, sir, it's Brian O'Toole. I just wanted to make a good impression, and I'm not hurting anyone by changing it."

"No one except maybe your family," Daniel said.

"My ma was all I had, and she's gone now, so I don't suppose it matters."

After taking Alexander Morton out to lunch to catch up on everything he knew, Daniel stopped by Conklin's Stationery to pick up the copy of *The Hound of the Baskervilles* they'd ordered for him. Byron had been recommending it for the last two years, and since it promised to be a lovely evening, he hoped he'd be able to get a little reading in after his interview with the Brissedons' groom. Sometimes it helped to step away from a puzzle for a bit to get a better look at where the pieces belonged, and that would be the perfect way to do it.

Loath to bother the family during their father's wake, Daniel headed straight for the stables when he arrived at the Brissedons', intent on talking to the groom, Trevor Kilpatrick.

"And what can we do for you today, Doc?" Mickey Duggan said, his lips turned up in a snarl.

"Is Mr. Kilpatrick here today?" Daniel kept his eyes on Mickey's face, which seemed to make the man uncomfortable.

"Yeah, he's over by the horses." Willie came to stand by his friend, presenting a united front, no doubt. "He's giving Miss Charlotte her lesson. Miss Kathleen's trying to keep everything as normal as she can for the young ones."

"Thank you, gentlemen," he said, using the term loosely. He headed over to Trevor Kilpatrick, and the man looked up.

"Run along, now, darlin'," the handsome Irishman instructed Charlotte. "We'll have another lesson tomorrow."

Charlotte glanced at Daniel as she passed, then turned around sharply. "Are you the man who's going to find out who killed my papa?"

"I'm going to do my best, miss."

The girl pulled him down to her height and whispered. "It's probably Patrick. He didn't get on with Papa at all. Sometimes he wouldn't behave, and Papa would have to hit him so hard he'd get sick and cry."

"Did he?" Daniel's heart ached for Patrick. Once again, he realized how lucky he was to have his mother and father.

"Yes." The girl nodded, clearly determined to defend her father. "He probably wanted to hurt Papa back."

"I'll check that out as soon as I can." Daniel wondered if Kathleen would ever tell them what a wicked man their father had been. The girl hurried off, and both Daniel and Trevor just stood for a moment looking after her.

"She doesn't know any better," Trevor finally said. "She idolizes Mr. Colin, so whatever he says, she believes. Sometimes she even gets angry at Miss Kathleen over it."

"Sounds like you don't think much of Colin Brissedon."

"I think he's been Mr. Desmond's ruin. He was a good lad before the Brissedons came along."

"And now he's not?"

"Well, let's just say virtue isn't among his stronger points."

"He likes the ladies as well as his booze, I gather."

"That he does, and he'll take either wherever and whenever he can get them. 'Tis such a waste."

"Why do you blame Colin Brissedon for Patrick's behavior?"

"Who else is he to look to, with his own father gone and all? He was barely eighteen when his da died, then just two years later, his ma. For the life of me, though, I can't understand why he wants to be like that scoundrel."

"Because of the beatings, you mean?"

Trevor nodded, a bit hesitant. "That and the way they treat him. There are times those stable hands are dealt with better than he is."

"When you speak of these beatings, Mr. Kilpatrick, what exactly do you mean? A few whacks at the end of his stepfather's strap?"

"Why do I get the feeling you already know the answer to that?" Trevor said. "But no. I mean just what I say. Beatings! At first it was just the strap, all right, like any da might, but over the last few months, it's intensified. The old man would still use his strap, but he took to using his fists more, even kicked the lad a time or two, and he didn't watch where the strap landed either. The lad started showing up at the stables with a black eye or a swollen lip, things like that. And once Mrs. Desmond . . . Brissedon . . . passed on, things changed yet again, and not for the better."

"Why didn't you stop him? Call the authorities?"

"Stop him? And how was I to do that? 'Twas his son, by law, to discipline as he saw fit."

"Discipline that severe is frowned upon," Daniel said. "Even by the authorities."

"It wouldn't have done any good even if I had. Lord knows why, but the lad would have just denied it, said he'd fallen from his horse or some such foolishness. Without his cooperation, nothing could be done."

Trevor walked over and handed his horse off to Mickey Sutton, then waited for him to get out of earshot before he spoke again. "This last time he really gave the boy what you would call a good beating . . ." He rubbed his hand across his mouth and took a deep breath. "'Twas only recently, mind you. I thought he was going to kill the lad. Then he handed him off to those two," he motioned to the stable hands, "so they could finish it up."

"And they never questioned it?" Daniel asked, feeling nauseous at the thought of all Thomas Brissedon had subjected Patrick to. He couldn't say he'd blame the young man if he had killed the bastard.

"Them two?" Trevor shook his head. "They got a right kick out of it, didn't they? Beating the lad till he couldn't stand, taunting him like some sort of animal."

"How often did it happen?"

"That bad? Just the once that I know of. Dear God, forgive me. I could hear him crying, gagging on his own vomit, and I couldn't bring myself to go help him. I was that scared."

"Afraid of what they might do to you if they found out you knew?"

"That's part of it, I suppose," Trevor said, "but to be honest, more afraid of what Brissedon would do to him. He'd think nothing of putting the boy in an asylum just to get rid of him."

"But you didn't know of the beatings, at least not to that extent, until after Mrs. Brissedon died?"

"No, can't say I did, though I suppose he wouldn't be doing it before, now would he, not with the missus alive. She loved that boy more than her own life."

"Do you think Brissedon might have hastened her death?"

"I'd like nothing more than to swear he did, but I can't say I saw him act anything but loving toward her. Myself, I just think she was heartsick after losing Mr. Desmond."

Daniel made a note in his little book, wanting to wait a moment or so out of respect for the memory of Patrick's mother. Finally, he returned the conversation to the issue at hand.

"Patrick must have truly hated the Brissedons, especially Thomas."

"I suppose he did," Trevor said. "All except Miss Kathleen, that is, and who could blame him? But you're not suggesting the lad murdered his stepfather, are you? I won't believe that, not for a minute. He doesn't have it in him."

"Did Colin Brissedon beat Patrick as well?"

"From time to time, they'd get into fisticuffs, but since Mrs. Des . . . Brissedon passed on . . . yeah he's given the lad a good beating a time or two as well, or at least, let them two worthless pieces of shit do it. Truth be told, though, I don't think it would have even entered his mind if he hadn't seen his old man going at it."

"Colin saw the whole thing?"

"He did. That lad's always snooping round to see what dirt he can dig up. Filing it away, no doubt, to use to his advantage."

"Did anyone else know about the beatings?"

"Aside from Mickey and Willie, you mean? Not that I know of, not firsthand, anyway. I've spoken to most of the indoor staff about it, but they only know what I've told them, and they've been warned not to let Miss Kathleen hear of it. She doesn't know a thing about it, you see, and it would devastate her if she found out. Mr. Patrick swore me to secrecy a while back, and I in turn have done the same. Not one of us would do a thing to hurt that sweet lass, especially Patrick."

Daniel nodded and checked his notes once more. "This is an odd question, I know, but do you know if Mr. Brissedon . . . preferred the company of gentlemen?"

Trevor took his cap off and brushed back some dark strands that had fallen down over his eyes. "I hardly think so, not the way I've seen him acting around the ladies. More than a few have slipped through that door to the back stairs, Mrs. Langston, for one."

"You mean after Mrs. Brissedon passed."

"No, I don't. I mean while the poor woman was ill. I was on my rounds one night and caught him opening the door for her. Doesn't he send her on in and come over to speak to me."

"What did he say?"

"Not to look on him in a bad light. He had needs, and with his wife being so ill, the lady helped ease the tension. But what made you think he was that kind of *gentleman*? I mean, I've heard some marry to keep up appearances, but he's been wed three times, hasn't he?"

Daniel frowned. *So that matchbook likely wasn't his.* "We found the matchbox to a known Manhattan fairy club in his room."

"Well, if he was that way, he sure didn't show it." Trevor scratched the back of his head and sniffed, clearly hesitant about saying more.

"Please don't hold anything back," Daniel said. "It could cost someone their neck, and I do mean literally."

"'Tis just that . . . before me and Lizzie—" He stopped short, realizing what he'd said.

"We'll get to that in a minute. Finish what you were going to say."

"Well, back in the day, I'd occasion to visit a lady or two . . . of looser morals. I'd see Brissedon coming or going there as well, and you can be sure it wasn't no gent he was visiting. He always had them two bastards following someone, though." He gave a nod in the direction of the stables. "Truth is, that matchbox is probably just one of the little pieces of evidence he was collecting on some poor soul. I'm thinking that's how he won so many contracts. It certainly wasn't because the builders hereabouts loved him."

So, he probably knew about Edward Langston's sexual preferences. Daniel made a few additional notes as more of the puzzle fell into place.

"Did you hear anything about a deal with Mr. Stockbridge?"

"Only that he'd been done dirty by Mr. Brissedon, and Mr. Talbot wasn't too happy about it. Seems Brissedon tricked him into signing a contract, thinking he was helping out Stockbridge, only to find out the latter had been cut out of the project completely."

"Did you see Kathleen Brissedon the night of the murder?"

"I did, about twelve thirty or so, as usual. I was making my rounds, checking things out."

"That's when she met with Brighton Templeton."

Trevor nodded. "They met out by the woods at the edge of the lawn." He let out a little laugh. "I don't think Brighton was allowed in the house any more than I was."

"Do you know when she came back in?"

"No, but I don't think she ever stays with him for long, and she's never alone. Molly was with her that night. I saw Brighton down at the lake somewhere round three in the morning as well. He looked like he was trying to cool off. I reckon he expected more than he got from the lady. He should have known better by now."

"Are you always up around three in the morning?"

"From time to time," Trevor said, though he hesitated a bit. "Me quarters can get a bit stuffy, especially on a warm summer night."

"And that was an unusually warm night."

"It was that." Trevor shrugged.

"But you were there all night . . . in your quarters?"

"I was, though I don't suppose anyone saw me there."

Daniel sighed and leaned against the gate. And just when he thought Trevor had been the most forthcoming of everyone he'd questioned. "I have witnesses who will swear you were not in your room on that particular night, Mr. Kilpatrick, but up at the main house with one of the maids."

"I can't imagine who that could be." Trevor tried to sound lighthearted, but Daniel could hear the tremble in his voice.

"Then perhaps I should go up and talk to Miss O'Shea herself. I wonder what she would say when I informed her you'd told me the truth."

Trevor hung his head and released a deep sigh. "There's no need of that. I'll tell you myself. I don't want to upset the poor lass any more than she already is. I was with Lizzie that night, and I'm not ashamed of it. She's carrying our child, and she was having a bad time of it, stomach upset and all, so I went to stay with her. There's a small room with a bed off the kitchen. Mrs. Quinn usually uses it, but with Liz being so sick and all . . ." He hung his head again, taking a breath to compose himself and likely to organize his thoughts.

"Where did Mrs. Quinn go?"

"There's an extra room upstairs in the staff quarters. She's been awful kind to us. Anyway, about three o'clock Lizzie spewed up something awful, so I went down to the lake to clean her basin out and cool off a bit. I know it's the babe, but I blame Brissedon for it as well. Lizzie was sore worried he'd find out. Not over herself being let go, mind you. I won't want her working as a maid after the babe is born anyway. 'Twas worry over him firing me as well that had her so concerned. 'Tis a good job, and if I was put out without references . . . Well, you know how that is." He took another deep breath. "The thing is, we were secretly married before she'd even lie with me. Lizzie was firm about that. Said she didn't want to make the same mistake Molly was."

Molly. He'd have to come back to her. "What were you going to do?"

"Turn in me papers, I suppose, and see if I could get a reference and find another job before he found out. But then the other morning, Miss Kathleen told Lizzie not to be fretting over it. Said she'd talk to her father about it, and if she couldn't convince him to at least let me stay on, she'd help find me another position and see we both got good references. Lizzie's right good at needlepoint, and she planned on taking in laundry from home, you see, but if she was dismissed without references . . . well, who'd want to hire her services? Of course, that was the morning they found Mr. Brissedon dead, so I don't suppose we need be worrying over it now. 'Twas kind of Miss Kathleen, though. She's a bit of a romantic, I think, and has a kind heart."

Daniel was pleased to hear that Trevor and Lizzie were wed and that Kathleen had been so understanding, but he wasn't quite through with the man yet. "I hope that news made Lizzie feel a bit better. Was she all right for the rest of the night, then?"

"She was for a while, till round five or so. She got ill again, poor lass, and ran up to change her clothes while I went back down to the lake. That's when I saw Mr. Patrick. He was just sitting there, his head in his hands. I asked if he was all right, but he said he'd just needed some air. Him and his ma used to take a walk along the shore every evening, so I reckon it brings back memories of better times."

"Who was Molly seeing that caused Brissedon to fire her?"

Trevor cursed just loud enough for Daniel to hear. "You know about that, do you? Lizzie's tried speaking to her, but she says she's in love. Says Mr. Radcliffe promised to marry her. Well, you know what'll happen there, now, don't you?"

"I'm afraid I do, Mr. Kilpatrick, all too well. Thank you for your help."

"Dr. O'Halleran, sir?"

Daniel had started to walk away but turned back to face the groom. He already knew what Trevor was going to say. "All I can promise is to follow the evidence, but if it leads to Patrick . . . After all that was done to him, though, I suspect the court will go easy on him."

"Not the death penalty, then?"

"I doubt it, but I thought you didn't believe he did it?"

Trevor frowned. "I don't, sir, but there's no denying the lad had more than enough reason. What would you have done?"

Daniel nodded and headed back toward his buggy. Hadn't he convinced himself last night that Patrick was more likely to try to expose his stepfather's crimes than kill him? Yet thinking back to the fury he felt every time Arthur called his mama a whore. . . He shook his head. No, he might beat the bastard to death, but use a knife . . . highly unlikely.

CHAPTER 29

Thursday, June 30, 1904 – 2:00 p.m.

Daniel found Dr. Tennyson sprawled on his porch swing the next morning, snoring away. It seemed Mrs. Jennings had gone into labor late last night and took her time about it. While both mother and daughter were doing well this morning, it appeared Sam hadn't fared so well. Taking pity on his mentor, Daniel told Nell to leave him be and saw to his scheduled patients.

As a result, it was almost one when he picked up the sergeant and headed back for the Brissedons'. He wanted another go at those two stable hands, certain the charge of assault would be a stronger incentive than any loyalty they might feel for a dead Thomas Brissedon. They'd just pulled up to the stables when Pete Rooney, the Brissedons' gardener, came rushing over.

"I was hoping you'd come by today, Doc."

"Is Clara all right?" Daniel asked. "She isn't due for another three months yet."

"Oh, she's fine, feeling better than ever. That's not what I wanted to see you about." He hesitated a minute, a frown crossing his tanned brow. "It's just that I was working in one of the flower beds over by the house this morning when I came across a bloody knife that wasn't there last week."

"Can you show us where?"

The gardener nodded and led the way up to the house, pointing to one of the flower beds set up against the porch. Daniel bent down and picked up the pearl-handled knife, his heart sinking. Taking a deep breath, he looked up at the window above.

"Do you know whose bedroom that is, Mr. Rooney?"

"I'm not rightly sure, sir, but I think it's Mr. Desmond's new room. I've never been farther than the hallway, you see. Forbes comes out to pay me when I finish up for the day. I have seen the lad at the window quite a few times, though, pacing back and forth. It's almost like he was in some kind of prison."

"And what about the first floor?"

"Well, this window here is Mr. Brissedon's study. I know that because I did manage to make my way into the entry hall once or twice and saw Mr. Brissedon sitting at his desk. You can see for yourself that the front entrance is the only thing to the left. I reckon anybody could have tossed it here."

"I suppose you're right. Thank you, Mr. Rooney." Daniel turned to walk up the steps to the house, feeling as though he'd been gut-punched.

"You look like a man who's bound to do something he wished he didn't have to," the sergeant said. "May I inquire as to what it is, Doc?"

"I think we need to search Patrick Desmond's room, and I'm afraid of what I may find."

"I don't suppose this looks very good for the lad, but perhaps we'll find nothing at all."

"Actually, I'm hoping we do find something. Miss Brissedon mentioned Patrick kept a knife under his mattress, a pearl-handled one that was his father's, much like this one."

"Then I hope you're right, because if not, this is the knife, and you know what that suggests."

Daniel gave a solemn nod. "That Patrick Desmond may very well be our murderer."

Daniel walked into the parlor and found Kathleen praying before her father's coffin. Her face was pale and stained with tears, but even in her grief she remained almost angelic. He could only imagine the emotional turmoil she was going through. In spite of everything she knew, Thomas was her father, and he had done right by her. How could he disturb her prayers? For Thomas Brissedon likely needed all he could get.

Folding his hands in front of him, he stood by one of the mourners and bowed his head. He was glad he'd thought to wear his black suit today. Peeking from beneath his eyelashes, he scanned the room, not quite sure what he was looking for. Patrick sat toward the back of the room, staring into space. Probably bored to tears. Colin already looked like he was half in the bag. Jeremy seemed miles away, clearly preoccupied. The Langstons had come to pay their respects, as had the Stockbridges; even Mr. Talbot was there. All just doing their duty, he supposed, and adhering to proper etiquette. God, he hoped when he passed on, people would remember him fondly and not just show up because it was the right thing to do.

At last, Kathleen glanced in his direction, and, rising gracefully, she came to stand by his side. "I just can't believe he's gone," she said, a lone tear trickling down her ivory cheek. "I keep expecting him to sit up and scold us for being so foolish."

"It must be very hard for you."

"More than I ever thought it would be," she said, keeping her voice low. "But not simply because he's gone. I want to know why he did what he did, and now I can't even ask him. Did he think the money made any difference?"

"Some people think it does." He hesitated, wishing he didn't have to ask the questions he did. *Work your way up to it, lad,* he could hear his uncle Timothy saying. "I'm sorry I have to keep intruding on you, especially at a time like this, but they're to hold the inquest on Wednesday, and if I'm to find your father's murderer, there are still some questions I must ask."

"Yes, of course. I completely understand." She indicated that he was to follow her and led the way across the hall to the study, which was much more orderly than the last time he'd been there.

He stopped just inside the doors, waiting for her to close them, but didn't realize how close he was standing to her. When she turned, she stumbled into him, and he grabbed her waist. Their eyes met, and for a moment he forgot why he was there. She put her hand to his cheek, and a wave of desire coursed through him like nothing he'd ever felt before.

"I only wish we could have come to know one another under more pleasant circumstances," she said. "But even so, I'm glad you're here with me now. I don't think I could have faced all this alone."

He nodded, using every ounce of restraint he could muster to keep from taking her in his arms and kissing her pale pink lips. But he knew he mustn't. Not here. Not now. Filled with dread, he led her to the light green couch that stood to the side of Thomas's desk and sat down beside her. He rubbed his hand across his face, taking a breath in a feeble attempt to keep his voice steady.

"Miss Brissedon." That sounded wrong somehow. "Kathleen, please forgive me for what I'm about to ask."

"Yes, of course." She flashed an understanding smile. "I'm a much stronger woman than most men imagine."

"I think you're an incredibly strong woman, and under ordinary circumstances I would even now be contemplating how I might ask if I could call upon you."

"Why have you not asked, then?" she said, her soft blue eyes gazing into his once more.

Daniel found his concentration shattered. He could sense himself drawing closer to her, feel her breath warm against his cheek. It was against all reason. *Watch yerself, laddie!* Uncle Timothy's voice echoed through his mind, and he pulled back, jumping from the couch.

"I beg your pardon, Miss Brissedon. That was completely unprofessional of me."

Rejection and embarrassment transformed her expression, and she bowed her head, blinking to keep the tears at bay. "No, it's completely my fault. I shouldn't have expected . . ."

Daniel couldn't stand to see the pain on her face and dropped down to kneel before her. "I'm not saying I didn't want to, Kathleen, just that I can't. It wouldn't be right. I'm on a case, and I can't let my feelings for you interfere with that."

"Of course. I'm sorry. I should never have put you in such a compromising position."

He stood up and walked toward the window, staring through the sparkling glass a moment before turning to face her. "Besides, after you hear what I have to say, you may not wish for my company. It would be wrong of me to take advantage of you that way."

She took a deep breath and went to stand on the other side of her father's desk. She fiddled with his cigar box, and Daniel could tell she was considering whether or not to say something. Her mind made up, she looked up into his eyes, a soft smile playing across her lips.

"Over the past few days, I've come to the opinion that whatever steps you take are well considered and without malice. In short, I trust you not to jump to conclusions. Now, what questions do you have for me?"

"I didn't mean the situation would be forever," he said. When she raised a questioning eyebrow, he continued. "While it would be inappropriate for us to see each other under the current circumstances, I see no reason why two sensible adults could not consider doing so at some future time . . . if you would still find it agreeable, that is, given what I have to say."

"And what is it you have to say, Doctor, that seems to have you so upset?"

Daniel wanted to end the case right there and then, for he realized what he said within the next fifteen minutes or so could alter their budding relationship drastically. He sat back down on the sofa, trying to still the impending headache, and Kathleen sat beside him once more.

"Ask what you must. I will understand."

Daniel nodded, then fumbled through his notebook, trying desperately to prolong the inevitable as long as possible. "Is it true that you were looking for employment on behalf of Trevor Kilpatrick?"

"Well, I just found out about their situation Friday morning, but yes, I told Lizzie I would if my father let him go. They're married and expecting their first child, but clearly Trevor's explained all that to you."

"Just verifying what he told me."

"Do you verify everyone's information?"

"If possible. People tend to be most honest when they find out you do. But your father really wouldn't have kept them on if they were married?"

"Not unless they swore there would be no children, and that ship has certainly sailed in their case." She dabbed the corner of her eye with a hankie. "I guess some good has come out of this, after all."

"What do you mean?"

"Well, now that Father is gone, they'll be able to stay on here. I've spoken to Colin about it, and he agrees there's no need for either one of them to be let go."

Daniel nodded. "I'm happy for them." He fiddled with his notebook again, knowing his next question would be far more telling. "Is Molly around? I'd like to get into one of the rooms upstairs."

"Yes, of course, but there's no need to disturb Molly. I'll take you up myself."

"But your family will be looking for you. You have mourners to attend to."

"Mrs. Quinn will see no one goes hungry, and it's about time Colin stepped up as head of the family."

As they started up, Kathleen asked him to remove his boots, which he did obligingly, waiting for the other shoe to drop, so to speak.

"I suppose there's no need of that anymore," she said. "It's just force of habit."

"I'm sure it will get easier as time goes on." But not for him, not today. Within a few short steps, she would be asking what room he needed to see, and she may no longer be so agreeable. Still, if he were to be an honorable man, it must be done, no matter how much he wished he could avoid it altogether.

"Kathleen." He touched his hand to the small of her back as they neared the top of the stairs, "I need to have some of the sergeant's men search Patrick's room."

Before she could answer, however, Patrick came bolting up the stairs, boots and all, demanding an explanation. Unfortunately, Daniel felt an answer might compromise his investigation, and so he simply informed the boy that the task could be accomplished just as easily with or without his cooperation.

"Fine, then!" Patrick said, his eyes flashing with anger. "Look all you want! There's nothing to find, but if that's the only reason you have your hands on my sister, please remove them!"

"Patrick!" Kathleen called after her stepbrother, but he took off down the stairs in a huff.

"It's all right," Daniel said. "I don't really blame him."

"Then why do you feel you have to do it? Why not my room or Colin's?"

"You have to trust me on this, Kathleen. I can't explain it all just yet."

The young woman sighed, uncertainly darkening her eyes. She looked down the stairs to find the sergeant and his constables standing at the foot. "You'd best have them come up, then," she said before walking ahead to Patrick's bedroom. Opening the door, she entered and stood off to the side. "What do you hope to find?"

"I'm not sure I know. It may be nothing." He walked over and opened the window, letting in the warm summer air. "It's a beautiful day, isn't it?"

But he didn't fool her for a moment. "Please don't insult my intelligence. What are you looking for, Daniel?"

"Let's go into the hallway for a moment and give the officers a chance to search." But they had barely moved away from the room when Sergeant Owens came back out.

"If I could talk to you a moment alone, Doc?"

Kathleen eyed Daniel warily, but being a lady, she politely excused herself and headed downstairs. She shot one or two looks up in his direction as she descended, her eyes filled with concern, but much to Daniel's relief, she said nothing. If it was bad news, he'd break it to her later, gently, and if it was good news, she would find out soon enough. But what could the good news possibly be? That Patrick was guilty and her father's murderer found, or that her stepbrother was innocent and her father's murderer still on the loose? He sighed wearily, then turned to the sergeant.

"What did you find?"

"She's not going to be happy about this," the sergeant said. "Can't say I am either, for that matter. I've known the lad a long time and don't see him as a murderer, but we found some evidence in his room that seems to back up that theory."

"Go on, what have you got?"

"There was this note from that Alexander Morton."

"What?" He took the bit of singed paper. Alexander Morton's name was written across the top, along with the name Tommy Breslin. "But Kathleen found the note

Morton sent, and the man himself said Patrick hadn't come to see him."

"Perhaps they're both covering for the lad. The note was thrown in the fireplace. I guess with it being summer and all, he didn't think to keep the fire going, so there's enough of it left to see it was dated the Wednesday before the murder. But that's the least of it."

Something didn't feel right about this, and yet . . . "What else did you find?"

"There was blood on the washstand scarf. Looks like he tried to hide it under the basin, probably hoping no one would notice. We also found his shirt, wadded up and stuffed in the corner of his wardrobe. It's covered with blood as well. On top of that, we found some mud on his rug, not a footprint, but . . ." He shrugged. "Under the circumstances."

"What about the knife?"

"No sign of any under his mattress or anywhere else, Doc."

Daniel closed his eyes, an ache clutching his heart. How would he tell Kathleen? The evidence against Patrick was overwhelming. Maybe too overwhelming. Even the sergeant didn't think Patrick capable of such a heinous act. Still, he had a job to do, and he couldn't ignore the evidence, no matter what his gut was telling him.

He opened his eyes. "Find Patrick Desmond and place him under arrest, Sergeant."

"But—"

"I have no choice. I agree with your instincts, but the evidence says otherwise. He had more than enough reason to want the man dead and could have easily slipped into his room undetected. And now his knife turns up covered in blood, not to mention the shirt and that note from Morton. I just don't have any choice, Sergeant."

"I know that, Doc. It just doesn't seem right somehow."

"Don't give up just yet. It doesn't mean I'm going to stop investigating."

The sergeant nodded, then, after giving Daniel a pat on the back, he took his men and headed out to look for Patrick while Daniel started down the stairs, intent on returning to the parlor. The last of the mourners had just left for the afternoon and Kathleen was closing the door behind them when a shot rang out and Daniel staggered, doubling over and clutching his side.

Kathleen caught hold of his arm, calling for the sergeant. Daniel was already sitting on the stairs, groaning and gazing at his side. He uttered a rather vulgar curse, probably hoping she hadn't heard it. Oddly enough, it made her breathe a bit easier.

"Good Lord in heaven." The sergeant and his men came barreling through the door. "We heard a shot."

But Kathleen was already delivering orders. "He's still alive," she told the sergeant. "Go to the sideboard in the parlor and demand whatever my brother is drinking. Forbes, send Trevor for the doctor."

"I am a doctor," Daniel hissed through clenched teeth, but Kathleen ignored him.

"Well, go on," she said to Forbes. "Jeremy, you and Colin help him up to the guest bedroom across from mine."

"Now see here, Kate," Colin said, "what do you plan on doing with this whiskey?"

She had no time for this. Though she was barely holding back tears, she had no intention of losing her composure. Nor did she have any patience for her brother's petty complaints. Daniel was injured.

"Help him upstairs, Colin, or so help me, I'll give you a good swift kick in the balls."

The men's eyes all widened, but Sergeant Owens spoke up. "All right, boys, looks like the lady has things in hand. Let's get a move on and see if we can find who did this."

"Thank you, Sergeant," Kathleen said. "Molly, have Mrs. Quinn bring up some clean rags and a basin of water."

Daniel shoved Colin away. "I can take care of this myself. It's only a graze."

"That goes for you too, Doctor. You may be large, but I would imagine you'd fall just as hard."

Daniel pressed his lips together. Golden rims highlighted the inner part of his irises, and a small patch of red flared on his forehead, but he did as she said. Taking a deep breath, she followed him up, Mrs. Quinn behind her with the basin and rags. As soon as he sat on the bed, she helped him take his jacket off and pushed him back on the quilted coverlet.

A subtle smile crossed his lips, but she was in no mood for any shenanigans. "Don't!" She narrowed her eyes and gave him a look that always seemed to quiet the rowdy students in the library. It must have worked, for he rested his head back against the pillow and tugged at his shirt.

A large red patch stained the white material, and Daniel craned his neck to get a look at it. "Give me a wet rag so I can wash the blood away and see how bad it is."

"Lie back and let me do it, for heaven's sake. Don't be so stubborn."

He winced as she pulled the cotton material away from the wound but didn't argue. At least he wasn't going to be difficult about it. Dipping the rag in the water, she ran it over his taut muscles, her fingers tingling each time they touched his smooth, warm skin. He definitely was in good shape. *Concentrate, Kathleen!*

"Do you have any carbolic acid, iodine . . ." he said, gritting his teeth as she ran the rag along the laceration.

She was glad to see it wasn't as bad as it had looked at first glance. "Yes, I'm sure we must. Mrs. Quinn . . ."

"I've already sent Forbes for it."

"What's happened?" Dr. Tennyson barreled through the door, his face pale except for a few patchy spots on his cheeks and forehead, a sure sign he was concerned. "Mr. Kilpatrick said Daniel had been shot."

"It's only a flesh wound." He tried to sit up, but Kathleen pressed him down again.

"A very deep one. I've cleaned it the best I could and sent Forbes for the carbolic acid."

"Let's have a look, then." The doctor sat in the chair beside the bed, calling for this and that, a frown creasing his ordinarily pleasant countenance.

Daniel looked pale, his usually healthy complexion devoid of all color. No one asked her to leave, so she stood at the end of the bed, twisting the bloodied rag she still held in her hand. At last, Dr. Tennyson bandaged the wound and stood up, stretching his back.

"Don't look so worried," he said. "The bullet left a nasty wound, but it's clean and just grazed his side. He'll be up and around in no time. He's bound to be a little sore, but he should be right as rain by the morning. Don't let him do anything too physical for a few days so as not to tear those stitches out."

"I am right here, you know," Daniel said, but Dr. Tennyson continued speaking to Kathleen.

"And I've left some of his headache powders should he need them. Don't fret, Kathleen, he'll be fine. He's stronger than he looks."

Daniel frowned. "What's that supposed to mean?"

"It means you're to do as you're told and don't give this young lady any more trouble. Had you not been standing exactly where you were, this could have been a lot more serious."

Kathleen had a sudden, urgent need to cry, and without warning, tears trickled down her cheeks. "I'm so sorry. I don't know what's wrong with me."

Dr. Tennyson leaned over to whisper in her ear. "Don't you now?" He straightened up and patted her shoulder. *Is it that obvious?* She rubbed her wet cheeks with the back of her hand, and Mrs. Quinn handed her a dry cloth.

"Here you go, Miss Kathleen."

Colin stuck his head around the door. "Why don't you come downstairs now? He's not dying, and there's nothing further you can do here."

"Just go back to the parlor and drink yourself into oblivion, like you always do," she said. She felt guilty even as the words left her lips, but she'd had enough of his irresponsible behavior. Her father was dead and likely responsible for the death of Cornelius Desmond, and now Patrick was going to be charged with his murder. But foremost in her mind was the fear that she might lose Daniel before they even had a chance for the love he'd only hinted at. She was tired of lies, tired of secrets, and tired of being sheltered from the truth.

Patrick climbed the tree and stepped off onto the porch roof, casting a glance around the darkened street before creeping his way over to Lydia's window. He shouldn't be here, shouldn't put her reputation in danger, and yet he needed to talk to her. If he were found guilty, he wanted her to know the truth. It was better for her to hear it all now, before the newspapers got ahold of it and sensationalized everything.

Pressing himself against the shutter, he tapped on her open window, whispering her name.

A moment later, a shadowy form appeared inside. "Patrick? What are you doing out there? Do you know what time it is?"

"No, I've just been driving around, trying to clear my head. They're going to blame me for his death, Lydia. I'm scared."

"You'd better come in before you fall and break your neck."

He climbed over the windowsill and pulled off his cap. "What if your brother hears me?"

"He won't. A friend called for him, and they've gone to spend the night on Fire Island. As for Mother, she drank herself into oblivion about two hours ago. You can hear her snoring if you listen."

"That's one of the things I want to speak to you about." He sat down on her bed and put his face in his hands. Where was he supposed to begin? "If they arrest me, I need you to know the truth."

She sat down next to him and wrapped her arm around his. "Then you do care about me. I knew you didn't mean any of those horrible things you said."

"I'm no good, Lydia. Things are going to come out, hurtful things, and I won't be able to stop them. Everything I told you about Thomas was true. I'm sure he killed my father, and I might even have the proof I needed, but now it just makes me look more guilty."

"Did you?" she asked, though she didn't lift her head from his shoulder. "Kill him, I mean?"

He stood up, nearly causing her to fall from the bed, but he caught her in time and knelt down before her. "God, no! But they were searching my room. No one else's. Just mine."

"But you have an alibi. I told Dr. O'Halleran I was with you that night."

"You what?" He shook his head before laying it in her lap. He couldn't have her lying for him. "They'll think we were in it together. We have to tell O'Halleran the truth." He got up and sat on the bed, leaning back against the headboard, and she snuggled up against him, her head resting on his chest. "I just need to rest here for a bit first, though."

"Of course, stay as long as you need, and we'll go to the doctor together."

They must have sat there like that for hours, talking about one thing or another, until finally, the first hint of morning touched the horizon. Time had run out. He had to tell her and be on his way before anyone could know he was there.

Nudging her aside, he stood and walked to the window once more. It was all so peaceful. If he could only freeze time and forget the tumult that swirled in his gut. Her hand rested on his shoulder, but he didn't turn around. He had to get this out, and if he looked in her eyes, he would never have the strength to say what he must.

"I had no choice in any of it, not really. When he called me into his office, he informed me I had no money, that my father was practically penniless, and if not for him, my mother and I would have ended up in the alms house . . . or worse."

"I don't care about any of that."

"Just hear me out, please," he said, still not daring to look at her. "He threatened to put me out on the streets or see me locked away in some asylum if I didn't do what he wanted. I did refuse at first, but then he dragged me out to the stables and beat the shit out of me. I just wanted to die, but that would have been letting him win. I had to keep trying to prove my father's innocence, prove Thomas had killed him."

"Oh, Patrick." She led him back to the bed and sat him down before handing him a glass of water. "I could slip downstairs and find something stronger if you feel you need it."

"No, just sit, please. I have to get through this before I lose my nerve."

She did as he asked, taking his free hand in hers, and after drinking the water, he placed the empty glass on the bedside table. "I finally did agree, though, much to my shame."

"But why did he want you sleeping around?"

"No, I did that on my own, to get back at him, just like I told you the other day. What he asked of me was far more sinister. He planned to expand his business by blackmailing potential customers into giving him all their trade."

"I don't understand. How did he intend to do that?"

"By having me entertain their wives, in whatever way the ladies saw fit. In return, they'd supply Thomas with information he could use against their husbands."

She frowned for a moment, and then a wave of understanding crossed her face, just as surely as the morning tide broke along the shore. "Oh . . . you were to sleep with them?"

He nodded, certain what he said next would be so repulsive to her she would never want to see him again. "I was with your mother the night my stepfather was killed."

"My mother?" She started to laugh but must have seen the sincerity in his eyes, for she turned away and walked back to the window. "You slept with my mother?"

"I had no choice." After hesitating a moment, he got up and stood behind her, reaching out to touch her arm, but as he feared, she pulled away. "That's what the piano lessons were   about."

"Stop! I don't want to hear any more of your lies."

"I wish they were lies. The last thing I want to do is hurt you, but it's all going to come out. They'll arrest me, and . . . She was willing to betray her husband just to go to bed with me."

Lydia spun around and slapped his face, her gorgeous crystal-blue eyes flashing with anger. "You'd destroy my mother's name just to give yourself an alibi? My brother was wrong about you. He said you were nothing more than a rake, but you're far worse than that. You're the most despicable creature I've ever met. Now get out before I call Standish and have him throw you out. I'm sure Edward will love hearing what you have to say about our mother."

Patrick could barely breathe. "I'm sorry, Lydia. I'll do my best to keep it from coming out, but I'll not hang to preserve her reputation." He climbed back out on the roof and gazed through the window at her petite form, almost ethereal in the pale moonlight. Any further words would fall on deaf ears. A pain wracked his chest, though it had nothing to do with any physical ailment. Even from his grave, Thomas Brissedon had found a way to rip them apart.

Shimmying back down the tree, he ran the three blocks to where he'd left his stepfather's automobile and drove back to Oak Street, where he settled down beside the lake to contemplate his dubious future . . . or lack thereof. He'd never been so scared in his life, and now he truly didn't have anyone to turn to. Maybe he should have just let them hang him and kept his secret to himself. At least then, he would still have Lydia's love. But would it really have mattered? In the end, the truth always wins out, his mother used to say. And then, he would have died for nothing.

CHAPTER 30

Friday, July 1, 1904 – 8:00 a.m.

When Daniel opened his eyes, Dr. Tennyson was closing up his medical bag. "He slept through the night, then?"

"Yes," Kathleen said. "I had Forbes keep an eye on him."

"That's good. He hasn't developed a fever and his color has returned, so he should be fine, albeit a bit sore."

"I could have told you that yesterday." Daniel pushed himself up in the bed, only to realize he was wearing nothing but his drawers. He pulled the covers up over his chest, glaring at Kathleen.

"Don't look so shocked. What were we to do, leave you in your bloodstained shirt? It even spread onto your pants. Lizzie's trying to get the stain out, but I'm afraid you may have to shop for some new ones when you're up to it. There are some fine shops in the village."

"Well, I'm off," Sam said. "You, young man, do as the lady tells you. I still want you to take it easy for a day or two. Sergeant Owens has things well in hand."

Daniel frowned after the doctor, waiting for the door to shut before speaking again. "Where is the sergeant, anyway?"

"Sergeant Owens and his men are out looking for Patrick." Her brow furrowed, and she sat back in the chair by the bed. "Daniel, what's going on?"

He rubbed his head, deciding it was time to tell Kathleen what they had discovered, but she jumped up, pouring some of the headache powder into a glass of water.

"I don't need that." He reached out to take her hand and sat her back down in the chair. "It's just a little tension. It will ease in a minute. Don't worry about the stain, just get me my pants and what's left of my shirt, will you?"

"Absolutely not! Didn't you hear what the doctor said? You need to rest."

"He said not to do anything too physical, and I hardly think getting out of bed constitutes excess exertion."

There was a knock on the door, and the sergeant stuck his head in. "I brought you some clean clothes, Doc."

"Sergeant, you're a saint. The lady refused to retrieve my clothing," he said with a pointed stare. "Now, miss, I suggest you either leave the room or turn your back unless you'd like to see me in all my glory."

"What, not shy anymore?"

"That was just because I thought you'd undressed me, and I wasn't awake to enjoy it."

Kathleen's jaw dropped, and she stood up, but then she must have thought better of it. "No, I think I'll stay." Her lip quirked up in a smile that dared him to object. "After all, I have already seen your bare midriff." She turned her back and walked over to the window, staring outside at the early morning sun.

"I think she called your bluff, Doc." The sergeant stifled a laugh, then sat down in the chair and sighed. "In all seriousness, perhaps you're getting a little too close to the truth for comfort."

"Have you found the young man yet?"

"Patrick?" Kathleen spun around, clearly oblivious to Daniel's state of dress. Fortunately, he had already donned everything but his collar, tie, and jacket. "Don't worry about him. He'll come back soon enough. He always does after he finishes pouting, though he's never stayed out all night before. I'm sure he has an explanation."

Daniel motioned to the sergeant, and the kindhearted man picked up the bag holding the evidence they'd found the previous day. "Are you sure about this, sir?" But when Daniel nodded, the sergeant opened the sack, took out the bloodstained garment, and handed it to Daniel.

"Do you recognize this shirt?" he asked Kathleen, though it pained him to do so.

"I don't know. It's just a gentleman's shirt. It could be anyone's."

Daniel sat on the edge of the bed and took her hands in his. "Except that we found it stuffed in the corner of Patrick's wardrobe. Does it look like something he would wear?"

"I don't know. It looks like it could be, but why would it be covered with blood?"

Daniel's heart ached, but she had to see the evidence, had to know why they were looking for her stepbrother, or she'd never believe it possible. Taking the knife from the sergeant, he held it out before her. "What about this knife? Do you recognize it?"

She nodded, questions flashing in her eyes. "That's Patrick's. I told you; he keeps it under his mattress."

"We found it in the flower bed beneath his window, covered with blood. There's also blood on the scarf beneath his washbasin, and a note from Alexander Morton dated the Wednesday before your father's murder."

"But no, Morton said Patrick never came to see him."

"Maybe he lied. Patrick was his client, after all. It wouldn't be stretching the imagination too much to think the man would stick up for him. I hate to admit it, but you and I both know your stepbrother has more than enough reason to wish your father dead. Then, to make matters worse, somebody takes a shot at me not half an hour after he finds out we're going to search his room."

"That's exactly it! *Somebody!* You don't know it was Patrick. And he's not even here to defend himself. I refuse to believe it! I don't care what so-called evidence you have. That boy is not capable of murder!"

She pulled her hands from his, and he would have sworn someone had just yanked his heart from his chest. There was no hope for them now. He could only pray she'd forgive him one day. The door had slammed, and he pinched the bridge of his nose.

"It had to be done," the sergeant said.

"I know, but that didn't make it any easier. Tell me something: Would your sister stand up for you like that?"

The sergeant straightened up, a fondness in his eyes that spoke of a close bond. "She would, without even thinking about it."

Daniel nodded. "Mine would as well, and she'd never speak to my accuser again."

"Oh, I don't know. Mine might when she realized he was only doing what he knew was right. Don't go worrying yourself over it. That one will come around. I feel it in my bones."

He'd no sooner spoken the words than the door flew open. "No!" Kathleen exclaimed. "It couldn't be Patrick. He would never have left his father's watch behind."

"What watch?" Daniel ran his hand through his hair, wincing as the action stretched the skin around his wound.

"I'm going to head back out." The sergeant slapped Daniel on the back. "You seem to have things well in hand here."

Kathleen pulled a watch from her pocket and handed it to him. "I found it on my father's bureau. I should have given it to you right away, I know, but . . ."

"Yes, you should have." It was a handsome watch, engraved with three golden shamrocks set in Connemara marble, one of the clovers holding a diamond in its center. There was no doubt it matched the cuff link they'd found at the crime scene. Daniel wound it, for it appeared to have stopped at ten o'clock, and there, on the inside lid, were engraved the initials *CD*.

He looked up to find Kathleen sitting on the edge of the green upholstered Morris chair, her face devoid of all color. His heart nearly stopped, and he fell to his knee before her, resting his hand against her cheek.

"Kathleen, are you all right? What is it? Should I have Forbes go for my medical bag?"

She blinked, looking at him as tears trickled down her cheeks. "It's just finally hitting me. That proves beyond all doubt that my father killed Cornelius Desmond."

He tucked a stray lock of hair behind her ear, swallowing the bitter taste that had risen in his throat. "What do you mean?"

"Patrick said his father always carried that watch with him."

"Maybe he was mistaken."

She shook her head. "Why would he lie about that, and not the rest of the set? He was sure whoever murdered his father had stolen the watch. Brigid was troubled about it too. She was convinced it hadn't been among her husband's things and that his assailant had taken it."

"She wasn't wrong about it not being returned. It wasn't listed in the police report. Was that why she hired a private investigator?"

"Part of the reason, I suppose, but mostly she just wanted to prove Cornelius was innocent."

"What did she say when she saw your father wearing it?"

"She never did. He didn't start carrying it until after she'd passed away."

"And Patrick never recognized it?"

"Of course he did. He outright accused him of murdering his father to get it."

Daniel pinched the bridge of his nose. How on earth did Kathleen think this information could help Patrick? It only made him look more guilty. "How did your father react to the accusation?"

"He told Patrick he was delusional. That it was in a box of things the police had returned. He claimed Brigid had never gone through it, being so upset and all. When Patrick insisted it belonged to him, my father told him to considerate it partial payment for all the money he'd handed out to cover Cornelius's debts."

Daniel squeezed her hands. As painful as it was, he had to make her see what it meant. "Don't you see? That only gives Patrick another reason for wanting your father dead."

"No," she said, her dusk-blue eyes pleading with him to understand. "In fact, it proves his innocence. If he had murdered my father, he never would have left the watch behind for my brother to claim. Bad enough Colin would inherit the rest of the set."

She had a point, a weak one, but a point, nonetheless. He was just afraid it wouldn't be enough.

"You said it was part of a set? What were the other pieces?"

"The cuff links, but we've already located them, and there was a tie pin and a watch fob as well, I think. At least that's what Patrick says. My father would wear the tie pin now and then, but I never saw him wearing the fob. It wasn't listed in the inventory either."

"What inventory?" Her cheeks had flushed a deep carnation pink, and he groaned inwardly. "Kathleen!"

"It's just an old box my father kept for documents. There's nothing to do with his death in there. I'll show it to you later. Right now I'm more concerned about Patrick. That watch proves he didn't kill my father."

Daniel looked into her eyes. He wanted to believe she was right, but he couldn't let himself go down that path. He had to remain professional. "I have to follow the evidence, Kathleen, and the fact that he left a watch behind doesn't prove anything. If he'd just murdered your father, the last thing he'd be thinking of was that watch. And if he knew it was there, why not go back to get it later? The rooms haven't been sealed off, as you know so well. All this tells me is that he didn't realize it was there, or maybe he thought taking it might point the finger at himself. I have to be honest, it doesn't look very good for Patrick, but I promise you I'm not going to stop investigating. Not until I have the whole story."

Kathleen nodded but didn't say another word. Instead, she stared down at the open watch, running her finger over the ornate initials.

At a loss for anything else to say, he stood and walked to the window, gazing out at the tranquil scenery. That knife and bloody shirt were just too hard to discount. But why leave them where they could be found? Perhaps Patrick had acted out of anger and panicked after the deed was done?

Though his gut still told him the boy was innocent, his head was beginning to doubt it. He could easily imagine the young man's anger festering after seeing Brissedon with his father's watch, the emotion growing when he'd lost his mother, only to come to a head when he discovered Lydia was to be taken from him as well. There were any number of reasons he might have left that watch behind, and he'd wager Patrick had thought of them all.

A thump sounded in the hallway, and Daniel turned just in time to see Sergeant Owens shove Patrick Desmond through the door ahead of him.

"We found him down by the lake, sir. Sitting there, just as calm as you please."

"Why wouldn't I be?"

Daniel sighed. "Where have you been, Patrick?"

"I spent the night with a lady friend, not that it's any of your business."

"And what was the lady's name?"

Patrick shrugged. "I don't remember, Yvette or something like that."

Daniel nodded. "That kind of lady. What time did you get there?"

"Go fuck yourself!"

"Patrick!" Kathleen had the same look in her eyes Daniel's mother got when he or his brothers had been extremely rude. It was one they never dared challenge. Nor did Patrick, apparently, for his face had turned a blotchy red.

"I'm sorry, Kate. It's just . . ."

"There is no excuse for that language. Now apologize to the doctor and answer his questions, or I shall be very cross with you."

He took a breath and nodded. "I don't know exactly. I took the automobile into town and walked around for a bit. Then drove a few towns over to this bawdy house Colin told me about."

"And you were there all night."

He looked at Kathleen, the blotches darkening to a deep crimson. "Yes, sir, until about six this morning."

"What did you do then?"

"I stopped at Newins for breakfast, but I wasn't very hungry, so after a few bites, I went to sit by the lake. That's where I was when the sergeant grabbed me and dragged me up here."

"Why were you so agitated about us searching your room yesterday?" Daniel asked, secretly wishing the man had a viable explanation.

"Don't pretend Colin didn't put you up to it. Why else would you be searching my room and no one else's?"

"Because we found this knife below *your* window . . . covered in blood. Do you have any idea how it could have gotten there?"

The red in his cheeks paled to a pink blush. "What? No! That can't be." He turned to Kathleen, his eyes begging her to believe him. "Kate, no, it's not true. I don't know how they got my knife. Honestly, I don't."

"I know, darling." Coming to stand next to her stepbrother, Kathleen looked over to Daniel, a pleading in her eyes that caused him physical pain. "Can't you let him go? He won't run, will you, Patrick?"

"No, I'll tell you whatever you want to know."

"We found this gun lying in the water among some rocks," the sergeant said, "not five feet from the very spot where he was sitting. I don't think it could have been there too long, not from the looks of it."

"I don't know anything about a gun," Patrick said. "And what has that got to do with my stepfather's murder? His throat was cut. I saw it."

"Someone shot Daniel yesterday afternoon," Kathleen said. "Right after he told you he was going to search your room."

All the red had drained from Patrick's face now. He looked toward the door, probably with the intention of making a run for it, but two constables stepped in and grabbed him, each taking him by an arm.

"And you think I did it? Anyone could have thrown that gun there. Everybody knows I sit down by the lake sometimes, especially when I'm upset."

"I'm sorry, Kathleen," Daniel said. "There's just too much evidence, and with the inquest on Wednesday, I can't justify releasing him."

"Patrick Desmond," Sergeant Owens said, "I'm placing you under arrest for the murder of your stepfather, Thomas Brissedon, and the attempted murder of Doctor Daniel O'Halleran. Get him out of here, Constable."

"No," Patrick said, his turquoise eyes brimming with tears. "Please, Kate, I didn't do it. I couldn't do anything to hurt you."

"Daniel, please," she said, "where are you taking him?"

"He'll stay in the village lockup until after the inquest. Then, he'll be transferred up to Riverhead to await trial."

She touched Daniel's arm, her eyes imploring him. "At least let him stay here until my father's been laid to rest and we've had time to mourn properly. The sergeant could leave one of his men outside Patrick's door."

Daniel groaned and threw a glance in his sergeant's direction.

"I reckon we could guard him here just as well as in the lockup," the man said, "and it would be a whole lot more comfortable at that."

Daniel didn't have the heart to refuse her request, and so he agreed that Patrick could be held under house arrest until his hearing. "Make sure the door is locked, Sergeant." With that, the young man was torn from his sister and escorted back to his room, but before the sergeant followed his men down the hallway, Daniel took him aside just outside the guest room door. "Make sure there's a guard beneath his window and one outside that back stairway door as well, just in case."

"That'll mean asking the night watch to do overtime."

"I'll pay for it myself if I have to. He's scared and thinks we're all against him. I wouldn't be surprised if he tries to bolt, and I don't want to make it easy for him."

"We could just take him down to the lockup."

"No, he'll be more relaxed here. Maybe I can get him to trust me, and truth be told, I still don't think he did it."

The sergeant and his constables escorted Patrick back to the west wing, and when Daniel returned to his room, he found Kathleen sitting on the damask-covered armchair next to the window, her eyes brimming with tears.

"I just know he's not guilty," she said. "I don't think I could bear it if I lost him too."

"Did anyone else know about his knife?"

"I don't know. I suppose Molly might have come across it while straightening his room." She shook her head, pulling a handkerchief from her pocket to blow her nose.

"Were the rooms always kept locked?"

"Generally, yes."

"So it's unlikely anyone was rummaging around Patrick's room and just stumbled across it."

"I didn't say that. The staff all have keys, and the locks are incredibly easy to pick even without one. I've come across Colin sneaking into my father's room on a number of occasions."

"What did he say when you caught him?"

"After telling me it was none of my affair, you mean." She sniffled and blew her nose again. "Usually, it was about money, I believe, or the keys to the liquor cabinet. Father kept the best liquor locked up, you see, for when we had guests. Colin didn't appreciate that. It wasn't quite so easy to break into as Father's rooms."

"He drinks a considerable amount, I've noticed."

"You're being kind, Doctor. My brother is a drunkard. I'm under no illusions. Patrick and Jeremy aren't far behind."

Before Daniel could comment on the statement, the door flew open, and the sergeant dragged Patrick in by the scruff of the neck. "He tried to go out the back door, sir, just as you feared, though for the life of me, I don't know how he got there. I had a man right outside his door."

Kathleen stifled a sob with her handkerchief, but Daniel was angry. For her sake, he'd hoped the boy had more sense. "Why, Patrick? Your sister went out on a limb for you."

"Because you're all in on it. I don't stand a chance. They'll hang me, and then I'll be out of the way, leaving them free to do as they please."

Daniel frowned, and he was finding it increasingly difficult to hold his temper. "You think Kathleen would do such a thing?"

The man at least had the decency to bow his head and blush. "No, not Kathleen. But that won't stop the rest of you."

Daniel breathed in a long breath through his nose, trying to quell the fury that was rising. "How did you do it, then? Is there another secret panel?" When Patrick turned his head, refusing to answer, Daniel grabbed ahold of him and shoved him into the ladder-back chair by the side of his bed. "So help me, I'll beat the living daylights out of you before I let you hurt Kathleen. Tell me, you little bastard. How did you get to that staircase without anyone seeing you?"

Patrick pressed himself back against the chair, squeezing his eyes closed as if he were waiting for the first blow to hit. Daniel might have obliged him, but he felt Kathleen's hand on his shoulder.

"Please, Daniel, hasn't he been through enough?"

It took every ounce of reserve Daniel could muster to keep his tone even. "Sergeant, would you please escort Miss Brissedon to the kitchen and ask Mrs. Quinn to make her a cup of tea?"

"I don't need tea . . ."

Daniel nodded to the sergeant and turned to face Patrick, ignoring any further pleas Kathleen might have had. She would be angry with him, but he needed to do this alone. He waited for a moment, glaring at the young man before him until he heard the door close and footsteps on the staircase. Only then did Patrick open his eyes.

"For God's sake, Patrick, I want to help you, but you're not making it easy." He bent down, grabbing him by the collar so that their faces were inches apart. "For your sister's sake, you're going to tell me the truth because I will do whatever it takes to see you never hurt her again."

The young man swallowed. "It's not a secret panel, really. Just the back panel to the built-in closet in the guest room. It was never finished off right, so you can push it aside and get to the back hall."

"And your room has a door into the guest room?"

Patrick nodded, and Daniel bit back his temper. He walked over and swung the door wide. "Constable, could you please take Mr. Desmond back to his room and keep guard from inside this time, both you and your associate? He's not to leave under any circumstances."

"But what if . . ." Patrick began.

"You can use a chamber pot for the bathroom. For Kathleen's sake, I'm giving you another chance, but if you try to escape again, I'll see you hang myself. Is that clear, Mr. Desmond?"

"Yes, sir, perfectly." The words almost seemed rehearsed, devoid of all emotion, as if he'd said them a hundred times before.

"Tell me one thing, Patrick. Why didn't you take your father's watch? It was sitting right on the bureau." He held his breath, wondering if the boy would slip up.

Patrick frowned. "I can assure you, Doctor, if I had killed my stepfather, not only would I have taken my father's watch, but I would have secured the matching cuff links and watch fob, as well as the stick pin, if I could have found them."

"But your stepfather's dead now. Why didn't you just go look for them?"

"And have Colin accuse me of stealing them? Or worse?" He let out a sarcastic laugh. "But what does it matter? He's going to see me hang anyway."

Daniel rubbed his forehead and watched as the officer pulled the young man out the door. Patrick didn't know they'd found the cuff links? He'd have to question that boy again later. Something just wasn't adding up, but more than ever, Daniel's gut was telling him Patrick was innocent.

CHAPTER 31

Saturday, July 2, 1904 – 8:00 a.m.

Patrick sat staring out his window. It truly had become a prison for him now, and there was nothing he could do to escape. Thomas Brissedon's destruction of his family was complete. At least the doctor had relented and allowed the constables to move back outside his room to keep guard, though he was still required to use the chamber pot when nature called. A knock sounded at the door, and one of the officers opened it.

"You're to get ready for your stepfather's funeral, Mr. Desmond," he said, completely devoid of all emotion. Probably annoyed that he had to do a double shift.

"I'm not going," Patrick said in the same dry tone.

"That's not one of your options, sir. Miss Brissedon has asked that you be permitted to attend, and you will be, even if I have to dress you myself."

"Patrick, please!" Katheen nudged her way into the room. "It took me all evening to convince Dr. O'Halleran and Sergeant Owens that you had yet to be proven guilty, and it would be prejudicial to your case for you not to appear."

"Perhaps so, but it would be hypocritical for me to do so. More to the point, do you think your father really would have wanted me there?"

"It makes no difference." O'Halleran came to stand beside Kathleen. "It's what your sister wants, so I suggest you prepare yourself, or I'll do more than take you to the local lockup. I'll drag you up to Riverhead this minute, and you can await trial in the county jail. Rest assured, your bedroom is the more comfortable of the accommodations."

"Give me a moment alone with him. Please, Daniel." Kathleen rested her hand on the doctor's forearm, and once again he acquiesced to her demands. Interesting. Perhaps there was more going on there than they wanted to admit . . . even to themselves. He hoped there was. Kathleen deserved someone better than Brighton Templeton, and except for the fact that he wanted to lock him up, the doctor seemed like a decent sort.

Kathleen turned to Patrick, placing her hand on his cheek just like his mother had when she wanted him to behave. But he spoke before she could say a word. "I've been accused of his murder. Do you truly think it appropriate that I be there? I'm sure the others would rather I didn't make an appearance."

"You've been accused, not found guilty, and in spite of Dr. O'Halleran's stern demeanor, he has assured me he will continue to search for evidence in the case."

"And you believe him?"

"I do. The truth is, I don't think he believes you're guilty either."

"You don't believe I did this, then?" A gentle wave of hope washed over his heart. Oddly enough, the hardest part of this whole ordeal was the thought that she suspected him as well.

She brushed his hair back and kissed his forehead. "Of course not, darling. But you must tell the doctor everything you know so he can discover who really did. Promise me you will do that."

He hung his head. "I may not have killed your father, but I have done things I'm ashamed of. I couldn't bear it if you thought badly of me. You may find some of the things I say . . . painful."

"Nothing could be more painful for me than seeing you blamed for an act you didn't commit. The person who killed my father must pay the consequences, but that's not you. I feel that in my heart. And while my heart hasn't been the best judge of late, I know in this case, it speaks true."

Patrick could barely speak. Kathleen's approval meant so much to him. With his parents gone, she was the only one he truly trusted or cared for. "I'll do as you ask, but are you sure I can trust the doctor?"

She straightened her shoulders, a glow suffusing her flawless skin. "Daniel is an honorable man. If you are innocent, you have nothing to fear from him. Now, about my father's funeral."

"I'll go for you, but don't ask me to be happy about it." Even she couldn't expect that much from him.

Daniel stood beside Sam Tennyson at the gravesite, far more interested in the attendees' reactions than the actual burial. Monsignor Cronin said the usual prayers as they lowered Thomas Brissedon down into the damp earth. A momentary image of his mama's grave flashed through his mind. He'd been remiss in visiting it of late. *I must go next time I'm home.*

He focused his attention on the mourners once more. The servants all stood by properly, though not one tear was shed amongst them. Granted, they didn't know the full extent of their employer's treachery, but they did know he was a ruthless man who, at times, treated his stepson no better than a dog—and a mistreated one at that.

To most of those present, however, this side was clearly hidden away, along with Thomas Brissedon's other secrets. Daniel had managed to speak to a few of them over the previous week, and while they knew Thomas to be a cold, calculating businessman, they believed he had done right when it came to Patrick. Some even thought he'd done more than could be expected. "After all," one had said, "the boy does have a drinking problem, not to mention his penchant for the ladies."

Before long, the priest finished speaking, and it was time for the family to say their goodbyes. Colin went up first, holding seven-year-old Ryan by the hand. Gently, they each tossed a rose down on the oak coffin, then bowed their heads for a moment of prayer. The elder staggered slightly as he walked away. Daniel shook his head. Clearly, the man had already been at the liquor, a habit he indulged in all too frequently.

Next Kathleen walked up, her arm around her younger sister, Charlotte. The younger girl clung to Kathleen as they, too, threw roses on their father's final resting place. They were both crying softly, and Kathleen kissed her rose before tossing it into the grave. An ache clutched Daniel's heart. How would she ever manage to reconcile the memory of her loving father with the reality of the man he truly was?

He couldn't help but wonder why she'd insisted on coming in the first place. His mother and sister never attended funerals, though of late, he'd heard of more women doing so. Nell Tennyson had even accompanied her husband.

Bringing his thoughts back to the moment, he watched as Patrick was nudged forward. Since he was under arrest and handcuffed to the sergeant, both men approached the grave. Daniel could hear the other mourners, mostly men, whispering as Patrick gazed down at the coffin. Some believed he was guilty, though of those, few thought he'd been in his right mind at the time. "The boy clearly wasn't in control of his senses," a man in a topper said, while his companions nodded in agreement.

"Losing both his parents in the span of two years had to take a toll. Especially when he found himself penniless as well," another said.

Daniel shifted his position a bit to hear what others were saying. "Well, I'll not believe a word of it," a third man said, "any more than I believe his father murdered that girl and died in a drunken stupor."

Then, of course, there were those, like Jeremy Radcliffe and Edward Langston, who were more concerned about their own dirty little secrets coming to light with the boy's trial. However, Daniel would have bet a month's pay not one of them expected Patrick to react the way he did.

With an obvious contempt for the man who lay before him, he threw his rose on the ground and, crushing it with his foot, angrily spat into the grave. A hushed murmur engulfed the crowd, and all stood relatively quiet until a painful cry broke the stillness. Patrick hung his head, tears erupting from his eyes as he reached out to beg Kathleen's forgiveness.

Sergeant Owens, however, apparently thought such a show of disrespect was uncalled for and dragged Patrick away from the gravesite, even as his fingers brushed Kathleen's. The sergeant threw the young man into the carriage and, without a word, took off for Oak Street.

Kathleen brought her black rimmed hankie to her face, sobbing into it, and though Daniel felt like whisking her into his arms, he held back, letting Mrs. Quinn step in and guide her to the waiting carriage.

"She will get over it," Jeremy said. "We'll all have to, won't we? I'm just not sure . . . Will they be hanging him, do you think? Surely he wasn't in his right mind when he did it. A few years in an asylum, perhaps?"

"I couldn't say," Daniel said. "But you're jumping the gun a bit, aren't you? He hasn't been convicted yet."

"No, of course not. I just meant . . . Well, there is quite a bit of evidence against him, isn't there? I . . ." Jeremy's droopy eyes seemed to droop even more, and he shook his head. "I am truly sorry."

Jeremy had no sooner rushed off than Daniel felt a tug at his jacket and turned to see seven-year-old Ryan gazing up at him. "Are you going to get the man who hurt my papa?"

"I hope to." Daniel's heart ached. He knew all too well the pain the child must be feeling.

"I don't think it was Patrick."

The sentiment surprised Daniel, and he bent down to look the boy in the eyes. "Why not?"

"That knife you found, it was Patrick's."

Not being sure where this was going, he nodded. "Yes, I'm aware of that."

"But Patrick didn't throw it in the bushes."

Now Daniel's interest was aroused. "Who did, then?"

The boy frowned and looked around, as if he was about to tell a huge secret, which perhaps he was. "Jeremy took it from Patrick's room and tossed it there."

"When did he do this?"

"After Papa had . . . been killed. The next day, maybe."

"And you saw him do this?"

The boy nodded, a mischievous grin crossing his lips. "They don't pay me any mind, on account of I'm only seven. But I'm not stupid." He shrugged. "Anyway, I thought you should know."

"Thank you, Master Ryan, I truly appreciate that."

The boy started to turn away, then stopped and faced Daniel again. "Will it help Patrick?"

"You didn't make it up to help him, did you?"

"No, sir. My sister taught me it's not good to lie. She says you always get found out in the end, and then it will be worse than if you just told the truth in the first place. What I don't understand is why so many grown-ups haven't figured that out."

Daniel couldn't help but chuckle. *Out of the mouths of babes.* "I don't have the answer to that either."

Ryan shrugged again and ran off toward Colin, who seemed uncharacteristically gentle with the boy. His mother always said there was good in everyone. It was just buried deeper in some people than others. To which his father would inevitably reply, "Yes, my dear, and to find it in some, you need a pickax." At that moment, he wondered if he'd need that pickax to get the truth out of Jeremy Radcliffe.

When he arrived back at the house, Jeremy was talking to some of the mourners who had returned for refreshments. But Daniel had no time for the niceties of social behavior. Monday was a holiday, and two days later the inquest was to be held. Excusing himself with all the finesse his mother had taught him, he asked if he could see Jeremy alone.

"Now? It's really not a convenient time. We have mourners to attend."

"I'm sure Kathleen and Colin are more than able to handle the situation, and it is urgent that I speak with you."

"Very well. I suppose I could spare a few moments. We can go into my uncle's study, or I suppose I should say Colin's study now."

Daniel nodded and allowed the man to lead the way, not wanting to even hint at what was so urgent. As soon as they entered, he closed the doors and turned to face the man.

"Tell me one thing, Mr. Radcliffe: Did you see where Patrick kept his knife the night you tried to force yourself on Kathleen, or did you happen across it by accident, perhaps while you were planting evidence in his room?"

"I beg your pardon. I've no idea what you're talking about."

"Kathleen doesn't believe in lying, does she? Surely you're aware of that."

Jeremy collapsed in his uncle's chair, leaning on the desk and resting his face in his hands. Daniel waited until, at last, the man looked up.

"I never meant her any harm. I'm afraid I'd had a bit too much to drink, and seeing her with Brighton . . . I knew what a wastrel he was, remembered him from the city."

"Knew him well, did you?"

"Brighton? No, not at all. But I heard things, about his penchant for gambling, for instance. That's where Colin came across him. Kathleen deserves better."

"Yes, she does. Imagine what she thought when she found out it was you who sent Cornelius Desmond to the tenement that day. Did you know what your uncle had in mind?"

Jeremy shot up from his chair. "What? No, I . . ." He closed his eyes and sank back in the chair, deflating like a punctured balloon. Opening his eyes again, he took a deep breath. "Will they hang me?"

"I can't say for sure, but I suspect much of your future depends on what you tell me here today and whether or not it's the truth."

He nodded. "What is it you want to know?"

"I believe the first question is already before you. Did you know what your uncle was about?"

"I knew he was up to no good. We'd run the same sort of scam on a number of swells. I'd play the messenger, then send them off somewhere on urgent business. When they got there, Tommy would clunk them over the head and rob them."

"So why was this different?"

"I didn't know it was, not till well after it was done. I just thought he'd slammed the fella a bit too hard and he'd fallen over that banister. But then I started hearing about the dead girl and how they were blaming it on that gent. I knew that lass. Tommy was always going to see her."

Daniel felt ill. Thomas must have killed his own child. "Why didn't you go to the police?"

"I wasn't a complete dolt. What if someone heard me talking to that swell? I could be sure of one thing: Tommy wasn't going to defend me, now, was he? Not if it meant his ass was on the line. And what proof did I have? He'd already taken on that new identity for himself, rented a sweet set of rooms and all."

"He'd been garnering a lot more money from those jobs you helped him with than he let on, hadn't he?"

"Enough to send his kids to fancy schools and all, while I spent my days doing his bidding."

"Why did you stay, then?"

"'Cause he was there for me when no one else was. And he always made sure I had food to eat and a decent roof over my head. Then after Desmond died, he said we had enough to live comfortably for the rest of our lives. He bought me new clothes and had me come live with him, even put a few dollars in my pocket. All I had to do was keep my mouth shut."

"Who doctored the books for the mill? Found a way to transfer all of Desmond's assets?"

Jeremy actually grinned. "I did that. I've always been right good with numbers. And Tommy made it well worth my while."

"Did he kill Brigid Desmond?"

For the first time since Daniel had met him, the man's eyelids sprang open, making him look wide awake for a change. "I don't know, and that's the God's honest truth. He seemed to be fond of her, and the doc, he didn't think there was any foul play, but then . . . Tommy was a canny one. I just don't know."

"Did you know about the rest of it—the beatings and such?"

He hung his head, his eyes droopy once more. "Not all of it, but I suspected. Tommy had a way of keeping people in line."

"Why did you steal Patrick's knife and plant it under the window?"

Jeremy's head shot up again, and he swallowed deeply. "I was afraid it would all come out. Patrick had an investigator looking into it, didn't he? But if he was in jail, that'd be an end to it."

"And if they'd hanged him?"

"I didn't think that far ahead. I just got scared and panicked." He stopped speaking, and Daniel could see the shame in his eyes. "I knew what they'd do to me. No one would believe I didn't know."

"Did you hide the bloody shirt in his wardrobe as well?"

"Shirt? No, I swear, just the knife and that note I burned and left in his grate."

"Where did you get the note?"

Jeremy smiled again, a bit of pride touching his eyes. "Still a right pickpocket. I lifted it from Colin's jacket. It was only fair since I spied Colin going through Patrick's pockets on a number of occasions. When I saw it was from a detective agency, I knew what it was about."

"May I presume the burned part referred to yourself?"

He nodded again, the shame returning. "Tommy tried to shield them from it all, you see. But I had to let everyone know somehow, maybe let them see the connection between Tommy Breslin and Thomas Brissedon. I suppose I figured maybe the courts would go easy on Patrick if they read that."

"And you truly believed no one would look any further?"

"I told you, I panicked. I hadn't thought any of it through. I'm not proud of my behavior, Doctor. I'm a coward. Always have been, I suppose, or I would have stood up to Tommy. He wasn't a nice man, but I didn't kill him. I might have wanted to, but I didn't have the nerve."

Somehow Daniel felt sorry for him. If not for his uncle Timothy and his adoptive family, that might have been him. He liked to think he had more moral fiber, but his mother and father had instilled that in him. Jeremy had only Tommy Breslin to look to.

"Or maybe you're just not a killer. You knew Mary O'Neill saw you speaking to Cornelius Desmond, didn't you?"

Jeremy's mouth quirked a bit at the side. "I couldn't be sure he said anything to her, though, or even that she'd recognize me. I followed her to the trolley one day, just to see if she did. But that little creep got there ahead of me."

"Brighton?"

"Yeah, he was trying to find out what she knew about Desmond's murder. Guess he figured he could dig up some dirt and use it as blackmail. She got all nervous and called the conductor, so I took off. But you're right; I wouldn't have hurt her. I just wanted to know if I had to keep an eye out, come up with some story."

"She married that conductor, you know."

A spark twinkled from under the droopy lids. "My ma always said something good comes out of everything." He took a deep breath and sat up straighter in the chair, as if a load had been lifted from his shoulders. "Are you going to arrest me now? It's only fair, I suppose, after everything I've done."

"For what, the murder of Cornelius Desmond? I don't believe you did know what Tommy was up to. The murder of Thomas Brissedon? Miss Brissedon and Miss Buchanan have given you a plausible alibi for most of the evening, so while it's still possible, it's highly unlikely."

"Molly spoke up for me? She's a good lass."

Daniel could feel his anger rise again, with thoughts of how his father had wooed his mama only to toss her aside when he'd gotten what he wanted. "Yes, she is, and I'd hate to see her hurt, her reputation ruined, or worse."

"Oh, you misunderstand. I love the lass and plan to ask her to marry me. Tommy wouldn't have permitted it, but he's not here now, is he? I don't know who murdered him, but I won't say I'm sorry. Molly makes me a better person." Something must have struck him because his eyes widened again, their droopy lids lifting. "You won't have to tell her about what I did, will you?"

"No, but it will likely come out, so I suggest you tell her. If you care for her as much as you say, you'll be honest with her."

"I've not been popular with the ladies, not like Patrick or Colin. I never thought it mattered until I met Molly. If I lose her . . ."

"You most certainly will, if you lie to her."

"If you're done with me, then, I'd best be going and packing my bags. Patrick won't want me here once he finds out what I did. I'll make sure to tell Molly before I leave, though."

"You're not going anywhere just yet. Not until this case is wrapped up. I do have a few more questions. Back to Brighton for a minute. How did he come to be courting Kathleen?"

"That law firm he works for wanted some help out here for the summer, and as I said, he met Colin while he was out gambling. The two hit it off, and the next thing you know, he's bringing Brighton over for dinner. Of course, he was taken with Kathleen and started coming round more often. Thomas wanted me to look into the kid, see if he was on the up and up. He wasn't."

"What do you mean?"

"Turns out he was just another guttersnipe. His old man died with a bottle in his hand, and his ma was sickly. Desmond came along and bought him a decent suit of

426

clothes—made sure his ma got her medicines too. He was all set to send the kid to college, from what I heard. Maybe that's why the bastard was so intent on finding out who did Desmond in."

"Do you think he could have found out it was you who sent Cornelius to that tenement?"

"I don't know how. From what I could tell, Mary had no idea who I was. And if he'd seen me himself, he wouldn't have been asking her about me, now, would he?"

"I wouldn't think so." Daniel closed his notebook and stood up. "Except for Molly, I'd appreciate it if you kept this conversation between us, at least until we've located the real killer."

"You really believe I didn't do it?"

"I didn't say that, but between Kathleen and Molly, your whereabouts for most of the night do seem to be accounted for, except for a small window around five thirty or so."

Jeremy frowned, a look of uncertainty on his face. "But surely it would take longer than that to kill a man."

"Would it? How many have you killed, Mr. Radcliffe?"

Jeremy's face blanched. "None! I didn't mean to imply . . . I never . . . I just thought . . ."

Daniel held up his hand to put a halt to Jeremy's sputtering. "For now, you can go, but a word of advice. Do right by Molly and be honest with her."

"Oh, I will, Doctor. You know, I can't help but wonder if I would have been a better man if someone like Cornelius Desmond had raised me. I'm not saying I'm without fault. Lord knows I lost my innocence a long time ago. But I just wonder sometimes."

"It's never too late to change, Mr. Radcliffe. Try doing it for Molly."

CHAPTER 32

Sunday, July 3, 1904 – 9:00 a.m.

Patrick watched solemnly from his bedroom prison as his family returned from church. After the spectacle at the grave the previous day, the sergeant had decided it was best he didn't attend church that morning. Instead, Monsignor Cronin had come by earlier to hear his confession and give him Communion. The priest made no judgment, though he did ask three times if Patrick had anything else to confess. He was a kind man and seemed almost relieved when Patrick said he didn't.

The smell of bacon wafted up the stairs, and he was just wondering if he would be receiving any when a knock sounded at his door. Dr. O'Halleran entered a moment later, though much to Patrick's dismay, he wasn't carrying a breakfast tray. It was just as well, for the doctor wore a solemn expression as he pulled up a chair and sat down, motioning for Patrick to do the same.

"We need to speak, Mr. Desmond."

"About what? You already have me tried and convicted. How much is Colin paying you?"

The doctor shot out of his chair, pulling Patrick up by the collar as he did. "I don't care what you think of me, Mr. Desmond, but don't ever accuse me of taking a bribe. You were placed under arrest because the evidence pointed toward your guilt. It's only your dear sister's intervention that keeps me from throwing you in the lockup. Do not press my generosity."

He shoved Patrick back into his chair and walked over to the window. After staring through the glass for a few minutes, not saying a word, he straightened his jacket and returned to his own seat once more, his calm demeanor recovered.

"I beg your pardon for my outburst, Mr. Desmond, but you should be careful about accusing a man of such behavior. It could ruin their reputation. My honor is important to me, and I can assure you, no matter what you may have heard, not everyone in law enforcement accepts bribes. I have some questions for you, and you're going to answer them honestly this time. Is that clear?"

Patrick just nodded, figuring the man was sure to give him a good thrashing before their conversation was over. But then, Kathleen had trusted him. Perhaps he should as well?

"Good. Let's start with why you were so upset when I asked to search your room."

"I told you. Because I knew it was all Colin's doing. It would suit him just fine if I was out of the picture."

"Where did you go when you left the house that day?"

He wasn't about to mention his visit to Lydia, so he stuck with his original story, even though not a word of it was true. "We've been over this. I walked around, like I always do, then drove my stepfather's automobile a few towns over to get a bit of snatch. Getting away from here helps me forget what bastards they all are."

"Kathleen included?"

"No, not Kate, but I've already told you that as well. I'd probably be dead by now if it wasn't for her. They had to keep up appearances, make sure she didn't find out, didn't they?"

"What do you mean, appearances?"

"That of the loving stepfather, tolerating his disobedient, irreverent stepson."

"So you left to calm down. I can understand that. Kathleen mentioned you'd done it before; however, she also said you never stayed out all night. What made you do it this time, and how did you end up down by the lake?"

"I went where I could get some sympathy." Well, at least that part was partially true. "The lady was especially attentive."

"Was she expensive?"

Patrick pretended to stifle a laugh. What difference did it make? It's what they all thought anyway. "Extremely, and very discreet."

"So if I went to speak to her, she'd deny everything. How convenient. Of course, that leaves you with no alibi. You do realize that."

He shrugged. "Her discretion is what makes her so popular."

"Of course. And when you returned the next day?" The doctor sat back in his chair, his eyebrow lifted in an inquisitive arc.

"It was early. I went down to the lake to think. It was peaceful and helped me put things in perspective."

"Were you there long?"

"I don't know; I lose track of time when I'm out like that. What does it matter?"

"We found that gun in the water not far from where you were sitting."

"That doesn't mean it was mine. So if that's all you have, I'll be leaving." Patrick stood and started for the door, but the doctor grabbed him by the arm.

"Sit down, Mr. Desmond!" he said, his voice the menacing purr of a tiger about to pounce. He picked up a small bag, taking out the knife and laying it on the floor.

Patrick flopped back down in the chair and shook his head. "I told you; someone must have stolen it. It was the only thing I had left from my father. Brissedon sold everything else . . . or kept it for himself."

"Kathleen said the rooms were generally locked, so how did anyone manage to break into yours?"

"I don't know. Ask Colin. He was always snooping about, but I suppose it could have been anyone. It's harder to pick the lock on Kathleen's diary then the ones on those doors." The doctor lifted an eyebrow, and Patrick could feel the heat rising in his cheeks. "It was right after she moved in. I just wanted to see how she really felt about me."

"And?" A soft spark lit the doctor's eyes.

Patrick shrugged. No sense adding any more lies. "I couldn't get into it, but after a while, I didn't need to. I could see she really did care."

The doctor nodded and pulled a shirt from the bag, the sparkle fading from his eyes. "What about this? Is it yours?"

Patrick's mouth dropped open as he looked at the bloodied material, a lump settling in his throat. "Maybe, I guess. It could be, but I don't know how it would have gotten that way. I'll admit I threw one on the floor by my bed. I meant to have Molly take it for the laundry, but I guess in the confusion I forgot about it. I never even noticed it was missing."

"It wasn't missing, Mr. Desmond. It was shoved in the corner of your wardrobe, but of course, you don't know how it got there."

"No, I don't. I told you; I threw it on the floor by my bed, and there was only a spot of blood on it. I'd cut myself shaving. My stepfather was having Stockbridge and his wife over for dinner that night, and I was running late, as usual."

"What about this note? Do you deny receiving it?"

Patrick looked at the folded note carefully, shaking his head as he did. "I don't know what it's about. I never got any message from Mr. Morton. I talked to him on Wednesday, it's true, but he never sent me any note."

"What about this one?"

Daniel handed him another piece of paper, this one singed, and Patrick recognized it at once. "No, this isn't from Mr. Morton. These are the notes I took while I was there."

"Do you recall what he told you?"

"Yes, a woman named Mary O'Neill saw a man speaking to my father, but she didn't know him. And Brissedon Mills didn't exist until a few months before my father died."

"That's all?"

"Someone thought Thomas was a man called Tommy Breslin, but he denied it."

"Mr. Morton sent you that other note Thursday night, asking you to contact him as soon as possible. It seems he had reason to believe the man Mary O'Neill saw your father speaking to was Jeremy. He wanted to see if you could get him photographs of both men."

"Jeremy! That bastard!" In his heart, he'd always known the truth. And now here was the proof he needed, but it had been turned back against him. "Then it's true. Thomas

Brissedon was behind my father's murder, and my mother's, for that matter. Whether he actually did anything to harm her or not, I can't be sure, but Father's death sealed her fate just as surely as if my stepfather had taken a knife to her throat."

"An interesting choice of words, Mr. Desmond, considering that is the very method that ended Thomas Brissedon's life."

"But I didn't kill him! I didn't even know about the note. Surely you must see that now. Besides, you said it came Thursday night? When would I have had time to speak to him?"

"You might have made an assumption. After all, you'd asked him to look into Thomas Brissedon's past. It would only be natural that you'd take it to mean he'd found proof of your suspicions. Besides, even without this note, you had more than enough motive. There was your obvious hatred for your stepfather, and the belief, founded or unfounded, that he murdered your father and stole your inheritance— not to mention the beatings."

"I told you. He didn't beat me."

"For God's sake, Patrick. I'm a doctor. Do you think I don't know what the bruises from a fall look like? You may be able to fool your sister, but you can't fool me. And if you have any hope of being cleared of your stepfather's murder, you had better start being honest with me."

Patrick didn't know what to say. To confirm the doctor's suspicions would just give them more reason to suspect him, and yet to lie did much the same. The doctor cursed under his breath before getting up and returning to the window. Though the day had barely begun, the man looked tired. His patience was clearly drawing thin. The silence was becoming nerve-racking when the man turned around and changed the direction of his questioning.

"Tell me why you felt the need to hide the bloodstains on your washstand scarf, or more to the point, how did they even get there?"

"The stains on my scarf? That was my blood! I told you. I cut myself shaving. When the blood dripped on the scarf, I panicked. It was one of my mother's better ones, and I knew how difficult it would be to get a bloodstain out of such fine linen. Mrs. Quinn would be furious with me, so I decided to hide it until I could get into town and purchase another one."

"Mrs. Quinn strikes such fear in your soul, does she?"

"Yes, she can strike fear in my soul, but not for the reasons you think. Mrs. Quinn has been with my family for as long as I can remember. She's always been a kind of grandmother to me. If you'd grown up with someone like her, you'd understand." A tear trickled down Patrick's cheek, and he quickly wiped it away.

The doctor sat back down in the chair, a smile transforming his face for the first time since he'd come through Patrick's door. "As it happens, Mr. Desmond, I understand completely. My parents' housekeeper is called Hattie, and she can still put the fear of God in me, though I love her as if she were part of my own family."

Patrick was surprised. Somehow he'd pictured the doctor growing up on the Lower East Side, where some kindhearted soul had sponsored his education, the way his father had for others. "Then you'll understand what went through my mind that morning."

"Yes, I do," the doctor said, his tone noticeably softer. "But I need to know the truth about that night if I'm to help you. Who were you with the night of the murder?"

"I already told you. I called—"

"Lying about it isn't getting us anywhere, and it serves no purpose. Kathleen stopped by your room that night."

"What? Why was she there?"

"For now, it's not important. She needed to talk to you. The point is, you weren't there. Did you meet Lydia Langston somewhere? She's admitted to spending the night with you. I'll do my best to protect her reputation, if that's what you're worried about, but—"

"No, it's not true! She's just lying to protect me."

"Look, Patrick, you're in a lot of trouble! The evidence is building against you. We've already established you had sufficient motive, not to mention an available weapon. And it certainly appears you had the opportunity. With the case we have against you right now, you'll hang within the week. Is that what you want?"

A wave of nausea engulfed him, and he swallowed to keep the bile from surging up his throat. "No, but I'll not sully Lydia's reputation to save my own neck. I didn't spend the night with her. I swear that on whatever honor I have left."

"No, but it was a Langston, wasn't it? Elizabeth, to be precise."

Patrick looked up in shock. How could the doctor possibly know about Elizabeth, and what was more, did that mean he knew about the threats Thomas had made? He felt as if someone were strangling him, and he began to gasp for air. He was going to hang for sure. This would be another nail in his coffin. Spots appeared before his eyes as sweat beaded across his forehead.

The next thing Patrick knew, Dr. O'Halleran was grasping his neck and pressing his head down between his knees. Slowly, the heat that had been rising in his face receded and his vision cleared. He tried to sit up, but the doctor held him there a bit longer, and when he sat up, he thrust a glass of water in his hands.

"Drink this!" he said, his tone transformed into that of the concerned doctor rather than the stern detective.

Patrick did as he was told before asking, "How did you know?"

"Your life may be on the line here, Patrick," the doctor said. "How I learned isn't important, but I need to understand how it all came about."

Patrick shook his head. "It doesn't matter."

"Do you want to die, Patrick?"

"Sometimes, but you wouldn't understand that, would you?"

"I understand that there's at least one person in this house who cares a great deal for you—more than that, from what I hear. Doesn't that mean anything?"

"I won't hurt Kate. I don't care what you do to me."

"Dear God! This is all to protect Kathleen, isn't it?"

"Leave her alone, please. She's innocent of everything. She doesn't deserve any more pain."

"You really do care for her, don't you?"

"Kate's been like a real sister to me, not a stepsister. She's the only family I have left, and I won't hurt her, no matter what. Knowing the truth would devastate her. Thomas Brissedon may have been a bastard, but he was a good father to her, and she loved him."

"She loves you as well. Do you think it will hurt her any less believing that the brother she loved murdered her father? She's far stronger than you suspect."

Patrick's heart ached, and tears crept down his cheeks, though he swiped them away as fast as they fell. Somehow he trusted this man. Maybe it was the admiration in

Kathleen's eyes when he'd caught her gazing at him. Or the pride he saw in the doctor's eyes now as he spoke of her strength. It was the same tenderness he remembered seeing when his parents had watched each other from afar.

"Please help me. I don't know what to do," he finally said.

"The only way I can help you, Patrick, is if you tell me the truth, starting with how your servicing of Elizabeth Langston came about."

"It all started a few days after Mother died. Brissedon called me into his office and told me what I was going to do. That if I didn't obey, he'd disinherit me or worse."

"You refused, so he brought you out to the stables, where he gave you a severe beating."

Patrick started to gag, and the doctor shoved a washbasin under his chin, but there was nothing to come up. Taking a deep breath, he pushed the basin away and answered. "He said he'd throw me out on the streets, or lock me away in an asylum, where I'd never see anyone I loved again. As disturbing as lying with Elizabeth Langston was, the alternative was far worse. At least here I had Kathleen." Patrick bowed his head in shame.

"I'm just a bit puzzled, though. What was it about sleeping with Elizabeth that so disgusted you? You're not exactly known for your chastity."

Patrick couldn't help but smile at that. "No, it wasn't that. Aside from the fact that I don't like being used like a cheap whore, she's Lydia's mother. Can you imagine sleeping with your sweetheart's mother?"

"Ah, I see your point. You really do care for Lydia, which explains why you were so upset when you learned she was to be married to Colin."

"I've just knotted my own rope, haven't I?"

The doctor let a smile catch the corner of his mouth. "Let's not go there just yet. What about the beatings? They didn't stop after you'd agreed to service Elizabeth, did they?" The doctor rubbed his thumb across the yellowing bruise on Patrick's cheek. "And don't tell me some jealous brother caught you with your pants down. I want the truth this time."

"Colin did this. He didn't like something I'd let slip to his father."

Daniel nodded. "Regardless of Colin's threats, you need to tell me the truth now. I can protect you from Colin, but unless you're honest with me, I can't help you beat this murder charge."

"You really do want to help me, don't you?"

"Yes, I do. The fact is, my gut's telling me you didn't do it. And I always pay attention to my gut, whether it's on a case or at dinnertime." Daniel smiled and rustled Patrick's hair the way his father used to. "I need you to confirm—or deny—that you were with Elizabeth Langston the night of the murder."

In spite of the man's assurances, Patrick hesitated for a moment, the anger and hate in Lydia's eyes still fresh in his memory. If he told the truth, Colin would beat the shit out of him and Lydia would despise him, but if he continued to lie, he was sure to face the hangman's noose. He opted for the former. Perhaps Lydia would forgive him one day.

"Yes, I was with her for a good bit of the night. She won't admit it, though. It's not very proper for a lady of her standing, now, is it?"

"Tell me about that night. You used the bedroom next to your own, I'm presuming?"

Patrick nodded in resignation. "I'm not proud of it, but I didn't know what else to do."

"Yes, I can imagine. What did you think about Edward marrying your sister?"

The doctor certainly did jump from one subject to another, but Patrick supposed it was an effective tactic when attempting to throw a suspect off guard. "I was furious. Katie deserves better. She's so much love to give, and Edward . . ."

"Prefers the company of gentlemen."

God! Was there anything this man hadn't found out? "Yes, but don't tell anyone. Edward's a decent sort, and he watches over Lydia. He'll marry one day and raise a family. I'm sure of it."

"Won't that be a bit unfair to the woman he marries?"

"She'll never know. He'll be a good husband. Duty and respect come first with him."

"You just don't want that woman to be Kathleen."

"I want her to have someone she can share everything with. It wouldn't matter to some women. They'd be content just to have an attentive husband, but Kathleen . . . she'll want more. Lydia doesn't have to know about him, does she? That's where I went the other night. When I heard you wanted to search my room, I knew you were going to arrest me, and I wanted to tell her everything before it came out at a trial or something. Needless to say, she didn't take it well. Finding out about Edward as well would devastate her."

"For what it's worth, I believe she already knows about that." The doctor leaned back in his chair and let out a long breath. "So you spent that night with Lydia?"

"No, not that way. I swear, we didn't do anything. I was scared and just wanted someone to talk to. I didn't tell her about her mother until just before dawn. And then I left."

Daniel frowned. "I'll do my best to keep both that secret and Edward's, but I won't risk letting a murderer escape to do it."

"You can't think Edward did it? Just over the marriage arrangements? All he had to do was refuse to go through with it. He hadn't agreed to any of it."

"Unless your father found out his secret and threatened to make it public."

Could it be possible? Such knowledge made public would certainly ruin Edward. In a way, he would have been defending his life.

The doctor abruptly changed the subject once again.

"Your stepfather insisted on having the only keys to the back stairway door. Is that correct?"

"Yes, except for Forbes." Where was he going with this?

"And the one you still have from your father."

Patrick felt ill again, so he just nodded. He'd been a fool to think he could keep anything from this man.

"I'm assuming it was a way for your stepfather to keep track of everyone's movements, or so he thought."

"I suppose that was his intent." Patrick blew out a breath and tried to relax. "He might as well have left it wide open that night, though."

"Why is that?"

"It was used at least three times that I know of."

"Did you see who used it?"

He hesitated once again but continued when the doctor lifted an eyebrow. "The first was Kathleen. I assume she was returning from meeting Brighton."

"Yes, I understand he wasn't allowed in the house."

"No, and of course, being a lady, she would be forbidden to go to his place, so they met out by the woods next to the lake, though she never went alone."

"You don't have to defend the lady's honor. She's already explained the situation to me herself. Who else do you think used it?"

"The next time I heard noise in the hallway, it was Colin."

"Colin? He was heading out, I suppose?"

"No, he was heading down to his father's study. You found the secret entrance, I believe."

"Yes, we've come across it, but what was Colin doing in the study?"

"I'm not sure. He was ruffling through some papers, so I presume he was looking for something. Gambling tickets or money, most likely. Probably both. He'd also want the key to the back door. We all knew where Thomas kept it."

"Do you think he found what he was looking for?"

"I've no idea. The floor creaked, and he stopped to listen. I was sure I was going to end up in the stables again, so when he seemed to ignore it and went back to his rummaging, I hurried upstairs as fast as I could. He must have found something, though, for he headed back through the hallway a while later, and I didn't hear any grumbling. He would have been muttering to himself if he hadn't found what he wanted."

The doctor tilted his head to the side. "You saw him heading back through the hallway? What time was that?"

"No, not exactly. It must have been around four, maybe a bit earlier. After watching Colin in the study, I went back to my own room, but since I still couldn't get to sleep, I took one of the sleeping pills Dr. Tennyson had given me a few weeks ago. I was finally starting to doze off when I heard the footsteps, so I didn't bother getting up to see who the third person was, but it makes sense that it was Colin. Who else could it have been?"

"I don't know, but I think whoever it was may have been our murderer." The doctor stood and walked over to the window once again. "Colin argued with your stepfather about some stolen money on Wednesday, didn't he? Do you think he did steal it?"

"I know he did! I mean, I didn't at first, but then he beat the sh—" Patrick stopped and rephrased his sentence. "That's why he gave me this." He pointed to the bruise on his cheek. "He said it was because I'd informed on him, but all I told Thomas was that I'd seen him in the study the day before. Colin didn't believe the old man had figured it out himself, so once again, I bore the brunt of it."

"So you went to sleep a little before four. I suppose you have no way of knowing whether or not Elizabeth slept along with you?"

"No, though I couldn't have slept more than an hour or so in spite of the sleeping pill. Something woke me up. It almost sounded like my door closing, but there was no one there. I couldn't get back to sleep, so I got up and went out to sit by the lake awhile. Of course, I dozed off there a bit, and ended up being late for breakfast again."

"I understand your stepfather demanded punctuality."

"He demanded a lot more than that."

"He ridiculed you a lot, did he?"

"He seemed to derive some sort of perverted pleasure from it."

"So you went to breakfast fairly sure the man would humiliate you yet again, still nauseous over having to lie with the mother of someone you cared for, and well aware that Lydia was destined to marry Colin."

"That marriage would never have taken place any more than the one between Edward and Kathleen. Edward Langston hated Colin, and there was no way he was going to let his sister marry him. He was furious over his mother arranging it, though he blamed it all on me."

"Because of your afternoon visit with Lydia?"

The doctor certainly had been busy the past few days. "More than likely. Mrs. Langston called on Thomas a few hours later, and they hatched the plan, though I imagine Elizabeth was more of a reluctant participant than one of the masterminds."

"You think he threatened to disclose her secret trysts if she didn't agree?"

"Possibly, though I suspect there are more than a few in the village who are aware of her escapades. I'm sure Edward must be. No, I think there was more to it than that. Thomas had secrets on everyone, and he never hesitated to use them."

"Why not just arrange a marriage between you and Lydia, then?"

"Because I wasn't really one of his own. Besides, he knew he'd never be able to control me the way he would Colin. Once I got my degree and could support us properly, I planned on taking Lydia and moving away from here. He could stick his trust fund."

"But your stepfather put a wrench in the works when he arranged for Lydia to marry Colin. Of course, now that he's dead, Colin won't go through with the wedding, so you'll be free to marry."

"I thought your gut told you I was innocent?"

Daniel leaned back in his chair and chuckled. "It does, but my brain needs to believe it as well. I like to cover all the possibilities."

"It doesn't matter whether Thomas is alive or not. Aside from the fact that Lydia will never go against her brother's will, she despises me for what I said about her mother. Even if she didn't, it's only a matter of time before Colin gives me my walking papers. If not for Kate, he probably would have done so already.

"Well, for the time being, anyway, you're not to go anywhere. Is that understood, Patrick? Trying to escape only makes it look as though you are guilty. Why would an innocent man run?"

"Perhaps because he's being framed!"

"You have to trust me on this, Patrick. I haven't stopped investigating. Do I have your word as an honorable man?"

Dr. O'Halleran's obvious belief in him touched Patrick's heart, and after all, Kathleen seemed to trust him, and Dr. Tennyson as well. "I won't try to escape again, but may I be allowed to walk around the house freely? Using the chamber pot is not pleasant, especially as Molly is only permitted to empty it once a day." The doctor looked up, a frown crossing his brow, so he clarified. "It's Colin's doing. He says she's far too busy to do it more than that."

"All right, I'll let the constables know; however, if you try to run again, I will ask the sergeant to instruct his men to shoot you on the spot, innocent or not. Are we in agreement?"

Patrick nodded, albeit reluctantly. He wasn't thrilled with the shoot-you-on-the-spot part, but he was smart enough to realize his only real chance at freedom lay in Dr. O'Halleran's hands.

CHAPTER 33

"Kathleen, I need to speak to you, if you wouldn't mind."
A few more neighbors had stopped by to pay their respects,
and she was just seeing them out the door.

"Yes, of course, Daniel. I'll have Mrs. Quinn bring us
some tea." She led the way to the garden but had barely
settled herself when she spoke. "How is Patrick holding
up? I've been so worried about him. Perhaps if you could
just let him take some fresh air?"

"I've told him he can have free run of the house as long
as he doesn't try to escape again. That includes the garden,
though not beyond. He's given me his word, but should he
break it, it could be worth his life. The sergeant's men have
orders to shoot on sight if he leaves the grounds."

"Let me talk to him. Just to make sure he understands."

"You're free to speak to him anytime you like, but first I
need you to answer a few questions. What do you know
about Brighton Templeton?"

"He's Colin's friend, and he's studying to be an
attorney. He works at Grayson and Brice."

"Do you know how he and Colin became acquainted?"

"At the gambling hells, I suppose, though Colin says
Brighton plays much better than he does." She frowned.
"That's one of the reasons I became disenchanted with
him. I could never marry a man who frequented such

disreputable places. A card game now and then, or an occasional trip to the track, is one thing, but that is quite another."

"Was that the only reason?"

"Why do you ask, Doctor? I can't imagine it having anything to do with the case." The sweetest smile he'd ever seen crossed her lips, and a warmth tingled in his cheeks. He was not about to play coy with her this time, however.

"I'm not sure it does, Miss Brissedon, but I fear that discussion must wait for another day. Had he asked for your hand?"

Curiosity lit her eyes, but she answered. "Yes, on a number of occasions. I told him I'd need my father's permission, though in truth, I wasn't at all sure I wanted to accept regardless. A bit cowardly of me, as I've already admitted, but I knew Father would never agree."

"Why did he dislike Brighton so?"

"I don't really know. All he'd say was he knew that lad, and he was nothing but a rounder."

"Do you think now he might have known him from his time on the Lower East Side?"

She sipped the tea Mrs. Quinn had left for them and stared out across the garden. "I suppose it's possible, though I wouldn't think so. Brighton's parents must have had money if he was studying to become an attorney. Besides, they never showed any signs of recognition."

"Kathleen?" He hesitated for a minute, debating whether the next question was necessary or not.

"Say what's on your mind, Daniel. Your honesty is a point in your favor."

That relaxed him a bit. "We're on a point system, are we?" She laughed, and he asked before he lost his nerve.

"Who were you trying to protect when you said you were with Brighton all night?"

"I'm not really sure," she said. "Perhaps it was only myself. After all, I would be just as much a suspect as anyone else. And Brighton and I had a terrible argument over my father that night. He wanted me to run away with him, but I told him that was impossible, that I couldn't hurt my father. We were both upset. Then to make matters worse, my depraved cousin, Jeremy, was waiting for me when I got in."

"I never asked. How did you know where Patrick's knife was hidden?"

"He showed it to me once, as a sort of insurance, I think. If my father tried to take possession of it, I could honestly testify that it belonged to Patrick."

"And you're certain Jeremy headed up to Molly's room after he left you?"

"No, I can't be certain, but Molly is. The poor girl believes he's going to ask her to marry him one day, but my father would never have permitted it."

"For what it's worth, I believe Jeremy truly does care for her, and with your father gone, he might ask for her hand."

Her eyes widened, filled with distress. "You don't think he could have murdered my father so they could marry, do you?"

"The thought has crossed my mind, but I need a few more pieces to the puzzle first. What did you do after Jeremy left?"

"I waited a few moments until I was sure he was gone. No, wait. He didn't go directly up to Molly's room. I saw him pacing back and forth on the front lawn. He seemed to be chiding himself for being such a hopeless cad."

Daniel narrowed his eyes. "How do you know that's what he was saying?"

"You recall how brutally hot that night was. The window was open, and my cousin is not subtle. I caught more than a few words. By the time I got back in my room, I heard him heading up the stairs to the third floor, to Molly's room, I presumed. I was so angry with him. I was determined to tell my father in the morning. Not to send him away, but to force him to stop drinking so heavily. He would never have done anything like that if he wasn't in his cups, as you gentlemen say."

Daniel smiled. She was such a caring person, much like his mother and sister. "You could hear him going up the back stairs from your room?"

"I probably could have. This is an old house, and everything creaks, but no. The main stair continues up to the children's hallway. There's just a door between that and the staff's quarters."

"Had he ever tried anything like that before?"

"No, never." Pain filled her eyes, and she reached out to touch Daniel's arm. "You don't think he was forcing himself on Molly? I should have inquired. Made sure she was all right."

"No, I'm fairly sure Molly's in love with him. You said yourself she thought he was going to ask her to marry him."

"Yes, that is true."

"Who else is up on the third floor?"

"The rest of the indoor help, except Mrs. Quinn, who usually sleeps off the kitchen; the nursemaid, Moira; and the children."

"Was Mrs. Quinn up there that night?"

A smile ticked her lips, though she tried to suppress it. "Now, Daniel, why do I get the impression you already know the answer to that?" Heat rose in Daniel's cheeks again, and he cleared his throat to answer, but he stopped short. Her smile had dropped away as quickly as it had sprouted, replaced by concern. "It just can't have been Jeremy."

"He had more than enough motive and could have easily snuck back downstairs."

"But why? Father's always been so kind to him."

"Jealousy, perhaps, or anger. He risked a lot when he sent Cornelius Desmond to that tenement but reaped few of the benefits."

"Perhaps, but Father continued to take care of him. He was treated like one of the family."

"But Colin would inherit the bulk of the estate when it was Jeremy who took the chance. And on top of that, your father would deny him the first woman to truly care for him."

"Oh, I hadn't thought of it that way, but then, I'm still coming to terms with what my father did." Her eyes filled with tears, and she pulled a handkerchief from her pocket to blow her nose. "We will have to inform everyone when this is over. Nothing is truly ours."

Daniel reached across the table to touch her cheek. He knew he shouldn't, knew he had to remain professional, but his heart ached at seeing her distress. "We'll deal with that later. For now, we have to find out who did this."

She straightened up, dabbing her nose once more before speaking again. "Yes, you're right, of course. You must help Patrick, for in my heart I'm sure he's innocent."

Daniel nodded and, squeezing her hand, continued his questions. "Did you see Mr. Templeton again later that night?"

"No, in fact, I didn't see him again until the wake was held. He came to pay his respects."

"How did he find out about the murder?"

"The papers, I presume. That's all they spoke about that next day, as if Father's death was some kind of amusement."

"He must have been furious when he heard you were to marry Edward Langston."

"Yes, as I said, we had a terrible argument. But when I saw him the day of the wake . . . well, it wasn't an issue anymore, was it. He assured me that he and Colin had sorted it all out. He even laughed about the prospect of such a marriage taking place, as if the idea of Edward and I marrying was a joke."

"Perhaps he thought it was, although I think he was mistaken about Edward."

"I wish you wouldn't be so cryptic, Daniel." Kathleen huffed, her pretty face squished up in annoyance. "I am sorry I lied to you at first and held a few things back, but I swear what I tell you now is the truth. Please do me the same courtesy."

Daniel smiled, throwing caution to the wind, and leaned over to kiss her on the forehead. "Just a few more people to speak to, and you'll have your answers. Right now, however, I need to speak with Colin again. Is he here?"

"Yes, he's in the study—drinking, I presume."

Kathleen was correct on both counts, for Daniel found him sitting with his feet up on his father's beautiful mahogany desk, a bottle of whiskey by his side. Daniel knocked twice on the open door before entering, and the man had the decency to sit up straight.

"Yes, Doctor, what is it?"

"I'm hoping to conclude my investigations shortly, but I have a few loose ends to tie up first, if you wouldn't mind."

"I shall be happy to oblige," Colin said with a slight slur as he took another drink. "Would you like one?"

"No, thank you. I try to avoid overindulging, not knowing when I'll be called upon in my capacity as a physician."

"Of course, quite understandable. That's why I went into law. As long as you win the case, no one cares if you're up the pole or not, especially since I seem to be much more effective when I've had a few."

Daniel didn't say anything, so Colin rested back against the chair and surveyed his surroundings. "Can you imagine? This is all mine now. Aren't I the lucky one?"

"From what I understand, you're a very rich man."

"But they'll expect me to handle everything now. Kathleen wants to know if Molly can stay, Talbot needs to be sure his lumber will be ready on schedule, Brighton wants to marry my sister! They actually expect me to show up for meetings at the mill."

"That does usually go with the territory."

"Well, I think I liked the old territory better. Patrick can handle this part. He should have to earn his allowance, don't you think?"

"I thought he was already employed . . . working nights, from what I understand. Something to do with entertaining the wives of prospective clients."

"That little bastard!" Colin cursed, just loud enough for Daniel to catch. "I warned him to keep his mouth shut!"

"When you beat him, you mean? Or did you let the stable hands do that for you?"

"That fucking little weasel. You can't trust him. He'll say anything to hurt my family."

"In this case, I think it's his own neck he's worried about. He fears the hangman's noose far more than he fears you. It's clear you knew about the *arrangement* your father had with Patrick. In fact, you informed him that things would continue as usual as soon as the commotion over your father's death died down, didn't you?"

"I did no such thing!" Colin's face had lost all trace of color.

"Mr. Brissedon, I have you in the vicinity of your father's rooms between two and six on the morning of his death, so you have opportunity. You inherit the bulk of his estate, making you a very wealthy young man. Your father was also demanding you marry a naive young girl in return for paying off your enormous gambling debts. That's quite a motive. Shall I go on?"

"But you found the evidence in Patrick's room, not mine."

"That could have very well been planted there by someone such as yourself. Someone who'd like to make sure Patrick was no longer a threat to their fortune."

"That's preposterous!"

"Is it? I find it quite plausible myself, so unless you begin telling me the truth, you may find yourself behind bars."

"That little bastard never did know when to keep his mouth shut." Colin emptied his glass, refilling it before he spoke again. "All right, I knew what Father had him doing, and I did rough him up a bit now and then, but I didn't

452

murder my father. I may have argued with him about money on occasion . . ."

"Even stolen from him," Daniel said, finding this was the first time he was actually enjoying making accusations.

"Yes, even stolen from him, but I didn't want this responsibility. In case you haven't noticed, Dr. O'Halleran, I'm not fond of dealing with reality."

"As you said, Patrick could handle it for you . . . or Jeremy. Perhaps that's what you had planned all along? Get rid of your father, frame Patrick, and let your cousin handle the responsibilities, leaving you free to do whatever you wanted . . . and with the money to do it."

Colin sat up, gently placing his glass down on the polished wood. All the fight seemed to have drained out of him, leaving him oddly sober. "I'm going to have to deal with this, aren't I?"

"I'm afraid so, sir. You can begin by telling me what you were doing in your father's study at two thirty on the morning of his murder."

"I was looking for the gambling receipts he'd just paid. I thought if I got ahold of them, he couldn't use them to force me into a marriage with Lydia."

"Were you looking for this as well?" Daniel held up the note Patrick had scribbled during his meeting with Alexander Morton.

"Perhaps," Colin said in surprise, "but where did you find it?"

"More to the point, where did you get it?"

Colin shrugged and took the note from Daniel's outstretched hand. "It was delivered for Patrick, but he wasn't available, so . . . Wait, no! This isn't the note I thought it was."

"The one you clearly neglected to give to Patrick, you mean?"

"I never had the chance. It was missing from my pocket when I went to look for it the next morning, and then all hell broke loose."

"I'd wager that one didn't go missing until after you'd ransacked your father's office. Kathleen found it stuck against the side of the bottom left-hand drawer." Colin cursed again, so Daniel continued. "You took this note out of Patrick's pocket the day before when you roughed him up, didn't you?"

"So what if I did? I knew he was up to something. His mother had hired a detective to snoop around in my father's affairs. I just wanted to know what he found out. But how did you get it?"

"It turned up in Patrick's fireplace grate."

"So the little ratbag stole it back?"

It was all Daniel could do to keep from laughing out loud. "No, Jeremy planted it there."

"Jeremy, but . . . How did he . . . ?"

"I understand he was quite a talented pickpocket in his day."

"Jeremy?" Colin took another drink. It was evident he had no idea what had gone on while he was away at boarding school.

"What did you do when you read this note?"

"Nothing at first, but when Father informed me I was to marry Lydia Langston, I thought maybe I could use it to my advantage. He was always holding secrets over people's heads, threatening to reveal them. This time I held the winning card, so I showed it to him Thursday night after everyone left and demanded an explanation." He swore again, taking another drink. "I never have been a very good gambler. He just laughed at me, saying it was nothing more than Patrick's feeble attempt to clear his father's name at our expense, and I'd fallen for it."

Daniel frowned. "So your father was the last one to have the note?"

"No, he told me to get rid of it before Patrick found somebody more gullible than me. I shoved it back in my pocket, had another drink or two, and then went to bed."

"What did Jeremy think about the whole thing?"

Colin took another drink and shrugged. "All he was worried about was making sure he wasn't blamed for anything. Only God knows why."

"Why indeed?" Daniel said. "Didn't you ask him about it?"

"Lord, no! Why would I? Jeremy was always afraid he'd done something to displease my father, whether he had or not. Of course, I can't say I blame him. Father treated him like one of the help most of the time."

Daniel loved switching up his line of questioning to throw people off guard, and he did that now. "How did you feel about Kathleen being promised to a man like Edward Langston?"

Colin twisted his lips in disgust. "Found out about him, did you? Then you're well aware there was no way I was going to let that marriage take place, not that Langston would have gone through with it anyway. Besides, Kathleen loves Brighton, and he loves her, no matter what anyone says. He's not just after her money."

"He gambles quite heavily, and yet his debts are always paid in cash . . . by you, I believe."

"Yes, so what if they are? Since when is it illegal for one friend to help another out?"

"Ordinarily, it's not, but when that friend has to steal in order to come up with the money. . ."

"Father hated Brighton because he wasn't wealthy enough. I begged him to just lend me the money, but he would never hear of it. He said I needed to keep better company. Wealth and prestige were all that mattered to him, not friendship."

"Mr. Templeton must have been furious when he heard about Kathleen's proposed marriage."

"He was duly upset, but I told him I'd take care of things, just like I always did. He knew I'd come through for him."

"Your father's death would certainly take care of that particular problem."

"No! That's not what I meant. Father hated seeing Kate unhappy. All I needed to do was point that out. He'd bluster a bit about it, but eventually he'd give in."

"And when did you deliver these encouraging words?"

"About two thirty, quarter to three, I guess, maybe a bit later. Kathleen had gone in—"

"Through the back hallway," Daniel added.

"Yes, through the back hallway." Colin frowned before continuing. "Brighton was upset and had slid down against the wall by the door . . ."

"What key did she use?"

"The one from his study, I suppose, but you can't possibly think—"

"Calm yourself, Mr. Brissedon. I'm convinced Kathleen came in far too early to have killed your father. Did she give you the key, or did you locate it while ransacking your father's study?"

"I didn't ransack it," Colin said. "I left it in perfect order. I'll admit I opened the window so it would look like a theft, but I didn't leave things in the state we found them."

"Fair enough, but you saw Brighton after that."

"Yes," Colin replied, having the good grace to show some remorse. "We talked for a few moments, and he calmed down. I asked him if he wanted to come with me, but he said he was just going to sit down at the lake for a bit and cool off, so I went off to the beer hall for a quick drink, bought a bottle, then stopped by to see a certain lady for a bit. Patrick told you about me being in the study that night, didn't he?" He huffed an ironic laugh. "I thought I heard someone in the hallway. I should have known it was him."

"But you didn't return from the beer hall that way, did you?"

"No, I tried to, but then I realized the key was missing, along with a good bit of cash, so I was forced to use the main stairs. No doubt I was robbed at the beer hall. I was quite inebriated. Do you think someone there is responsible for murdering my father as well?"

It did put a new spin on things, but somehow Daniel thought this was far more personal. "I doubt that. What time did you get home?"

"About five. I can prove that," he said with a sudden eagerness, as if he saw a beacon of hope. "I didn't take my boots off. Forbes must have seen me stumbling in because when I headed down to breakfast, it was already cleaned up."

"Mrs. Quinn did, actually. Of course, as your father was killed between the hours of two and six, that doesn't completely let you off the hook. Tell me, when you were in the wing, did you hear anything unusual coming from the bedrooms? Patrick claims he was with Elizabeth Langston, but she adamantly denies it."

"Oh, she was there all right. I'd recognize that bergamot perfume she drenched herself in anywhere."

Daniel looked at him curiously, and Colin didn't hesitate to clarify. "Yes, I slept with her as well, so did Father. For an older woman, she has an insatiable appetite. I dare say, she'd even teach you a few tricks, Doctor. It was fun while it lasted, but then Father started seeing her, and, well . . . She lost her appeal."

"Interesting! Well, thank you for being so candid, Mr. Brissedon. Now, if I could just speak with Molly Buchanan, I'll conclude my investigation for the evening."

"Molly! What on earth for?"

"Please, Mr. Brissedon, I believe you know precisely why."

"Yes, of course, I'll have Forbes send for her." He called the butler at once, and a few moments later Molly was standing in the study, her face as white as her apron.

"I would like to speak to the young lady alone, if you wouldn't mind, Mr. Brissedon."

"Ah yes, of course. I'll be in the parlor if you need anything."

With a bottle of whiskey, no doubt. Daniel shook his head and turned to Miss Buchanan, not wanting to cause her any more anxiety than necessary. "Please calm yourself, Miss Buchanan. You are in no trouble. I have only one question for you, but I need you to be honest. A young man's life may very well depend on your answer."

"Mr. Desmond's, ye mean?"

"Perhaps, or Mr. Radcliffe's."

Her eyes widened, and her hands began to shake. "Jeremy was with me all night. I already told ye that. We're going to be wed and all."

"Yes, I recall, but I need to know what time he arrived in your room and when he left."

"Must have been about one or so, when he got there. Lizzie had just fixed her bed about a half hour before, so it looked like she was still there, and headed downstairs."

"Fixed her bed? Why? Mrs. Quinn clearly knew what was going on."

"'Cause she didn't want Jerry to be finding out about her and Trev, now, did she?"

The amount of subterfuge that went on was giving Daniel a headache. "I see. And what time did he leave?"

"Round about five. Lizzie'd been sick and came back up to get clean clothes. Sure, she was real quiet like, not wanting to wake Jerry while she was still there, but it was about time for us to be up and about anyway, so he didn't think nothing o' it. He had a right headache, though."

"Thank you, Molly. I do have one more question. You bring the shoes to Forbes for cleaning, do you not?"

"Sure, I do that."

"Did you ever notice a chip on one of the men's heels, on the corner of the right shoe?"

"Can't say I have, sir, though Jeremy's is nearly worn down to the nub, and Mr. Patrick's is always scratched along the inside. From the bicycle riding, ye see."

"Yes, of course." The girl saw far more than she realized. "Thank you again, Miss Buchanan. You may go back to work."

"Jerry's in the clear now, isn't he, sir?"

"I can't give you any information about that yet, but rest assured the information you gave me was extremely useful."

Colin was pacing in the entrance hall when Daniel came out of the study. "Was she of any help?"

"Yes, thank you."

"And do you have your answer? Do you know who killed my father?"

"I'm afraid I still have a bit more to look into, but I feel confident I'll have an answer by tomorrow. Please give my regards to Kathleen."

"Yes, about Kathleen. We're having a picnic tomorrow for the holiday. I know it's not in keeping with proper etiquette, but she feels it will be good for the children, and I have to agree. She's hoping you can join us. Dr. Tennyson and his family are coming as well."

His first instinct was to decline, considering they were virtually all suspects, but then he thought better of it. This would give him a perfect opportunity to observe them all in one place. "It would be my pleasure."

CHAPTER 34

Monday, July 4, 1904 – 7:00 a.m.

"Brighton?" Kathleen smiled as she looked across the garden. "You could have come in the front door, you know. There's no one to object anymore. Certainly, Colin won't."

"I heard your voice and wanted to surprise you."

"I'll be done here in a minute, and we can go in. I'm just gathering flowers for the picnic."

"I was surprised you were celebrating at all, with your father being buried so recently. Won't the gossips be wagging their tongues?"

Kathleen laughed. She should be concerned for their reputations, she supposed, but after all her father had done, breaking the mourning code was the least of her worries. "We're just having family and a few close friends. The children need some happiness and normalcy back in their lives. They don't really understand any of it."

"Yes, you're right, of course. Before we go in, will you take a walk with me down to the carriage house?"

"The carriage house? Why on earth . . ."

"I have a surprise for you. Please indulge me."

"Yes, of course. But we can't take too long. There's still a lot to be done."

Brighton wrapped his arm around her waist as they walked across the lawn. She really needed to be truthful with him, but he looked so happy. They reached the large wooden building, and he opened the doors to reveal a bright red automobile with a black roof, similar to her father's except that it had only a front seat.

"Do you like it?" he asked.

"It's lovely, but it must have been quite expensive."

"I have a small trust fund. Come take a ride with me. We won't be long."

"Oh, Brighton, I'd love to, but maybe later. I've so much to do up at the house."

"It's the doctor, isn't it?"

"I beg your pardon?"

"You've fallen for that doctor, haven't you?" He grabbed her arm and squeezed it. "What has he been telling you about me?"

"Brighton, you're hurting me. Let go."

"Answer me. What has he told you?"

"Nothing. He just asks questions." She tried to pull away, but his grip only tightened. "I'm going to scream for help if you don't release me. What's gotten into you?"

"Oh, Kathleen. It could have all been so nice."

Something hard poked her in the ribs, and she looked down to see a gun. "Brighton, what are you doing?"

"Taking what's mine, what your father took from me. Now get in the automobile, and don't think of running, please. I'm an excellent shot."

"I don't believe you'd do it."

"I slit your father's throat and never lost a night's sleep over it. Now, you can come with me and be my wife, or you can die right here. It would be unfortunate, but with the money I've stolen, I'm sure I'd get over it in time."

He motioned with the gun and gave her a lift up into the seat. All the while, her mind was racing. Could she chance jumping from the vehicle? She cast a quick look around. There wasn't even anything to hit him with. Where were the stable hands? The engine turned over, and Brighton hopped in beside her.

"What have you done with Mickey and Willie?"

"Those two idiots? Two bits and a cheap bottle of whiskey will have them sleeping until tomorrow. You weren't hoping they'd rescue you, were you?"

"Where are we going?"

"Far away from here. That doctor of yours will put it all together sooner or later. He was there the day Neily died, you know. He tried to tell them it wasn't right, that poor Neily didn't hurt anybody. But them coppers, they just wouldn't listen."

They were on the road now, heading where? Toward the village, it seemed. The railroad, of course, but where then? Her heart was pounding against her rib cage, her pulse racing, but she had to keep her wits about her.

He pressed the gun against her waist. "Anybody waves, you just smile nice and wave back."

She nodded, happy to oblige. The more people who noticed them, the better chance Daniel would have of finding them. Smiling cheerfully, she waved to everyone they saw. Mrs. Jeffries was out with the children; the Whitlocks were enjoying a quiet walk. When they pulled up in front of the railroad station, he leaned over and squeezed her arm.

"Remember, one word, and I end it all right here and now. I have nothing more to lose." He reached down and pulled open a bag he'd thrown on the floor. "Here, put these on." Handing her a hat, gloves, and a small bag, he motioned for her to walk ahead of him into the station.

"Good morning, Mr. Templeton, Miss Brissedon," the ticket agent said. "I was sorry to hear about your father."

"Yes, awful affair," Brighton said. "I'm taking Miss Brissedon out for the day. She needs to get away from the house."

"Yes, I can imagine. Just the two of you?"

"Miss Brissedon and I plan to announce our engagement as soon as it's appropriate. Her father's death has unfortunately delayed our plans."

"Well, may I be the first to offer my congratulations."

Kathleen felt a poke in her ribs. "Thank you. You're very kind."

The train hadn't arrived yet, so they sat on a bench. "What about your car? And clothes? We have no clothes or money."

"I've been planning this since I learned that doctor had taken over the investigation. I was afraid he'd pick up on things, just like he did with Neily. What are the odds of the same doctor examining both him and your father? And then you had to go ask him to take another look into Neily's death as well. That stupid detective poking around wasn't enough?"

"I know my father killed Patrick's father, but how did that affect you? I don't understand." *Pretend to care, Kathleen. Daniel will figure this out.* "Please, Brighton, I want to know."

"Neily Desmond was a good chap. He cared about people, not like Tommy or even Jerry."

"Tommy or Jerry?"

"Don't pretend you don't know. That doctor came sniffing around, asking questions about your old man and such. He's not the type to keep things from you."

No sense in playing ignorant. "You mean my father and Jeremy."

"I knew he told you. Neily was helping my mother and me, buying the medicine she needed, and it was working. He was even going to send me to college."

"That's how you're able to go to law school."

"Guess he didn't tell you that, then, did he? I'm not in law school. I'm not even a clerk. I run messages. My college career went down the drain when your old man killed Neily Desmond. So did my mother's life. We couldn't afford the medicine anymore. The measly bit I brought in could barely put food on the table. She died two months later, in agony. And every day I watched her suffer, I swore I was going to get even with the man who did it. I have to admit it took me a bit to put all the pieces together. But I'd seen him, hadn't I?"

"What do you mean?"

"I heard Neily telling Mary O'Neill he was off to one of the tenements way downtown. I didn't like the idea of him going down there on his own, so I followed. I got caught up in traffic, but I wasn't too worried since I had the address. I got there just in time to see this man kicking Neily in the side. He knelt down, taking his watch and telling him he'd have his wife as well. Neily always said that watch was meant for Patrick."

"We should go back and make sure he gets it, then."

"Nice try, darling, but that's not going to happen." He sat quietly for a moment, staring down the track. She had to keep his mind occupied and maybe throw him off guard in the process.

"So if you didn't know the man's name, what made you think it was my father?"

He smiled and ran his finger against her cheek. "Fate, my love. The planets aligning. Call it what you will. I discovered that I had a talent for gambling and came across your brother in one of the gambling hells. Imagine my surprise when, not a year later, I see the announcement in the newspaper. 'Lumber magnate Thomas Brissedon to wed Patchogue widow Brigid Desmond.' I knew it couldn't be a coincidence. That very day, Mr. Brice asked if I'd be interested in working at his Patchogue office for the summer. So you see, darling, it was meant to be. I took the position and headed out to Patchogue to meet Colin's father. Your brother really was quite obliging. When I saw your old man, I knew what I had to do."

"But why not just go to the police, tell them what you knew?"

The train came, and he took her arm, nearly dragging her on board. When they were settled, she asked him again. "Why not tell the police?"

"Tell them what? That I saw some swell send Neily to his death in that tenement?" He let out a cold, bitter laugh. "He begged, you know, your old man. Offered me a drawer full of cash. Did you know the bottom drawer of his bureau was full of crisp hundred-dollar bills? I took it all, of course, plus those blasted cuff links. I must have dropped them, though."

"You did. I found one out by the trees."

"You should have just married me, Kate. We could have avoided all this unpleasantness."

"Would it have really made a difference?"

"No, I suppose not. He took Neily's life. He had to give his in return. I had planned on dragging it out a bit more. Making him watch as I slowly drove a wedge between him and his children. Making him suffer, just like my mother did. It was easy with Colin. Get him so boozed up he had no idea how much he'd lost. Half the debts your father paid out on his behalf went to me." He grinned, a hideous, lecherous smile. "You, my darling, were a bit more of a challenge. I would have won you in the end, though. But then he ruined everything again."

Anger flared in Kathleen's chest. Her father had thought nothing of who he'd hurt, but neither did Brighton. "And what about you? You took a life as well."

"I was taking what was owed. Doing what Cornelius Desmond couldn't do. Your father didn't care about Brigid or Patrick or anybody else who was left to mourn Neily."

"And did you care about me or Colin or the children? No matter what Father was, he took care of us. But you didn't think about that, did you? It was only your pain that mattered."

"Shut your mouth!" He hissed the words so low she almost didn't hear them. "You're nothing but a spoiled brat. You'll get over it soon enough, and if you give me any trouble, I'll stick you in an asylum somewhere in Europe where no one will ever find you."

"Europe? Is that where we're going? But we have no luggage, no money."

"I told you," he said through clenched teeth. "I've been arranging this since that doctor of yours showed up on the case. And if he gets too close, I'll kill him too. He's no different than the rest of you. Everything handed to you on a silver platter. But when I had my chance, your father took it all away."

"You shot Daniel, didn't you?"

"He shouldn't have been nosing around in my business. I just sent him a little warning. Worked out well, don't you think?" He rested back against the seat and chuckled. "I hardly had to do anything. I couldn't believe it when they arrested Patrick. The news was all over town."

"He was Neily's son," she said, unable to keep the disdain from her voice. "I thought you killed my father for him?"

"And I thought I told you to shut up? I didn't want to hurt Patrick, but that was all your father's doing too. If he hadn't killed Neily, I wouldn't have had to kill him, and then that fucking doctor never would have been nosing around. Besides, he'll figure it all out now and Paddy will be off the hook. Of course, we'll be long gone by then."

He took a calming breath and glanced down the aisle. "I really didn't mean to leave that shirt in Patrick's room. I was very careful to avoid getting blood all over myself, but I couldn't keep from getting some on my hands, and there was the knife, of course. Couldn't have that, now, could I? What if someone spotted me darting back down the hallway? My plan had been to say I was looking for your room."

"So you slipped into Patrick's room and wiped your hands on his shirt." Kathleen couldn't keep the tears from budding in her eyes, but she swallowed, struggling to hold them at bay.

"What? No. I wiped my hands on my own shirt. Didn't want to leave any smudges behind when I robbed old Tommy, now, did I? Afterward, I stopped by Patrick's room." He frowned. "I truly thought the little lecher would be out, but there he was, spread out across his sheets in nothing but his drawers. Made me stop short, but then I realized he was dead to the world. Probably had a busy night.

"Not that it mattered. When I was a kid, my old man used to take me to swells' houses and slip me through their windows so I could open the door for him. He always had a light foot, my old man, even when he was up the pole. This was easy. I put on one of Patrick's shirts and threw mine in his wardrobe. He never even budged. Fate stepping in once again," he said with a maniacal grin.

"He's not in, Doc," Sergeant Owens stood looking up at the two-story house. "The landlady says he went out early this morning. Didn't say where he was going or when he'd be back."

Daniel hissed a curse. He should have followed his gut and come to question the man last night. Why hadn't he remembered it sooner? Brighton had mentioned Desmond's clothing had been saturated with whiskey. The newspapers hadn't reported anything about that. There was only one way he could have known. He'd been there. A fiery knot formed in Daniel's stomach.

"Search his rooms, would you, Sergeant? I'm going to see if he headed to the Brissedons'."

Daniel walked into the landlady's pleasant sitting room, and Mrs. Newins looked up. "Anything I can help you with, Doctor?"

"Do you have a telephone, ma'am?"

"'Course I do. Have to keep this place up-to-date or people would stop wanting to rent rooms, now, wouldn't they?"

"I suppose you're right." He smiled his most endearing smile. "May I use it to phone the Brissedons'? It's official business. I'll be happy to reimburse you whatever you think is fair."

"Don't be silly. You go on ahead and use it. Just head down the hallway, and you'll see it, right off the kitchen."

Daniel's fingers trembled as he dialed for the operator and asked to be put through to the Brissedon household. He swore his heart was pounding twenty beats for each ring, and his mouth had gone so dry he could barely swallow. At last, after the fourth ring, Forbes picked up.

"The Brissedon household. May I help you?"

"Forbes, it's Dr. O'Halleran. Is Miss Brissedon available?"

"No, sir, I'm afraid she's taken a spin in Mr. Templeton's new automobile."

"Fuck!"

"I beg your pardon, sir? Is everything all right?"

"I'm terribly sorry, Forbes. When did they leave?"

"About an hour ago now, sir. Quite unlike Miss Brissedon, with company coming and all. She didn't even take her hat."

Daniel's heart rose into his throat, and he could barely catch his breath. "Thank you, Forbes. Please call Dr. Tennyson when she returns." New automobile? On a messenger's wages? He supposed there might be a perfectly good explanation for everything, but his gut was sending off all sorts of alarms.

"Yes, sir. Of course. Pardon my asking, sir, but is anything wrong?"

"I'm not sure. I'll be in touch as soon as I can."

Daniel had no sooner hung up the phone than Sergeant Owens came in, his expression looking almost as dire as Daniel felt. "I'm hoping I'm wrong, Doc, but we found this key up in his room. Looks an awful lot like that one we found in Brissedon's nightstand. And that's not all." He handed Daniel a watch fob. "I'll eat my hat if this isn't part of that watch and cuff link set that belonged to Cornelius Desmond."

"Dear God! Brighton must have taken it off Desmond's corpse."

"You think he killed the man?"

"No, but I think he saw who did. Except he didn't know who he was—not until Colin introduced him to his father. He lost everything when Cornelius Desmond died, and now Brissedon was doing it all over again. Templeton wanted revenge. He killed Thomas Brissedon, and now he's taken Kathleen."

"Sergeant," one of the constables said, "I found this pad tossed in Templeton's garbage. Whatever he wrote left an imprint, but . . ."

Daniel pulled the pencil from his pocket and grabbed the pad. He was acting almost out of habit now, without thinking, for the only thought in his mind was finding Kathleen. As he rubbed over the imprint with the side of his pencil, the lettering stood out. Pier 48 – White Star 1:00 p.m. Without asking this time, he picked up the phone.

"Adams residence."

"Byron! It's Daniel. Is my uncle there?"

"Yes, he just arrived. I gather you wish to speak with him?"

He didn't have to answer. A moment later, Timothy picked up the phone. "Danny, me boy. I hope ye took the day off to relax a bit with that lovely lass."

"She's in trouble, Uncle. I need your help."

"O' course, what can I do?"

"He's taken her. They're likely coming into the Long Island City station to get the ferry. They're to take the White Star Line out of Pier 48 at 1:00 p.m. If the ship sails . . ."

"All right, Danny, but who has her?"

"Brighton Templeton. He murdered Brissedon, and now he's taken Kathleen. He's got about an hour-and-a-half head start on me, I think." He flipped through his notebook. "His real name's Brian O'Toole."

"O'Toole! He's naught but a petty thief. So that's where he's been keeping himself."

"Well, he upgraded to murderer, and he's kidnapped Kathleen."

"All right, Danny. I'll get me men on it. Ye just get to the ferry as soon as ye can, lad."

Daniel hung up and shot out the door, Owens on his heels. "Where are we going, Doc?"

"The railroad. You don't have to—"

"The heck I don't! You can fill me in on the way. One of the constables can get word to Milly. She'll understand."

Five minutes later, Daniel stood at the ticket counter. "When's the next train out?"

"It's about to leave. You just made it. We put on some extra trains due to the holiday."

"When was the last one?"

"About an hour ago. It was running a few minutes late."

He almost wanted to kiss the man. Each delay brought him closer to Kathleen. As he settled in the seat, he filled the sergeant in on what had happened. Then he turned to stare out the window and prayed.

Kathleen held her breath as the train slowed to a stop between two stations. Perhaps they'd get stuck and give Daniel time to catch up with them. Surely someone must have seen her leaving with Brighton and been concerned that she hadn't returned.

"What's going on?" Brighton asked as the conductor passed by.

"One of them newfangled automobiles got stuck on the track. He's lucky we saw him in time, the dang fool."

"How long are we going to be delayed? I have a ship to catch."

The conductor rolled his eyes. Kathleen could almost hear him saying, *Well, la dee da.* Instead, he said, "We're working as fast as we can, sir."

"When is the ship leaving?" Kathleen asked.

"What?" Brighton looked at her as if he'd forgotten she was there. "Oh, one o'clock. We still have plenty of time." His lip turned up in a snide bow. "Don't worry. We won't miss it, and once we're out to sea, there won't be a thing Doctor Dan can do about it. I've even had an acquaintance of mine make something called passports in phony names. They'll never find us."

"Why are you so determined to take me along? You clearly have no feelings for me. Was it all just an act?"

He frowned, the sneer dropping from his lips. "No, of course not. You were a wonderful surprise, but your father wouldn't have it. He tried to take you away from me, just as he had everything else. Well, he's the one who's lost everything now. It's only right, don't you think?"

"But what about me? Don't I have anything to say about it?"

"Of course, darling." He touched her cheek, but when he leaned over to kiss her, she turned away. "Well, no doubt about what you think, is there? That's really too bad." He sat back in his seat. "You've allowed your father to turn you against me, so now you're no more than collateral damage, just as I was. Get used to it, Katie, dear. Who knows, you may even grow to care for me . . . in time. I've been told I'm an excellent lover."

"I'll never give myself to you."

He laughed. "Don't be so foolish, darling. I have no intention of asking your permission. According to our *passports*, you're my wife. I'll do as I please."

"You're a wicked creature."

Anger suffused his face, turning it a sickly red. "*I'm* a wicked creature? Your father is the one who killed an innocent man and ruined countless lives, mine included."

"And that's really the only reason you care, isn't it? Because Mr. Desmond was giving your mother medicine and sending you to college. If not for that, it wouldn't have mattered to you whether he lived or died."

He shrugged. "True enough, I suppose, but he *was* doing all that, so your old man had to pay for his crime."

"It's not the first time you've killed, is it?"

He looked at her for a moment, a hint of remorse in his eye. "Oh, what does it matter? If you try to tell tales, I'll just have you put in an asylum somewhere. No, it's not. But that was all your father's fault as well. I do regret having to leave Jeremy alive, though. And that's your fault. If you hadn't called that wisenheimer doctor in, everything would have gone according to plan."

"You were going to kill Jeremy as well?"

"Of course I was. He sent Neily to that tenement, after all, knowing your old man would be waiting there for him. Though I doubt the fool had any idea what Tommy had in mind." He pulled out his watch and cursed. "My fob!"

"Did you lose it?"

He sneered at her again. "It would appear so. But don't fret, darling. I have enough money to buy a new one."

Clearly, it had annoyed him, though, for he cursed under his breath again as he shoved the watch back in his pocket and called for the conductor.

"Any news about that confounded automobile?"

"Looks like they almost have it off, sir. Shouldn't be a minute or so more."

A moment later, the train started to move again, and Brighton sat back against the seat, releasing a long, calming breath. He was nervous, and that could work to Kathleen's advantage.

CHAPTER 35

They pulled into Long Island City, and Kathleen threw a quick glance at the clock, trying to calculate if Daniel could possibly catch up with them. They had lost time waiting for the automobile to be removed from the track. Still . . . Brighton shoved her across Borden Avenue toward the ferry station.

Tears came to her eyes. Crowds of people were waiting to get onto the ferry to travel across to Manhattan for the Fourth of July celebrations.

"Shit!" Brighton hissed, his grip on her tightening. He had a lightweight woman's shawl thrown over his arm where the gun met her ribs. Would he dare shoot in the ferry terminal? Of course he would. He'd admitted her father wasn't the first person he'd killed.

He stood with his hand squeezed around her arm, sweat glistening on his forehead as his eyes shot around the dock. Apparently, he hadn't planned as well as he thought. He took his watch out again, cursing just loud enough for her to hear.

She didn't utter a word, not wanting to aggravate him any more than he already was and cause him to do something rash. They stood waiting amidst a sea of humanity to get the tickets, the minutes ticking away, the sweat on Brighton's brow increasing with each passing second, while Kathleen's hope grew.

Even after they had the tickets, they'd have to wait their turn to get on the ferry, just like everyone else who stood holding a ticket. More of a delay, more time for Daniel to arrive.

"Katie, darlin', is it yerself I'm seeing?" She looked up, and the ember of hope that was nestled in her heart sparked to life. It was Daniel's uncle. She was sure of it.

Brighton pressed the gun harder against her ribs and cursed in her ear. "Just say hello and exchange a few pleasantries. Don't even think of crying for help."

"Timothy, how are you?" It was all she could do to keep her voice from shaking.

"I'm fine, darlin'. Are ye heading over to the city for the festivities, then?"

"Yes, we thought it would be nice to get away." She could feel Brighton's hot breath on her neck, the barrel of his gun pressing ever firmer against her back.

"Ah, sure, it will be. And who is this ye have with ye?"

"Just a friend," Brighton said, his smile as phony as a wooden nickel. "If you'll excuse us, I do believe there's some room opening up over there, darling."

"Sure, there is. Why don't I just be going over there with ye, and we can catch up a wee bit. How are yer brothers doing, Katie, darlin'? It must be two years or more since I've seen them."

"No!" Brighton's face had turned a bright tomato red. "I remember you. That day Neily Desmond was murdered. You were the copper." He pulled the gun out from under the shawl and pressed it to Kathleen's head.

"Now hold on there, lad," Timothy said, raising his hand as if to calm a frightened animal.

People all around had taken notice and moved out of the way as Brighton dragged her toward the ferry. Women were screaming, children crying, but he kept moving backward, his arm tight around her waist, the gun jammed firmly behind her ear.

She didn't know where he came from or when it happened, exactly, but like an avenging angel, he came out of nowhere, slamming into Brighton. They lay sprawled out on the floor, the gun skidding across the wooden boards. Daniel had flipped him over and was pounding his fist into Brighton's face. Timothy was trying to pull him off.

"Danny, lad. That's enough, Danny!"

She stepped forward, still half-dazed, and gently placed her hand on Daniel's shoulder. "That's enough, Daniel. Please."

He stopped at once and stood up, dragging Brighton with him and tossing him toward his uncle. His chest was still heaving with exertion, his deep brown eyes highlighted in gold, his white shirt splashed with blood, but he pulled her to him, holding her tightly as her tears came.

She didn't remember much about the ride home except that she'd never felt safer. Though her nerves remained shaken, the tears had stopped, and her muscles were no longer tied in knots.

There was a lot of fuss when she arrived home, but he stood by, her guardian even then, asking everyone to give her some time to relax. Eventually, they all ate, and most of the family headed down toward the bay to enjoy the fireworks, but Daniel sat beside her on the porch swing, watching the light show from afar.

"It was him all along," she finally said. "But how did you know?"

"I started to suspect when I found out he wasn't in law school at all, and that Cornelius Desmond had intended to pay for his college education."

"Which all went away when Patrick's father was killed."

Daniel nodded. "Then last night, while I was going over everyone's testimony, I realized that Brighton had mentioned something about Desmond's murder scene. Something he wouldn't have known unless he was there. When Owens found Desmond's watch fob in Brighton's room, it confirmed my suspicions. It must have broken off when your father grabbed the watch."

She sighed, clutching her hankie in her hands. "And Brighton retrieved it. He saw my father that day, you know, but didn't have any idea who he was, not until Colin introduced them."

Daniel put his arm around her and kissed her forehead. "To be honest, I think it was the marriage announcement between your father and Brigid Desmond that tipped him off. Meeting your brother was just a lucky coincidence."

"Will they hang him?"

"I don't know. Sam thinks he may not have been in his right mind. Not only did Brighton lose his dreams of a law degree when Desmond was murdered, but he lost his mother as well. She was the only family he had. The judge may commit him to an asylum for the rest of his life. Though Uncle Timothy's not so sure."

"Why is that?"

"His real name is Brian O'Toole. My uncle said he was well-known as a petty thief. Probably the real reason he never reported what he saw the day Desmond was killed. He figured the police would likely see it as a robbery gone wrong and blame him."

"So he decided to take care of it himself." She took a moment to blow her nose. "Had he really killed before?"

"He did, but it wasn't deliberate. To put his plan into action, he needed some money for decent clothes and such, so he got himself a job delivering groceries to a few of the wealthier homes, ingratiating himself with the staff and learning the comings and goings of the inhabitants. As he'd always been a petty thief, it seemed right up his street, until someone arrived home early. Brighton panicked and, in his rush to get away, he shoved the old gent down the stairs. The man died."

"It's all so sad, and all because of my father's greed. Why didn't Brighton just use the money he stole to pay for his own education? Surely as an attorney, he could have found some evidence against my father and held him accountable."

Daniel reached up and touched her cheek, a dimpled smile crossing his handsome face. "First of all, he didn't manage to steal near enough to cover the tuition. And secondly, it takes more than money to get into NYU or Columbia. It takes recommendations from prominent men, something he didn't have."

"He lost that with Cornelius as well."

Daniel nodded. "But more than that, he wanted revenge, to make your father suffer for everything he took from him. I think he was very close to his mother. Losing her took away whatever stability he had in his life."

Kathleen sighed. "So what now? None of this belongs to Colin. It has to be sorted out."

"I've asked my brother Joe to come out tomorrow and go over the books. He's been looking for an excuse to take a day off and see what it's like out here. But don't think about that now. We'll deal with everything tomorrow. Tonight, let's just sit here and enjoy the fireworks."

Kathleen smiled and rested her head against his shoulder. She couldn't remember when she'd last felt so much at peace.

Tuesday, July 5, 1904 – 9:00 a.m.

Sam Tennyson accompanied Daniel to Riverhead the next morning for the inquest. It was short and sweet. Brighton was transferred to the county jail to await his trial, and the entire proceeding was over by noon.

"Can I buy you lunch?" Sam climbed up into the buggy and took the reins.

"Thank you, but Joe's at the Brissedon Mill this morning, going over their books." Daniel hopped in beside his friend and mentor. "I want to stop by and see what he's discovered. I have a hunch most of the fortune belongs to Patrick. I've asked them all to meet me at the house later today."

"Will Joe be able to figure it out that quickly?"

Daniel laughed. "He is a whiz with numbers, but Jeremy is going to guide him through it. He's the one that set the whole thing up in the first place. I think he's trying to make amends, probably hoping Patrick won't press charges. But even more than that, I truly think he loves Molly and wants to be the man she deserves."

"You don't think he had anything to do with Neily's murder, then?"

"No, I think Tommy was the only family he had, and he was just used to doing whatever he told him. In a way, he was just as much a prisoner as Patrick was."

"Well, I don't envy you having to deal with them all. I'm not sure Colin is going to go quietly into the night."

"Truthfully, I don't think he wants the responsibilities. He likes the money, of course, but he's got a law degree and should be able to make a decent living for himself."

"You think Patrick will ask them all to leave?"

Daniel scrubbed a hand across his face. "Not Kathleen, but I'm not sure what she'll do if he puts the others out."

"What would you do if you were in Patrick's place?"

"I'm not really sure."

"Oh, I think you are, and I'd wager Patrick's thinking along the same lines. Of course, I could be wrong, though I usually do all right when I follow my gut." He cast a glance in Daniel's direction, a sly grin on his face.

"Now you sound like my uncle Timothy."

"Well then, I couldn't do much better, now, could I?"

"You never told me, Sam. I know you met my father during your college days, but how do you know Uncle Timothy?"

"Drunk and disorderly, I believe." Sam chuckled and stared straight ahead, a smile breaking out on his lips as he clicked the reins.

Daniel grinned. He'd get nothing more out of him that day, but there was always tomorrow.

As planned, Daniel met his brother at Newins Restaurant at two o'clock. "So what do you think?"

"He may not have a degree in finance, but I think Jeremy will make a damn good accounting clerk. If he uses his talents for good, that is."

Daniel laughed. "I suppose he is trying to now."

Joe shrugged and shoved a potato in his mouth. "The entire estate belongs to Patrick Desmond. Brissedon must have used whatever money he had setting up the scam. There were some payments to loan sharks, so that was clearly one way he got some money, but they were paid back in cash with withdrawals from Desmond's accounts. There was even a safe full of jewelry. Jeremy said it was Brigid's, but Thomas pretended he had to sell it to pay her debts."

"Well, I'd better get to it, then. Can you take care of all the legalities?"

"Already started."

"Thanks, Joe. You heading home tonight?"

He nodded, a slight smile causing his lips to quirk up in the corner. "I don't want to come between you and your lady."

Daniel had started to get up, but he sat back down. "I'm going to back off for a while. She needs time to get adjusted to all of this."

"Don't tell me you're still on your 'not worthy' kick. She's not Pru, Danny"

"I know, and Izzy's already given me that speech, so save your breath. I'm just not ready yet, and to be honest, I'm afraid she might want to get away or something."

"Seems to me you're two peas in a pod. Both thinking you're not good enough. Tell her, Danny, and let her make up her own mind."

"I will, just not yet."

"Yeah, I know. You're just giving her some time to adjust. Well, don't wait too long, little brother, or she may think you don't care and look elsewhere."

Daniel gazed up at the stately house, its shingles the same color as Kathleen's eyes. It never ceased to amaze him how much the actions of one man could alter the course of so many lives. His own father had changed the course of his mother's life and, ultimately, his and his uncle's as well. Thomas Brissedon had ruined Patrick's life and Brigid's and deprived countless others of the benefit of Cornelius Desmond's kindness. And Brighton Templeton had changed the lives of the Brissedons, though in this case, perhaps it was for the best.

The front door opened, and Forbes came out on the porch. "Shall I announce you, sir?"

"Is everyone here?"

"Yes, sir, everyone you asked."

Daniel picked up the satchel Joe had given him and headed into the parlor.

"Thank you all for coming. Recent events have brought some interesting information to light."

"None of it's ours, is it?" Colin was standing against the sideboard, a glass of whiskey in his hand. "How could that be? My father was a shrewd businessman, and while a good portion of it might be Patrick's, surely he made some money of his own in the last year or so."

"You really are an imbecile," Jeremy said, most uncharacteristically. It seemed the recent events might have given him some backbone. "Even if he did, it was made with Patrick's money. It still doesn't belong to us."

Phillip Stockbridge stood up and rubbed the back of his neck. "This seems like family business to me. I really don't know why you asked me to be here."

"Please, sir," Daniel said, "just indulge me a bit longer."

Patrick sat on the small sofa next to Kathleen. "So my father's name really is cleared?"

"Yes, he was on a mission of kindness when he was killed."

Patrick sighed and ran his thumb over the shamrocks on his father's watch. No one said anything for a moment, and then Jeremy spoke up.

"There are a few recent deals you may want to revisit. I've left them on the desk in your study. Now, if there's nothing else, I'll pack my things and be on my way."

A sob came from the hallway, and Forbes called the girl in. "For heaven's sake, Miss Buchanan. I daresay this involves you as well."

"Oh, you'll always have a job here, Molly," Patrick said, the full impact of Daniel's statement clearly beginning to hit him. But Molly looked to Jeremy, her eyes full of tears.

The droopy-eyed man went to her side, wiping the tears from her cheek. "I'm not leaving you, darling. I mean to find a job in a nearby town and send for you once I've established myself. That is, if you'll still have me after all I've done. I need to make myself worthy of you first."

Patrick looked up, a confused expression on his face. "Don't you like working for the mill?"

"Of course I do, but . . ." He shook his head, true sorrow filling his eyes. "I was the one who sent your father to his death."

"What choice did you have? If I know anything about Thomas Brissedon, it's that he knew how to manipulate people, force them to do as he wished. Kathleen says you had no idea what he meant to do. I believe that's true. Thomas would never have shared that information with you."

"But I tried to frame you."

"I have to admit that still gets my dander up a bit, but then you had no one save Thomas to teach you right from wrong. Dr. O'Halleran says you're trying to make amends. I believe my father would want to give you a second chance."

"Thank you, Patrick. You're very much like your father, I think."

Patrick's cheeks blushed. "I doubt my father ever had the reputation I do."

"That was my father's doing as well," Kathleen said. "But you all have a second chance now to make things right."

"You'll stay, then, Jeremy," Patrick said. "Here at the house. At least until you and Molly start a family of your own."

"Yes, I will. I promise you won't regret it." He leaned down and gave Molly a kiss.

"I will be going," Colin said. "I spoke to Mr. Brice this morning. It seems he has a vacancy for a law clerk."

"But you have your degree," Kathleen said. "And Patrick will need someone to look into the legal aspects of things."

Patrick frowned. Though he didn't say anything, it was clear it was going to take far more than an apology to forgive all that Colin had done.

"I'm sure he'll find someone suitable. It's for the best, I think, and Mr. Brice has promised me an associate's position once I prove myself. After all, you're always telling me I should be more responsible. This is a chance to do so." He turned to Daniel. "If there's nothing else, I really must pack." When neither Daniel nor anyone else objected, he downed his whiskey and left the room.

"Now, Mrs. Langston," Daniel said, undeterred by Colin's departure. "Considering the recent developments, you shouldn't have any objections to Patrick courting your daughter."

"I most certainly do."

"Let it be, Mother," Edward said. "For once in your life, learn when to cut your losses and leave with dignity. We have no objection at all. I truly am sorry for my behavior, Patrick. Please feel free to call upon Lydia whenever you like." Giving a nod to Kathleen, he turned to Daniel. "If you have finished with us, we'll be going as well. And thank you, sir, for your discretion." He walked to the door and nodded to Forbes. "Oh, there is one more thing." A moment later, Lydia walked into the parlor.

"Perhaps we could take a stroll and talk things over," she said, a shy smile struggling to break out on her lovely face. "Within sight of the house, of course."

"Yes, of course." Patrick jumped up. "If the doctor has finished up here . . ."

"Now, just wait one moment." Phillip Stockbridge jumped up from his seat. "I still don't know why I was asked to be here. I have business to attend to."

"Oh!" Patrick said. "I am terribly sorry. I'm not used to dealing with the everyday running of the mill yet, but I'd like to renegotiate our contract with Mr. Talbot. I'm sure you'll find the new arrangement far more to your liking."

"You would? I mean, yes, of course."

"We could meet tomorrow morning, if that's convenient."

"Yes, it is. I'll see you then. Good day, gentlemen, ladies."

Patrick took Lydia's hand and followed Stockbridge out the door, talking enthusiastically about his plans for the mill.

Kathleen let out a contented sigh and stood up, a twinkle in her eye. "Well, now that's all settled, I could use a walk as well. Would you care to accompany me, Doctor?"

"It would be my pleasure."

They walked down toward the lake and sat on the bench that surrounded the old willow tree. He knew what he intended to say, but was he being foolish? No, they both needed time.

"Kathleen . . ." Even as her name left his lips, she held her fingers up against them.

"I know. We both need time. Well, I do, anyway. To sort things out, get used to my new role here. I really don't have anything of my own at all now, not even a dowry."

"Patrick's not about to let you or the children go without. He's even letting Jeremy stay."

"Though not Colin."

"That's going to take a bit more time, I think. Jeremy was as much a victim as Patrick was, but Colin . . ."

"I know." Kathleen dabbed her eyes with a hankie. "Perhaps it will do him good to be out on his own, and they might reconcile one day, don't you think?"

"Possibly, if Colin can change his ways and show a little remorse."

She nodded. "As to myself, regardless of how Patrick feels about me, I'm simply his stepsister, one who's not entitled to anything. I need to find where I fit into all of this."

"You're more than that to him. You were there when no one else was, and he'll always see you as his sister."

"True enough, but even sisters have to find their way. I need to do that before I make any further commitments." She took a deep breath and smiled, her dainty nose twitching. "So I've told you the reason I need time. What's your excuse, Doctor? Are you still in love with the woman who left you at the altar?" He lifted his eyebrows, and she continued. "Your sister mentioned it the day we went to see Mary Brady."

He was going to give Izzy a good tongue-lashing the next time he saw her. "Prudence?" He let out a hearty laugh. "No, not at all. I think I dodged a bullet there."

"What, then?"

"I'm not ready to share that just yet, but know it has nothing to do with how I feel for you. I'll get there. I just need to work through it all."

"Maybe we can work through things together . . . as friends, at least for now."

He leaned over and kissed her cheek, a hint of what he hoped may someday come. "Or until the next adventure," he said as they made their way back to the house.

HISTORICAL NOTES

With a new century came new industries and innovation, and Patchogue was right in the center of it. Conklin's Pharmacy was the headquarters for the central office of the New York and New Jersey Telephone Company as early as 1893, and by 1904, the drug store had installed the village's first public telephone. Quite convenient for our detective, Alexander Morton. The phone number was listed as 36. Yes, that's it, a far cry from today's phone numbers.

Automobiles remained few and far between, but by 1904, they were gaining in popularity, so I have a few dotting the streets here and there. Horse and buggy was still the main mode of transportation for our characters, though Thomas might have purchased a 1903 Ford Model A four-seat tonneau, while Brighton most likely opted for the two-seat runabout version of the 1904 Model C, popularly known as "the doctor's car."

The village had electric lights, as well as gas. The Mills Building on West Main Street housed the Patchogue Electric Light Company, while the Syndicate Building held the office of the Patchogue Gas Company, as well as the Patchogue Post Office. In the bathroom, Kohler had introduced the flush toilet, and cast iron bathtubs with running water were becoming more prevalent.

Advances were being made in photography as well. In 1900, Kodak had just come out with its classic box camera, the Brownie, making it easy for anyone to take a picture. Portrait studios were still popular, but the inexpensive little Brownie made photography fun for all.

Sitting on the Great South Bay, Patchogue boasted a number of fine hotels. I chose Roe's Hotel for Daniel to stay at because it was one of the few that was open all year round, the Central Hotel on West Main Street being another. Located in the center of the village on East Main Street, Roe's Hotel could accommodate two hundred guests and had a nearby livery. Along with a bar, billiard room, and dining room, it advertised steam heat and electric lighting, though it being the height of summer, Daniel hasn't had need of the heat as yet. The original Roe's Tavern, located on the corner of Ocean Avenue and East Main Street, was built around 1790 by Austin Roe of Culper Spy Ring fame. It played an important role as a stagecoach stop in the early years, but eventually the family built a new hotel a bit further east on Main Street, and the original tavern was taken down. Around 1892, the new hotel was expanded, and it remained a popular spot throughout the early nineteenth century. During the off-season, it was a frequent location for hunting parties, business conventions, and traveling salesmen. Sadly, not much remains of Roe's Hotel today, as a huge fire in 1934 destroyed a good portion of the block, and it was replaced by a variety of storefronts.

Cycling had become a popular sport during the late 1890s into the early 1900s, and Roe's Hotel was a choice destination for cycling clubs. The bicyclers, or "wheelmen" as they were popularly known, would pedal out from Manhattan to spend the weekend. After some fun at the beach, they'd head back to the city on Sunday. Some pedaled their way home, but many stowed their bicycles on special racks provided by the Long Island Railroad and enjoyed the leisurely hour-and-a-half ride back to the city. Actually, the trip didn't really take much longer than it does today.

The Long Island Railroad first came to Patchogue in 1869, bringing with it a flux of Manhattan residents who saw the village as a popular resort area and a way to escape the hustle and bustle of the city for a few days. In 1904, however, the railroad still didn't have a direct rail connection to Manhattan, which would entail a bridge across the East River. Instead, riders would disembark at Long Island City and take a ferry over to one of three docks in Manhattan. By the 1890s, there was a rail connection across the East River from Brooklyn to Manhattan, but as this El Connection was nowhere near the LIRR terminal, it too required disembarking and boarding another train. In the end, taking it was just as time consuming and troublesome as using the ferry, so most people opted to take the latter. It wasn't until 1910 that the LIRR finally constructed a bridge across the East River, thus making Patchogue even more accessible to city dwellers. Fortunately for Kathleen, this new bridge had not yet been constructed. Being one of the only methods to cross over to Manhattan, the ferry terminal did often become a bottleneck, crowded with eager riders, so Brighton's dilemma would have been quite real.

Wanting to give the novel the feel of what life was like in a small Long Island village just after the turn of the century, I tried to include some of the local businesses my characters might frequent in their everyday lives. There were two pharmacies located near Daniel's hotel where he might stop to pick up his headache powders. Conklin's Pharmacy, which was across the street, is mentioned above, but there was another on the corner of East Main Street and Ocean Avenue, which he might also visit. McBride's Pharmacy claimed to have the "largest and best soda fountain in the county." Today, O'Neill's Jewelry and Sales Exchange stands on that corner.

Kathleen, of course, volunteers at the library, which in 1904 was located in the George M. Ackerley Block on South Ocean Avenue. After a number of temporary locations like this, it finally received a permanent home in 1908, when the Carnegie Library was built on Lake Street with land donated by Edwin Bailey and funds provided by Andrew Carnegie. Today, the building is used for the Young Adult department, while the Main Library is located on the south side of East Main Street.

Daniel frequented Newins Restaurant on Ocean Avenue, run by Mrs. Emma Newins, and C. H. Murdock's Family Restaurant, known as "The Old Homestead," on West Main Street, neither of which remain today. Mrs. Frank Newins did run a boarding house on North Ocean Avenue, where Brighton rented a room. And how could I forget to mention Swezey & Newins' Department Store, which stood on the corner of North Ocean Avenue and West Main Street. For over a hundred years, the store served the people of Patchogue with everything from household furniture to clothing. With the advent of the large shopping mall on Long Island, however, sales dropped, and the store closed its doors in 2003. The building was used by various tenants for the next ten years and was ultimately demolished in 2013 to be replaced by an upscale apartment complex.

I also tried to mention some local people of note in the narrative. Edwin Bailey, for example, did have a successful lumber mill in Patchogue. In fact, many a South Shore business and private home built during the period was constructed with lumber from Bailey and Sons. By 1904, it was a huge enterprise built along the Patchogue River, which included a number of specialized buildings. The mill had direct access to the railroad, and as the Patchogue River was Long Island's only deepwater port, Bailey and Sons also employed a small fleet of vessels for use in shipping its products. Alas, today a bowling alley stands where it once did, though after the pandemic, it too has been closed down. As for Mr. Stockbridge and Mr. Talbot, neither of them ever existed, at least not that I know of.

C. W. Ruland was an undertaker and embalmer in 1904. The family established the first purpose-built funeral home on Long Island in 1908 on the corner of Lake and North Ocean. Before that, funeral directors worked out of old Victorian homes, which didn't offer spaces conducive to preparing a body for burial. In the 1950s, at the bequest of grieving families who required more room for parking, etc., a new building was built further up on North Ocean Avenue. The Ruland Funeral Home still exists at that location, though it was purchased by the Romeo family in the late 1970s. The name, however, remains the same. The original building, on Lake Street and North Ocean, now houses the Reese's 1900 pub.

And Monsignor James Cronin would have heard Patrick's confession. He was the pastor of St. Francis de Sales Roman Catholic Church in 1904. The church at that point in time was located on East Main and Conklin Avenue, though the building was moved to its current location at Amity Street and South Ocean Avenue in the winter of 1907. It took three to four months, from December 1906 to February or March 1907, to actually get the building moved.

There was a small brick jail, or lockup, located on the east side of Havens Avenue, until the 1920s, when a two-cell building was built behind the firehouse on Lake Street. The newer jail was popularly known as "Hangover House," most likely due to the fact that most of its occupants were nursing just that. In searching the newspapers from 1900 to 1905, I found only two or three murders in the area for the entire period, and perhaps a theft or two, so such serious crime was not something the local authorities were used to dealing with on a daily basis. There was not yet a police force in Patchogue in the sense we know it today, though they did have a police chief, a sergeant, and a few police officers or constables. They were hired by the people of Patchogue to keep a watch over things. What little serious crime there was seemed to be handled by the Suffolk County District Attorney (who was Livingston Smith in 1904), the county coroner, and the justice of the peace. Samuel Tennyson, however, was not a real person, nor was Sergeant Owens, but Dr. Scholer was the Manhattan coroner. The trial would likely have been held in Riverhead, which was and still is the county seat of Brookhaven Township, of which Patchogue continues to be a part. The county jail is still located in Riverhead.

There's so much more I could talk about, such as the Suffolk County Alms House, which was located in Yaphank, but I'll save some for another book. These are the main names and places you might have come across in this book, so I'll leave it there for now.

While Patchogue faced some hard times during the latter part of the twentieth century, it has reinvented itself yet again. Revitalized, it is flourishing once more, becoming a home to fashionable stores and restaurants as well as a center for cultural events, while retaining the flavor of the quaint Long Island village it once was at its peak in the early twentieth century. For more information on Patchogue, visit the Celia M. Hastings Local History Room's website at https://history.pmlib.org.

About the Author

I. M. Foster is a Long Island historian and librarian who loves to read and write and search around for her roots, genealogically speaking. She has a BA in History and an MLS in Library Science and enjoys the research almost as much as she does writing the story. In fact, many of her ideas come to her while doing casual research or digging into her family history. She also writes under the pen name Andrea Matthews, and is the author of the Thunder on the Moor series, a historical romance set on the sixteenth-century Anglo-Scottish Border, and the Cross of Ciaran series, a paranormal romance where a fifteen-hundred-year-old Celt finds himself in the twentieth century. She is a member of the Long Island Romance Writers and the Historical Novel Society.

You can keep track of her upcoming historical mysteries and tidbits about the books at the following sites:
Website: https://imfostermysteries.com
Facebook: IMFosterMysteries

Keep track of her romances, published under the pen name Andrea Matthews, at:
Website: www.andrea-matthews.com
Facebook: Andrea Matthews Historical Romance

Made in the USA
Middletown, DE
20 February 2023

24548309R00298